Tell It to the Bees

Fiona Shaw

This edition published in 2019 by Serpent's Tail,
an imprint of Profile Books Ltd
3 Holford Yard
Bevin Way
London
WC1X 9HD
www.serpentstail.com

First published in 2009 by Tindal Street Press, UK

1 3 5 7 9 10 8 6 4 2

Typeset by Country Setting, Kingsdown, Kent, UK.

Printed and bound in the USA.

ISBN 978 1 78816 407 8
eISBN 978 1 78283 004 7

To Karen, for all

Tell It to the Bees

The town was so small, just a dent in the landscape. Charlie could have held it in his fist. He drove carefully on this side of the road, down from the hills, down from the sky, towards the puddle of trees and buildings, the green and the grey that had made his home.

He was taller of course, at least two foot taller. But the town was smaller by leagues. By acres and oceans. This he had not been expecting.

He picked the calico bag off the back seat and slung it over his shoulder. He put money in the meter and locked the car. There was something he had got to do, but not at once. First he needed to walk.

So he walked through the town, from remembered place to remembered place. His street and his house. The blue bridge, which was red now. The towpath where there was still broken glass, still dirt and tired weeds, and across the river, the factory. He stood and stared across the brown water like he used to do twenty years ago, watching for his mother, but it was too early for the hooter and the women coming out in their crowds, and the factory only purred to itself.

He walked round the park, tagging the railings as he'd done as a boy, then rubbing the dry dirt from his fingers like salt. He looked in at the ornamental beds where the same flowers grew in lozenges of purple and yellow and red.

Beyond the park, up on the hill, was the doctor's house. When he was a boy it was miles away. It was much closer now. He was there in ten minutes. But there were gates at the end of the drive and he couldn't see in. So he walked on up, alongside the garden wall, and high above were the branches of the beech tree, fresh with the year's new green. He stopped and put a hand to the wall.

'You're putting it off,' he told himself. 'Go now.'

It took longer to walk back again. His feet dragged and the calico bag banged awkwardly. He'd felt quite calm so far, but now his mouth was dry.

'It's nothing,' he told himself. 'There's nothing to lose.'

The waste ground at the top of the street had gone. He'd played there as a boy, or watched other boys play, more often. Once he'd seen a cat run howling, tin cans tied to its tail. Now, where there had been wild trees and dead arm-chairs, there were maisonettes in brown brick.

Charlie walked on down the street and everything went quiet. His heart beat hard. He stopped at a door. It was still green; the paint scuffed on the weatherboard. Though his pulse echoed in his ears, he felt nothing. Perhaps the house was empty. There was no sign of life in the windows.

'Knock then, Charlie,' he said, and he took his hands from his pockets.

Perhaps it was only a minute he stood there, perhaps it was longer but finally he knocked. Nothing happened.

'Just go,' he told himself. 'There's nothing left here.'

He waited a moment longer.

'Come on,' he said. The meter would be running out and he had a long drive ahead. 'It doesn't matter.'

But as he turned to go, there was a sound from inside, a door banging. Then footsteps, dragging and slow, and some-body was turning a key in the lock.

'Dead trouble now, Charlie,' he said.

Slowly the door opened. The air from inside smelled of dust and cabbage. The old man smelled of something else. He wore slippers on his feet and his trousers were hitched high above his belly. He looked at Charlie.

'What do you want?' he said at last.

I

You came upon the pond quite suddenly, if you didn't know it was there. It lay in a dip of grass, like a sixpence in the palm of the hand. A ring of water that carried the sky in its eye.

This day, at this time, it was busy. Ducks cruised in the green water, courted by children and their bags of stale bread. Pigeons crowded at the children's feet, hammering their heads for crumbs, their beaks worrying, disrespectful. Squatted at the pond's lip, several girls fished with nets in the shallows, and tricycles and scooters rode the gentle curve with all the speed their small riders could muster. Three or four boys sailed their boats.

As always, there were people who took the pond in their stride, cresting the hill without that pause of pleasure. They had their sights set somewhere else and the park was the fastest route to get there. At this hour, which was between three and four o'clock in the afternoon, there were only occasional figures like this, whose working costumes rested heavy and conspicuous on their shoulders as they passed by. They carried briefcases, or important bags, and wore suits and shiny shoes and serious expressions. The women among them often found the wind tricky and some blushed as their skirts played about, or wished for a moment for the harsh limits of their old Utility clothes, which the wind couldn't toy with. So the women would walk even faster than the men to be gone and away, safely back indoors again.

Sometimes something gave one of these brisk people pause. A broken heel, or a friend. Very occasionally one of them would stop to sit on a bench for a minute. Today a woman with a Gladstone bag and careful shoes checked her stride, though she didn't appear to have broken a heel, turned an ankle, or to know anyone. Sitting on the bench edge, bag beside her, she nodded politely to the old men with their talk of dirty carburettors, and they nodded in return. One of them thought to greet her by name and then thought better of it, finding her head already turned away.

The woman glanced about her, checked her watch and then, coming to some decision with herself, she put the bag on the ground, leaned back into the municipal curve of wood and looked at the pond.

The breeze was whippy and the boats were struggling, even with their sails trimmed right back. The woman watched. There was one especially that caught her eye. It had a white sail with the number 431 and a blue fish leaping, and it was flirting with disaster, heeled so far over that capsize seemed the only course. She looked across at the boys on the far side. She could see at once which one's boat this was.

While the others ran and danced this way and that, chipping and jeering into the wind, their voices high and slight, willing their boats across, one boy stood quite still, his body keen and tight, with eyes only for the blue fish. He must be about ten years old, one of those boys so skinny, all elbow and knee in flannel shorts and short-sleeved shirt, that you're surprised when they move at their grace.

But it was his boat that came in first, scudding sharp and fast into the pond edge and he kneeled and leaned forward, arms wide in a cradle, lifting it clear in a single fluid movement, so that it seemed for a moment as though boy and boat were part of the same force.

Once he had it safe, the boy's concentration was broken, and he flaunted his victory in a whooping dance. Absently, the woman checked her watch again. There was time yet. For these last minutes, the boat and boy had filled the woman's sight. When she stood up, all else would muscle in and she'd be back on the path, back in her brisk walk. She glanced around. The sun had gone off the pond and children were being called to put on sweaters and cardigans. The old men stashed their pipes and nodded their leave. She searched for her boat boy and found him again, slouching slowly up the hill not so very far from her bench, boat beneath one arm.

On the hill a young woman stood waiting. She held a book in her hand, a finger still between the pages. His mother, she must be – the same tousled hair, the same way of standing, body alert. Only where he had waited for his boat, she waited for her boy.

She was smiling and he came up to her, like a foal to the mare, bucking a little as if to show his own separate spirit, but eager to be close. The mother took the boat from his unwilling arms and placed it on the grass, untied the sweater from the boy's middle and gathered it up, easing it down over his reluctant head before he ducked away, pulling his arms through the sleeves, running now towards the trees behind.

The woman with the bag watched them. It had been the boy who had caught her eye, and now it was his mother. She looked the sort who worked in the electrical factory. She probably wore her working clothes beneath her coat. The woman would bet on it. And she didn't know her own beauty. That was there in the offhand way she had with herself.

The woman shook her head, as if to break some connection. Picking up the Gladstone bag, she left the bench and took up her stride again, away and off. She stopped at the top of the rise, before the pond was out of sight, turned and looked, but the boy and his mother were gone.

2

Charlie Weekes sat at the table and waited for his mother. It was late in the day and the air in there was warm and old. The room was nearly empty, which suited Charlie, but still he'd been waiting for ever and he wanted to go now.

The library stood on the north side of the high street and although the sky was clear and the sun shone in on other places, it had long since gone from here. So the lights were turned on and they hung above Charlie's head like dull yellow planets.

The librarian leaned to her books and a couple of old men slept over old news. Hidden among the novels, his mother pulled out spines and shushed them in again, a slight shuffle of sound that Charlie knew like he knew the rattle of a box of matches in his father's pocket.

He had a book propped up on his lap, its covers opened flat against the table edge. The corners dug into his midriff. He stared across at the clock on the wall. In the stilly warmth, the pages gave off a faint musty smell that Charlie recognized from his mother's books.

He looked down. Leant against the table leg, out of its bag, his blue fish leaped into the dead air. He pressed his finger to the tip of the mast. It had been good when his boat came in first, and his mother there to watch his triumph. His mother there to see him. Now he waited for her in the library; a promise made. But he was getting to an age where waiting for your mother is no longer a simple thing to do.

A fly swung lazily above him, knocking against the light. He got to his feet, leaving the book on the table. He could see the lamp curve crusted inside with the husks of so many others, and he wondered how they got in there. He shut his eyes. They'd be going home soon. Home to where the heart is. That's what his mother said, but he wondered about it.

'Can we go now?' he whispered, too quietly for his mother to hear. But she must have because then she was there, at the desk, handing over her tickets.

Lydia Weekes swung her basket as she walked, the wicker brush-brushing against the pleats of her skirt. She walked lightly, her toes peeping red in her slingbacks, turning slightly with each step as if on the point of dancing. She was smiling, or dreaming, Charlie didn't know which, but he thought of it as her Friday face. He glanced up at her, seeing the point of her chin, her brown eyes and her summer freckles, like his. Dot had told him, when he was smaller, that his mother was very pretty and now he felt a thrill of understanding.

She hummed a tune, something she had heard on the radio, something unobtrusive and catchy that she couldn't have named. Beside her, Charlie walked in that quickstep children must adopt to keep up with an adult: three strides and a skip, three strides and a skip. He carried his boat in an old satchel of his father's, the strap fastened to its shortest hole. The mast, jutting up, caught his ear as he walked, and the hull banged against his hip. When he could, he watched the walls, kept what his dad called a weather eye out for what he might see. But they were walking too briskly for him to glimpse anything. And besides, he couldn't stop and look.

Charlie had a question for his mother. It was a question that he'd carried about with him for a few days. Walking alongside her, he tried it out in his mouth again, felt the words form and bulge against his tongue. He didn't really understand why it should be so, but he knew that it was a question she wouldn't want to hear. They'd said as much, the ones who'd told him it, and so he hadn't been able to ask it yet. If he could, he would forget the question altogether and just ask her what was for supper, or whether he could listen to Dick Barton on the wireless. But he had heard it too often now to get rid of it, and so he would have to say it to her.

There was a group of girls in the playground that all the boys kept a distance from. They were older than Charlie, but not a great deal older, and though they were bigger than him, it wasn't their size that made them alarming. He'd tried just the once to describe them, but his mother hadn't understood.

'They don't like you,' he'd said. 'They don't even like the other girls.'

She was chopping onions, her eyes streaming.

'Well, you can't like everyone,' she'd said. 'Anyway, they're only girls,' and that had made him look at his mother wide-eyed. Because she'd been a girl once, he supposed, and surely she knew what he meant.

Now the question was like a feather in Charlie's throat. It tickled and scratched and he couldn't quite catch hold of it.

Charlie knew the name of the tune she was singing, and if she asked him for it, then maybe he could ask her his question in exchange. A trade. But before they were home. It had to be before they were home.

The fish for supper shifted in Lydia's basket, the smell of it catching in the air with each back swing.

'Poached or fried?' she said.

'It hasn't got a head, has it?'

'It used to. That's as bad, surely?' she said, in a voice that wasn't meant to, but which nevertheless carried a touch of disparagement.

Charlie shrugged.

'Is Dad having it too?'

'When he gets in, yes.'

Charlie swallowed. His heart banged in his chest.

'Is he out, then? Now, I mean?'

He knew the answer.

'Football practice,' she said. He looked up at her carefully, sidelong. There was no other thought in her face.

'And then the pub. He'll have a good appetite when he gets in.'

The question loomed in Charlie's mouth. Lydia was thinking on something, lips puckered with concentration.

'Mum, what's it mean, when . . .'

'I could make a crumble,' she said, as if he wasn't there. 'There's apples galore. His favourite.'

'Mum?'

She looked down at him, her face bright, eager, unwilling to let in anything else.

'Shall I do that? Put cloves with the apple. Sugar on top and brown it under the grill. For when he comes in.'

Charlie nodded. The boat had been good. The park had been good, and his mother on the hill there, watching. She was looking at him now. He squeezed her hand, something he wouldn't do often now in public.

'Charlie?'

They were nearly home. He'd wanted to ask her something but he wouldn't say it. No need. It was Friday, he wouldn't be at school till Monday. He could see the tree outside their house, half empty of leaves already.

'I'll help you,' he said. 'I'll peel the apples.'

'Peel them carefully and you can toss the skins. Find out the letter of your love.'

He grimaced. 'I'm not going to marry. I don't like girls very much.'

Lydia laughed. 'Everyone says that at your age.'

'So what do they say at yours, then?'

'Don't be so rude,' she said, and she cuffed him gently on the ear and then they were home.

3

Jean Markham wanted no more that evening than to sit for twenty minutes and watch her bees. There was nothing she needed to say, but she'd have liked just to sit. Then she'd put Peggy Lee on the gramophone and pour herself a Scotch. But she was late and there was no time for any of that. The house was quiet. Mrs Sandringham had gone a couple of hours earlier, home to her large boys and their impossible appetites, so nothing now disturbed the empty spaces.

She stopped in the hall and stood still, listening, waiting for the noises of her arrival to subside – the door slam, her footsteps on the tiles, the bump of her heart in its cavity, the dull echo from her dropped bag. The silence gathered itself around her shoulders, warm and possessive, and she put a hand to it as you might to a cat that had settled there, then climbed the stairs to her bedroom.

It was five years since Jean took on this house but it hadn't yet let her take possession. Built for a different cast and at a different time, with its breakfast room and dining room, servants' bells, maids' attic rooms papered in faded flowers, it seemed still to resist her efforts and her living. She occupied properly only a few rooms: her bedroom, the kitchen, sitting room. Her father's books in what she called, for a joke, her library. For the rest, the house rebuked her and her solitary state, needling her in vulnerable moments with things still found, left behind in corners and cupboards, children's things especially – a marble under the doormat, a tin car mysteriously high up on the pantry shelf, a rubber duck in the airing cupboard, its dusty rump leaving a tideline in the basin when she rinsed it clean. It seemed to Jean as if these things had a will to be hidden. They had escaped her first-time clearing and cleaning and then come to light as if by their own volition, catching her unawares later.

Strangest of all to find was the lock of hair. She had been reading in a small room at the back of the house that caught the last of the late summer sun. The room was empty save for an old armchair, just bare boards and dust flowers in the corners, and two faded rectangles on the papered walls – tiny pink buds in green tracery – where two pictures must have once hung.

The cat had sat for a while on her lap, arranging herself, as cats do, to absorb the sun as best she could, till Jean had got too hot and lifted her down. She'd gone back to her reading then, till some odd movement had caught her eye and she'd looked up to see the cat across the room sitting back on her furry haunches, cuffing a paw in the air, as if half playing, half annoyed. Something was caught on her claw and, kneeling to her, Jean saw a snatch of red. Holding the cat firm, she unhooked a bow of dusty ribbon, shot with a thread of silver, and tied within it, a lock of fine, blond hair.

Probably the slip of hair and its ribbon had been caught between the floorboards. Probably that was what it was. But still, this particular scrap of other life unnerved her, as if she'd been playing peeping Tom to the strangers living here before her. As if she'd seen something she shouldn't.

It was Friday night and Jean was tired. Her neck hurt. She arched her shoulder blades back and round, hoping for some ease. A bath would have been nice, but she was invited for supper at eight so it would have to wait.

Perhaps because she looked so much at other people's bodies, Jean wasn't usually interested in her own. But tonight, changing out of her working clothes, she undressed entirely, dropped her underwear on the rug, and stood naked before the wardrobe glass. She looked at all the length of her.

'Too tall to find a husband easily,' she said out loud with that rueful tilt of the mouth that even those who knew her well found so hard to read. The words had the status of an old truth, like other things understood in her family: that her grandmother had died without saying farewell to her daughter; that her mother had married beneath her; that they'd rather Jean had been born pretty than clever.

Wheeling her bicycle the short distance to supper, Jean paced her mood against the trees spreading high over the road. Their leaves shushed her feet, brittle and soft, and the clear, darkening sky was visible through their branches. Laying down her worries like this was an old trick, learned from something Jim had told her about, a Russian who couldn't stop remembering things and had made it into his trade. He'd remember lists of words by placing them in his mind up and down the streets of his home town, until his head was so full that he'd have to do the same thing to forget them, walking round the streets in his mind till he'd cleared the words away again.

So Jean leaned her worries up against the trees as she walked her way to supper, and by the time she had reached the twelfth elm, she had shrugged herself free, for now.

In the normal way of things, supper with Jim and Sarah Marston was as close to a family affair as Jean came. Jim opened the door to her before she could turn the handle, and held out a glass.

'It's a weak one now; been waiting for you so long, the ice's melted.'

Jean shrugged off her coat and swapped him the glass for her bag.

'You know not to put ice in my whisky,' she said.

'You likely to be out tonight?'

She took a long sip. 'No, but you never know.' She pointed up the stairs. 'Are they?'

'Waiting for you. Go and send them off.'

'Them or me.' She blew him a kiss and went up the stairs.

The children smelled sweet and warm in their beds, doe-eyed with near sleep.

'Buzzz, buzzz,' Meg murmured as Jean took the book from the shelf. She kissed each of them on the forehead and sat on the chair between the beds.

'From where we stopped before,' she said. 'You remember, there's Wild Man and Wild Woman in their cave and Wild Dog has gone to them on account of the delicious smell of the mutton. You both listening?'

The two little girls nodded their heads into their pillows, and Jean began to read:

'. . . Wild Horse stamped with his foot and said, "I will go and see and say why Wild Dog has not returned. Cat, come with me."

'"Nenni!" said the Cat. "I am the Cat who walks by himself, and all places are alike to me. I will not come." But all the same he followed Wild Horse softly, very softly, and hid himself where he could hear everything.'

She read on until the Cat went far, far away and then, with another light kiss for each sleeping girl, she stopped, put the book back in the shelf and turned off the light.

'Sleep tight,' she said.

Jim watched Jean as she told them how their children slept. She spoke to the pair of them, but in truth she spoke only to Jim. He took his time, as she talked, watching her, gauging how she was. He saw that she had changed her clothes for the evening. She wore stern two-piece suits for doctoring, but now she wore a summer dress that Sarah would probably tell him later had gone out of fashion several years ago. She had on the earrings her grandmother had left her, and her curly hair was getting long, so that she had to push it from her eyes more than once.

He watched her roll her shoulders and sweep her hands over her face. He noticed her put her fingers to her neck and rub. Her gestures were as familiar to him as his own children's. He stroked the side of his glass, the smooth, sheer cool. Jean told how Emma had nuzzled into her pillow and pretended to be Wild Horse, her child's soft hair as his wild, long mane, and he laughed, and saw how now, when Jean smiled, the wrinkles round her eyes were strong. He hadn't noticed them before.

'Shall we eat, then?' Sarah was taking the food to the table, her forehead puckered, busy.

He asked Jean about her bees, and she talked as she ate, her speech and her eating cutting across each other.

'The queens have gone out of lay and nearly all the brood combs are covered. Not much more to do now till spring. I'll creosote the hives in the next week or so and there's a few knot holes to plug. Keep the weather out.'

'Slow down! You're getting faster,' Jim said. 'Isn't she, darling?'

'You always say that,' Sarah said.

'I don't,' Jim said. 'Do I?'

The two women exchanged a look, and Jim leaned across to his wife and cupped a hand to the back of her head, a gesture so habitual to him, he didn't know he'd made it.

'I don't,' Jim said again, stroking his wife's hair.

Sarah pressed her head back against his hand. 'My love, since our first date, almost.'

Jean laughed. 'Such a gooseberry I was. Only your mother could have made me do it.'

'Which first date?'

'Eating ice creams, by the beach. Jean was talking about medicine, I expect. You got out your watch. Timed her speech.'

Jim put his hands up. 'My oldest friend and my wife. What chance do I have?'

They knew the colour of old jealousy, each of them at the table. Their stories were like incantations, to keep it at bay.

It was one of Jean's few real regrets, that she couldn't have married Jim. But when, all those years ago, he had put a proprietorial hand to her head, cupped it to him, his fingers in her hair, she had felt caged, possessed, and she had fought wildly, cruelly perhaps, against him.

Yet even now, eating supper in his house, with his children asleep above, she couldn't help a twist of desire. Not for this man who was her closest friend, but for the life here that she could only ever visit.

And so the three of them talked on, chewing the fat until the warm light of the kitchen was cut by a ring on the doorbell.

Mrs Sandringham's boy was pink with exertion and he spoke in bursts, so that the message came out like small gusts of wind, the vowels and consonants tossed about inside it.

'Robson's worse . . . missus says noise you told her . . . it's there.'

Mrs Sandringham had been housekeeper and factotum to the doctor years before Jean became the doctor in question and inherited her, and she was a stickler for certain kinds of etiquette. Young John had been coached from a young age on how to deliver these messages, but the fact was that he was more at ease with crankshafts and inner tubes than he ever would be with people. All this Jean understood, and so she thanked him gravely before taking Jim's car and setting off into the November dark to see the dying man.

It wasn't much over the half-hour before she returned. Jim had kept the pudding warm for her. Jean put her spoon into the hot apple.

'These first cold nights,' she said. 'They take bodies by surprise.'

'Anything you could do?'

'It was really his wife that needed me. To tell her there was nothing she could do. That you can't stop a dying man from dying, not with all the will in the world.'

'That's what you said to her?'

'Course not. I gave Mr Robson a shot of morphine, told her the lemon cake was delicious and that he'd smiled when I said I'd been well looked after.'

'Had he smiled?'

'Then I reminded her that the world and its wife would be through her parlour very soon paying its last. So we sat back, she and I, and talked about food and wakes, and who could be counted on for what, daughters and sisters and such. She made a list; and told me how there were those who said her baking had brought them back from death's door, and her man upstairs more than once even.'

Jim smiled. 'Clever.'

Jean shook her head. 'So little I can do. Ease the pain for a moment, hers as well as his. That's all.'

'Eat your pudding.'

'But he has what he needs,' Jean said, the spoon of apple in her hand. 'You know.' And she made a small gesture with her free hand which took in this whole dense knit of the world she had just left – the small house and the dying man and his wife; her cake and the parlour; children, grandchildren, relatives and friends; the list just begun of all those who were part of this man's living and now of his dying.

She stood again, the apple still untasted.

'I'm tired, Jim. Say goodnight to Sarah for me. And come and drink tea tomorrow, if you can.'

4

Charlie hadn't meant to walk so far. It was only that he'd been intent on following things and they'd taken him on and on. It never started like that. But then one thing became something else and now, here he was, looking up at last to find himself on a broad road he didn't know, where the town seemed about to give out on itself altogether.

He could see a couple of houses ahead and then beyond only fields, black and featureless in the darkening of the afternoon.

'The first field, just touch a gate,' he told himself. 'And then go back.'

So he walked on, past a cat in a lit window looking out, pert and unimpressed, and then in the next house a mother's voice calling a girl's name, a tinny, small sound in the freezing air. There was the mother, too – her head moving across the window, a yellow scarf like his mother's, and wild eyes to the boy outside as she called again in this tired afternoon hour.

Charlie hurried. He must be quick.

The grass at the roadside was long and wet, limp with the weariness of the old year. His shoes glistened as he stepped up to the gate, and he felt the cool damp of it through to his skin.

'Touch,' he said, and he put his hand out to the wooden bar. It was icy cold and his fingers made trails on the wood.

'Frosty Jack'll be here soon,' he said, and he gave the smile his mother gave, of a secret known.

Charlie found the river on his way home. He crossed over on the blue bridge and walked the other side from the factory, along the towpath, being careful with his feet as best he could in the half-dark, because you got a pile of broken glass and dog dirt along here. He ran past the dark barges lying low against the bank – they had dogs that hated boys – and was almost beyond the factory when the hooter went off.

'Dead trouble now, Charlie,' he said, which was a phrase he liked, because now he knew what time it must be.

But he stopped, there on the other side, and stood watching. Everything was quiet, really quiet, and Charlie almost held his breath. Then doors opened in the walls, making drifts of light, and the girls came out, like a flood. So many of them. Somewhere in there was his mother. Their voices crossed the water, tumbling, released. He pictured her, head down and leaning forward as if walking in a wind, tying on her scarf as she went, her bag banging against her side. She'd be heading for her bike, rushing, he'd guess, because she was always rushing, to be home and on with the tea.

The street lights were on by the time Charlie reached the marketplace, dropping small pools of light through the darkness. Cats skulked round the edges and every now and then one would flit across a pool with a fish-head or some tattered wrapper, then disappear again into the dark.

He liked the market when it was empty like this, the tarpaulins sagged and flapping. The air was acrid with new fires lit, and he took shallow, short breaths to keep it out as best he could. He was thinking hard, looking for an excuse for where he'd been. It wasn't that his mother wanted him indoors all the time, but she always seemed to know when he hadn't just been playing out.

He'd pushed the sounds a long way off now. The whispers that snatched at his skin; the singsong voices that ran up the back of his neck, calling after him, the jeer that winded him, beating up his fear, till he had run and run, and finally come to the sombre fields and the cold gate.

You've been to another boy's house. There's a boy with new Meccano, or he's got some insects. Collected them. He shook his head. He didn't know any boys that collected insects. Cigarette cards, marbles, matchboxes. But not insects. Anyway, he didn't collect those things so his mum wouldn't believe him.

Down the high street and they were locking the doors and pulling the shutters across, snapping the light from the windows. Charlie's feet were sore, chafing with the wet from the grass. He was tired now, and very hungry.

His mother would be angry with him and rough like she was when she was angry, pulling his jacket off and putting his shoes by the fire. She'd point to the footprints on the lino and tell him to change his socks for dry. Then she'd ask him what he'd eaten since school and maybe make him bread and jam, or bread and dripping if he was lucky, stand over him while he ate it.

He hurried on, his thoughts striding ahead of his feet, and for now, all worry of how to account for himself was put away.

'Tide you over,' she'd say, giving him the bread and jam, and she'd put her hand through his hair. Which he'd half wriggle from, but part of him loved it when she did that. 'Tide you over till your father's back.'

Charlie stopped. His skin prickled. Words came back to him. He didn't know where to go. He stared at his shoes. A leaf was stuck to one heel.

An old man in a brown coat was sweeping the pavement with a broom as wide as a table. Charlie looked at him unseeing. The man swept his day away in long, straight strokes, down towards the road and into the gutter. Twice he swept to the gutter and Charlie still stood. Then the man leaned on his broom and looked at the boy. When Charlie lifted his head, he wagged his finger.

'Out of my way,' he said. 'Won't be as bad when you get there.'

And Charlie nodded, though he hadn't heard, and walked home.

The wireless was on when Charlie let himself in and his father was home already, his coat and hat on the hook, his shoes in the hall. His father was back, so no bread and jam. Charlie headed for the stairs and his satchel caught the hung coat and he smelled his father's smells of smoke and sweat and something else.

Kicking off his shoes, he lay on his bed for a bit, his tummy rumbling, picking at the ridges in the counterpane, rolling the cotton fray between his fingers. It was Christmas in another month and he wanted the earth. That's what he'd told Bobby for a joke. The earth. It was what he meant. But he wouldn't get the earth, so he was hoping for a fish tank.

He'd taken Bobby to see an ants' nest once, a really good one he'd found down the side of the allotments. Lifted these slabs and shown him.

'Look there, and there. See the tunnels and chambers? For food, and there's the egg chambers, see, and they're going berserk because we've lifted their roof off.'

The two boys had watched the ants rushing with the white oval eggs in their jaws, tugging them below and into the earth, out of sight, away from the terrible light and the threat.

'They're gossiping,' Bobby had said. 'Heads together, just like my ma and my aunts, heads together.'

'D'you see it now?' Charlie had said.

'They're a bit like us, then. Humans. With the gossip and the bother and them all worked up, getting fierce over the eggs.'

But it wasn't that at all for Charlie. It was just exactly not that. It was because they were so far from him that he watched them. Because they lived in another world from his. But Bobby was his best friend, so Charlie didn't answer him.

It was cold on his bed and he was nearly tempted to climb in under, feel the slow warming through and the slip towards sleep. But that would bother his mum, and his dad might clip him. He didn't like it when you did things out of turn. Charlie stared at the wall, eyes wide as they'd go, willed himself to see the wallpaper, the line where the roses didn't meet, petals flying into stems.

'Why've you got roses in your room if you're a boy?' Bobby had said when he saw it. Charlie didn't know, but he liked them.

He couldn't smell the fish on, which was odd, but he could see it on its plate, done over in flour, ready. He'd go downstairs now. His mum would be glad to see him, and he'd like that, even without the bread and jam. Fish would be a halfway house. Fish would do for now.

Pushing open the door to the living room, Charlie saw his mother and his father. His father sat at the table, fingertips resting on the evening paper, a beer bottle running rings around the headlines. He'd have been in the pub already. He didn't look up when Charlie came in, and this was just the same as always. His mother was there too, hands wedged into the small of her back against the length of day. Her apron strings made a butterfly at her waist and there was a dark patch on her left calf where she'd darned the stocking. She didn't hear Charlie there and this was not the same as always.

He wondered if they had been speaking before he opened the door, because after a moment with him still saying nothing and his father picking up the beer bottle and drinking from it, his mother crossed the room to the kitchen.

'Hello,' Charlie said, because otherwise she'd be gone into the kitchen and she still wouldn't know he was there, and she turned and gave him a bright, bright smile, like he didn't know what.

He waited for her to ask him where he'd been, to be cross, to put her hands on his cheeks to feel for the outdoors on him and then put a hand through his hair; to tell him that supper was all but ready and didn't he know how worried she got, and who had he been with out so late, and was it that Bobby again, she'd have to talk to his mother, and his supper nearly ruined, and would he go and wash, please, look at his nails. But she only walked to him, dropped a peck on his cheek and then went into the kitchen so quickly, to her cooking and the jolly wireless sounds, and pushed the kitchen door to so hard that he turned to his father to see if he'd noticed.

But his father sat with his eyes on the newspaper, his finger tracking a story. Charlie saw the strong line of his shoulders, the shove of flesh against his collar and the dark bristle of hair that threaded down his neck.

The bowl of cockles on the table made Charlie's mouth water. The wince of vinegar on his tongue. He watched as his father's fingers made delicate work of them, lifting each one clear with a slight shake before slipping it between his lips. Charlie wondered why his father ate them one by one, such little things.

Friday night food, they were his mother's treat for her husband, and Charlie knew better than to ask for one for himself. Anyway, he could smell the beer on his father.

'You up to much, then, Charlie?' his father said without raising his eyes from the paper.

Charlie wasn't sure what his father wanted, so he muttered something, and then waited. His father looked up at his son, rubbed his brow as if to clear it of something.

'Getting out, are you? Like boys ought to.' He picked another cockle from the bowl and Charlie watched a drip of vinegar darken the football news.

'Maybe there'll be snow soon, and we can take trays out,' Charlie said, remembering, pleased to have thought of something to say.

'Snow,' his father said, as though considering the word, and he shook his head. 'We'd have fun Charlie, wouldn't we? But not on trays.'

'But on the hill, like before, with Annie? You remember, so fast and off at the end into it, all over, down your sleeves and everything? And Annie got laughing so hard, she couldn't stand up and you put her back on the tray and gave her a push . . .'

'Your mother doesn't like it,' his father said.

'But it was Auntie Pam who wasn't pleased,' Charlie said, frowning. 'Because Annie brought the tray.'

Through the kitchen door Charlie could hear his mother moving pans about. He thought about her not liking it, and he wasn't sure. It didn't seem the kind of thing she minded. He looked at his dad. He had his head down with the football again, and then Charlie remembered something he really wanted.

'Dad,' he said, and Robert looked up.

'*The Gunfighter*'s on at the Regent.' Charlie said. 'Bobby said so at school. We could go. Bobby's going to the four-thirty with his dad.'

Bobby had been to a Western before with his father and Charlie thought it sounded like the best.

'Why don't you ask your father?' Bobby said, and Charlie didn't reply. But he had now, and he waited to see what his father would say.

Robert took a swig of beer and set the bottle down on the same ring mark.

'School,' his father said at last. 'You behaving?'

Charlie looked down at the floor and blinked hard. His dad got angry if Charlie showed he minded things. After a moment, he answered.

'Miss Phelps says it'll be a world war any minute, if we're not careful,' he said.

'If we're not careful?'

'Yes, and then it'll all be over, with the bomb.'

'How are we going to be careful then? For Miss Phelps?'

'Don't know. Because it got Lizzie Ashton so worked up, we had to get out our sums then.'

His father laughed, but it hadn't been funny. Lizzie Ashton screaming hadn't been funny.

'We all need to do our sums,' his father said. 'Get them wrong, and then where are we?'

Charlie put Lizzie Ashton's screams out of his mind.

'Miss Phelps is good at showing us. She's good at doing sums.'

'Miss Phelps is good at doing sums?'

'But she took Lizzie to the corridor because of the noise, and Miss Withers stood at the front. Everyone thinks she's pretty, but she's not as good at sums.'

'Aha, but that's it, Charlie,' said his father, his tapping finger making a nubby sound on the table.

'That's the thing about girls. There's the ones that are good at sums and the ones that are pretty. You marry the first, and they get your dinner on the table and your children scrubbed and brought up. And you don't marry the second.'

'But how do you know which are which?' Charlie said.

His father gave a hard laugh. 'Oh, you'll know that when the time comes.' He gave him a wink. 'Only your mother doesn't agree.'

'So what happens to the ones you don't marry? Don't they get to? Don't they get to have some children?'

His father tweaked a cockle clear, gave it a little squeeze.

'They're fine and dandy, Charlie. Fine and dandy. You'll see. Works out best for everyone.'

'And is Mum . . .'

'Is what?'

Something in his father's voice made Charlie flinch. He shrugged. 'She's not so good at sums,' he said. 'She's pretty too.'

Charlie didn't know what it was he'd done, but, pushing his chair back, his father stood up and turned an angry face towards his son.

'Did I say she wasn't? Ever? It's her who's done the saying. Did I say she wasn't?'

Charlie took a step towards the kitchen. 'I have to help with the vegetables. Mum asks me to,' he said, his voice soft with anxiety. His father walked to the living-room door.

'Tell her not to bother waiting up,' he said.

Charlie heard his coat fetched from its hook and the scuff as he pulled on his shoes. Then the frill of cold shuffling the newspaper pages, chilling his knees, and the door slam and the quiet. He was gone.

Lydia had her book propped open with the two-pound weight. On the hob, the potatoes boiled. Charlie looked down at the floury water. He warmed his hands in the steam, though they were cold again afterwards. Next to the hob was a plate with three pieces of steak.

'It's Friday, Mum.'

'Treat.'

'What for?'

Lydia chopped at the potatoes. Charlie went and stood beside her, leaning in against her waist. He felt her apron ticklish against his shin.

She nudged him with her elbow and swept the potato pieces into a saucepan.

'Hungry?'

He shrugged.

'School all right?'

'Dad said could you keep his supper over till later.'

Lydia didn't reply. Charlie looked at the book. 'I could read to you,' he said, picking it up. 'From where you got to. Page ninety.'

Lydia closed her eyes. Then she smiled. 'Go on then.'

He hefted the book in his hand, as if its worth could be felt in its weight, and started to read:

Slowly the world returned, black and cold. But where was he? No voices, no motor cars. Not a bird's cry, not a dog's bark. He tried moving his hands. Pain shot through him and he lay still again.

They came so quietly, he didn't hear until their whispered voices were just above him like snatches of a bad dream.

'He's alive.'

'Get him up and hold him.'

Someone lifted and he screamed in agony.

'Where's the Rigger, Georgie?'

The question came again and again, different voices speaking into the icy quiet, till the pain felled him and everything was still against the soil.

Charlie read carefully. He stumbled occasionally, but Lydia didn't interrupt. She carried on with what she was doing, taking care to be quiet. So she scrubbed the carrots more tenderly than she might. And laying them out on the chopping board, end-to-end like so many bodies, she was gentle with the knife.

But an action is an action, however it is performed, and

in the end Lydia's carrots were as sliced in one way as they would have been in another. After a short time she put a soft hand on the book.

'I might not make gravy,' she said.

Charlie lifted his eyes. He smiled and nodded his understanding. It was what his father liked, and his father had gone out. Sometimes his mother would put the wireless on and dance a little, but she wouldn't do that tonight either. She didn't dance very much any more.

'But read me some more,' she said.

'What's a rigger?' he said.

Lydia crunched up her forehead, thinking.

'We don't know yet. But I'd hazard a guess that it's a nickname.'

So Charlie read on a while longer, leaned back against the counter, as his mother got the supper ready. He read slowly and sometimes, if he asked, Lydia helped him out on a word. He didn't know what they were up to, but soon his head was full of figures monstrous in the London smog, and the plight of Georgie, who sounded like a gentleman and who was worried about catching the 6.48 boat train for Boulogne.

Lost with his mother in this strange, half-lit world, he forgot for a time that his father had gone out and that his mother had been crying when he came in.

5

The month before Christmas was bitter and wet. The sky lay low and grey on the town, pegged like a blanket to the hills in the west and dipping down in the east to meet the sea. By day people muffled themselves against it as best they could, buttoning coats high, pulling hats low down on the brow, tying plastic headscarves tight beneath the chin. Fires were banked high and reluctant children wrapped up, so that the town was full of swaddled figures. But each night, when the river mist rose and the sky dropped down below the trees to greet it, then people were caught unawares. The damp air eased between sheets tossed and loosened with dreams, kissing uncovered throats, slipping in with unguarded breaths to lie snugly in the lungs and wait for day.

Jean knew how the air did its work, and she was either strong or lucky, but her health stayed clear while her waiting room was filled during those winter months with people sickened by the lowering sky.

With the bees asleep, and the days cinched in so tight you could barely draw a proper breath, Jean dug herself into her work and waited for the coming of spring. She knew how the winters took her and it was best to be busy. Her time was filled with surgeries and clinics, with the impersonal light of hospital wards and the intimate fug of illness that brought her into people's homes.

'Doctor and priest,' Jim had joked once. 'You're the only ones invited into the bedroom.'

'For God's sake, Jim.' Jean had been a little irritated at the time, but it was true that sometimes a shiver did run across her skin when she crossed a threshold.

Mostly, when she visited her patients, she'd find the best linen out, on the bed and on the patient. The bedroom would have been tidied, and even the sickest person would have had a warm flannel over them before they saw the doctor. So when she lifted a wrist for the pulse or bent close to listen to a heartbeat, she was most likely to smell soap, and sometimes fever, and sometimes, unavoidably, the smell of death.

But occasionally she'd push the door open and there would be a glimpse of something else. It might be nothing more than a nightgown tossed over the end of the bed, or a drawer ajar. Or an unplumped pillow, still moulded by the head that had slept there. Or the room would carry the stale, intimate odour that eventually she grew to recognize.

Jean's parents had cultivated the romance of their marriage to the exclusion of all others, including their children, and made few bones about it. All through her childhood there had been conversations in which her mother and father would remind her of her place. Her father, reading an article in the newspaper about a ship foundered on rocks, would remark on how strange it was that the children should be got off first.

'I'd have been beating all back to get you to safety, my love,' he'd say.

And his wife would respond in kind: 'But if you drowned saving me, then there would be no point in living.' This would often be followed by Jean's father rising from his chair to kiss her mother at length on the mouth, while their daughter continued to eat her soft-boiled egg, or haddock in white sauce.

Jean had always known that the door to her parents' bedroom was not only shut, but usually locked, the key turned against all comers. Only dire emergency warranted a knock on the door, and on the rare occasion on which she had knocked, she'd been too scared to do more than stand on the threshold and cry, glimpsing behind an irritated parent the altar of their rough and tumbled double bed.

Perhaps this was why she didn't pursue Jim's remark about doctor and priest as she would normally have done. But neither did she examine the feeling these bedroom visits gave rise to, which was some strange mixture of embarrassment and envy.

Jean spent Christmas with Jim and his family. There had been a token invitation from her mother, but she wasn't expected to accept it, and she declined, as always, with a professional excuse.

'Only unmarried GP in town. Makes sense for me to be on call on Christmas Day,' she said.

Her mother made no reply. This was old history. Nothing new to be said.

Jean was free on New Year's Day to do whatever she wished. Without any particular reason, she decided that she wanted to feel the weight of the sky and to see no one.

She'd have travelled to the sea, if it had been the right sea. But the beaches nearest to this town were all wrong, with their pavements of rock and their crumbling earth cliffs.

Driving out of the town, Jean thought of her childhood coast with its deep hinterland of marsh and brackish lakes, and miles of dunes before you reached the sea. She longed to whittle time as she did then, spending the day hidden up, snug inside the sand, in sight of no one. Make a driftwood fire for warmth, this time of year.

She headed out for the hills. A beat was playing in her head, something by Duke Ellington, left over from the night before. She was determined to walk hard today; she had a route planned that meant she would have to, once she'd set out, if she were to get back to her motor car before dark. She'd walk herself out of the mood she was in, and into something different.

Last night everyone had laughed and toasted in the New Year, and Jean had swung around a dozen faces and kissed them. But later, home in her bed and lying in the dawn, curled around her own belly, hands tucked warm between her legs, she had cried her loneliness into the pillow before she slept. That's why today, the first day of the year, she was determined to walk herself straight again.

Jean had a lot of sympathy for other people's sadness. It accompanied illnesses and accidents into her surgery every day and she knew better than to set them up on a scale. The death of a father was a terrible sorrow for one person, but liberation for another. A son failing grammar school entrance, a daughter who played loose, a miscarriage, the failure of the potato crop – you couldn't set a scale to the sadness by knowing what gave rise to it. She didn't understand why some were struck harder than others, but she knew that it was so.

Setting out, Jean had little patience with her own feelings. She had a map and compass and a good sense of direction to guide her through this walk.

You're a fortunate woman, she told herself. You deserve short shrift. And she checked her bootlaces, humped up her haversack and set out.

All day the sky stayed low and every so often the thin mist that had followed her from the town would drift up from the valleys and hang in a desultory kind of way over the high moorland, laying a fine drift of wet over everything: plant, stone, solitary walker, the sheep that huddled in the lee of the rocks. Occasionally Jean heard the bristle of a small creature in the gorse and later, when she had dropped down lower into the valley, she heard deer.

Unpacking her lunch, she found her haversack wet with dew. She stood by a stream to eat and watched the long-tailed tits, their feathers dirty in the mist, skitter about the tall, dead stems of willow-herb. The rushes were half-dead and half-green, bundled untidily at the edge of the water. She saw a single fern pushing through the fallen leaves, its green so green it was like an interloper in this landscape.

The last miles were heavy weather. Her feet were wet; the haversack straps dug into her shoulders and her knees had started to ache with every downhill step.

'Bloody hell,' she said. She looked around her, peering into the empty, sodden air. 'Bloody hell,' she yelled, and she laughed, cold and alone and on a walk that was too long of her own devising.

When Jean bent over the bed and saw the little boy's sore eyes and runny nose and heard his cough; and when she coaxed his mouth open and saw the tiny tell-tale spots clustered in his soft cheek; when she felt the heat of his brow, she knew they were in for a bad run.

'Keep him in bed, keep the room cool and dark and encourage him to drink as much liquid as you can. Water, Ribena, doesn't matter. You'll notice a rash appear in the next day or so. That's normal. Stomach pain, diarrhoea is normal. The high temperature is normal. But if it stays high, beyond Friday, call and I'll be out to check on him.'

'Can't you give him some medicine? Or some of those anti things?'

Jean shook her head. 'Won't help. It's a nasty disease and he'll need the best care you can give. But most likely in a week or so's time he'll be well on the way to recovery.'

In the course of the day, Jean made house calls to two more mothers with four children between them, and gave each of them the same advice, explaining that measles was highly infectious and warning them to keep other children away.

By the end of the week, she had seen several dozen children and the town was in the grip of an epidemic. When another doctor went down with the disease, she took on his calls too; her evenings were filled with the sharp cries and racking coughs of sick children. She was exhausted and exhilarated.

'It's blown away my winter blues,' she said to Jim.

'I'm sure they're delighted to be helping you out.'

She swiped at him. 'I mean that I'm good at this. It's what I was trained for.'

'Mrs Sandringham moved in?'

Jean nodded. 'For now. She's a saint. Hot food and warm house when I come in at night. Her humming. Some cheerful noise.'

She reached over and tapped Jim's hand.

'Your girls all right?'

'Right as rain.'

'It's a horrid disease, Jim. Lock them up for now if you have to.'

The telephone rang.

'Dr Markham here,' Jean said, and when the voice at the other end spoke, her shoulders slumped.

It was a woman's voice, its telephone cadence high and tinny, urgent. Jean shut her eyes and for nearly a minute the voice went on. Finally, opening them again and squaring her shoulders, as though for a fight, Jean broke into the stream.

'You're doing everything you can, and as I said last night, you're doing it very well and . . .'

She rolled her eyes at Jim.

'No, it is only the measles,' she said in a voice which sounded almost the parody of calm. 'It would be no wonder if Connie caught them too. But at least you know now

what to expect. High temperature, tummy upset, rash . . .
No, there's nothing else I can do. I know she's only little
but . . .'

Following another spate of sound, Jean compromised.

'I'll call by in a couple of days, Monday afternoon.
She might be through the worst of it by then, with any
luck. You're doing a grand job. Keep it up. Excuse me
now. Yes.'

And then she brought the conversation to a close, banging her fist quietly on the table for emphasis.

'I think we'll find her temperature is on its way down by
then,' she said. 'Yes. A couple of days. Afternoon.'

She put the telephone down hard on its cradle with a
snap of plastic.

'Mrs Bewick,' she said. She slumped into her chair. 'She
called yesterday, too, to tell me about her little girl. She
didn't sound like a very happy mite, but that's how it is.'

'Measles?'

'Four children, gone down like ninepins, eldest to youngest. Three boys first, and now Connie. Only girl and her
mother's pride and joy. Father's away, working on the roads,
so Mrs Bewick's exhausted. I don't think that helps.'

'No family to help out? Neighbours?'

'No family near by. Also she's a bit strange. Won't let
anyone else do for them. Calls me, and calls me out, all the
time, but doesn't even like me examining them.'

'You sound fed up.'

'I'm tired is all, and she's a worrier. She always thinks
they're ill. I don't know how many times I've been into
that house.'

'And now they are.'

Jean frowned. 'The boys are on the road to recovery.
The eldest two will be back to school in a day or two.'

'She wants you to do some of your magic, my dear,' Jim
said.

'Don't tease me. I'm too tired. She doesn't want magic from me.'

'So what does she want?'

She shrugged and got to her feet. 'I don't know, but it's not a cure for her daughter's measles.'

With Mrs Sandringham living in, the big house felt quite different. There were lights on when Jean came home, and curtains drawn. She opened the front door to different sounds and smells. The wireless on and Mrs Sandringham humming at the stove, a pot of stew bubbling. The smell of her powder. Sometimes the pungent odour of young man, and there would be Mrs Sandringham laughing and chiding in the kitchen with one of her boys.

'Look at you,' Mrs Sandringham would exclaim when Jean pushed open the kitchen door. 'Well, look at you.' And she'd cluck around Jean, her nylon housecoat bristling, chivvying a son, pulling out a chair for her, lighting the gas under the kettle for tea, slicing and buttering a chunk from the loaf, and all the while chatting of something and nothing. Jean would sit, bone-weary, and be glad of the diversion.

'You can buy it sliced now,' Mrs Sandringham would say. 'It's off the ration. But I don't know what people see in it.'

Then she'd take the honey from the larder and dip a teaspoon with great ceremony.

'Not too thick, Mrs S,' Jean would say, and Mrs Sandringham would tut, but scrape the honey back.

'You'll fade away, you're not careful,' Mrs Sandringham said that Sunday evening, the second Sunday of her moving in. 'You were a man, you'd have a wife doing things properly for you, not this halfway house.' She leaned back against the counter, arms folded, and watched Jean, who was finishing an early supper at the kitchen table. 'It's the day of rest. Your eyes are on stalks and you can't stop yawning.'

'I'm fine,' Jean said, filling her bowl full of Mrs Sandringham's sponge pudding with a show of enthusiasm. 'Hale and hearty, with the best housekeeper in the world. The measles won't go on for ever. Another month, I'd give it.'

Mrs Sandringham pulled a chair out from the table.

'If you don't mind?' she said, and Jean nodded, smiling slightly at the unusual formality.

Mrs Sandringham shook her head.

'It's too much for a woman, all this. It was different, with Dr Browning. He had a wife as well as me. Mark you, he had his run-ins with illnesses too. But it's not the same.'

'I'm doing the same job a man would do, and I'm not doing it badly.'

Mrs Sandringham sat up straight in her chair. She checked her hair, re-pinning it with expert fingers, then put her hands on her lap.

'Can I speak plainly to you, Dr Markham? As one to another?'

'Of course,' Jean said.

'Well, then, it's not the point, is it? That you can do the job the same? In a war and that, then women are needed in men's place. They do the job as well. We all of us know that, specially the women. But the war's well over, the men are back, and there's no need for you to be working your fingers to the bone, out all hours, and home to a house big enough for a great pile of a family, and it's got nothing but you and your cat. It's a shame, you being as you are.'

Jean looked across the table. Mrs Sandringham's hands had come untethered from her lap and she was rubbing at a mark on the table, the stone in her ring catching the wooden surface with a faint *cratch* sound. As Jean watched, she lifted her head and focused somewhere off near the sink, as if summoning herself again.

'First of all, I have to be frank, when you arrived, you didn't seem the thing at all, after Dr Browning, and him there so long. Your own ways and so forth. I thought, to be honest, you'd only be here till you'd got the ring on your finger. But it hasn't gone like that, and besides, we rub along well enough now?'

Jean nodded.

'You've been good to my boys, and you like my casseroles, which is a thing Dr Browning never was so keen on.'

'Best housekeeper any doctor could wish for,' Jean said.

But Mrs Sandringham's thoughts were intent upon something, and Jean wasn't sure she'd heard her.

'I thought of writing it in a letter,' the housekeeper said, 'but then it wouldn't come out right. The thing is, and I know it's not the best time to be saying it. But there never is in your line of work. The thing is, I'm thinking I'll move to my sister's. Not right now. Later in the year, after the summer.'

'The one living on the farm?'

'I've always wanted to live in the countryside. The boys are grown now. It's not so much a farm. More of a smallholding. But it's too much work for her on her own, and you know her husband passed away.'

'You'd be going for good?' Jean said.

'She's got a man can help her this summer, but she can't afford him much beyond. So I thought it best to tell you soon as I could. So there's plenty of time.'

'Yes,' Jean said. 'Of course. That'll be quite a change for you.'

Mrs Sandringham got up and busied herself with the kettle.

'I've helped out often enough.' She shimmied it over the hob. 'I know what's needed. But I wouldn't go before you'd found someone else.' She lifted the kettle, on the poise of its boil. 'I wouldn't dream of doing that.'

*

Jean slept through that night. The doorbell was rigged up so that it rang inside her bedroom, but there were no call-outs. Yet something still brought her out of sleep with a start as if an electric shock had run through her. Head heavy on the pillow, she lay still, coming round. One of her hands was wedged between her legs, the other cradled beneath her head.

The light was bleary so it seemed not so much that the day was dawning as that the night was, in some essential way, undone. There was no more sleep to be had, but the morning was hard and unyielding, and Jean got up into it slowly, her limbs freighted with reluctance.

As her body surfaced, Mrs Sandringham's words came back to her and a wash of sadness ran across her, that it was only ever her own hands that caressed or cradled her.

The consulting room was warm, as always, by the time she arrived, the gas hissing quietly below its breath. Her desk was ordered, pens and prescription pad ready, and the teapot was under its cosy. The wireless was on in the waiting room, magazines straightened, chairs aligned. Two patients were waiting when Jean looked in. They kept their eyes down on the pages of *My Home* and *Practical Householder*, as if to avoid her notice, stay safe.

Jean knew that for every man or woman who came to see her, and put their bag down, or took off their hat, or unfastened their coat, and sat in the buttoned brown upholstered chair, there came into the consulting room with them a whole life lived, and a cluster of human intimacies. She knew that very often the sore arm, or the asthma, the bronchitis or the shingles, the infected finger or the worry over another pregnancy, carried the fray of that life. She would listen, and she would treat, and often she was sure that the first did more good than the second.

That Monday in January she did as she always did when she arrived at the surgery; shaking down her cuffs, a habit learned from her father, positioning the desk lamp, tearing yesterday from the calendar and gathering herself.

As a doctor, Jean was unruffled and authoritative. She listened attentively and learned over time that different kinds of performance worked better for men and women, so unless she knew to do otherwise, she would school her manner for each.

Formality worked better with most men, so she would sit behind her desk, pen poised when they came in, and when she examined them, she'd make a point of turning up her cuffs crisply. As though they were a business to be managed, not a human being with a body. She'd always get straight down to it, making it clear that any questions she asked had a bearing on the problem brought, and when it was necessary to ask about things that might embarrass, she would do so with her eyes down, intent on the notes she was taking. Only later, once her examination and assessment was made and the man was breathing easier again, adjusting his braces, or tying laces, would she ask him if he had any other worries.

With women she did things differently, shutting the door more carefully and then perhaps pouring herself some stewed tea. She'd listen with her head on one side, and when the consultation was finished, she'd ask them about somebody else, their children or their mother. She might even remark on their hairdo, and put a rueful hand to her own.

That Monday morning she saw a knee injury, back pain, haemorrhoids, a possibly tumorous lump and a duodenal ulcer. She saw a man with a bad heart and a young woman who stroked the arms of the buttoned chair and said the problem was that she couldn't breathe. Five minutes a life was the rule, and Jean was proud of her ability to give people the time they needed, and to keep to the schedule. Still, she allowed some slack to those who couldn't fit their pain into the minutes provided and, by the time she arrived on her first house call, she was, as usual, running behind.

It was gone four o'clock when she got to the Bewick home. She'd heard nothing, no message left, which was a good sign. A scurry of fingers opened the front door to her and she smiled wearily at the small, grave boy in underthings who stood back against the wall, his face still riddled with rash.

'You feeling a bit better?' Jean said, and he nodded. 'Good. Upstairs?'

He nodded again.

Last time Jean had seen Connie had been only three days ago. She'd stood at the front door scuffled in her mother's skirts, bright-eyed and shy. Jean remembered her apple-round face solemn at the threshold, and then wide in a smile as Jean bent to pick her up.

'Let me have a hold of you, you little sugar plum,' she'd said as she swung the small chunk of girl up level with her eyes and then turned her round and carried her up the stairs before her.

Today Jean found Mrs Bewick sitting on her bed with Connie a swaddled bundle in her tight arms. She looked unkempt, her lank hair bundled up roughly, a grubby beige cardigan pulled over a thin cotton shift dress. Jean could see that she was shivering.

'Mrs Bewick?' Jean said. 'It's Dr Markham. Can I come in?'

She didn't lift her head, didn't reply. Jean could hear the child's breathing, laboured and rough. The room was stuffy and the bed unmade. A bedside lamp cast a brackish light into the room, as though it were underwater. A bucket of dirty nappies stood by the chest of drawers, and a baby's bottle lay beside it. The bottle rocked slightly as Jean walked across the floorboards to the bed.

Crouching beside mother and child, Jean put a hand to the woman's elbow.

'Let me see her,' she said softly.

Mrs Bewick made no reply, only held her child closer to her.

Jean put a hand to the small brow. She was burning with fever.

'Has she been like this for long?'

Mrs Bewick turned the cradled child away.

'I need to see her, Mrs Bewick. I'll only be a minute.'

Jean could smell the little girl's hair, that sweet, milky smell. She could hear her struggle for air.

'A couple of things. I must check a couple of things.'

'I didn't call you.'

'I know.'

'You said not to call you.'

'Let me examine her, please.'

She tried to keep the panic from her voice, and maybe that persuaded Mrs Bewick and she placed Connie on her lap and allowed Jean to loosen the swaddling.

The three brothers were crowded in the doorway, shoving for a better view, but silently, as though they knew that something in this visit was very different from the last, and so they met it with their own, childish gravitas.

Jean turned to them. They looked like the three wise monkeys there, one tousled head below another, below another. She wanted to close the door against them. She didn't want them to see their sister like this. She didn't want them to see their mother's fear. She didn't want them to see her own. Forcing a smile, she waved her arms as if they were some quizzy pups.

'Go on, you lot. Git.'

Even in the silty light Jean could see the blue shadow at the girl's lips, and when she lifted a small hand free of the blanket, the same chilly shadow at the fingertips.

'She was looking at me so oddly,' Mrs Bewick said. 'Her eyes really wide, but not like usual. Her hands so icy and her head so hot. But now she won't look at all.'

'How long has she been like this? Struggling for breath?'

'You think I bother you. You think I make things up.'

'I think we need to get her to the hospital.'

Mrs Bewick and Connie had a side room in the hospital while they waited for the penicillin to take effect. Neighbours looked after the boys, who wished their sister could be ill more often, what with the jelly and fruit pastilles.

When Connie opened her eyes and smiled at her mother, Mrs Bewick looked as though she would break. But then her eyes closed again and though her body continued its struggle for air for two more days, her spirit seemed already to have drifted beyond reach.

When they trained you for doctoring, they didn't teach you how to cope with death. Only how to do all you could to rescue men and women from it. But death was a very present fact of life in Jean's line of work. People were born to die. She'd made her mother very angry once, saying that.

Despite all her best efforts, despite all medical knowledge and expertise, people would die and there was nothing she could do to prevent them. She knew by now that some, by the time it happened, were glad of it, but that many were not.

However they stood, Jean was surprised by how many people seemed to know when death was holding out its hand. Even young men and women. But not Connie Bewick. She had been out of the womb too short a time to know she might be going already. The caul still clung to her, soft and mother-smelling. But when her lungs were finally covered and she took her last breath, she seemed to slip into death so easily. Her fingers twitched, her eyelids quivered and then she was gone. There was nothing Jean could have done to hold her there, but when Mrs Bewick turned and looked at her above the small dead body, that made no difference. Despite herself, despite what she knew, Jean railed that night at she knew not what.

6

Charlie didn't keep step with his father on the way to the doctor's. It was partly his ribs, partly not, and both of them knew it, though Robert didn't know it as much as Charlie did.

Robert would go ahead for a bit, then stop and turn. His son walking so slowly, one arm held in to his side, head down, made him scowl. The boy made him angry. He wanted to shake him, tell him to stand up straight, stand up for himself. But he remembered Lydia's look as they had left, and he lit a cigarette instead and told himself to be patient, to wait it out till tonight.

Charlie told his mother he had tripped on the steps to the river, where the stone never dried and it was green and slippery. But she didn't believe him.

'You don't get ribs that sore by falling on the steps. Not at your age, Charlie.'

He shrugged and she tried again.

'Will you tell me? What happened?'

She waited; her eyes on her needle as she stitched at the tear in his shirt. Charlie didn't reply.

'You're going to see the doctor tomorrow morning,' she said.

'But you've got to go to work.'

'Your father's taking you.'

He looked at her; alarmed or angry, she couldn't tell.

'Not Dad. Please will you take me?'

'He can take the time. I can't.'

'Then couldn't Annie?'

'She's at work too now. Remember?'

'Please, Mum.'

She shook her head. Charlie willed her to look at him, but she kept her eyes fixed on the sewing.

He didn't blame the boy. Fred Dawson. It was the girls had done it with their skipping. He wouldn't think about it and he wouldn't answer his mum, so he might as well keep quiet as make something up for her.

Dinnertimes, he and Bobby had a place they went to between the boys' and the girls' playgrounds, down the side of the school. It was narrow there, and often windy; the sun didn't get in till nearly summertime. The school seemed to reach to the sky if you looked straight up.

It made Charlie dizzy, leaning his head that far back, and he'd put a hand to the bricks to steady himself. When it was summer the bricks were warm. But not the day he hurt his ribs and when he lifted his hand, his palm was cold and gritty. A drainpipe dropped the full height of the building down to a gutter channel, and sometimes there'd be foam there, left high and dry, to be flecked up by the wind across your face and arms.

The building stepped in behind the gutter so there was a space where the boys could be hidden, and mostly they were left alone. They played marbles, heads squinting in concentration over cat's-eyes and bombsies in the dust, and Charlie would tell himself that if he could just roll his marble the closest to the lag line, or win Bobby's favourite cat's-eye, then he'd get home without any trouble, or there'd be treacle pudding for tea.

Sometimes they hunched back against the school wall and made up stories. Bobby's about war or cowboys, and

Charlie's about masterful criminals outwitted by masterful detectives, always in fedoras and smoking Pall Malls. Yesterday they'd been playing for keeps, and Bobby had been winning.

He didn't listen to the girls. They weren't singing at him. They were skipping, the rope swinging high and hard, with a *whoosh* and then a whip across the ground with a tight, neat crack. *Whoosh* crack – *whoosh* crack – and the girls beating out the rhythm with dancing feet.

Down in the valley where the green grass grows,
There sat Biddy pretty as a rose.
Up came Johnny and kissed her on the cheek,
How many kisses did she get this week?
One, two, three, four . . .

Bobby was hunched forward, his attention focused on the colours in the dust.

'I've got you on the run, Charlie. Four that was, out of the ring.'

The girls' rhymes, swung with the rope, were as familiar a drone of girl-sound to Charlie as the small, shrill shouts thrown out by the boys playing football. They stopped and then started again.

Down in the valley where the green grass grows,
There sat Irene pretty as a rose.
Up came Robert and kissed her on the cheek,
How many kisses did she get this week?

Charlie looked down at the circle. The marbles waited in their pools of dust. Bobby waited. The girls started again, but it was different this time. Their voices were sneery and knowing. This time they sang it for him to hear, not for the rope. They sang his father's name again. They sang the other name again. The name he'd heard between his parents. The name he knew but didn't know why.

Down by the river where the green weeds grow,
There sat Irene giving him a blow.
Up came Robert and kissed her on the bum,
How many babies did he put in her tum?
One, two, three, four . . .

Charlie stood up, his bare knees gritty. Something was drumming inside him, drumming along with the rope turn.

'Charlie? It's your turn.'

Bobby was pointing. Charlie looked down, and the marbles stared up like so many eyes watching, waiting.

Still the rope hit the ground and still the girls sang.

Later, Charlie couldn't remember how the fight had started, or how it had gone on. He remembered running to stop the rope swinging, to stop the girls singing, away from the marble eyes, away from his wondering friend. He remembered crossing the white line and a teacher's voice shouting. He remembered the girls' faces grinning as he ran at them, then shocked and surprised.

But after that it was fragments, like a picture cut into pieces. He didn't know how come he'd fought with this boy. The white skin of Fred's hairline, the skew of his tie, a scab beneath his chin, bleeding from one of Charlie's blows.

He didn't know he'd been hurt until the teacher stopped them. But standing in the corridor, waiting to see the headmaster, then he knew, and he moved gingerly, guarding his body against any sudden moves, anything that might take it by surprise.

'Took that like a man,' Fred said and, to his surprise, Charlie could hear respect in his voice. 'Your first time, seeing Mr Wilks?'

54

Charlie nodded.

'He'll go on a bit, but he doesn't like hitting us.' The bigger boy rubbed at his jaw. 'Got me good and proper. You were pretty angry.'

Charlie put a hand to his own mouth. His top lip was swollen and his mouth tasted of metal. One ear was hot, as if somebody was holding a glowing coal close up. But it was his chest and his back that felt the strangest. He put a finger to his ribcage and pressed. The pain was sharp. It made pinpricks in his scalp; it made him dizzy and he shut his eyes.

'You all right?' Fred's voice sounded as if it were in another room.

Fred was right and the headmaster didn't hit them. He was disappointed, he said, and he looked at Charlie with eyes that reminded the boy of an old dog.

Charlie's body ached. It hurt if he breathed in too much, and it hurt if he moved too quickly. But he didn't want to go straight home. Fred would leave him alone, but the girls wouldn't. They'd be looking out for him after school, so he decided to risk it and slip through the kitchen and then out past the bins. You could do it without being noticed if you were quick enough. Then he went with Bobby to the old pipe factory that lay back from the river.

The factory had been bombed in the war, and now the low lengths of brick building stood chopped up and open to the sky. Here and there corrugated iron sheets stretched across and the wind would string itself over their ridges with a low whistling croon.

Chunks of concrete pipe lay flung about in the weeds, some wide enough to crawl inside, and Charlie used to hope that they might find a grass snake basking in one some day.

When darkness fell, the place belonged to courting couples. Sometimes somebody would clear a corner under a corrugated strip and sleep there for a while. There'd be the remnants of a fire, some newspaper and empty cans. But mostly, after school, the boys had it all to themselves.

Bobby chinked the marbles in his pockets.

'I'll give you back your best ones if you tell what happened.'

Charlie shook his head. Bobby kicked a can against the bricks.

'If you won't tell, I get to choose the game.'

Charlie shrugged.

'Right then,' Bobby said. He leaned back against a wall and stared across the scrubby ground.

'It's the Blitz. I'm going to be the air-raid warden, and you be the wounded man.'

Charlie nodded.

'And you wouldn't go into the shelter.'

'Long as I don't have to run,' Charlie said.

'And I rescue you, and then I have to go and rescue these other people.'

So they played in the rubble for a while. Bobby found a vast sink, the enamel gone green with mould.

'We might find a snake here soon,' Charlie said. 'It's getting warmer. They'll be waking up end of March time. We could put it in here, make a place for it.'

'What are you going to tell your mum? About your shirt? And why you're walking funny?'

Charlie ran his fingers over the sink. The enamel was slippery and smooth.

'Don't know. That I tripped by the river. Something.'

He rubbed his green fingers over the tear in his shirt, and then across his trousers. Eventually the boys grew cold and went home.

Charlie and his father had to wait a while at the doctor's, so Robert stood at the magazine table and flipped the pages. Charlie sat and listened to the gas hiss and wondered whether, if he gave him his favourite shooter, Bobby would look for a snake with him.

Then the door to the consulting room opened and they were called in, and it was a lady doctor sitting behind the desk. She had green eyes and dark, curly hair, but not like Auntie Pam's. The doctor's curls looked like they had just grown like that. Auntie Pam made hers on curlers. He'd seen her in them, like big worms all over her head. The doctor didn't smile much and she asked Charlie, not Robert, to sit down in the chair. Charlie hesitated and looked up.

'It's Charlie that's here to see me. Isn't it?' she said.

The doctor's voice was firm, and she sounded serious. Charlie nodded.

'Then you're the one the chair is for. I don't expect your father will mind standing?'

'Sit down,' Robert said, and so Charlie sat, carefully, into the deep chair.

The lady doctor asked him to tell her what was wrong. He explained about falling near the river and hurting his ribs.

'And your lip? Did you hurt that in the fall too?'

He nodded. He knew she didn't think it was a fall, but she didn't ask him any more.

'But it's the ribs that are causing you some pain?'

'Yes.'

'I'd better have a look then,' she said.

When she stood up, Charlie saw that she was tall, as tall as his dad. She was wearing a skirt and a jacket made out of rough brown material with green and red checks. His teacher sometimes wore clothes like this. They made him feel itchy, just to look at. Although she wasn't smiling, she didn't look unfriendly and he didn't feel nervous. He noticed that she barely looked at his dad.

She had him stand up and take off his sweater, unbutton

his shirt and then lift his vest, so his chest and back were bare. She rubbed her hands together.

'They're not very warm, I'm afraid.'

Charlie could feel the blush across his face as she went to touch his ribs. He looked across towards the fireplace. There were some china figures on the mantelpiece and a glass vase, and something that looked like a piece of honeycomb except it was much bigger than the real thing and in an odd shape.

His mother had bought a jar of comb honey once when someone told her it would help his father's hay fever. It was expensive and Charlie hadn't been allowed more than a taste. But the comb had fascinated him. He'd turned the jar around and around at the table, staring through the glass at the impeccable hexagons, until he was ordered on with his porridge.

The honeycomb on the mantelpiece looked as if it was made of wood. Polished, smooth. If he could only get a bit closer.

'You've got some nasty bruising, Charlie. Now, this might hurt a bit.'

Charlie wondered about the wooden comb. He wondered whether he could touch it. It would be a bit like touching the real thing, only he could fit his finger in these wooden cells. The man who made this, he'd have chisels and sandpaper, and tools to measure with. But the bees did it with their mouths. They made the wax out of their own bodies and then built their perfect shapes. That's what his mum had told him.

'It might hurt a bit, Charlie,' the doctor's voice said, and then a pain scorched its way through his chest, so that his sight went blue and silver and he cried out.

Her voice was soft in its wake.

'Must have been quite a fall.'

And in the quiet, his father's voice.

'Least it's not another one with measles.'

Charlie heard his father's rough laugh, and after it silence. Then the doctor's voice, very low, and sounding like the word had been dragged out of her.

'No.'

Charlie opened his eyes.

'That hurt a lot, didn't it?'

The doctor was still crouched beside him. He wouldn't look at her. He looked across the room at the burnished comb.

'You looking at the honeycomb?' she said.

He nodded.

'Stop staring.' His father's voice was impatient. 'Come on and get dressed. You're wasting the doctor's time.'

'It's all right, Mr Weekes. Go and take a closer look, Charlie, if you want to.'

Charlie took a step, and then paused. How did she know what he was looking at?

'If you pick it up, you'll feel it's quite heavy. Very different from the real thing.'

Charlie walked across and picked it up. He heard the doctor say something to his father, and his father reply. He counted the cells – seven wide and five deep. Behind him, they went on talking, but he didn't hear. He wasn't listening. He traced the contours with his finger, then the doctor's voice cut in.

'It's modelled on a piece of comb from wild bees,' she said.

'So, do they make wild honey?' he said.

'Charlie, will you tell me how you got these hurt ribs?' she said.

He put the comb back on the mantelpiece and began to button up his shirt. He didn't turn and he didn't reply.

'Answer the doctor,' Robert said, and Charlie turned then, his face tight, and picked up his sweater.

'You'll be in more trouble once you're out of here if you don't answer,' his father said, but Charlie knew he only said it to sound proper to the doctor, not because he really cared how Charlie had got hurt.

The doctor was leaning back against her big desk, arms folded.

'A friend made it for me, because I keep bees,' she said, nodding towards the mantelpiece.

Despite himself, Charlie turned to her, his eyes alive with questions. The doctor smiled, not at him, quite, but more as if she understood something.

'Have you ever seen a hive?' she said, her face serious again.

Charlie shook his head.

'The bees wake up about now, with the weather getting warmer. I'll be doing a first inspection soon. You could come and have a look.'

Charlie looked from the doctor to his father, his face a shock of anticipation.

She turned to Robert. 'With your father's permission.'

Robert stared at Jean, his expression shifting like water. Charlie knew better than to say anything, or make any move. He stood where he was, his sweater still in his hands, waiting.

Robert got to his feet and shook down his jacket, adjusted his scarf, put on his hat. Motioning to Charlie to follow, he walked to the door.

'All right then. About the bees.'

7

The doctor's house was huge. Big as a ship. Big as a castle. All on its own, with its own hedge around and a driveway with gravel that wouldn't last a minute if it was on his street. Butterflies kicked up a storm in Charlie's stomach. What if she didn't remember him? What if she didn't really mean it?

He nearly turned around and went, except that a big lady saw him and marched at him like a tank and so he froze instead of running. She wore a thin coat like Auntie Pam did, over the top of everything else, so he could see her dress peeping out at the top and from underneath. You could get an electric shock off Auntie Pam's and when she stood under the electric light, the coat shone like plastic. This lady's had a pattern on it that looked like tongues in blue and red that swirled and flipped about in the wind.

'It's not anyone that's ill,' he said. 'It's about the bees. She said I could see the bees.'

And Mrs Sandringham got him by the collar and took him round the side of the house and shouted for the doctor.

She was wearing old trousers and a pullover with holes and she had a scarf around her head. When she got nearer, he saw she was smiling.

'Charlie Weekes. I'm glad you're here,' she said. 'Come and see what's going on.'

The bees had things to fear in the winter. Mice, which

crept in at the door and ate their sweet food. Woodpeckers that could shred the hive to splinters. Canny blue tits that came tap-tapping at the entrance to snap up any curious bees. Dr Markham told Charlie how the warm February sun could lure them from the hive with a promise, like the ice queen, then freeze them to death. How they could lose their way home in the snow, bewildered by its brightness. He watched her heft each hive to know its weight, and she told him how careful you must be, when it was still wintry, not to disturb the bees or they might kill their queen, though she didn't know why.

She gave him a notebook with a red cover and a leather loop to hold the slender pencil.

'Might be useful,' she said.

He wrote down that a slice of onion was good for bee stings. He wrote down that bee stings were good for arthritis. He wrote down that honey was heavier than water. He wrote down that you could talk to the bees and tell them about important things. But you must do it quietly, else they might fly away.

Before he left that day, Charlie ran back to where the hives stood. The doctor hadn't told him how he should speak and he wasn't sure how near to be, or what he should say. So in the end he stood at one side and put his head close, as if listening at a door. Covering his mouth with his hand, he told the bees he would be back next weekend and that he was glad now about the fight at school. Then, very quietly, he told them that his mum was sad but he didn't know why.

8

Lydia cycled through the town with the noise of the wind in her ears and the sight of her son in her mind's eye. The sun shone a thin light and the day promised to be warm, though it wasn't yet. Down the hill and over the criss-cross of streets, past men and women washed and combed and brushed for the day. Hair sliced into lines, scarves tight beneath the chin against the messy air, walking on and on, seeing and not seeing, ready and not ready for daylight business. Or queuing, checking watches, leaning and careful against a corner, rocking on heels still pink from between the sheets. Or heads ducked into newspapers to find a retreat from the rise of the day here and now in this place, these pavements, this weather, this town.

She'd been cross with Charlie this morning. He'd had his breakfast in front of him for ten minutes and not started on it yet and she was impatient with his dreaminess.

'Get on and eat, otherwise . . .'

And she'd turned with a shake of the head and gone for more water for the tea, so that Charlie had finished the sentence behind her back.

'Otherwise I won't grow tall and strong like my dad.'

She hadn't been sure, from the way he said it, whether she was meant to hear him, or not. It was what she used to tell him when he was little, and it was true that she hadn't found the new thing to say now he was bigger. But there was something in Charlie's tone that sounded bitter, not amused or jokey, and Lydia didn't know how to respond to that. So she'd sat down with the tea and settled on something else instead.

'Charlie, you're not making yourself a nuisance over the bees, are you?'

Which had got Charlie's head up from the threads of jam he was patterning over his bread. He'd stared at her, his mouth slightly open, in something that looked like alarm.

'She hasn't said that? She hasn't said it to you?'

'No, she hasn't. I haven't spoken with her. Haven't clapped eyes on her yet. But you're there every week almost,' Lydia said, and then, trying to make light: 'I barely see you weekends, these days.'

'She's said I can go after school today. If I want.'

He waited, eyes down again on his plate till he caught her nod, then he started eating his bread and jam, taking large bites and swallowing fast.

'Perhaps I better go and get ill,' Lydia said, smiling, watching him, 'so at least I could meet her. Thank her for her trouble.'

'It's not trouble,' Charlie said. 'She likes me being there. I like the bees. I can help her,' and he pushed back his chair to leave the table.

In that way parents have when they need to have the last word, Lydia called as he left the room, 'Wash your face before you go, and don't forget your dinner money.'

Afterwards, cycling, the early morning wind forced tears from her eyes. They scudded across her cheekbones, reluctant messengers from some unexamined pool. In her bag were a Thermos of tea, a clean pinafore and the square, clean corners of a book. She'd take it out at lunchtime if she could, and dip in like dipping in a stream, let the words carry her somewhere else, anywhere.

'Where'd you get the habit from?' her friend Dot asked once, as if reading was a bit like picking your nose.

'I had an uncle used to read to me.'

She looked down at her shoes, remembering, but not wanting Dot to ask about it.

Sitting side by side at the end of the vegetables, leaning against the shed. She used to put one hand behind her and snag at the splintery wood with her thumb, pressing just hard enough to feel the thread of nerve, and with the other hand she'd turn the pages, watching for her uncle's nod. She remembered how she'd liked to think nobody could see them, hidden behind the rhubarb leaves and ornamental thistles.

'So you got it from him, then.'

'Must have done.'

'What about his own kids?'

'He never married. Don't even remember any girlfriends. Then he was killed in the war. Ship got torpedoed.'

'Sounds like you were very fond of him.'

'He used to read me Sherlock Holmes.' Lydia laughed. 'Got me scared out of my wits.'

Dot rolled her eyes, as though it explained everything, that it was Sherlock Holmes, though Lydia knew she'd never read a book in her life.

'He promised to marry me when I was bigger. By the time he was killed I'd got old enough to know that you couldn't marry your uncle, but still . . .' Lydia shrugged.

She tailed off, and Dot nodded her understanding, not about the reading, but maybe about the rest.

When she could, Lydia got to work ahead of time. That way, she could find a good spot in one of the vast bike sheds and get away quick at the end of the day, pedal like fury back to her boy.

She was nearly in the factory door when the five-minute hooter sounded. You could hear it all the way across town, and Charlie used it as his signal to leave for school. She pictured him grabbing his satchel and his coat, pushing his arms into sleeves as he set off down the street, his socks halfway down already, his collar skewed.

This doctor bothered Lydia. She wasn't from the same place as them. She lived differently. She'd speak differently, and that mattered. Lydia wondered what they talked of, her son and this woman. She wondered what he'd think, that his mother worked in a factory and this woman was a doctor. She wondered why the doctor wanted Charlie there.

Around her the women gossiped and smoked. Somebody crooned 'Secret Love' till the bell sounded and the conveyor belt began its endless journey.

All through the morning Lydia wondered. Her head was tilted to the belt and her hands moved without thought, doing their dance with cable, clamp and screwdriver. When she first started in this room, she'd thought how pretty the boards looked with their patterns of coloured wire. Pretty after the grey on grey of the munitions. She didn't notice now. Only joined in the joke occasionally, when a girl left with her leaving gift, how the only thing she ever made and the one thing she never got from this place was a wireless.

The tea-trolley was rolled round and Lydia stood and drank her tea for ten while the tea-breaker took her place at the line.

Lunchtime, and she ate quickly in the blather of gossip and noise, the voices cutting this way and that. Cheap stockings to be got at a place behind the station. A girl got in the family way and flung out for it, till the problem disappeared and no more said.

'It's the mother should be ashamed. Girls die of that.'

'Least she can get herself a husband.'

'Might have queered the pitch for a baby, though. She won't be telling any hubby about that, now will she.'

Then it was on to a pair found carrying on in the wire store.

'Hard at it, they were, when the line controller came in. Bad luck. He'd lost his watch, only went in to search for it.'

'Locked, I heard they were.'

'Then she'll be needing more than new stockings,' Dot said, and Lydia laughed with the rest.

Arrangements were being made, for the pictures, and for dancing at the Grafton. Dot nudged her.

'You coming?'

'I don't think so.' Lydia looked down at her shoes.

'Come on. Charlie's old enough now. And there's always his aunt.'

Lydia followed Dot's glance across the cafeteria. Robert's sister Pam was sitting with an older group of women. Feeling their eyes on her, she looked across at them.

'Or Annie? She could come and sit in with Charlie. They're good pals, aren't they?'

'She gets precious little time free from her mother. I don't want to ask her to give up some more. Besides which I think there's a young man lurking somewhere.'

'Keeping his distance from Pam, I should think, if he's got his head screwed on right.' Dot nudged again. 'Look, she's going to give you a smile.' She made a wave with her hand and grinned.

'Don't,' Lydia said. 'Anyway, I don't want Charlie round there if he doesn't have to be.'

Pam must have said something to the women sitting with her, because Lydia saw several heads turn, quizzical, and Pam's in the middle, stony with dislike.

'She really has it in for you. Stealing her boy,' Dot said, her voice sarcastic.

'Leave it, Dot.'

'What is it, ten years since you moved here?'

'Pam doesn't get over things,' Lydia said.

'Yes, we all know that. We all know how her mum died and her dad died and how she kept her baby brother out of Park Hill single-handed with only the rats for company.' Dot's voice was singsong with scorn. 'Working nearly to death to bring him up.'

'But it's true,' Lydia said. 'I heard it all from Robert before I ever met Pam. And how her husband died in the first year of the war with Annie not even out of nappies.'

'Course it's true,' Dot said. 'Course it bloody is. We've all heard about her sacred Dennis. That's not the point.'

'You mustn't speak ill of the dead,' Lydia said, but there was a half-smile on her lips. 'It's just easier if I keep away from her as best I can,' she said, fingers on her tray, ready to leave.

'What I mean is, all that's nothing to do with you. You didn't even live here then. You don't even come from this town . . .'

'Which is something else she holds against me,' Lydia said. 'Thinks I'm stuck up. She thinks Robert should have married a local girl.'

'Once her Dennis was gone to the happy hunting ground she'd have married Robert herself if she could,' Dot said.

'Dot!' Lydia's exclamation brought looks from other tables, and she clapped a hand over her mouth. 'You can't say things like that,' she said from between her fingers.

'That's why she hates you,' Dot said slowly. 'She's jealous. She did all the hard work, brought him up, and then just when she's lost her husband, you waltzed in and stole Robert from her.'

'And had Robert's son,' Lydia said. 'She hates Charlie nearly as much as she hates me.'

'So come on,' Dot said. 'You can't change any of that. Forget your sorrows for a couple of hours.'

'I've got my book to forget in.'

'It used to be you suggesting it. Remember? Last-minute

Lydia. Remember them calling you that? We'd get to four o'clock on a Friday, or a Tuesday even, and it'd be you saying let's go dancing, or get a picnic up, or you'd have some mad thought because there was a full moon and we'd go off and do it and have a laugh.'

Lydia smiled.

'Come dancing tonight. It'll do you good. Besides, a dancer like you, you might get lucky. There's some lovely men on a Friday night.'

'I'm married. With a son.'

'I was joking, mostly,' Dot said. 'But with Robert and all. You need to look out for yourself.'

'And Charlie.'

'You don't look out for yourself, you can't look out for him.'

Lydia stood up. 'I need a bit of time,' she said, picking up her book, and Dot patted her arm by way of understanding, though whether it was understanding about the dancing, or about her wanting to read her book in the lunch hour, Lydia didn't know.

Robert was already home when Lydia came in from work. On the table were his shoes, dull with fresh polish. She heard his voice beyond the kitchen. He was in the bathroom, humming a tune from way back when.

A different time in our lives, she thought, and the smile in remembering was chased across her face by sadness.

As she started to prepare for supper, busy with pans and groceries, Charlie's breakfast plate and cup in the sink reminded her that he was late today because of the bees, and she stopped in her busyness a minute with thinking.

It was odd, Robert being home so early. She wondered about it. His spirits sounded high. She began on the washing, lifting clothes from the horse, folding and smoothing.

'. . . She is watching and longing and waiting
Where the long white roadway lies.'

He had a lovely voice. He used to sing a lot. It was the song he sang to her the day his leave was over and they stood on the platform in a throng of uniforms.

'And a song stirs in the silence,
As the wind in the boughs above . . .'

They were close up against one another, like all the other sweethearts, and he had one hand on her belly with its tiny comma of life swimming in there, and he sang into her ear.

'But there's one rose that dies not in Picardy!
'Tis the rose that I keep in my heart! . . .'

The laugh in her throat caught her by surprise, as she remembered how his voice had tickled. God, he had such a beautiful voice. She used to tease him that he could stand in for Vera Lynn any day, and he sang her 'Roses of Picardy' there on the platform and she loved him.

Lydia put the kettle on for tea and her chest felt tight with tenderness. This was the same man she had fallen for ten years ago. The same man whose voice saying her name made her stomach turn over with desire. Surely to goodness there was a way out of their present trouble? She knocked gently on the bathroom door.

'Robbie?'

The singing stopped abruptly, mid-line.

'I've got the kettle on. Do you want a cup?'

He answered yes, but even through the door she could tell he was surprised.

When he came out, she said she'd heard him singing.

'Reminds me of you going back to your ship that time. You sang that song then. Do you remember?'

He nodded slightly, hair tousled, skin warm and fresh,

his cologne sweet between them, and she glimpsed in the gesture, the way his dipped his head, eyes closed, the man she had fallen in love with.

'I was just pregnant,' she said, smiling, still caught in the memory. Something was in her mouth to say, something smooth and salt and solid. Something that might be a wish, or a promise, or both.

She watched him stare.

'Robbie,' she said.

He frowned.

'Why are you calling me Robbie?' he said.

'I always used to.' She could feel the shape of the words behind her lips, gathered in the space above her tongue. She could taste them. 'Remember?' she said, but to herself.

They might have made love now. She would have touched his warm, sweet skin; on the nape of his neck maybe, he always loved that. Or put her hands on to his shoulders, an invitation for his around her waist, them dancing there in the half-space, till his hands slipped down to her hips and he pulled her close and she felt the rise of his desire. They might have made love now.

Growing up, Lydia didn't know what a man's body looked like. Twice, or maybe three times, she'd glimpsed her father half-undressed in his heaved-up, woollen underthings, but the sight left her puzzled. Not at all like what she'd heard whispered at school. For a time during the war there was the American with the gentle smile. He charmed her, flirted with her and then he took her virginity. She'd given it willingly enough, and she did like him, though it wasn't more than liking. But she never saw him naked. He would take her clothes off carefully, folding them piece by piece on the chair, stroking her arm, her shoulder, her breast, till she stood bare, shivering. But then he'd be so coy, undressing with his back to her, having her turn away before slipping beneath the covers to join her, that all she knew of him was what she felt, and though he was lying hard up against her, somehow it didn't feel like him.

Then there was Robert. He wasn't like the American, not charming like that. He didn't treat her like royalty or even hold the door open for her. But from the first time she saw him, something got hold of her from the inside. She was standing outside a pub, stamping her feet for warmth, waiting for her friend and caught in her thoughts, when a voice broke in.

'Do you want a drink?'

She turned to find a sailor there, his neckerchief tied rakishly, with his brown face above and his white neck below. He was hungry-looking, thin as a wire, with a gaze that flicked over her shoulder and back.

'I'm waiting for someone,' she said with a shrug, but he didn't seem to mind and he leaned against the wall next to her, and said something about it saving him the price of a drink.

She couldn't place his accent, but he didn't come from anywhere she knew. She'd have stabbed a guess at somewhere in the middle of the country, which meant above London and below Yorkshire. He wasn't anything special to look at, but her heart was jumping in her chest and she could feel her body flush. She put her hand to her face in surprise. This had never happened to her before and she was glad of the half-dark to hide it.

'What about tomorrow?' he said, but in a manner so offhand, so different from her Yank, that she couldn't tell if he was serious or not, if he really wanted to.

'Maybe,' she said, trying to match his tone.

'I've got a week's leave.'

'I'm on a late tomorrow. Start at eight. And busy in the day.'

So the next night they met for an hour and he told her about his ship and the convoys and how boredom and fear snugged in together, making men do strange things while they waited for the U-boats in the middle of the sea. She watched him talk and nodded at the right places, asked the right things, but she couldn't stop her mind thinking other thoughts all of which went to the same place, which was that she wanted him.

Robert looked her up and down, as if he hadn't seen her for an age, and she waited, the cup of tea shaking a little in her hand, till finally he shook his head.

'It's too late,' he said.

Slowly she set the cup and saucer down on the floor. She didn't want the tea to spill. She had heard his words, but she didn't understand them.

'Why?' The word came out almost as a sigh, and she hurried to speak again in a plainer voice. 'What's too late?'

'I was so happy, that day. If I'd only known,' he said.

'It was the day I told you I was pregnant,' she said, her voice questioning, and he nodded.

'You were going back to your ship, but I was pregnant,' she said again.

He didn't answer, and Lydia leaned back into the wall. She could feel herself trembling.

'It was a good day. And the song. You remember? Every time I heard it after that, I thought of us close there, and of Charlie.'

She stopped and looked at him. Something in his face was closed. She wanted to reach across and touch him, put her fingers to his cheek as she hadn't done in so long. She wanted to waken something, in her and in him. Her hands felt empty and awkward at her side. Robert didn't move, didn't speak. She waited in the narrow spit between kitchen and bathroom, so close to him they nearly had to touch, and yet without touching.

She held her breath. It was like that moment before they

danced. When all it took was his finger on her hip, or the slight lift of her shoulder and they'd be away, off and away, and nothing more in the world existed, nothing more than their two bodies and the music and the dance.

When finally he spoke, Lydia saw him say the word, saw the shape of it in his mouth before she heard it, and she felt her palms grow sweaty and her scalp go cold.

'No,' he said.

The word was how she imagined a bullet to be. Spoken so precisely, as if it contained no more than its short sound, and then it was in her, exploding, unexpected, fired from a figure in a dark corner she only half suspected was there. The sound was silenced and dense.

'No,' he said again.

Then he spoke in a slow flood of anger, his voice at odds with his words, so calm and quiet, as if all this was something he had known so well for such a long while, that saying it was only a matter of letting the sentences out into the air.

'You didn't have anything left over once Charlie came along. Not for me. It was him from then on. Always picking the damn baby up straight off when he cried. Feeding him all hours of the day and night. Singing to him. Worrying over him.'

She wanted to put her hands over her ears. Wanted to shut his words out.

'He was my baby,' she said. 'Not my husband.'

'But you didn't want a husband after.'

You were jealous, she thought. You couldn't bear it that I loved him like that.

Robert crossed his arms and widened his stance, as though he were confronting her with something.

'My sister was right,' he said.

'He's your son too,' she said. 'You love him.'

'Pam said it from the first. That you wouldn't look at

74

anybody else, once he was there.'

'She hates anybody having eyes for anybody. She hated you having eyes for me, in the days when you used to.'

Lydia looked down at the tea in its circle: tranquil and brown. Still hot. She could pick up the cup and saucer. She could give it to Robert.

'She always said it was unnatural, letting him have his way that much.'

'You're talking as if he were a stranger,' she said.

'He'd be my boy if you'd let go of him. You've made him like he is.'

Lydia shook her head, side to side against the wall. Robert's words bludgeoned her. Like a boxer waiting for his opponent to gain his feet again, he stood waiting.

'Why didn't you say this before?' she said at last. 'You've never said it.'

'What was the point?' He tipped his chin up, his face still combative.

'But why now?' she said.

He looked down at his feet, brushed a wrinkle from his trousers.

'You shouldn't have said that about the song.'

'Charlie's older now. It's easier. He's not tied to my apron strings.' Despite herself, Lydia couldn't keep the rise from her voice, the plea. 'Maybe?'

Robert ran his hands over his face and up over his wet hair. He looked down at himself, his fresh shirt, his smart new trousers, and shook his head.

'I'm going out,' he said. 'Don't wait up, Lydia.'

It would be another hour before Charlie was back. The light was still strong and Lydia could hear children playing out in the back alley. But she couldn't keep hold of her fears, and her sadness fell into the potato water and on to the sausages.

She closed her eyes. A tune was playing somewhere, on

a gramophone maybe, or inside her head. A slow number for the end of the evening, couples so close you couldn't shine a light between them, swaying like riverweed, lost in each other. She hummed the notes, felt the music in her cheeks, in her hips. What if Dot was here in the kitchen and asked her now, asked her to come out dancing? She'd go like a shot. Get Annie in to mind Charlie, and go. But what about if it was Robert asking? What if she heard his key in the front door and then he came striding into the kitchen and over the lino, this great grin on his face, and took her by the hand, all in time with that tune playing somewhere, and he said, 'Let's go dancing,' or something. Something easy.

It was her that had always done that. Acted on the spur. Only that once, when Charlie wasn't more than two, or three maybe, Robert had come in after work, and she never found out why it was. But he'd come in with a wind behind him. She was sticky with bits of Charlie's egg, sticky with tiredness and he came in with a rush of excitement that had her on her feet with worry.

'Robert?'

'Get his tea finished. We're off to the Grafton.'

'What's happened?'

'I told you. We're going dancing. Pam's having Charlie for the night. We can fetch him back first thing.'

'Pam?'

And this once they'd laughed, both of them, because it was such a thought, Pam minding Charlie. Pam minding Charlie so they could go dancing. Lydia wondered what the bargain was, but she didn't wonder for long. She didn't care, not this once, because she'd never have dreamed it in a hundred years, and Charlie would be fine for a night. She didn't want to know how Robert had done it, what on earth he'd promised. She wiped her son's face clean and ran upstairs.

The foyer was jammed, the air dense with smoke and perfume. It had been a lifetime since she'd been here last. Groups of girls camped outside the Ladies, dipping in purses for compacts, giggling in the din behind their hands. Young men swaggered, touching their tie knot, checking their crotch, reeking of Dutch courage. Couples walked in, self-contained, demure, peeling apart to check coats and make-up.

Lydia breathed deep. She leaned back against the marbled pillar; put her palms flat against its cool. Somewhere behind her Robert was queuing for the cloakroom. Her husband. Her man. She glanced down at herself. The dress fitted like a glove. A tighter glove than before where Charlie had left his mark. But she liked her fuller hips. More curve, less bone. She liked her new-found cleavage.

'Fancy a drink?' Robert's voice was soft in her ear, and she took his hand.

They sat side by side on gilded chairs beneath the lights that were like vast wedding cakes, and watched the flurry and rush of the dancing. Lydia sipped her gin and lemon. Robert leaned towards her again.

'You're the most beautiful girl in this place,' he said, and she felt his hand slip over her bosom to rest on her thigh. 'I'd never have found the like of you in this town.'

Further down, beyond the bar, a line of girls waited, prinked and nervy. The cowshed. Robert said that's what they were called, the ones without escorts. They seemed so very young.

'Know any of them?' Robert said.

Lydia nodded. There were two she recognized from the factory. One worked in the valve room next door to hers. Now she looked again, maybe neither was any younger than she was. But she had a husband, and a child tucked up, and it set her apart so that she felt old, and shy.

Now the band had finished their set and for a moment

the dancers were becalmed. Then the sax player reached for his pint and the dancers broke apart and headed for the bar, flushed and bright and noisy.

When the sax player stood up again, Lydia took Robert's hand and they walked to the centre of the dance floor. She stood, back straight, head high.

'You ready?' Robert said, and it wasn't his words that brought her up short, but something from inside herself, kept down till now. A wave of nausea drifted through her quickly, like a summer fog. What if she couldn't dance any more? Now she was a mother? Not in the way she used to? She gripped Robert tightly, feeling for the bones, holding on. What if she couldn't get lost in it any more?

'Lydia?' Again Robert's voice, clear and solid. She looked up and caught the edge of his smile. The first notes of a song hit the air, the saxophone's easy complaint, and that was all it took.

She fell in love with Robert that night, all over again. The music filled the air beneath those wedding-cake lights and they danced inside it, their bodies close, turning and turning, their love suspended in the dance. Until at last the band fell silent and the swaggery boys and whispering girls found their coats and went on their way. Their strength spent and the dance still in them, arm in arm, Lydia and Robert walked home.

The house was no quieter than any other night, but something else was stilled for Lydia because Charlie was not there. While Robert stood on the back step for a last cigarette, she climbed the stairs and stood for a moment at the door to Charlie's room. She looked to where his sleeping form should be, the blanket smoothed flat, and then she turned and went to wait for Robert.

She undressed him as she had the first time they'd made love, sitting on the bed and standing him before her, tugging open his belt, unlacing his shoes, unbuttoning his shirt.

'You know me now,' he said. 'No surprises.'

But she quietened him with a finger to his lips, and slipped her hands over his hips.

In the morning she'd gone to pick up Charlie. Her better than Robert because he had to be into work first. Besides, she was hungry now, to see her boy. So, in getting over to Pam's early, she hadn't so much as washed her face, and maybe there was too much of the night before still on her, she didn't know. But Pam was in a rage with her, or with her child.

'Thank you for having him,' Lydia said on the doorstep.

'Mine never woke me in the night,' Pam said. 'Nor Robert neither when he was little.'

'We had a lovely evening,' Lydia said, holding Charlie close. He nuzzled his head into her collarbone and she could smell the sweet child sleep still on him.

'Robert told me it was important,' Pam said, her voice tight with resentment. 'He said it was very important.'

'The big band at the Grafton. It was wonderful. For Robert too.'

'You went dancing. I had him so you could go dancing.' Pam's voice was disbelieving.

'Our first time since –' Lydia began.

'He never needed to go before he met you. He'd never have had me watching his child for one of those girls.'

'I'm very grateful –' Lydia began, but Pam cut her short.

'I've got work to get ready for,' Pam said. 'Tell my brother I'll see him on Sunday. And you, I dare say.'

And she shut the door hard.

When Lydia heard the front door slam, she had only an instant to wipe her eyes before Charlie was there before her.

'Hello, love,' she said.

'I'm parched,' he said. 'I ran all the way home.'

He was out of breath and his eyes were big with excitement. She saw the earthy dust on his hands and pale streaks of yellow on his arms. His face was so bright and alive, it made her chest hurt to see it, and she turned away and stared out across the back yard at the gate and the dustbin and the flowerpots of old dock and dandelion.

She heard him open a cupboard and then he was next to her and she could feel his rapid boy gestures, turning on the tap, filling a glass with water, and she could smell the garden and his young sweat.

She turned and kissed him lightly on the forehead, but she wanted to wrap him to her, hold him tight so that he would never go.

'Is tea nearly ready?' he said.

'Did you have a nice time, in the bee garden?'

'I'm going to be her assistant. I've not to wear shorts when we take the top off the hives, on account of the stings, but it's all right if I'm just looking. She said she could get me my own suit in a little while.'

'Tea's ready in ten minutes. Go and wash, Charlie.'

The pond was still, the surface dull with twilight. In the time it had taken Lydia to walk here, the sky had slipped from a thin blue to something deeper and she could see the first stars.

The park was next to empty. In thirty minutes they would lock the gates. She had the pond to herself. She bent down and dipped her finger in the water. Ducks were dotted like small, oval rocks on the grass, heads tucked in, though here and there she saw the glint of a weather eye on her.

She wondered if Charlie would want to sail his boat this year. He was growing up in fits and starts, sometimes still her little boy and sometimes not any more.

Lydia felt a terrible weight on her shoulders, as if the clear sky had opened the way for all her grief. She wept, not only for her marriage, but also for her father lost to her, and for her dead mother, and for the memory of her uncle's voice, sunk beneath the cold Atlantic.

She crouched by the pond, motionless, until pins and needles forced her to stand, and then she found a bench to sit on. She wouldn't have been able to say what changed, or why, and perhaps it was nothing more than the memory of the day's warmth in the wood of the bench that eased her spirits. But as she sat, she thought of what she loved. Odd thoughts of planting the pots in the yard for summer flowers, of beginning a new book, when anything might happen; of laughing so hard, she made herself cry; of the grit of sand between her toes on a beach; of the taste of roasted chicken. Most of all, she thought of Charlie.

A bird flew across the pond. It looked like the spirit of something in the evening light, and it was a spirit that spoke in two voices. The first was rough and urgent, shouting a sharp 'keew, keew, keew' over the water. Then the bird landed, perching on the No Paddling sign on the far side of the pond, and Lydia heard the second voice. It was yearning and low, an owl's 'whoo, whoo', that caught at the hairs on the back of her neck.

They watched one another, bird and woman, till the park bell rang out, and the bird spirit rose on its wings again and was gone.

Charlie was in bed asleep when Lydia got in. She lifted the comic from his chest and bent to kiss him. His hair smelled of trees. As she tucked the covers round him, he opened his eyes.

'Mum,' he said.

She put a finger to her lips. 'Sleep tight my love,' she said.

'I forgot to say before. Dr Markham says will you come for tea on Saturday.'

Lydia smiled at him. 'That'll be lovely, Charlie. Now sleep.'

9

Go in close, walk slowly, tread lightly. Don't crush the grass, walk through it. The bees know you by your walk.

They are busy now, they will not stop. Careful where you stand. They'll bump you otherwise, air dodgems, making their bee-lines, each coming back with a sack full of pollen, belly full of nectar.

A bee sting hurts, but it's not the end of the world. You shouldn't pull it out, though. Dr Markham had shown him what to do. How to scrape it, with your fingernail or the hive tool, and it hurt still then, but not so badly.

He spoke to the bees in a low voice, so as not to alarm them. Made it smooth and flowing, like the smoke he pumped from the smoker. They knew his voice now. He fancied that they knew it for its colour and its smell, as they knew the flowers. He would speak to them of the garden and what he thought the weather would do, and sometimes he told them other things too.

10

Jean woke early on Saturday. She had slept with her
curtains open for just this, to be coaxed from dreaming
by the May light flooding the room. But she moved carefully. She had drunk too much the night before and her
head protested as she moved from her pillow. Down by her
feet, the cat slept on, curled around, one paw laid above
an ear.

At supper with the Dexters last night there had been
tennis, which she had enjoyed, and then drinks, which she
had not. On the way there, Jim had teased her about the
extra man. Who would he be? Where would they get him
from this time? Had she got her pearls on specially? Surely
they'd used up all the extra men available in the town?
Until Sarah had silenced him with a look.

The extra man proved to be a nice fellow who had con-
fided to Jean, as they made their way to the dinner table,
that he had a girl in Birmingham he intended to make an
honest woman of. After that, the two of them got on
famously, drinking too much whisky and exchanging tales
of childhood pranks, adult dreams and favourite jazz tunes.

Jean stroked a hand around the cat's warm spine.

'I wish they'd stop thinking that I wanted any extra man,'
she said, and the cat arched ever so slightly and slept on.

Charlie's mother was coming for tea today. It had been
Sarah who said Jean should ask her.

'If I was her, I'd want to meet this woman my child was spending so much time with.'

'But he's perfectly happy in the garden. I've said he can visit when he wants. He's not always with me. Usually not, in fact. I only know he's been because of his notes. I gave him a notebook, and he leaves me messages, about the bees mostly.'

'Not the point. You're making him a bee suit. He's going to help you get in your honey crop.'

'Harvest. And it's not a suit. It's my old veil and gloves, and a pair of Mrs Sandringham's son's old overalls. She's adjusting them.'

'How old is he?'

'Ten, I think.'

'So still at primary school?'

Jean nodded.

'Have his mother round for tea, then. Else you might find he doesn't come to visit any more.'

Jean had had Mrs Sandringham's son mend the old wooden gate at the bottom of the garden and oil the latch, so that Charlie could let himself in when he wanted, without needing to come to the house. The garden was bigger than Jean could manage, and she had let this part run wild. Ancient fruit trees took a knotted stand against the ivy and briar roses, brambles and wild raspberries. The grass grew deep and coarse, shot through with tiny wild colours. Buddleia flourished, kicking out from the tumbled stones of some old sheds down one side.

She knew Charlie loved the way that the door let him in to the wild parts. She had seen it on his face when she'd showed him it all. She'd seen him glance about and recognized his eagerness.

'We had a garden bigger than this when I was your age,' she said. 'And some of it grew wild.'

'Did you make dens there?' Charlie said. 'Or find strange things?'

'No. I stayed on the lawn.'

'Didn't you want to?'

She laughed. 'Very much, but I wasn't allowed. Girls weren't meant to go exploring or get dirty. I had a nanny to stop me.'

'You could have run away from her.'

'I did sometimes, but then I got into trouble.'

'Creatures hide themselves in here,' he said. 'I bet there's all kinds to find.'

'You can come whenever you like. As long as your mother knows, and as long as you're still my bee-keeping assistant.'

Jean knew Charlie had taken her at her word on this, though she'd only found him there once in the past few weeks.

It was about six o'clock one evening and the garden still warm and bright. Jean had got through her list of house calls more quickly than she'd expected, and now she walked down across the lawn towards the burning white may blossom that marked off the end of the tended garden. Coming close to the hedge the noise of the bees was dense in the tumble of flowers, and she stood a moment and let the hum, the incessant din of it, fill her head.

Walking round the end of the hedge, she glanced at the four hives. Workers were flying in at full tilt, pollen baskets heavy with white pollen. Jean was checking the hives each week now, and the queens were laying up the combs nicely. She'd been showing Charlie how to spread the brood, adding supers to the top of the hives as needed. Very soon the colonies would be built up, and the swarming season would be upon them. She must show Charlie how to clip a queen's wings, and how to control the swarm. Then it crossed her mind that Charlie wasn't more than a couple of years older than Meg and she wondered how Sarah would react if she were teaching these things to Meg.

'It's natural with him,' she told herself, and put the worry away.

The garden smelled full, as if it had spent the day gathering perfume, and if she were to walk to the bottom, to Charlie's gate, there would be the last traces of the bluebells beneath the trees, and wild garlic. She took a few steps into the deep, rough grass beyond the hives, thinking to go down and check the fruit trees, and then she noticed Charlie, standing with his back to her.

His shirt was untucked and his socks were adrift, runkled round his skinny boy calves. He stood with his arms down by his sides, motionless. With his head slightly to one side, he seemed to Jean either entranced or intent. She couldn't tell. Less than a foot away, a young blackbird pulled a worm from the ground. But Charlie wasn't looking at the bird. Jean stepped closer. She could see now that the boy was watching something. That for all he looked relaxed, his body was held like a spring, the tendons in the back of his knees jumping, his fingers braced against his legs, index fingers twitching. He reminded her of herself.

As a child, about Charlie's age, she had once watched a mouse cross the rug before the nursery fire. It was evening, she'd been reading and a movement had caught the corner of her eye. Without changing her position, she'd dropped the book slightly and raised her eyes from the page. The mouse was squatted back on its hind legs, as if surveying the field. Then it had crouched and run across the hearth in small flurries of movement, lifting its nose before each, black pin eyes sharp and unblinking. She had watched it all the way across and then, as it scampered to the skirting board and beyond her line of vision, she had returned to her reading.

Jean watched the boy for a minute or more, during which time he made no move. Then she turned and walked back towards the house.

Charlie had said his mother worked till dinnertime on a Saturday, so they were to come for tea at three-thirty. They would come to the house, but all being well with the weather, tea would be in the garden. Jean had consulted Mrs Sandringham as to the menu, and cucumber sandwiches, a Victoria sponge and ginger biscuits had been agreed on, with lemonade for Charlie.

As the time for tea drew closer, Jean was surprised to find herself nervous. She changed her tweed skirt for the green shirtwaister dress that Sarah had persuaded her to buy, thinking perhaps it looked less doctor-like. What if Mrs Weekes disliked her, or disapproved? She must think it strange, Charlie making friends with a doctor, and a woman doctor at that. She supposed it was quite strange. Certainly not something she had done before, or anticipated.

What if Mrs Weekes thought it was unsafe, Charlie working with the bees? She might think that, once she'd seen the hives and all the bees about them. She might think Charlie should be mixing more with children his own age. With boys instead of grown-up women. Jean thought that herself. She had suggested to Charlie he bring a friend to the garden at some point if he wanted.

'You're worried she'll stop him visiting,' she said to herself. 'That's why you're nervous.'

She had to own it to herself that this boy had become a companion to her in recent weeks, albeit a companion she rarely saw. Or something more than that. Something more like a friend. She laughed. How could a woman in her late thirties make friends with a boy still at primary school?

They arrived on the dot of three-thirty; Jean saw them through the upstairs window. Charlie was washed and brushed, comb-lines still visible through his hair, his shorts pressed sharp. He walked up the drive several strides ahead of his mother, beating at the bushes with a switch, then turning to wait. His mother walked slowly, hesitantly, stopping to look at something in the hedge, changing the position of her handbag.

Jean knew where Charlie lived. She'd looked it up on his medical notes. She could picture the house, number 43. She'd visited enough of those terraces. Charlie had told her that his mother worked in the wireless factory.

She watched Mrs Weekes look over at the house and she wondered what Charlie had told his mother. Had he mentioned the dozen tall chimneys? Or the gabled roof? Had he told her there was a driveway at the front? Did she already know the house had tall, sash windows, a cloakroom full of old photographs and wildflower sketches? A stair window of coloured panes? Did she already know that there was one person, just Jean, living in it all?

She moved like someone in pain. Jean knew the look of it, the hesitancy, the guarded movements. But close as she looked, Jean couldn't tell where the pain might be. As boy and mother came closer, she guessed that it wasn't so much in the body as somewhere else.

Jean wasn't very careful about her own appearance, and didn't necessarily notice the finer details of other women's. But she did take in that Charlie's mother wore a pale blue shift dress with a pattern of little flowers, perhaps not quite this year's fashion, but pretty and fresh, that she wore her hair like Katharine Hepburn, and that whatever Charlie had from his father, he had his eyes from his mother. Grey eyes and long, dark lashes that he would be bound to dislike when he was slightly older. That's where the pain in the woman was too. Behind the eyes. A shadow there that shaded her gestures.

As she made polite conversation – how nice to be meeting, the weather, tea in the garden – Jean led the way into the house. Mrs Weekes was nervous. It was there in her stiff movements and her short, monosyllabic replies. So

Jean moved swiftly, while continuing to talk lightly. She'd learned to do this with patients who were anxious about some procedure or examination, or about undressing before the doctor, and now, walking into her hall, she did it without thinking.

'It's a house built for lots of people. I took it on with the practice. Silly, living here alone. Except, of course, when there's a bit of a push on and then my housekeeper, Mrs Sandringham, moves in for a time. So as you can imagine, it's been a pleasure, and a tremendous help, having Charlie to assist me with the bee-keeping.'

Jean paused at the far side of the hall to draw breath.

'What about the garden, Dr Markham?'

'I have a man who does the hedges and lawn, and Mrs Sandringham is very good. The rest of it I do myself. But the bees are my kingdom. And Charlie's now, of course.'

She would take them straight out on to the terrace.

'The flowers are gorgeous.'

The irises had been a last-minute thought, cut hastily and thrust in the jug.

'I'm not much of an arranger,' Jean said.

'My uncle used to grow irises like these. Small purple ones,' Mrs Weekes said. She bent her head close to them. 'Reminds me of him. Funny how a perfume can do that. Take you straight back somewhere, or remind you of someone so much.'

Jean smiled and nodded. Something about the recollection, she supposed, but the woman seemed to have lost her nervousness.

Her voice wasn't what Jean had expected. It wasn't her accent exactly, which wasn't from round here, but wasn't unfamiliar either. It was more her way of speaking. She spoke as though she were unaware of what she ought to say, or not terribly interested in it. Instead she seemed to speak straight out of her thoughts.

None of this went through Jean's head then. Then it was only the moment's surprise at something and, almost as a reflex, the glance at Charlie.

He was stood in the middle of the hall with an expression she didn't immediately recognize.

'Mum,' he said in a fierce whisper, and Mrs Weekes looked across at him.

'Aren't they lovely, Charlie?' she said, and it was only when he nodded – a small, reluctant nod – that Jean understood. He was embarrassed.

'Charlie, will you show your mother round the garden? And remind me to cut a bunch of irises for you before you go.'

Jean watched mother and son through the kitchen window, Charlie taking his mother by the hand, tugging at her to be quicker. They were down by the pond by the time she'd taken out the tea things, Charlie pointing at the rushes. He picked something off a stem and held it in his palm for his mother to see, and she looked down at his hand and said something that made him butt her softly at the waist, like a calf with its mother.

Jean paused, walking down. She had seen these two together somewhere else and she stood absolutely still, trying to place the memory. But it wouldn't come, and so she carried on towards them, feeling like an extra, a walk-on part. She had an odd sensation that she didn't quite recognize, and if Charlie or his mother had turned round at this point, they would have seen a scowl on her face. She waited for Charlie to bend to the pond again before joining them.

The two women stood watching the boy, until Jean felt she should make conversation.

'Charlie said he's always lived in the town. But I'd hazard a guess that you're not from round here,' she said.

'I met Charlie's father in London during the war. It's him who comes from the town.'

'So Charlie's got family here?'

'Yes,' Mrs Weekes said, and her tone made Jean look round, but she didn't add anything more. 'We had an allotment, growing up,' she said instead. 'I loved it there. I've got pots in the yard now. They're pretty, but it's not the same.'

'I'm very lucky,' Jean said. 'I don't really have time to keep it under control, though I think Charlie likes this wild part best.'

Charlie stood up, hands cupped, elbows dripping pond water.

'Look, Mum,' he said.

She lifted his covering hand, and in his palm a tiny green frog sat. She looked at the frog, and the frog looked back.

She smiled. 'Reminds me of you.'

'Why?' Charlie said. 'It's an amphibian and it lives in a pond.'

'Because it's new and very small. When you were barely born you already had fingernails and eyelashes. Tiny but perfect.'

Charlie winced and wriggled his shoulders, then ducked under her arm and crouched back at the pond's edge.

Watching this easy intimacy, Jean knew what the earlier feeling was. She was jealous. Jealous that Charlie showed the small frog in her pond in her garden to his mother first. Jealous because if Mrs Weekes hadn't been here, he'd have shown it to her. Uncomfortable with the feeling, she became cheery.

'Come on now. The lemonade will be getting warm.'

Afterwards, Jean couldn't recall what they talked of during tea. She gave Charlie his beekeeping things – gloves, suit, veil – and his eyes went wide with pleasure.

'It's Mrs Sandringham you have to thank,' she said.

Thinking back afterwards, she fancied that Charlie did a lot of the talking. His mother told him he was like a king sitting there, and they his courtiers, and he laughed with pleasure and Jean smiled to herself, seeing her guests so at ease.

Later, the two women watched Charlie run full tilt the length of the lawn and disappear from sight, and at some point Mrs Weekes owned to being an avid reader.

'Detective novels mostly,' she said. 'But I'll try anything. Sometimes there's nothing new in the library, so I'll pick books out of the General Fiction.'

'Anything you don't like?' Jean said.

'The girls all swap romances at work.'

'Charlie told me you work at the wireless factory.'

'Nearly ten years there.'

'It must be the biggest employer in the town. For women.'

'Not many other places to get work. They know that too. No sick pay, and they're very tight if you've got a child sick, anything like that.'

'I've seen a fair few accidents from there,' Jean said. 'Soldering burns, wire cuts. That kind of thing.'

'I've been lucky so far with accidents,' Lydia said. 'It's dull work, but you need to concentrate. I've always been able to do that. Not get distracted.'

'Is that how you read books as well?'

Lydia laughed.

'I suppose so. How I do most things. Something Charlie's got from me. He gets lost in things too.'

She looked at Jean, such a direct look that Jean felt herself blush slightly.

'What about you? Do you like reading?'

And Jean confessed to having a whole library of books and never reading any of them.

'My father left them to me. Because, even if I didn't read them, he knew I wouldn't sell them.'

'And you haven't?'

Jean shook her head.

'They have a room all to themselves in the house. Only the cat sometimes for company, when the fancy takes her.'

They must have talked for quite a while, because eventually Charlie returned, impatient to try his new equipment.

Putting his mother in the best place to watch, he lit the smoker and puffed it gently to quieten the bees, as Jean had shown him.

'It's how I got my first stings,' Charlie said. 'Annoying the bees.'

'Annoying them?' Lydia said.

'I didn't do it on purpose.' Charlie's tone was a little weary, a little wise. 'I just didn't know how they liked things then. The smoke helps, if you've got to interfere with them.'

Opening the hive, Jean checked the queen, and they looked for any queen cells, and at the pattern of brood growth. They repeated this for each of the other three hives. Jean would nod for more smoke, or lift a hand to signal enough.

They were in the hall and nearly leaving when Charlie remembered the irises.

'You told me to remind you,' he said.

Jean found a pair of scissors. 'Cut the stems long, and at an angle,' she said.

The two women stood waiting, somewhat awkward, in the hall.

'Your husband might like some cake?' Jean said, and Mrs Weekes gave a shrug.

'He's a lovely boy. An unusual boy,' she said.

'Yes.' But Mrs Weekes seemed to have left already.

Afterwards Jean went into the garden. Charlie's switch of wood lay on the lawn. She picked it up and whipped it through the air. She remembered his excitement at the beekeeping things, and the way he had left the table and just run. She remembered that he had his mother's eyes.

And then she ran. Down across the grass, past the hives and through the rough tangle, till she reached the gate in the bottom wall and stopped, panting and scratch-legged, and leaned a palm against the warm, flaked paint.

She was laughing, elated, her breath catching in her chest, her eyes wide. Perhaps she had caught something of Charlie's pleasure, his exuberance, but she wanted to leap and shout out.

It might have been five minutes or fifty before Jean walked back to the house. She didn't know why, but as she carried the tea tray in, she could feel a pulse of exhilaration beating out beneath her ribs.

She had intended to cook herself an omelette and then do some paperwork that evening, but her appetite had gone and she couldn't settle to working. Instead she put Dinah Washington on the gramophone, poured herself a deep Scotch and stretched out on the sofa.

Later, before bed, she opened the door to her father's books. The room was dusty, warm with the stored heat of the day. She had grouped the books roughly by subject – history, science, literature, philosophy – but never got further. Now she ran her finger over the titles of old novels. Eventually the telephone put an end to it, but even a late-night call-out and the demands of an anxious and querulous patient couldn't entirely cover the pulse she still felt, and she slept finally, in the small hours, with a hand to her breast, nursing this new beat.

II

They didn't speak of the tea in the doctor's garden, either Lydia or Charlie. It was understood between them that it would be better if Robert did not know of it.

The day following, the Sunday, they went to eat dinner at Pam's house. They had done this almost every other Sunday since Lydia had moved to the town. It would take a bullet to stop Robert visiting his sister. Or something bigger even. An earthquake, or an H-bomb. Not such a bad idea, Lydia thought. But she winced.

It was a fifteen-minute walk. When Charlie was smaller, Robert would fret at the pace and hoist him up on his shoulders. Now it was Charlie who chafed at the speed, and ran on ahead. There was a patch of waste ground on Pam's street and Lydia knew they'd find him there when they arrived.

Robert walked in front and Lydia carried a bowl with trifle, her best Coronation tea towel keeping it decent. She watched Robert nod his greetings in the street, charming, genial. People would be thinking them such a fine pair, so well-suited.

The sun hid as they walked and a fine drizzle began to fall. It was humid. Lydia watched the tea towel darken and her arms mist with rain.

Since their conversation last week, he had stopped talking to her, answering her questions only with a yes or a no, or the shortest alternative. She wondered what people knew when they smiled at him, and greeted her.

He'd been out all Saturday evening and she found him asleep on the settee in the morning.

'I think it would be better if you and Charlie went to Pam's for lunch on your own,' she said. 'She'll wonder what's going on between us. She'll say something.'

'She'll wonder more if you don't turn up.'

'She doesn't even like me,' Lydia said.

'You're still coming.'

'You could make an excuse. I've got a headache. A cold. She doesn't like other people's sickness.'

'No,' he said.

So they walked together through the streets, each on their own, and when Robert went on to his sister's house, Lydia went to find Charlie.

The waste ground was in the space between number 19 and number 29. Four houses' worth. The council had said they would rebuild but the wind had seeded trees there now and it was green with wild growth, the bricks' torn edges softened by moss and elder. Charlie had seen a fox here once at twilight, and there were often hedgehogs. The woman at number 31 regularly called the council man about the rats.

Trails made by children, or tramps, or lovers, cut in and around the tangle, and there was the usual furniture – dead mattresses, a signboard for something, rusted wire, an armchair sprung with ferns.

Charlie was leant against a bit of wall, his back to the street, staring off into the waste ground, and he didn't see her approach. For a second Lydia saw him as the older boy he was becoming, slouched and lean, the softness in his body gone, his gaze off and out, away from her.

'Charlie?' she said.

She saw the start in his shoulders before he turned, as though she'd caught him out. It was Sunday dinnertime and she'd thought there was nobody about. But then beyond him, she noticed three bigger boys, huddled round something.

Charlie came towards her, eyes to the ground, scratching at his ear.

'Time to go,' she said.

They walked back towards the street in silence. The air smelled sweet, rising off the warm ground. As they reached the pavement, Charlie looked up.

'It was a cat,' he said, lengthening his stride to walk ahead.

Lydia couldn't make out his tone. She stopped and turned. The boys were laughing, their adolescent voices chopping high and low. One raised his arm and swung a small dark bundle high, then brought it back towards him, cradling it, then setting the bundle to the ground. He bent to it, then the three boys stood away, watching, waiting, silent now and expectant.

She couldn't tell, from her distance, whether the cat was standing on its legs, or whether it was lying down. Perhaps it was dead. It seemed very still. The boys moved away a step, almost in unison as if their action were choreographed, beautiful even, in the washy, wet light. Then the cat moved, and suddenly it was running, jolting and urgent over the waste ground, and three tin cans tied to its tail tossed and pitched in their own squall of sound.

They stood outside Pam's house and Lydia found she was shaking. She handed Charlie the trifle.

'You give it to her. Don't mention the cat.'

'I know that,' he said.

Annie opened the door. She grinned at Charlie, bearing the trifle before him like a tribute, and feinted a jab at his ribs.

'You can't touch me,' he said, 'else I'll drop your dessert.'

'What kind?'

'Trifle.' He spoke it like a trump card.

She tossed her head and winked at him.

'I'll have to get you after dinner, then,' she said, and Lydia saw her son bridle with pleasure.

In the kitchen Pam and Robert stood at the cooker together. The room was hot with whispered words and cabbage water.

'Dinner smells lovely,' Lydia said.

Pam put a quick hand to her brother's shoulder. She turned, her eyes sharp.

'You crept in very quiet. Didn't hear you.'

'Annie let us in. Charlie's got dessert.'

'It's trifle,' Charlie said.

Pam put her hand on his head. 'Isn't your mother marvellous?' she said, and Charlie flinched and was gone.

'What can I do?' Lydia said.

Pam shook her head. 'Annie's seen to it all.' She turned away with a disapproving mouth.

Ten years Lydia had been coming here for Sunday lunch, and still it brought her out in a sweat. Her blouse was sticking under her arms and the back of her neck prickled. Years back she'd tried to explain it to Robert, but he hadn't understood, only told her that Pam was a proud woman, and mother and father to him, all of which Lydia knew already.

Head bent to the gas, Robert lit himself a cigarette and stepped out of the back door, sucking the flame hard against the drizzle.

Lydia watched the door close. He'd always just walked out when he felt like it. Films, conversations, washing up. And in these last years after making love even. Didn't ask anybody, didn't wait to find out, just left. Now Lydia was waiting for him to walk out of their marriage, both dreading it and hoping he would do what he'd always done and simply go.

She turned back into the kitchen. She didn't know what to say to Pam, or what to do. She always put herself wrong, said or did something that changed the colour of the air, something she couldn't see beforehand. She looked at Pam's back, the hard angles of her hips and shoulders pushing at the nylon housecoat, the widowed grudge that clipped her movements and cast her voice with a fine mesh of grievance.

'Busy at the works, this last week,' Lydia said. 'We've been nearly frantic on our line. Mrs Levin's had our noses pressed down at the belt.'

Pam took the cruets from the shelf and put them on the table.

'Mrs Levin. Wouldn't expect anything else from her sort.'

'It's the new four-valve T110 model,' Lydia pressed on. 'It's in the magazines now. I saw an advertisement. There's a rush for them, so Mrs Levin is saying.'

Lydia hated the sound of herself. She didn't want to talk about the factory; it bored her rigid. But they both worked there, and it was safe to mention. Safer than most things.

'Mrs Levin can say as she likes. I haven't found it any different to the usual,' Pam said.

Through the window Lydia could see her husband's head, his curls tight in the damp air. She should say something now about how hard Pam worked and about how everyone at the factory knew it, name some names. That was her usual route back; that was the way to curry favour.

Robert flicked his wrist and Lydia caught the shift of his shoulders, so familiar, as he ground his cigarette butt into the concrete. That was what he did to her, she thought, and she shook her head, angry.

'Robert might not be so hungry. He wasn't back till the small hours,' she said, and she'd timed it well. Pam had time to turn but none to say a word, because a moment later Robert pushed open the back door.

'Dinner ready then?' he said.

'Hungry are you?'

He shrugged and kicked a foot against the table, making the forks and spoons ting. It irritated Lydia. He only behaved like this, like a boy, when he was with Pam, and where Lydia found it pathetic, Pam thought it charming. 'Plenty of women would give their eye teeth . . .' she'd told Lydia more than once.

'No,' Robert said, 'not very.'

Lydia stared at the blue Formica. It shone back at her; uniform, shiny. Her eyes swam and she blinked. Now there were tiny flecks of other colours; suspended, random.

'Smells delicious,' she said. 'I'll call them down.'

It was on their third date that Robert seduced her with his bringing up. He was late arriving at the café and she was angry, mashalling crumbs around the oilcloth with a finger. She was angry with him, and angry with herself for wanting him so badly. When he came through the door finally, she was on her second, slow cup and wishing she was with her girlfriends and on to her second gin and French instead of tea.

He hadn't apologized or made an excuse, and back then, though still angry, she'd been impressed by this. Even in that early time she hadn't thought he was much to look at. She'd been on the rebound from her lovely Yank with the gentle smile who danced like a dream and who'd gone away promising the earth, which he said was the best in the world, if she'd ever heard of Minnesota. He didn't turn her stomach over, didn't make her pulse jump, but he was so handsome and he treated her so well, until he left.

Robert was the first thing in trousers to say hello. Unlike her American's smile, Robert's seemed to take him by surprise. Unlike her American he didn't promise her the earth. He didn't promise her anything, but somehow that was a stronger lure. He didn't seem to care what anybody thought, and he didn't go away.

'I was just about to leave,' she said that day. 'I've been drinking this tea for an age. I'm getting looks.'

He sat down opposite and chafed at his hands.

'Thought you might have gone round to my digs,' she said, 'till I remembered you don't know where they are.'

'I'll get my hands warm and then I'll be here,' he said, and something in the way he said it made her look at his hands then, and stroke his knuckles, his fingers.

'No gloves,' she said, and he shook his head. 'Poor boy,' with only a little mockery in her voice and then, at last, he'd looked hard at her, frowning.

'I could knit you some. Like I did for my uncle. He's serving on a ship too, somewhere he says is very cold, and he gambled his gloves.' She looked down at Robert's hands, pink on the yellow oilcloth. 'He says it's like gambling away your future, what with frostbite. Silly man.' She laughed. 'Perhaps you'll meet him one day.'

Robert made no reply and she looked up. His gaze was over her shoulder, so intent that she thought God, perhaps a pretty girl had sat down behind her. She waited for him to look away, back to her, and when he didn't, she turned to see. But there was only an empty table and another bit of wall like theirs, with grubby silk flowers hung up in a vase.

Then he looked at her again and got to his feet.

'Shall we go somewhere else?' he said, and he took her hand and kissed her on the lips as she stood up.

I was so easy, she thought, standing at the bottom of the stairs, calling the children to dinner. Like jelly when he kissed me. I'd have killed to get inside his trousers. Then dead parents and a sister like a mother to him so there I was, nearly pleading to look after him.

*

He told her his tale in the first pub they came to, warming

his hands against the stove, and afterwards they'd walked all the way to her digs and his story had flowered in her breasts. When he sat down on her bed and looked away beyond her shoulder again, his gaze faced this time by the shelf beside the basin with its Colgate and Ponds, this time she didn't need to turn, but she felt such a heat inside that she held his head between her hands and pulled his gaze back and then found his mouth with her mouth, while her fingers touched his young man's hard belly and traced the thick line of hair downwards.

Then she sat down on her bed, stood him before her as a mother stands a child, and undressed him. Lifted things over his head, pulled them down around his ankles and off, till he stood, before her. She stared, wondering.

'I've never seen a naked man before,' she said. She touched his hip, ran her finger up to his nipple and he covered her hand and, gently, led it down.

Afterwards while she lay still, her fingers sticky with him, her skin growing cold in the grey light of wartime winter, he pulled his coat around his shoulders, and sang. She watched him, the sharpened profile of his nose, the curl of his hair breaking round his head, eyes invisible, looking out – she knew the view so well – to the flats across, beyond the plane tree, and dim-lit scraps of other lives made out between the branches. The unlit room grew dark and she climbed inside the counterpane and slept inside his voice.

They had only three more dates before he returned to his boat, and each time she asked him questions and he told her a bit more about himself and they came to her room and made love. Each time afterwards he sat and sang beyond the window while she lay beneath the covers and drifted. By the time he returned to his ship, she'd heard his favourite songs, especially all the thirties tunes, and she knew all about him. About his family and his old loves;

about the work he'd left for the war, and his plans for after it ended. She knew about his scorn for people who thought themselves better, and she loved that because her father was one of those people and it had left him with a bitter spirit.

She even knew something of his orphan heartsickness, and she didn't notice how little he wanted to know of her, didn't think about it. Not much more than her name, and that she was happy to listen to him. By the time he returned to his ship, Charlie was seeded in her womb, and now she was here, calling up these stairs for him to come for dinner, and the end of it all was pressing up close behind her.

They stood in their usual places; Robert at the table's head, Lydia and Pam at either side, Charlie and Annie opposite one another, a space at the foot where John would have been. Lydia noticed how pretty Annie looked, like a flower in its early flush. The food steamed and Charlie said grace with his eyes open.

'Bless thou this food dear Lord that we are about to eat . . .'

Lydia watched him, his crown of dark hair, the parting slender white. He lifted his head and glanced at Annie.

'. . . We thank thee for thy mercies.'

Annie winked at him, her face still held solemn.

'Amen.' Charlie's voice cracked slightly, and Pam's eyes were open, her glance like a claw, but he had his eyes down again, and Annie's were shut, and they sat down to eat with grace unchallenged.

Lydia made herself eat dinner like someone with an appetite. She would give Robert no quarter to think he had her sad. Roast pork slicked with gravy, potatoes, vegetables. The food caught in her throat, hurt her ribs, sat like lead in her stomach. Robert was solicitous, passing her the condiments, refilling her water, offering her more potatoes, more cabbage, keeping an eye out for his sister. She saw his hands – the veins proud, jutting, the square line of his fingertips. They would touch another woman's face tonight, and his mouth would kiss her lips. Another woman would hold the curve of his shoulder that she had once. Some other woman. Not Lydia. It would never be her again. She didn't want him, she didn't want to hold him, touch him as the other woman would, but this minute here, with Pam's coach clock ticking her days away on the mantelpiece, she couldn't bear the sadness of it. She couldn't bear the fury.

I don't want this, she said to herself. Everything in her tightened and she pressed her nails into her palms so fiercely that later she saw she had broken the skin.

Her father had cut her off when he found out about Robert.

'You come to me like this,' he said, butting his head towards her belly. 'I'm glad your mother's not alive to see it.'

'But I love him,' she said.

'It's not love's the question, and it's not the war,' he said, banging the table hard enough to make the cutlery jump. 'You think you can have your own way on everything, no mind for the family. Same as over your schooling, same as over your future.'

'I'm doing what's best for me,' Lydia said.

'You don't know what's best.' He was on his feet now. 'You barely know the man. You've said so yourself. You couldn't control yourself, girl. What does he know of you? Of your prospects? At least before you marched out of school and into the factory.'

'There's a war going on,' she said. 'They need girls in the factories.'

'But that's not why you went, is it. Not really.'

He leaned back against the wall and waited. She hated him doing this. She hated the waiting. He had everything so measured, so planned. That was how he lived, how everyone had to. Her schooling, her marriage, her prospects. Her children even. Her unborn children. He had their lives planned into his schedule already. If it was a girl, then she'd inherit her grandmother's sewing machine and marry someone with a good trade. If it was a boy, he'd go to the grammar and get a proper education.

'Dad,' Lydia said, 'please.'

'You did it on a whim, like everything else you do. You've got no staying power,' he said. 'So now you can live with it. I want respectability, family and what's right. He's not the man I intended for you, and I want nothing to do with him, or what he's got on you.'

'The baby,' she said, but her father had come round the table and taken her by the elbow.

She could still remember the feel of that; her father in his steely rage.

Lydia had never mourned her mother as hard as when her baby was born. Her father had been right, by more than a grain. She had acted on a whim, almost, and that was a sin in his eyes. Maybe falling in love was acting on a whim. But her mother would have forgiven her for the baby's sake, would have held him and looked at his eyes and told her how they looked like his grandfather's. Her father was unrelenting, and her letters were returned unopened.

It was so strange this Sunday, how everyone behaved as if nothing had changed. Pam went on talking about the church and her curtains and where John was now, only four months left to his National Service. She spoke of Annie as if the girl wasn't there, sitting at the table. And Lydia and Robert sat so close at that small table that their chair legs touched – so close, but with something sliced so cold between them that Lydia chafed her hands for warmth.

'Those young girls at the factory,' Pam said. 'The way they carry on.'

Lydia nodded. She had seen them. That was all her nod meant. They were girls doing what girls do. She liked it. Liked watching them, their puppy energy, their curves and turns, their laughs and cries.

'And their skirts! Have you seen their skirts! They'll be there in the small hours, foot on the treadle of their mother's machine and she asleep in bed and none the wiser. Then in the morning parading in the corridors as if there's not an inch more than before.'

'I hadn't noticed that,' Lydia said.

Pam looked to Robert for support, but he shrugged and got up from the table. He'd go for a cigarette in the yard instead of dessert. Lydia felt a bubble of laughter rise in her throat.

'Well,' Pam said after a pause. 'Annie knows proper obedience. She's got her girlfriends, but there's none of that carrying on. I'm her first port of call, and she obeys me. As does John – but being the boy, well, it's not the same.'

'I quite like those skirts,' Lydia said. 'Lots of the young girls are wearing them.'

Pam snorted. 'Doesn't matter what you like. They're only wearing them to catch the boys.'

'What's wrong with that?' Lydia said, surprised at her own daring. 'It's natural at their age. I'd shorten the skirt on this dress if I were younger,' she said, patting the skirt of her yellow dress, bought so long ago during the war.

This caught Pam short and she shuffled the knife and fork on her empty plate.

'I was running a house at their age and not much choice about it. Not any more than our mother had about dying.

Took all my energy to make sure my brother had cooked food and clean clothes. Not much over for fiddling with skirt hems and such. Good thing Dennis didn't care much for that sort of thing.'

'There's nothing wrong –' Lydia started, but Pam was on a roll and not about to stop.

'Teaches you a thing or two, that does. You grow up fast.'

'Pam,' Lydia said.

'Girls carrying on like that now, getting their claws into young men,' she said.

'They can't do it with a hemline,' Lydia said.

'And we know what men are. You let them look at you, next thing . . .' She made a gesture with her hands.

Lydia looked over at Annie. The girl had her eyes on her lap, a blush at her neck. Poor girl, Lydia thought.

'But the girls've only got themselves to blame . . .' Pam went on.

Lydia glanced at Charlie, but he was picking at something on the side of the table. There was a smile in his eyes and his lips were pursed with effort. He didn't seem to be listening.

'I knew Dennis all my life,' Pam said. 'All my life. Not some passing fancy, somebody you have a nice dance with one night. Not somebody you come home with only because –'

'Mum . . .' Annie said.

'What do you know?' Pam said, her voice tight. 'You were barely more than a baby when he . . . Where's the justice in that?'

'Why don't you clear the plates?' Lydia said to Annie. 'Poke Charlie to help. Bring the dessert in.'

'Charlie?' Annie said, pulling her chair back, keen to leave the conversation.

Lydia looked across at him again. He hadn't heard.

'Charlie!' Annie said again, more fiercely. He started

and put a finger to his collarbone, rubbing it slightly, the way he always did when he felt caught out at something.

'Clear the dishes,' Lydia said.

She saw his glance to Annie as he stood up, and the grin she returned. The two cousins had always been close, even though Charlie's idea of a good time still brought him in with muddy knees, and Annie was a young woman now.

Charlie stood and Lydia handed him the gravy jug.

'Shouldn't need asking, Lydia,' Pam said. 'Haven't got maids any more to pick up after you.'

'I never did have,' Lydia said in a rare moment of defiance. She held her breath for the retort, about how she was above herself, or too good for Pam and her sort.

'Shouldn't need asking,' Pam said again. 'Though men aren't cut out for the kitchen. Makes them all thumbs. But then no daughter, so needs must.'

Robert had been out for longer than a cigarette took to smoke, and as soon as Lydia had that thought, she knew he'd gone. Out the yard gate and down the alley, back God knows when, and what did she say to Charlie and to Pam? She served the trifle out and took the spare bowl back into the kitchen.

'Where's Robert?' Pam said.

'Must have been late for something,' Lydia said. 'I expect he went out the back gate.'

'Not even dessert? Not even a goodbye to his sister?'

Pam's voice was wheedling. If Lydia had been someone else, if her marriage wasn't ending, she might have mentioned that it was Pam who'd brought him up, taught him his bad manners. Instead, she dug down into the red jelly and spooned up the sugar sweetness.

'Going out this afternoon?' she said to Annie, but the girl shook her head.

'She's helping me with chores. We'll have a nice chat,' Pam said.

Once the dishes were done, Lydia could leave. Charlie had asked to go to the park, and Lydia wished he could be with her for ever, a child wanting only simple things.

'Don't go near the water. Be home before dark,' she said, thinking she would walk home alone now.

Pam had been talking the last ten minutes, but Lydia hadn't taken any of it in.

'Thank you for a lovely dinner,' she said when the talk stopped, keeping her voice steady. 'I'll see myself out.'

Outside Charlie and Annie stood close together. Annie was still catching her breath, hands on hips, chest heaving. She must have run round from the back alley so her mother didn't see her. Lydia saw her slip something red into Charlie's trouser pocket.

'Please, Aunt Lydia,' she said, and Lydia raised a finger to her lips.

Annie threw a flash of smile and squeezed Charlie's shoulder. 'Go on,' she said, and Charlie was off, running like only boys can.

Lydia kissed her niece on the cheek and walked slowly home, carrying the bowl empty of trifle, and the dishtowel folded neatly inside.

12

At home, everything was as Lydia had left it. Only of course Charlie wasn't there, because he was delivering a note for Annie and playing in the park.

The note was for a boy. Lydia was sure of that, and even with all her own worries, she hoped Annie would enjoy herself before her mother found out. Because it was only a matter of time, however careful Annie was, and then who knew what trouble there would be.

Robert wasn't there. Of course he wasn't. She knew he wouldn't be, but still she felt pained because of it and she cried out, standing in the dusty hall.

She opened the door into the living room and there was the Sunday mess and Charlie's clutch of toys and pieces of paper in a corner. In the kitchen the bowls on the draining board were dry.

She touched things. The table, the easy chair, a glass Charlie had drunk some milk out of, a watercolour picture they'd been given when they married. It was a highland scene with a stream and rocks. She'd never really looked at it. Now she saw there were sheep grazing, very small, just dabs of paint, and what might be a man – a stroke of grey paint by one of the rocks. The sun was behind a cloud, though the muddy yellow fringe hinted at its coming out. She didn't like the picture, and decided to get rid of it soon.

She sat on the sofa. It smelled of Robert. The cushions bore the mark of him. His body, his life in the house.

He'd nailed the photos to the wall. He'd chosen the fire irons. The neatness of the newspaper pile, the way the logs were stacked ready for autumn, the matchboxes at each end of the mantelpiece – these were all pieces of him, all pieces she had cherished. She'd laughed with her friends about his odd arrangings because they were part of her man. Now she wanted them gone, away.

If Charlie had been there beside her, if he'd known about all this, he'd have said it was like the *Mary Celeste*. His teacher had told the story recently, and he'd come back home haunted and watching the ordinary things around him differently for a day or two.

But she couldn't tell him, the boy that he was.

She pictured herself wrapping the fire irons in Robert's newspaper and strapping them to her bike, together with the photographs and the neat matchboxes. Then cycling to the oxbow field on the outskirts of town and tipping them over to join the old mattresses and bits of iron. How good that would feel.

Soon she'd have to ask her friends to laugh at that, and they would. They would, and they'd have someone buy her another drink and they'd lift their glasses to tell her they knew how she felt. But that was for later. Now she couldn't speak, not even to herself.

She sat on the floor by the window with her knees drawn high to her nose, hands around her shins, and watched the bar of afternoon sunlight pull across the room. She marked its movement inch by inch, over the carpet, picking out the fray of fibre, a crumb, till it edged on to her knee, settled on her thumb, and slowly moved its rays across her body. An ache grew in her back and her fingers were stiff with holding. She noticed, with a kind of pride, that the sunlight didn't warm her.

Lydia didn't know how long she sat there for, rigid and cold. She felt she was in some other place where thoughts and feelings had been burned away. Resolved to make no move for herself, to stay put in her discomfort, her pain was like ice. There was no consolation.

So when the doorknocker clapped through the empty air, the first thing she felt was relief. Because she must answer the door. It might be Charlie, it might be anything, and someone else had made her decision for her. She could stand up and straighten her aching body. She could move her limbs and rub the blood back to her hands again.

It wasn't Charlie at the door, or any of the emergencies that sit in a mother's library of fears. It wasn't Robert with a change of heart, or Pam to shock her with words of comfort. Jean Markham stood on the pavement, a duffel coat around her shoulders like an afterthought, a brown paper parcel in her hand.

'I hope I'm not disturbing your Sunday,' she said, and she gave what looked to Lydia, even in her numb state, like a nervous smile.

Lydia shook her head. She looked at the other woman, and then her heart jumped.

'It's not Charlie?'

'No, nothing to do with Charlie. I'm sorry, I should have said.' Jean lifted the brown paper parcel again. 'I'm not here as a doctor. Something I thought you might enjoy.'

'Oh,' Lydia said, puzzled, and then, as though remembering what you should do if a visitor called, she asked the doctor in.

Jean put the package on the living-room table.

'I thought, after you'd gone, how silly it was, my having all these books and not reading, and your being a reader and wanting books. I've brought you a couple.'

Although in general she was good at seeming cheerful, Lydia couldn't summon herself this time. She had no defence against this kindness from someone so close to being a stranger to her. She looked at the parcel, her name and address in neat ink on top.

'I was going to leave it with a neighbour if you'd been out,' Jean said.

'Thank you.'

'Wasn't exactly sure what you liked to read. So it's a couple of novels. One of my father's favourites, Wilkie Collins, and one by George Gissing because I liked the title.'

'You're very kind,' Lydia said.

Jean frowned. 'It's not kindness. You're helping me out. I feel that I ought to read some, for my father's sake. You're doing me a favour.'

Lydia closed her eyes to try and stop the tears, but when she opened them, a rogue drop fell and blurred the edges of the ink. She made a smile.

'I don't . . . it's . . .'

Jean shuffled her feet.

'I'm talking too much. I'm sorry for disturbing you. Please accept the books, if you haven't already read them. Or if you have I can choose different ones. Or you could –' Jean stopped herself mid-sentence.

'I haven't read them,' Lydia said. 'I'd like to.'

'Good, then. Keep them as long as you want. I won't fine you for returning them late,' Jean said with a laugh.

'Thank you,' Lydia said again.

'Come and get some more whenever you like. Thank God my father enjoyed reading novels. Unusual man. Or send them back with Charlie, and take your chance with my choosing.'

Lydia stood silently, and her visitor, anxious that she had outstayed herself, tapped the books gently and turned to go.

'I'll leave you in peace,' she said.

'Dr Markham, could you . . .' Lydia said, because suddenly she didn't want her to go. 'Wait while I unwrap them.'

So the doctor waited while Lydia opened the parcel, unknotting the string and untucking the corners, careful with this stranger's gift. She picked up the topmost book: green cloth covers, gilt lettering, and in the front, in a swooping hand: *James Markham, July 14th, 1890.*

Lydia ran her finger down the soft curve of the page edges. She opened the book and read a sentence. Jean watched her, saw pleasure in her eyes, saw her mouth relax.

'It's a beautiful book,' Lydia said. 'Lovely to hold.'

'My father would be pleased somebody was reading it,' Jean said. She knew there was something very wrong for Lydia, and she knew she couldn't ask. Enough to have raised that smile, she thought, and she left.

13

Dead trouble now, Charlie, the boy told himself. Dead trouble.

He had torn Annie's note out of his notebook as carefully as he could because the notebook was precious and shouldn't have ragged edges. He'd stuffed the note down his sock and now it itched. He shuffled a shoe against his shin, dug a toe into the thin grass on the side of the pitch. He'd deliver it safely for Annie's sake. He'd sworn to. But right now he didn't know how he was going to manage it. He picked up a pebble kicked clear in the soil and rubbed it clean. It felt good in his fingers. Small, round.

'Pocket stone,' he said, and slipped it in. He'd lost one the week before. He suspected his mother, going through the washing. She didn't understand about stones.

The sun had come through late today, and the world was picked out sharp in the wake of the rain. The piles of sweaters acting as goalposts, sweet wrappers stuck in the grass, and off behind him, higher up, the trees and near them a girl with a skipping rope dancing on the rise of the hill.

Squinting against the strong light, Charlie watched the football game and murmured Annie's description to himself.

'George. Curly brown hair. Grey eyes. Birthmark on his left cheek. Like a leaf. Say my name and you'll know it's him.'

The players were in their own kingdom a million miles away. They were jerky figures at the far end of the pitch, making darts and shifty runs, their hollering voices small and thin, and Charlie couldn't see their eyes, or cheeks, or anything much of that kind. He didn't know how long they'd been playing for, or when they would stop, and the waiting made him nervous. There were other boys around, older boys than him, scuffing up the grass, shouldering each other. If he stood there long, he'd get noticed.

He looked around him again. Perhaps he could make as if he was looking out for someone. The skipping girl danced down the hill, her rope alive and curving, and a man appeared above and threw a stick down the hill for a dog. Charlie watched the stick twist above the grass, a thin black line, turning and disappearing in the air, then drop beyond the girl.

He watched the dog go. It was big, an Alsatian maybe, and it looked lean and hungry, ears back, teeth bared. It ran towards the girl and she just skipped and skipped with eyes only for her feet and the rope turn.

Things were happening so slowly that Charlie could see it all – the dog hurtling, the girl skipping. He drew in his breath. The dog was nearly on her and at last she must have heard something because she jerked and turned her head around.

The man was running too now, calling out, arms wide against the pull of the hill.

The rope dropped dead to the ground and a high scream ran its way down Charlie's spine. The girl was like a jointed doll, her limbs flung about, the dog a wild rush of fur worrying and tossing this way and that, though whether it was the girl, or the stick, Charlie couldn't tell.

He stood; stuck, watching. He couldn't take his eyes away. The man had reached the girl and was bent and tugging, but still the dog and the girl seemed like one thing. If the dog had bitten the girl, if it had, she might not feel it yet; she'd be in shock.

He'd seen his father come home from work one day still green at the gills, because a man had got his arm cut through. There'd been a storm the night before and a tree had come down over a big road. Charlie's dad and the other man had been called in early to go and clear it. Charlie's dad was bracing the branch when the saw had slipped, or the man had slipped, Charlie wasn't sure which. But he remembered his dad saying how the man didn't feel it a bit then, didn't even know about it, didn't know how bad it was, till he caught sight of the face on Charlie's dad.

His mum had put her hands to her cheeks at the story, her eyes gone like marbles, and then reached and put a hand on his dad's arm.

Charlie liked watching. He liked being on the outside. It was something he liked about the bees. So much to watch, and being so far outside. He knew Dr Markham liked that too. They often stood by the hives together, not saying anything, just looking. He supposed she wasn't able to do much of that usually, not with all the sick people. But he didn't like watching the dog and the girl, so he turned back to the football game. The players had stopped and all except one were walking slowly, hands on hips, catching breath. All except one, with their heads turned up towards the hill.

Only one boy was still running as if his life depended on it. He ran past Charlie with feet like thunder, full tilt, his face desperate and his breath fierce. Everything in him was intent, driven, so that it was difficult to believe that only minutes before he'd been in a game of Sunday football, yelling with his mates, nearly ready for the pub. Only his red undershirt gave him away, flap-flapping this way and that behind him like it didn't give a monkey's, like it was clowning, fiddling while Rome burned.

That was what his mum said. Fiddling while Rome burned. Charlie, who had learned about Rome and Caesar, always pictured lots of men in togas sitting around in a Roman temple, white pillars and statues, fiddling with bits of string, or marbles, while outside the temple was a city on fire.

The boy ran towards the girl and the dog, and though he went by so fast, once he was beyond Charlie and into the middle ground, for an age he seemed to be running to nowhere. Then he reached the hill, and the girl, huddling over her before lifting her in his arms and walking away.

The footballers washed by Charlie as if he wasn't there. He knew how this was. That a small boy is next to invisible to the likes of them. He caught snatches of their chat – about the game, ended so suddenly, about the attacking dog and if it had been their sister, about a girlfriend here and a job there.

For thirty seconds maybe, he stood adrift in their sweat and noise, the gruff note of their male selves. Then he gathered his wits and looked for the curly brown hair and the birthmark.

At his first sighting of George, he felt his head go hot and his shoulders tighten, so he watched a moment before approaching, to cool himself. If he'd been older, he'd have known that this was jealousy.

George was slightly built and, Charlie reckoned, only a couple of inches taller than Annie. He had short legs and an abrupt walk. He was wearing a pair of football shorts and an old shirt, like the rest of the players, and his hair was uncombed and messy, but Charlie could tell the curls would be slicked and shiny in a few hours' time. In fact, he bet that George was what his dad called a sharp dresser.

The birthmark was like a small, red leaf, its tip towards his temple. It was an odd thing, and Charlie wondered what it would feel like to touch. Like ordinary skin, or different? He thought that maybe Annie could tell him, and he blushed at the thought.

The footballers had gathered up their things and were walking towards the road. If he didn't give George the note now, he'd lose his nerve. He tightened his fingers round the pocket stone, smooth and warm, and ran to catch up. Then he nubbed George on the back with a finger.

The back turned with a jerk and an 'Oy', and there was the face that Annie dreamed of in the factory, the face she thought of before she went to sleep. Charlie fished down his sock for the note, and George waited, arms crossed, weight leaned back, head cocked slightly.

'It's from Annie,' Charlie said, importantly. George pocketed the piece of paper with a nod and turned away, a yell in the air for his friends to wait and the messenger boy forgotten already.

Charlie knew about lots of things. He knew that his aunt would be very angry if she found out about Annie and George. He knew his father wasn't always in the pub like he said. He knew that his mother was sad. Charlie knew about animals, and the names of mountain ranges. He knew less about older girls and boys than he did about insects, but it was enough. He could tot it up on his fingers. That they went around in groups, like zebras or giraffes, boys in one group, girls in another. That at the weekend they would get dressed up to the nines, including the boys. He knew that the boys liked to swagger and the girls to preen. They used shop windows to check their faces in. He knew that in the evening, once darkness fell, you could glimpse them kissing in alleys, girl up against the wall and boy with legs planted either side of her, hands flat on the bricks at her head. It didn't look like fun to Charlie, especially if you were the girl. But he supposed that this was what Annie did with George, and he supposed that she must want to.

The footballers were tiny figures already, their strut and noise swallowed by big blocks of sky and grass. Charlie shut one eye and held his hand up in front of him. He could frame George inside his thumb and index finger, keep him there, and squash him in a second if he wanted to.

He closed his hand to a fist and swung his arm down and round, so that it tugged at his shoulder; he shook his head and stamped his feet on the grass. If he went to the pond now, maybe Bobby would still be there and they could play a game of wars and villains before it grew dark.

14

Lydia thought her life would stop right there and then. Collapse in and in till there was nothing beyond, no one outside. Even Charlie seemed somewhere very far off, swimming in another sea. After Dr Markham had gone, Lydia put the package of books safe behind the preserving pan. She went upstairs to the bedroom, took off her shoes and got in under the covers. As she dug down, her clothes dragged and caught against the sheets, rucking and bundling around her, so she felt awkward and encumbered. The soft fabrics dug at her hips and her ribs, and soon she would be too hot.

She hoped for sleep, but it wouldn't happen. So she picked up a book from the bedside.

Latimer stared at the corpse. So this was Dimitrios. This was the man who had, perhaps, slit the throat of Sholem, the Jew turned Moslem. This was the man who had connived at assassinations, who had spied for France. This was the man who had trafficked in drugs, who had given a gun to a Croat terrorist and who, in the end, had himself died by violence. This putty-coloured bulk was the end of an Odyssey . . .

From inside the thick of her grief, Lydia read. She read without lifting her eyes. She pinned her thoughts to Latimer and Dimitrios, Madam Preveza and Marukakis, only pausing when the ache in her shoulder or the pins and needles in her foot forced her to lift her eyes from the page, shift the pillows and turn the other way. Then her gaze would fall on the wallpaper with its pattern of roses and she would blink and wonder where in the world she was. Then, as she started to remember, thank God, there was the book, and she would slip under again, a sigh in her throat.

The terrible certainty Lydia had come to that Sunday sat like a bruise behind her eyes, invisible and absolute, so that although the form of life continued much as before, for Lydia the spirit in her marriage was dead.

Dead as a sap with a bullet in his neck, she told herself in a stab at Bogart, but it didn't raise a smile.

She was famished and hollow, heavy with the sadness of what had gone. And some nights she cried, her desire lost to itself, running her own fingers over her breasts, sliding her fingers high across the soft skin of her thigh, longing for someone else to touch her.

Lydia went through the motions. She went to work, she looked after Charlie; she shopped, visited the library, cleaned and cooked. She made excuses to her friends on the Friday, and then on the Saturday. Whenever she could, she took off her shoes and climbed inside the thrillers beside her bed. She took Dr Markham's books out from behind the preserving pan and read those too, then wrapped them back up in their brown paper and put them safe in a cupboard to return.

Robert came and went by degrees. A few days at a time at first, then for a week, then longer. After dinner that Sunday he didn't come home for three days. Not a word, not a glimpse; then on Wednesday, at the usual time, there was the sound of his key and he was coming through the front door, making the sounds he always made. And Lydia, despite her despair, was waiting. The grate of the latch, the jar of metal on the hall tiles as he dropped his lunchbox from his shoulder: these caught her pulse, making her jolt, so that she danced like a figure on strings in the middle of the kitchen, her feet rooted to the floor, her joints twitching, tugged by the ordinary, unseen sounds of her husband. For a moment she was paralysed and then, not thinking, she moved quickly.

She opened the fridge and took out a bottle of dark beer and a jar of cockles. She listened for his pause at the living-room door as he checked the hall for post, ran his fingers over his hair in front of the glass. These sounds, and gaps in sound, were as familiar to her as the creak of the fifth stair or the small animal noises Charlie made when sleeping. They were part of her life; and her body, carrying the beer and cockles, rose up to meet them.

Robert was sitting at the table, a holdall in one hand. He turned at Lydia's entry, and his face was a rage of emotion, so that she thought he would hit her, and then that he would wrap his arms around her, though it might be to smother or it might be to caress.

'What?' he said, and Lydia nearly wanted to laugh at him for pretending not to care.

She shrugged and put the jar and bottle on the table.

'How are you?' she said.

He looked what he was right then: a man on the run. Lydia knew it immediately. She'd read of enough such men in thrillers and they always looked like this: beads of sweat on the forehead, sitting on the edge of the chair, a large bag to fill fast, eyes darting, waiting for the bullet in the back, the cord around the neck, the cosh.

'Need to pick up some things,' he said.

'You're not staying then,' she said, fighting to keep her voice even, fighting not to plead, because he was too long gone and she didn't want him any more. It wasn't this last, short absence that was his going, but all the months, years of departure that had already been.

He looked at her as if she were a stranger. Her legs had started shaking, a quivery feeling she couldn't overcome, and she sat down. She took a cockle from the jar. It was rubbery and resistant, but the vinegar brought her up sharp. She picked up the beer bottle and the cockle jar and went into the kitchen. The one she emptied into the bin and the other she poured down the sink.

He still stood as if waiting for something.

She couldn't imagine touching him, couldn't imagine her fingers unbuttoning his shirt, or pulling at his belt buckle. She didn't want to lie with him, didn't want his caress. But this was still hard to bear.

'Charlie will be pleased to see you. He's upstairs.'

'Will he?' Robert said, and he turned away so quickly that Lydia didn't know what he meant. But when he went upstairs she heard him open Charlie's door.

Twenty minutes later and he had gone, leaving behind what she hadn't noticed during the time he was there, which was the smell of somewhere else.

During those next dark weeks, for the first time in Charlie's life, Lydia didn't see her boy. Or rather, with her eyes turned so much in, she saw only the outside form of him. She still had his food on the table and his clothes washed. She still chivvied him about his homework, made sure he washed behind his ears and she kissed him goodnight. But she no more saw how he was than she did the child across the street.

At first Charlie tried to make her see him. He told her stories from school, even made ones up that had him as the hero of the playground. He offered to read to her, downstairs, in the kitchen, where she ought to be, with her book propped open with the two-pound weight, like it ought to be. He ran willing errands to the corner shop to buy margarine or sardines from the fearful Mrs Edwards, and reorganized his shelf of curios, writing careful labels for each shell and lump of metal:

Venus shell. Found by Charles Weekes, Frampton beach, August 24th, 1953

Bit of bombed fireplace. Found by Charles Weekes, October 1954

Brittle star starfish. Found by Charles Weekes, Frampton beach, August 17th, 1953

Though he knew exactly where he had found things, Charlie had made up some of the dates. He took Lydia to his room to show her, holding her hand as if she were the child.

'Dad told me how the starfish would grow a new leg if it lost one. The shell was in the high tideline and you didn't like the smell because the seaweed was hot with the sun,' he said. 'And there were millions of sand-hoppers jumping, every step you took.' He looked up to see if his mother remembered, but he couldn't tell.

In that early summertime, with his mother as she was and his father not there, the balance of Charlie's life shifted too, and he spent longer in the park, and longer in the doctor's garden, sometimes coming home only when the light was almost gone from the day. He told himself that his mother knew where he was and that she'd said he could be out this late. But he knew that she hadn't, and that she hadn't noticed him gone.

In the garden Charlie was mostly on his own. He was happy like this. With the bees he was sure and clear in his actions and they were always calm with him. He wore his bee suit and veil, but after a while he left off the gauntlets. They made him clumsy and somehow he could see more clearly when his hands had their proper touch. He was stung a few more times, but he took it for a badge of honour, like Roger Race in his *Boys' Book of the World*.

Charlie told the bees what he was doing at home – the shelf with his precious things – and he told them that his mother wasn't happy. He didn't say very much about it. But it was important that he let them know. He didn't want them flying off because he had kept silent.

The bees were busy. Charlie watched them return to the hives heavy and slow with nectar, their wings beating a lower note, and so many in the air, even in the late afternoon, that it carried a low drone he could hear almost down to the pond.

'If the weather stays sweet, there'll be a strong honey-flow now,' Dr Markham had told him. 'Good for all our jam jars, Charlie.'

So he took pride in the bees' labour, encouraging them in whispers as they returned with their pockets full.

Mostly Dr Markham wasn't there. She was doctoring people, he supposed. But occasionally she'd come down the garden to look at the hives. One time she stood close up and sniffed like a dog, nose held high.

'They're still bringing in clover,' she said, and he'd sniffed to see what she meant.

A week later she'd done the same again. 'Smell, Charlie. They're getting in the lime now.' He'd sniffed and nodded, because if you stood near the hives in the evening, you could smell the honey, and it changed week by week as the bees found different flowers to suck. When early evening came, he'd stand close to hear the bees fanning the combs, and he'd wrinkle his nose to sniff the honey air.

Some afternoons Dr Markham would call down the garden to him to come and have tea and then they'd sit on the terrace steps on big, faded cushions that smelled old and drink perfumed tea from mugs.

At first, Charlie felt awkward. It was odd to see a grown-up sitting on the steps, not on a chair. Aunt Pam would never dream of it, or his mother much, unless they were at the seaside maybe. But he became used to it and then enjoyed telling her what he'd noticed. Sometimes they talked about the seaside, or the war.

She usually asked after his mother at these times, and he usually said she was a bit under the weather, which seemed to make Dr Markham smile. Sometimes she had Mrs Sandringham wrap up a piece of cake for him to take home, or she would cut some flowers. But she didn't ask him more questions, which he was glad of.

He knew she had called on his mother, but then she was a doctor and though his mother didn't seem to be ill exactly, she didn't seem well either. Not her usual self. That's what she would say if it was one of their neighbours. He understood why Dr Markham would visit her; he simply couldn't imagine what they'd find to talk about.

Getting to and from the factory wasn't so bad. Lydia pushed the pedals hard and fast.

'Cycle really quickly and don't look around you. Once you're here, we'll look after you,' Dot said.

So she kept her eyes on the road and set up a race with herself, a best time to reach the factory gates in.

'I might have passed him on the street and not known. I might have passed him with –'

'Don't. Don't think about it.' Dot took Lydia's hand, shaking it with each word. 'You're better off without him. You've known that a good while.'

'It doesn't help,' Lydia said. 'Not at all.'

Dot was as good as her word and in the factory Lydia was one of a crowd. She had her own barricade, joking and joshing, daring any other woman to shout out after her down the corridor.

'But you need to get out a bit,' Dot said as they walked towards the cafeteria. 'I know what's up, but it must have been weeks by now and you still shut in there. Let's have a trip. Next Sunday, a few of us girls. Take the bus into the countryside. Or walk out a way along the river maybe. Take some cake, tea in a Thermos. Or even go in all together for a bottle of port.'

She nudged Lydia, but Lydia shook her head.

'Not yet, Dot,' she said, and Dot turned away, her shoulders rigid with exasperation.

'You don't know what's good for you, love.'

'I've got Charlie,' Lydia said. 'And I've been to the library a lot.'

'The library. It isn't books are going to keep you company. It's summertime. The sun's out and you're shut in. Look how pale you are. It'd be good for you, get some sun on your face. That won't cost you.'

'I don't want to go out with the girls. Not even with cake and port.'

'Charlie's only a boy. You don't want to be weighing him down, do you?'

'What makes you think I am?' Lydia said. 'I'm not saying anything to him.'

They reached the cafeteria queue and Dot dropped her voice.

'Saying, not saying, doesn't matter. It's that his dad has upped and left. That's what's happened to him, whatever you're doing. He's a boy and probably doing what boys do.'

'Which is?' Lydia said, her voice raised and angry. The woman in front shifted slightly and she felt herself blush. Dirty linen, she thought. 'Which is?' she said again, more quietly.

'Which is keeping to himself and keeping that self busy. I'll bet you he's out of the house more than ever, and when he's in, nearly doesn't come out of his room. I bet he's dead quiet. More than usual.'

Lydia shrugged. 'Doesn't mean I want him to be,' she said.

'No, but you're moping in there every time he puts his head up. You'll make him feel it's his fault, you're not careful.'

'Robert's been back a few times,' Lydia said.

'What for?'

'What do you mean, what for? We've been man and wife the last ten years.'

'Probably to pick up his clean underpants.'

The woman in front snorted.

'Dot!' Lydia said, shocked. 'Now you keep your voice down,' she added, then a giggle caught her and suddenly the two of them were convulsed over their dinner trays.

'Look, Lydia,' Dot said when they had calmed, her voice close, quiet. 'I'm only down once in the week with Paul to the Crown for a quick one. A half a lager, a game of bar billiards. But twice in as many weeks there he's been, at a corner table.'

They were up to the front now, Dot first; and it was trays on the counter for cauliflower cheese and a slice of ham, or beef and salad.

'Looks all right today,' Dot said and, getting no reply, she looked back.

Lydia stood motionless, tray still down by her side, staring at the vat of cauliflower. On the other side of the counter, the ladling woman waited.

'What are you having?' Dot said.

'Was he with –?'

'Let's get our dinner and sit down,' Dot said.

'Was he?' Lydia said, her voice dangerously thin.

Dot reached and took Lydia's tray.

'The cauliflower, thanks,' she said to the woman. 'Come

on, love. There's plenty here are happy to hear us, but we're holding up the queue.'

Dot found them seats at the end of one table.

'Don't know any of this lot,' she said. 'They won't be wanting to listen in.'

'Robert's stopped paying into the rent,' Lydia said, shaking salt over her cauliflower in angry jabs.

'God, Lydia! What are you going to do?'

'I don't know.'

'The man's a bastard. Is he giving you anything for groceries, that kind of thing?'

Lydia shook her head.

'Can your family help out?'

Another shake.

'You can take him to the court.'

Lydia set the salt cellar down hard.

'Come on,' she said. 'Who do you know who's managed that? Name me one.'

'But you can do it. I heard someone say so.'

'It's not women like us that manage it.'

Dot's face crunched with frustration. 'You don't think, do you? Don't look ahead. It's fine, dancing when the sun's shining. You can dance the socks off anyone. But things have been going this way for quite a while. You knew where Robert was heading and even if you hoped he wasn't, you should have made some plans. Done something. Got a blinking umbrella. Or at least gone to look for one. You can't just not do anything, not think about it,' Dot said.

'Was he with her?' Lydia said. 'In the pub?'

'Course he was. Buying her bloody Martinis, what's more, on your bloody rent money. So now I'll tell you one thing about her and only one. She's not a looker. Not compared to you.'

Lydia picked at her food, pushing it this way and that.

She had no appetite. A thousand thoughts, a thousand questions rushed her mind.

'You don't eat, you won't be strong enough to sort things out, look after your boy,' Dot said.

So Lydia ate, willed the food down, swallowed against the hard lump of her life.

The two friends had got up to leave, when Pam came upon them, mouth gritted in a smile, netted hair swinging like a club, elbows braced, ready for battle.

'Lydia,' she said, nodding.

Lydia didn't reply.

'Hello, Pam,' Dot said.

Pam stared at her. 'I've come to speak to Lydia. There's no need for you to listen in.'

Dot looked at her friend, then sat down. She wasn't going anywhere.

Turning a shoulder to Dot, Pam began her speech. Lydia watched her. Pam's stance reminded her so strongly of Robert, it was all she could do not to exclaim.

It's in the jut of her jaw, she thought, or maybe the way she has of standing, as if she's about to leap up on a wall.

By the time Lydia was listening again, Pam had almost finished up, leaning in so close that Lydia could hear the slight adjustment of her teeth as she spat out the words.

'. . . but it's been long enough now,' was all Lydia heard, and then Pam paused as if inviting Lydia to respond. Dot rolled her eyes.

'You had the beef salad, didn't you?' Dot said.

'What?' Pam said.

'The beef salad. You ate it for dinner.'

'What?' Pam said again.

'Pickled onions do leave such a strong aftertaste,' Dot said.

'Were you listening to me?' Pam said.

'You said it was long enough now for something,' Lydia said with a shrug.

'You should be thinking of the family at a time like this,' Pam said. 'Not only of yourself. It's very embarrassing for all of us. There's your son, and your duty as a wife.'

'*My* duty?' Lydia said, her voice incredulous. 'Do you know what your sacred brother has been getting up to? For years? Was that his duty?'

The words had come out unexpectedly. She'd never before let herself think about the reality of what Robert had been doing, but as she spoke she realized the terrible truth of all his infidelities, all his betrayals.

'Lydia?' Dot said.

'There's conjugal rights,' Pam said. 'Men don't just up and leave their wives.'

Lydia took a long breath. Different answers tumbled through her head.

'Tell that to Robert,' she said finally. She turned and walked away, not waiting for Dot, not caring, suddenly not able to bear any of it.

Dot caught her up at the end of the day and they walked back into the town together.

'She was furious,' Dot said. 'She didn't know what had got into you. Said you'd never said anything like that before. She said: "I don't see why she had to shout at me like that." '

Lydia laughed at Dot's imitation, but her voice was bitter.

'The woman is a monster,' she said. 'She has her reasons, losing her parents to one war and her husband to another. But even so. I've petted her and stroked her and sidled up to her for years. Listened to her lies about my husband. Now I don't have to any longer.'

The two women walked slowly, enjoying the light and

easy warmth of the late afternoon sun. Around them, hundreds of others, released by the same bell, made their way home, beginning to siphon off now to left and right as they walked through the town. Men, women, boys in overalls, and girls not long out of school. The girls with their headscarves ripped off, hair and gossip tumbled round their heads in clouds of permanent wave. They ran along the pavements, past Lydia and Dot, like colts, like sirens, like animals pent too long, jostling and laughing, shouting and whispering, mouths behind hands and their sweet voices littering the air.

'My Dave mentioned Annie last night,' Dot said. 'I meant to say.'

'Mentioned why?'

'He was dressed up smart, natty tie, those narrow trousers they're wearing now, the young men, hair slicked up, shoes polished. Said he didn't want any tea thanks, Ma, so I asked him where he was off to and if he'd be late in. He said it was a double date. He said Annie was in the other half.'

'Annie?' Lydia said.

'Turns out she's walking out with Dave's workmate, George Pemble. Been going on a while, but very hush-hush on account of her mother.'

'The note,' Lydia said. 'I knew it was something like that.'

'Does Pam know?'

Lydia shook her head.

'If she did, she'd move heaven and earth to stop it. Annie's the only decent creature to come out of that house, poor love.'

They'd reached the corner that marked the parting of their ways and Dot turned to go.

'George is a good type,' she said. 'Got a bit of mouth with a few pints in him, but he'll look out for Annie. Do what he can with her mother, too, though he's young to be much of a match.'

Lydia nodded, but her thoughts had turned again; she was weary to the core and longed to be alone.

'Thanks Dot,' she said, and she rode away.

15

The cat lay out in the bars of sunlight, limbs extended, eyes down to a sliver. Only her ears made any move, twitching slightly as Jean came in.

She ran her fingers through the soft fur, felt the slight arch of pleasure. She touched a paw, lifted a claw with her fingertip, drawing it from its soft sheath, and felt it tip at her skin, almost painful. The early summer had turned hot and Jean basked with the cat, sprawling her legs out on the floorboards in the study, loving the wood warmth on her skin.

She was excited, but she didn't know why. Her appetite, usually strong, had deserted her and for the last few nights even sleep had been hard to come by. Sometimes she got up and sat in an armchair with a mug of tea and Sarah Vaughan on the gramophone. Others she lay on her bed, eyes wide to the dark. Then night-time call-outs came as a relief, and she had to check the enthusiasm with which she answered the telephone, casting the worried and the fearful into the electric charge of her strange mood.

Mrs Sandringham chastised her daily for not clearing her plate and then wanted to make her sit still a while, or take her temperature.

'I'm a doctor, Mrs S,' Jean said impatiently, but it was true that she couldn't diagnose this condition.

This time of year, Jean's list was always lighter. She didn't know why it was. Perhaps people simply felt better and got ill less often when the sun shone. It could be as simple as that. Anyway, it meant more time, and so these summer months she was in the habit of slipping further into her friends' lives, making herself part of their family, a kind of fair-weather part, Jim teased her. Doing the shopping with Sarah, meeting Meg and Emma from school occasionally, taking them to the town pool for the afternoon, or into the country for a weekend picnic.

So Jean was on errands with Sarah when she saw Lydia Weekes again one Saturday afternoon, standing on the far side of the bustling street. But unlike every other woman, Lydia seemed to have no purpose. She held a basket like everyone else, and probably she had a list too. On the back of an envelope, Jean imagined, or hastily scribbled on the margin of the evening news. But she was doing nothing. In fact, she looked as if she'd been arrested midway to somewhere, her slight body lifted up and dropped there, inside a yellow shift dress, with her back to Marshall and Coop's, arms by her sides, neither standing nor walking quite, her head bowed, her face closed in, closed off.

It was a busy time of day on the high street and women shoved past, impatient, wielding baskets like battering rams, pushing prams like tanks. Jean watched as Lydia was pushed forward towards the gutter, and then back, till she stood hard up, back against the plate glass window, out of which a vast pair of spectacles glared at passers-by.

Standing outside the butcher's, waiting for her friend, Jean watched this woman, Charlie's mother, and her heart went out to her.

'What on earth?' Sarah said, setting down her basket and looking over to the far pavement.

Jean started. Her mind had gone elsewhere and it took her a moment and a careful look at Sarah's basket of meat to remember where she was.

'What are you looking at?'

'Nothing. A patient,' Jean said. 'I must visit her later.'

'You were miles away.' Sarah hefted up the basket. 'Miles and miles.'

As they walked off, Jean stole a last look and, though she barely knew what she was thinking, it crossed her mind how beautiful Lydia was, and how sad she looked.

They were nearly back to the house when Jean ventured an unfamiliar kind of comment.

'They're pretty, the dresses being worn, with the big buttons and open necks. The sleeves like that.' She shaped what she meant with her hands and Sarah laughed outright.

'Now this I don't believe. Dr Jean Markham commenting on ladies' fashion.'

Jean was put out.

'Just because I'm voicing my thoughts,' she said.

'Is there a reason you want a dress with big buttons? Or maybe some higher heels.'

'I don't want to wear them. I was only noticing what's being worn.'

But she saw her friend's shrug and her smile, as though Sarah knew something that she didn't.

A few days later, Jean was on her way across the park with her black bag and certain stride, making good time, almost to the west gate, when she saw Lydia again. It was late in the afternoon of a sunny day and the air was full of children's shouts, shrill by now and weary with the heat. People were spread like washing over the grass, the mothers with their jam sandwiches, the lovers, newly-met after work, still coy with one another, fingers full of daisies, marking the distance between their knees. But the bright colours were dulling at the edges, the flowers scuffed with their long day out, the grass crumpled. Already two men in clipped grey uniforms and resentful shoulders were laying out hoses for the evening's recovery, one eye to the park clock so that they could ring out the end of the day, expel the mothers and the lovers, lock the gates and have their park back to themselves.

Jean's thoughts that afternoon were as busy as her feet, worrying over Mrs Sandringham's departure in the autumn, which would come up sooner than she knew, and about how to refuse the rash of summer evening parties. Her mood was strange, she knew that, and she simply couldn't bear the prospect of so much gregarious obligation. So it was chance; or a familiar perfume; or some strange motion somewhere – a thing she had no faith in, but that Jim might call the gods – that meant she looked up just as her path approached Lydia's, at one corner of a bed of pink dahlias.

Lydia, still with her hair up tight from the factory, walked with her bicycle, a plastic mackintosh piled into the front basket, and her thoughts adrift. Jean watched her. She walked like a dancer. Jean hadn't noticed it before. Her spine was arched and her shoulders back and she held her hands almost slack on the handlebars. Even her feet were turned slightly, as if she were returning from a re-hearsal, not from a day on the production line.

There were things Lydia should be thinking about, like how to make ends meet, and Charlie, and a comment thrown her way at work about Annie, and what to say next time Robert came home. But she couldn't bear to think now. Her mind strayed, and she stared at the lovers, their glances playing tag across the grass, as if they were from another country.

Jean watched Lydia walk towards her slowly, carelessly, eyes down, shoes catching at the gravel, and she felt her heart jump. She had learned to keep other people's grief at bay, but now she didn't want to. Though she was unused to hesitation, this knowledge, this certainty, gave her pause.

'Mrs Weekes,' she said, and perhaps if she hadn't spoken, Lydia would have passed by, unseeing.

But Lydia stopped walking and looked up.

'How are you?' Jean said, and then, because this seemed too much to the point, 'How are the books?'

Lydia knitted her brow. 'Dr Markham,' she said finally, and she pursed her lips as though pleased to have made the connection. 'Yes, I like one of them. The thriller.'

Jean nodded. 'Good. That's good,' she said, more as though Lydia had told her that her leg no longer hurt, than that she'd enjoyed a novel.

Now that she had stopped, Lydia seemed planted there, at that point on the path, as if her key had unwound its spring entirely, as if the world had stopped in its tracks, the birds in the trees, the children and the lovers.

'It's a lovely afternoon,' Jean said, a little too loud. 'I like being able to walk through the park. I'm so often in my car,' she said, hefting up her black bag as if to explain.

Lydia looked across to where the grass rose in a slight hill. On the far side, behind the crest of trees, the pond lay, and even now distant shouts reminded her of Charlie and his triumphs on that small circle of water.

'But you're always on your way to other people's misery,' she said. 'Isn't that hard?'

'The cost of the job,' Jean said simply. 'Somebody needs to do it.'

Lydia looked back at the doctor, and her words came out in a rush.

'I'm sorry. That was very rude.'

'Well, sometimes I leave them with less misery than they had before,' Jean said, 'and sometimes I don't.'

'I really did like that book,' Lydia said.

'It was a guess, on my part.'

'I tried the other too . . .' Lydia paused and gestured to Jean's bag. 'But you're in a hurry. Ill people.'

'No, no, actually I'm not. In fact . . .' Jean cast around for anything she could offer, a way to make Lydia stay.

Inside the gate the ice-cream van gleamed. 'In fact, would you like a cone?'

She could see Lydia shy at this, begin to leave, but as if to back her up, the van tolled its bell and Jean grinned.

'All right then. Thank you,' Lydia said.

The women walked towards the trees. Lydia spread her plastic mackintosh on the grass and they sat down with their cones.

'How is the garden?' Lydia said.

Jean looked up, surprised.

'Hasn't Charlie said anything?'

Lydia shook her head slowly, but Jean, watching her face, noticed a slight fret to her eyes.

'I don't think he has,' Lydia said finally, 'but I've been preoccupied recently. So perhaps I simply don't remember.'

She put a hand to her cheek and stared down at the grass. Then, as if a thought had just come to her, she looked straight at Jean.

'Why have you stopped here with me? Is it because of Charlie? Something I should know?'

'No, only because I wanted to,' Jean said. 'As a matter of fact, I enjoy your company.'

Lydia looked at Jean, eyebrows raised.

'You enjoy my company?' she said slowly.

Jean nodded, serious, and then Lydia threw back her head and laughed.

'You find that funny?' Jean was nonplussed, and then she smiled, because it was a grand thing, to see this woman laugh.

'I must go now,' Lydia said.

'Come soon and choose another book,' Jean said as they got to their feet, and Lydia smiled this time and went on her way.

16

Charlie had left the books with Mrs Sandringham. They were carefully parcelled in brown paper and, when Jean unpacked them, she found the note.

Thank you for the novels. I am sorry to have been so long with them. Charlie has promised to return them safe. I walked in the park at the same time this Thursday, but perhaps more of your patients were ill this week. Anyway I did not see you.
Yours gratefully,
Lydia Weekes

Jean put the note away in her desk. She wished the books were not returned, because then she could imagine Mrs Weekes coming with them herself, and now she would not. She cursed herself for being far the other side of town at five o'clock today, when Mrs Weekes had walked again in the park. But something made her glad, too, though she couldn't put her finger on it, and she stood still in the room and shut her eyes to be calmer.

Jean sent Lydia two more packages of books in the weeks that followed, tying them round with string so that Charlie could carry them home. She wrote the briefest of notes each time, since Mrs Weekes clearly had enough on her plate without Jean calling in each time.

But as busy as she made her life, packing it so full that there was no time to ponder, once her head touched the pillow she would think of Lydia, wondering over her sadness and bemused by her own pleasure in the other woman's company.

She was in the garden the evening that Lydia came to find her. It was a Wednesday and she was digging hard, the grit cut of the blade striking down through the drying summer soil, breath and effort filling her thoughts.

The garden bell rang loud enough to raise the evening birds from the lawn. Jean opened the gate swiftly, efficiently, ready to reassure, to calm, ready to wash the soil from her hands and change her shoes, gather her black bag and go. But it was Lydia she found standing there; Lydia, her body half-turned to go, her face uncertain, holding a string bag jutting with Jean's books.

'I'm sorry to disturb you this time of an evening.'

'Is everything all right?' Jean said.

'I've brought back your books,' Lydia said, lifting the bag slightly. 'Seemed rude to have Charlie always bring them this way and that. I thought all of a sudden . . . it was a nice evening for a walk anyway.'

'I'm glad you've caught me. I'm on call tonight. I thought you were a call-out,' Jean said.

'You're gardening,' Lydia said, pointing to Jean's hands.

'Digging,' Jean said.

'Must be annoying. To have to drop everything when someone rings the bell.'

'Sometimes. Jean leaned against the gatepost. 'But I fought a battle with my parents and then studied very hard for the right to have my evenings and my nights interrupted.'

Lydia smiled. 'Well, then at least this time you can go back to your digging.' She held out the string bag. 'Thank you.'

'That big book was one of my father's favourites,' Jean said. The bag swung between them, awkward, unbalanced. She looked at Lydia, a question in her voice. 'I wasn't sure you'd like it, it being so long.'

'I haven't read anything like that before. It's got such a lovely cover. Not like a library book. But heavy to read in bed,' Lydia said with a small laugh. 'You know, holding your arms up.'

'So come and get some more,' Jean said. 'Now you're here, you can choose for yourself.'

Lydia glanced away, into the garden, then back to Jean. She looked at the doctor with her tousled hair, her muddy hands, the sweat beading where her shirt collar opened. She didn't know any other woman who would be easy, being seen like this by someone not much more than an acquaintance. You got your lipstick on and your hair sorted out quick, whether you'd knocked off work, or gone and had a baby, or been in an earthquake. Lydia grinned.

'Thanks.'

Neither mentioned Charlie, but both conjured him, and they walked through the vegetables and round into the house each in their own silence. Jean saw him running ahead like a puppy between the high lines of beans, then stopping on a pinhead to crouch and watch something tiny on the ground, on a leaf, something invisible to her. She pictured him calling to them and showing them his find, his child's brow furrowed for a moment with the effort to describe, as she had encouraged him to do. He had said his mother was happy with him visiting, but Jean was anxious that Lydia might be hurt if she found out how much time he spent in the garden, or about the growing assortment of things he'd shown her, or about how many teatime meals Mrs Sandringham had fed the hungry boy.

Lydia wondered how far into this house Charlie had

been. Had he been up these stairs? Had he stopped to look at the pictures? There were several that looked very old in big, gilt frames: solemn couples with children on their knee, one of a man with his dogs. She could imagine that one catching Charlie's eye. Had he seen the room with all the books? Played marbles on this landing? Had he been at home here?

'It's a lovely house,' she said, and as if she knew Lydia's mind, Jean answered.

'I don't believe Charlie's ever been upstairs. No cause. He lets himself in through the gate at the bottom of the garden.' She turned to Lydia. 'He's always happy to occupy himself in the garden. With the bees; watching down by the pond. No trouble. He seems quite a solitary fellow. We barely know he's here.'

Lydia nodded. It was strange to hear someone so nearly a stranger talk about your own boy like this. She supposed Jean was used to doing that, being a doctor. Jean opened a door off the landing and gestured to Lydia to go in.

The room was walled all round with books. Shelves from floor to ceiling. Lydia stood silent at the sight. Aside from the public library, she had never seen so many books in a single room; never seen so many in a single house. The room was lit pink with late, low sun, and the books glowed on their shelves, all their browns and reds and greens, all the gold lettering. Lydia wanted to run her fingers down their spines, feel the sun's warmth held in them. She wanted to stroke these lovely things.

Jean watched Lydia's face. Her expression wasn't hard to read, and Jean was abashed at the other woman's wonder.

'There are a good few to choose from,' she said.

'Had your father read them all?'

Jean shrugged. 'I don't know. A lot, certainly.'

Lydia thought of her uncle's precious books, tucked into

a corner of her wardrobe. She had read them all several times over years ago and now they were cherished objects: *The Thirty-nine Steps*, *Rogue Male*, *The Sign of Four*, and maybe a dozen others. But Dr Markham said she didn't read the books she'd inherited, so what was it that she held so precious?

'I've put all the novels on those shelves,' Jean said, pointing to one side of the room. 'Please, choose some more, if you'd like to.'

'I mustn't be too long,' Lydia said.

Jean sat down in the armchair by the window. She had pulled out a book she remembered her father reading and that she thought she might enjoy. Not a novel, more of a travelogue, Norman Douglas's *Old Calabria*. But now she didn't want to read, only to watch this other woman in her reverie, and so she sat, book on her lap, finger marking a random page, eyes lowered, Lydia's outline just in her sights.

Lydia ran her eyes along the shelves. She took out a book and read the first paragraph, replaced it just proud of its neighbours so as to find it again. She pulled out another and held it in her palm. Such a solid weight. Opening it near the middle, she scanned over the text. The print was tightly spaced and she turned towards the window for more light.

'I could stay in here for hours,' she said. 'Pull out every one.'

And for ten minutes or more they stayed like that. Then Lydia started and looked at her watch.

'I must get back to Charlie. I said I'd only be out an hour.'

'If you liked *Middlemarch*, there are more by her,' Jean said. 'You could take another one back with you.'

'Her?'

'She wrote under a man's name.'

'Why?'

'To be sure she was taken seriously.'

'But you haven't read her novels.'

'No. But my father knew I'd be interested by the name question. Did you like it?'

'I don't know,' she said. 'It's a million miles from detective novels.'

Jean waited.

'There's a character, one of the chief ones, and she's not like me, not at all. And her husband isn't like my husband, either.'

Lydia stopped, and again Jean waited. Waiting was something she was good at. She'd learned to be patient, to listen for what was important.

Lydia looked at the wall, at the floor. Then she turned towards the doctor and spoke in a dull voice.

'Her husband only has eyes for himself,' she said. 'He never really notices how she feels, so she despairs.'

Jean looked at her because her voice was full of grief, and she saw the tears on Lydia's cheeks.

'But does it end like that?' Jean said.

'No. It doesn't end like that. But it's what I felt most, about the book.'

The sun was almost gone; the evening was darkening into night. Jean turned on a lamp.

Still Lydia stood, her cheeks wet with tears, like someone bereft, Jean thought. It was not the same, she knew, but she thought of her father's dying and how empty she had felt when he was gone. How hard it had been, how painful, to have nothing to hold. How it had hurt, physically hurt. Nothing in the place of his body. Even a body which, by the end, was little more than skin and bone.

That memory, the terrible, numbing loneliness of it, took Jean a step forward and made her open her arms and hold this woman, standing so still and sad; and wrap her round and hold her as she wept.

17

Charlie had his head down, already running, out of the boys' cloakroom, along the corridor and out of the school. It was Friday and he was heading for the pipe factory with Bobby. Bobby said he'd seen a grass snake there, he swore he had, and they were going to find it and make a den. It was a hot day and the playground tarmac was soft beneath his sandals. It gave off a smell that made Charlie sad, though he couldn't have said why.

He was running hard and fast, satchel wrapped tight to him. His thoughts were already crouched low and still, watching the scrubby grass near the stream, watching for a snake's turn or fold, watching the water for the ripple coil it would make. He didn't see Lydia waiting outside the gate.

He was yards down the pavement when he heard his name called, but it brought him to a halt so fast that Bobby was into the back of him.

'Charlie,' Lydia called again.

'It's my mum,' Charlie said.

'Why's she here?'

Charlie shook his head. 'Don't know.'

'Come on then. Before anybody else finds it.'

But Charlie still stood there.

'It must be important, cos she doesn't finish at the factory till five.'

'I saw the snake, for real,' Bobby said. 'I bet it'll be there today.'

Charlie looked again, as if to be sure it was his mother.

'I'll catch you up. Soon as I can.' He turned and jogged back towards the school, his satchel banging careless on his hip, but his face sharp with apprehension.

'Mum?' he said.

Lydia was standing at the railings, a bag on her shoulder and a basket at her feet. But she was wearing a summer dress, the blue one he especially liked, not her factory clothes and he didn't understand. She took a step forward and Charlie felt his heart jolt and the back of his neck go hot.

'Charlie,' Lydia said, her voice excited, 'we're going on a trip. You and me.'

Fear had gripped him fast. But she was all right, and now it dropped and left him dazed. He looked back through the railings at the empty playground. Bobby was gone to find the grass snake, and Charlie wanted to be with him. More than anything in the world, he wanted to be with him.

'But you're at the factory,' he said. 'You're at work till gone five. And I'm going to see a snake. Bobby promised to show me.'

'We got given the afternoon off,' Lydia said. 'So I've planned us a trip. There's a bus in twenty minutes. Marion at work was talking about it. This big lake, outside Allendon.'

'But I want to find the snake.'

Lydia didn't seem to hear him. She hoisted the bag to her shoulder and passed him the basket.

'I'll get you an Orange Maid,' she said. 'The bus ride's not long.'

Charlie looked out of the window. The bus seat scratched and stippled his legs, so he put his hands under to protect them as he watched the town slip away. He was still cross with his mother, and sulking. He saw the river turn between the trees and the birds and the grazing animals, and the hills far off on the horizon, while beside him, his mother read a book. Something in a brown leather cover from Dr Markham's library.

Charlie watched for what he could see and he made a list in his head. When he got home, he'd write it down in his notebook:

Sheep with a limp
Island for den in river – can Bobby swim?
Girl with birthmark
Hawk diving, don't know if it got its prey
Cat in a field, no house near by

They were the only people to get out at Allendon. Lydia took a piece of paper from her basket.

'Our map,' she said. 'Marion did it out for me. She said it was about a mile from the village.'

'What's a mile from the village?' Charlie said, looking around. There was nothing here that he could see. Only some cottages and a church. Nothing that you'd take a bus to specially.

'The lake. I told you.' Lydia turned the map around and fixed herself with a finger. 'This way,' she said.

Try as he might, once they started walking, Charlie couldn't keep hold of his sulk. His satchel over his shoulder, he took turns with his mother to carry the basket.

'Tea,' was all she said when he asked what was under the cloth, but every now and then he smelled a sweet bread smell, and sometimes there was a bottle clink. The playground and the railings, Bobby and the snake, they all slipped away and he was here with his mother, walking down a dusty lane full of flowers and insects and dried-up dung.

They smelled the lake before they saw it. It smelled of wet places, something that Charlie knew from the river.

'There it is,' Lydia said, pointing through the trees to what Charlie could see only as an empty space, a hollow in the air. But he followed her along a small path trampled in the grass and suddenly there it was, a vast expanse of water. Charlie stood and stared. It was so big, and so hidden. He couldn't even see the end of it. Willows swung their fringes and birds scaggled around the rushes along one side. Moorhens ventured out into the open water, jerky little pedalos, only to turn suddenly and duck back in behind the greenery at invisible perils. There were big lilies and high trees. On the other side of the lake there was a tumbled line of flat stones reaching into the water and, behind them, a piece of rough grass.

'It's bigger than Marion gave out,' Lydia said. 'And so still.'

'There'll be fish in here. Could be big ones if it goes deep,' Charlie said. He picked up the basket. 'I can get close over there, on those stones. You could sit on the grass, like you do in the park.'

Lydia laughed.

'I might want to paddle,' she said. 'Can't do that in the park.'

'But then you'll frighten the fish.'

Charlie crouched on the broad stones and looked down through the clear, brown water. Weed swayed, dancing like girls, caressing itself. Pebbles sat clear and still on the bottom and a shoal of tiny fish skittered about in the sun lines.

'You could fit forty ponds in here,' Charlie said. 'Fifty.'

He put his hand in slowly. The water lipped at his wrist, cool and unassuming, and he felt in his spread fingers the faint echoes and vibrations of the lake's life far in deep and out of sight.

'I bet there's pike,' he said. 'And perch and trout, and other fish.'

His feet firm on the warm, flat stones, Charlie watched the water. He looked across its surface, his gaze skimming past the insects dancing and the lily flowers, letting in the space and the light and the air. He looked up at his mother, standing barefoot, smiling, then back down at his hand, cradled in the shallows.

'You know what,' he said, suddenly excited; then he paused, unsure.

'What?' Lydia said, so Charlie said it.

'You know what, Dad would love this place. He'd know the fish all right. He'd bring his rod and we could stand right here.'

He looked up when there was no reply. But Lydia had walked away, lugging the basket and the bag like dead weights. Charlie stood, taking his hand sharp from the lake as if from some danger so that water spangled the air. He opened his mouth and his voice shouted across the water, lifting the birds, shocking the trees.

'Mum!'

Lydia stopped dead.

'Mum!' he shouted again, and his mother turned back and came and held him, arms around his back, his head against her breast so that his ear pulsed with the beat of her heart.

'Charlie,' she said quietly, just to him, and he felt the fingers of her hand against his ribs. 'I'm sorry, Charlie.' And then the birds settled and the trees grew calm.

After they had eaten their picnic, Lydia opened the shoulder bag she'd brought with her. Wrapped in several tea towels was Charlie's boat.

'Thought you might like to sail it here,' she said. 'I know there's not much wind today. But the pond's too small now.'

So Charlie took the boat to the flat stones and set it to sail, steadying, and then launching it into the breeze with even hands.

They watched it to the middle of the lake, and sometimes the blue fish leaped taut at the wind, and other times it drifted on its canvas plain.

Charlie's thoughts drifted with it, the keel of his mind cutting clear, because right now, beside this lake with his mother, things seemed better. Easier. He wondered whether Bobby had found the snake, and he thought about the bees and the honey harvest. A lot of the supers would be full by now and Dr Markham had set the date for the first weekend in September and had asked him to be her right-hand man. She had shown him the extractor, the uncapping knife and all the jars, washed clean and waiting. She had aprons ready and said it would be hard work. It would be something to tell Bobby about. It would be something to tell his dad.

He dreamed of his dad. He'd even had the same dream a few times, of playing football, being dead good at it, and his dad coming by and seeing him and being proud. The girls at school had stopped with their songs now. Old news maybe, like his dad used to say. But he didn't return. Or if he did it was only to take more things away. His mum didn't lay a third place any more.

'Going to be a hard job, getting it back.' Lydia's voice broke in and Charlie looked up confused.

'We'd better start walking round. It's sailing to the farthest point.'

Charlie stared round the lake edge, with its deep reeds and brambles and steep trees dropping to the bank. It would take them an age to get round, especially his mother, scrabbling and scrambling. He looked again at the boat. It was far down the lake now, running with the wind, free.

'We could leave it here,' he said. 'Let it sail to where it wants. Maybe another boy will find it.'

Lydia looked across the lake. She looked at her son.

They stood on the stones and watched the little boat sail almost out of sight, then they walked back along the path and through the trees to the road to find a bus home.

18

It was the last day in school and when the headmaster did his speech, the floor was a sea of fidgets and twists. The hall was warm as warm, and pretty Miss Withers began to fall asleep. Charlie noticed the rock-rock-rock of her head out of the corner of his eye. Some hair had fallen out of its pins and was straggled over her face and he turned away, embarrassed for her.

The headmaster spoke of trial and service. He spoke of boys who had gone before and of the ultimate sacrifice. He pointed to the wooden board with names cut in gold, and spoke of responsibility and reward. The children waited to be released, they waited to be gone; the teachers tutted and dozed and scratched their hot stockings as discreetly as so many pairs of eyes would allow. Finally the headmaster spoke of respect for elders and the holidays ahead, and of the day for their return ready for the new school year, a day so far into the future that it had no meaning for any child sat there, and at last they filed impatiently out and were gloriously away into the long summer afternoon.

The days stretched out endlessly. Charlie had all the time in the world, and it thrilled him and it weighed heavy. His mother was gone early and often working overtime now, taking any spare hours she could as other women took their holidays. She arranged with old Mrs Davis down the street that he could call in on her on an afternoon, if it was raining, or in case of emergency. She was a kind old lady, but there would have to be volcanoes spewing before Charlie knocked on her door.

So he spent his days around the edges of the town, a sandwich in his pocket for his lunch, maybe a coin for an ice cream. Sometimes on his own, sometimes with Bobby, sometimes in the gang of boys that would gather and knot around the park memorial.

Twice now Charlie had seen a snake at the pipe factory. Once basking near an end wall till he surprised it, and another time near the water. He was sure they'd been grass snakes and he still held out hopes of catching one.

'You've got to be patient,' he said to Bobby. 'They're shy, won't come out if you move about.'

But Bobby couldn't sit still for long, so mostly Charlie watched on his own.

The boys built a den there deep in the brambles. Charlie had filched some of his father's nails and brought over his hammer and crowbar and saw. His dad wouldn't have allowed it, but his dad wasn't there. There was a passage in, observation post, dug-in shelter with boards and corrugated iron and tarpaulin over, a place to keep equipment and maps, and another for supplies. They'd got supplies in a biscuit tin. A tin of sardines, some crackers and the end of a cornflakes packet. A jam jar to drink from. Bobby had even rigged up something for collecting rainwater. The den took days to build, and they celebrated with a bottle of lemonade, Bobby shaking it up and spraying it over the corrugated iron in zigzag patterns like he said he'd seen them do at his cousin's wedding.

'We're on our holidays next week,' Bobby said as they drank the remainder. 'Dad's got the whole of it off. Let's get down here loads before then.'

Charlie dug his heels down into the trampled earth.

'I know it's got to be top secret, but I want to bring my

dad to see it,' Bobby said. 'Only him. After he's back from work one evening. I'll get him to stand a foot away, over by the big bush, and you be inside it and he won't know it's there. Only him, Charlie. Cos he's not going to tell anyone else, is he.'

Charlie flipped a marble, watched it roll out of sight. Going home that evening, he saw his own dad. The first time in weeks. He was running, not to be late, and flicking over the day in his head, picking out the things to tell his mum when she asked; picking out the things not to tell her. She'd started asking him again, as if she'd started noticing he was there again and sometimes it was a bit much. Sometimes it felt as if he couldn't get his breath.

He only saw his dad when he was nearly past him. His dad, cigarette in his fingers, head turning to the left and then to the right, like he always did; his walk, like it always was, as if he was one part cowboy and wearing those leather trousers.

All these things his dad did that Charlie had never noticed before, but that he knew him by in the flash of the second he saw him. Just as Charlie knew him by the scar on his finger where the dog had bitten him when he was a boy; or by the way he set off singing in the bath; here he was, walking down the street like he had the right to be here, walking down the street smiling, with a woman on his arm that was not Charlie's mother.

All this Charlie saw and understood in the time it took to run by. All this Charlie saw, and his father saw nothing.

Then he was round the corner and past the pub, which was probably where his dad was heading, running, banging his feet at the pavement, not looking, not caring, only wanting to be gone and free, till suddenly he stopped dead and stood, looking straight out at everything – front doors, net curtains, the moon, a dog – and at nothing at all. He sniffed the air. He could still smell his father, the cigarettes and hair-cream, and the woman's perfume, and all the mixed-up smells made him sad, made him furious.

Across the street a lady stared at him and he stared right back, stuck his tongue out, and then he was running again.

The air was damp with cooking vegetables when he got in. Lydia had the wireless on, but she must have been listening for him, because he'd barely climbed the stairs when she was there calling up, her voice chirpy as if everything was all right now.

'Hello. What have you been up to? Did you eat your sandwich? I saw a hedgehog on the way to work, snuffling it was. I said to it: "You're out late, dear." Wish you'd seen it.'

Charlie buried his face in the pillow. His cheeks were burning and his head pounded. His mother went on talking up the stairs.

'I've got a nice dinner cooking. Come and read a page of my book to me while I finish off.'

When Charlie went down, she had the book propped open under the two-pound weight, like usual, and she was washing up, humming something.

'What sort of story is it?' Charlie said.

Lydia turned at his voice. She scrutinized his face and put down the wet brush.

'What's happened?' she said.

He picked up the book. The writing blurred before him.

'Charlie.' Lydia's voice was measured but insistent. 'What happened?'

'Just played.'

'Who with?'

'Bobby.'

'Did you finish the den?'

He nodded.

'Bobby's bringing his dad to see it.'

'Ah,' Lydia said. She paused, then asked, 'Anything else happen?'

He held the book and stared at the daze of small black letters.

'Charlie,' she said again, softly.

He looked up at her.

'Did you meet anyone else?' Lydia said, and he looked at her eyes to see if she knew. Then he slammed the book to the ground. There was a moment between them before he yelled, 'Your books are stupid,' and he ran from the room.

Later Lydia came up to find him. She sat on his bed and stroked his hair.

'Will you let me see your den?' she said.

'Don't know.' The feel of her hand stroking his head was good and he shut his eyes again.

'I know I'm not your dad, but . . .'

'You have to crawl, then you have to crouch. In one place I can nearly stand up, but you couldn't.'

'Are there different bits to it then? Different rooms?'

'I suppose so. But you don't have rooms in a den.'

'No, of course not.' Lydia thought for a moment. 'What about you taking me to see your den and then me taking you to Fontini's for ice cream?'

'Why?'

'Why not? We're not getting much in the way of holiday, what with me working all the time.'

'Will you wear perfume? Like you do going out with Dad?'

Lydia looked at him, puzzled.

'If you want me to, yes.'

'And paint your nails?'

'Charlie?' Lydia said.

He didn't say anything.

'Charlie?' she said again.

He shrugged. Then, in a throwaway kind of voice, 'Maybe Dad would come back if . . .'

'If what?'

He wouldn't look at her.

'If I painted my nails again and wore perfume?' she said.

She rubbed her hands across her face, as though to clear her mind.

'Have you seen him today?' she said, and after a pause Charlie nodded.

'And perhaps he wasn't on his own?'

Charlie didn't move.

'Was he with another lady?'

'You don't know any of the things I do,' he said.

Charlie would have struggled if he'd had to think back later about what he filled his time with in those next weeks. Much of it he spent on his own. Some days, as long as it was dry, he would let himself into the doctor's garden. First of all he would go and talk to the bees, each of the four hives, let them know he was there and tell them anything important that had gone on. Quickly and quietly. He tried to speak to them in the way they understood. The rest of the day he would spend on his own, watching insects or clouds, inventing schemes and stratagems in the tangled privacy beyond the hives. Although he didn't once see Dr Markham, he would leave something for her each time, with a note telling her where he had found it and anything else about it he thought was interesting. Like the skeleton of a dragonfly nymph, sharp feet clinging for dear life to a reed, which he placed on the garden table and covered with an empty flowerpot. Or an owl pellet, its oval black surface shiny like varnish, from under the oak tree at the bottom of the garden, placed beside the watering can in the greenhouse. He knew she would like these things and that she would know what he thought about them.

Some of the other days he spent in the park. Most of the boys who gathered there were older than Charlie and already running on the edge of adolescence, one moment picking stubs from the paths to roll into dangerous-looking cigarettes, the next pulling faces at the park attendants or chasing the pigeons. Charlie hung about at one corner of the group, affecting his own slouch, torn in his own way. He watched the young boys with their boats on the pond and for two pins he would have run down the hill and joined them. But he'd left his boat for someone else to find and he couldn't go back.

He went out to the woods beyond the town. Robert had taken him and Annie there on a couple of Sunday trips a few years back, Charlie riding proud on the crossbar of his father's bike.

The first time, when they arrived, they stood beneath the green ceiling of trees and Robert didn't know what to do. He shuffled his feet and said that his own father used to bring him and Pam here on a Sunday, as if that somehow explained his doing so now.

'I can't imagine Mum here,' Annie said. 'All the earth and undergrowth.'

Robert grinned. 'Wasn't her favourite place,' he said, 'but Father insisted.'

In the end they played hide and seek, then searched for the stream that ran through the middle of the woods, and it became one of the best times Charlie had ever had with his dad.

On his own in the woods, Charlie wandered with a will to be lost. Seeing no one all day, he played his solitary games, imagined himself shipwrecked, cast out, with only his resourcefulness to survive on. He picked blackberries for food and made a shelter beneath a slanted rock. He guessed at the time from the height of the sun and then made his way home, late and footsore.

The second time Charlie went to the woods, Lydia lent him her bicycle.

'You were back too late last time. No excuse now,' she said.

Again he wandered in the woods and told himself tales. He found the stream and made a dam, and decided to bring Bobby here, the first chance he had. Twice he heard the sound of other people, and ran in the other direction, inventing a story for himself of the lone outlaw boy, seen by none, respected by all. As the sun got low, Charlie slowly found his way back towards the stile and the bike waiting in the ditch. Then he heard a third lot of voices, but this time he didn't run. This time he stood and listened, and a smile creased his face.

Charlie would have known Annie's voice anywhere, and here she was, in these woods at the same time as him. It went through his mind that it must be later than he'd thought, if she'd come after work. He was about to call out when something made him pause. Annie was speaking in a tone he'd never heard her use before, and the other voice was George's.

Charlie found an eyehole through the undergrowth and looked through to see a clearing, a patch of mossy ground, hidden all round by holly and brambles. A rug had been spread over and on it lay Annie, and over Annie was George.

It wasn't Charlie returning with a puncture that bothered Lydia, or even that he was later than he should have been. It was that he seemed so withdrawn and uncommunicative. He came into the yard, pushing the bike, like someone who's been struck a hard blow. Walking through the kitchen, he slumped himself down on the sofa.

'You didn't have to walk too far? With the puncture?'

Lydia said. She wondered whether he'd had a falling-out with Bobby, except of course Bobby was at the seaside. Or whether he'd seen his father again, except his father should have been working.

Charlie shook his head.

'So you went to the woods?' she said.

He nodded.

'On your own?'

Again, a nod.

'And you had a good day?'

Charlie crossed his arms over his chest.

'Has the cat got your tongue, Charlie?' she said.

'George can mend the puncture,' he said.

'Is that Annie's George, do you mean?'

'He'll do it tonight if I ask him.'

'He might be busy, Charlie.'

'He'll do it.'

'Have you met him?' she said, and Charlie nodded again.

'It'd take quite a boy to be worth her,' she added, as much to herself as to Charlie, but when she saw his face, jaw clenched, eyes narrowed, she was taken aback. Then it dawned on her. Charlie was jealous. Her ten-year-old boy had been jilted for the first time.

19

Lydia felt clumsy. The woollen socks were itchy and the boots heavier than anything she'd ever worn. Her feet caught every root, every knuckle of stone on the path. She couldn't swing her elbows like Jean did, and though it was Jean who had the heavy haversack, it was Lydia that had to call a short halt at the top of the first hill.

She bent forward, hands on her thighs, while her heart slowed.

'You should have brought someone used to this,' she said when she'd caught her breath. 'Making bits for wirelesses doesn't help much.'

Jean looked across the moorland, the brown coloured in here and there with purple heather, slender sheep trails dipping away to invisibility, the pale sky and curtain of shadow on the hill, waiting for the sun to lift higher. She listened to the sound of small birds at work.

'You'll soon find your walking legs. Eat this,' she said, handing Lydia a piece of oatcake. 'And the shoes will ease up.'

'You sound like someone's mother,' Lydia said, but Jean didn't reply and they walked on in silence.

The landscape was vast and endless. It unnerved Lydia. No hedges or railings or trees. No other people. No animals – none that she could see, anyway. She hadn't been on a walk like this before and she was unsure of herself.

She wondered whether there was something more she ought to be doing.

The sun drew higher in the sky and the day grew warmer. Jean stripped off her sweater and tied it around her waist. Lydia opened the buttons on her cardigan. They walked steadily and Lydia discovered that Jean was right and that her heart and lungs had found their own rhythm.

Walking like this, not for any other reason than to walk, and in easy silence, Lydia's thoughts roamed. She wondered where Robert would be today, what he might be doing. She wondered if he'd be having lunch at Pam's tomorrow, like usual.

Bastard, she said to herself, and Old cow, and then she laughed beneath her breath. Least you don't have to do that any more.

She wondered how Annie was getting on, whether Pam knew about George. She must do by now, and come to think of it, Annie had been looking a bit down in the mouth the last couple of times Lydia had seen her. Nothing to stop and ask about, you couldn't in that place, all those people, but definitely not her usual self. Grey about the gills. If Lydia didn't have her own affairs to worry over, she'd have gone and had a word, asked her over for a cup of tea. But it wasn't so straightforward now, now Robert was gone.

Robert gone. Straight words. Hard ones. But walking here, high up in the light, she felt her mind begin to lift away from loss; to stretch itself and open up with possibilities. Daydreams they were, she knew that. But they were the first she'd had for a long, long time. She imagined giving up her job in the factory and doing something else. She imagined a new home, a different front door. She'd go on an adventure with Charlie. To a foreign country, or to an island. Do something she'd never dared think of before.

She thought of never returning.

She could just never go back, she told herself. As easy as

that. Drive on in the car and leave everything behind her. Get to the seaside, get a job, forget about Robert, forget about the rent. Maybe she'd even meet someone else some day. Bring Charlie out there. He'd love to live by the sea.

But her thoughts faltered with Charlie. It didn't feel as simple when she thought of him and her mind swung away.

She looked out across the moorland scrub and quickened her pace. Jean had promised a valley to her, with cows in fields, a stream and trees. A greener, softer landscape, and Lydia wanted to be there now.

'I can't see any trees,' she said. 'Not proper ones. Are you sure about the valley?'

'We'll be dropping down to it in about a mile,' Jean said.

'My dad used to go off hiking. But he wouldn't take me. It was fine, women walking to work. But they weren't to do it for recreation. Then it was only for boys.'

'Did he tell you that?'

'I think he simply didn't want me along. He always dressed up his dislikes into morals. I've never done this before,' Lydia said. 'Never just walked.'

Jean looked at Lydia, and Lydia had the feeling that she had shocked Jean with this.

'Not even when you were little?' Jean said. 'Not even with your uncle?'

'Of course we walked. But it was always to school or the shops or the park. For something. You don't wear special shoes for that.'

Jean laughed. 'But are you regretting it?' she said. 'Wishing you were home with a book?'

'It's good for letting your thoughts run,' Lydia said. 'Daydreaming. I haven't done that in a long while.'

Jean took off her haversack and fished out the water bottle. She passed it to Lydia.

'The more you drink, the lighter my load,' she said,

stretching her arms back behind her head and dropping them forward.

Lydia drank. It felt wonderful to be this thirsty and then to drink. She looked over at Jean, squatted down, looking at the path. The back of her shirt was dark with sweat. Lydia watched as Jean reached to pick up a pebble. She watched her muscles dance beneath the cotton; she watched the strong, slender rise of her spine and she wondered if she'd ever been in love. If she'd ever had a man touch her.

Jean's voice broke across Lydia's thoughts.

'I often find myself thinking when I'm walking,' Jean said. 'Sometimes I lean my worries up against the rocks as I walk. But sometimes something comes to me, about a difficult case maybe, that I hadn't thought of in the surgery. A diagnosis. An answer.'

Lydia saw how the curls at the nape of her neck were tight and damp. She passed her the bottle.

'You'll have to come dancing, in return,' she said. 'Come out on a Friday night with the girls. I bet you've never done that.'

Jean laughed. 'I'm not a great one for dancing.'

'It doesn't matter how you do it. Get dressed up, forget about the week, enjoy yourself.'

'What were you daydreaming about?' Jean said, and they both laughed because they knew she was changing the subject.

'This and that.' Lydia looked away. 'A different life.'

'What kind of different life?'

Lydia shrugged. 'I don't know. One in a different place. Me and Charlie.'

Jean gave what Lydia had come to think of as her doctor's nod and didn't ask more, only hoisted the haversack.

The sun was hot. Jean tied a scarf around her head. Lydia's legs were weary with walking and she longed to sit down in some shade and eat.

But she felt at ease. Happy even, and she smiled to herself.

'See there, below us,' Jean said, and Lydia looked down to see the slice of deep green far below.

At the start of the walk, Jean had spread the map on the car bonnet and shown Lydia their route, tracing it over and around the lines and shadings, and Lydia had watched Jean's finger finally curve its way down into a wooded valley. It hadn't meant much to her then.

'Fifteen minutes,' Jean said, and now Lydia imagined the cool beneath the trees, stream water and a rock to sit on.

As the path dipped, it curved its way through a high moor meadow flecked with yellows and greens and tiny, brazen pinks. Despite the summer days, the ground here was still boggy and the two women picked their way carefully, branching their arms for balance. They were almost there, almost to the tumbled wall that marked the start of the woodland, when Lydia, doing some fancy footwork to avoid the glisten of standing water, caught her foot in a root, or a branch, or in the tangle of half-thoughts and new sensations, and stumbled hard forwards.

She must have cried out, because in the moment of her falling, Jean turned and caught her, stepping back with the force of Lydia's fall to keep her own footing.

She held her so close, arms around her body, braced against her weight, that Lydia could feel Jean's heartbeat. She could feel her breath against her cheek, her fingers pressed into her side. Doctor's fingers. Impersonal fingers.

'I'm glad you turned so quickly,' Lydia said.

'So am I. I don't want to be doctoring on my day off.'

Lydia laughed. 'Let's go on. I'm longing for my lunch.'

Slowly, gently, Jean set her on her feet again. Lydia felt Jean's hand brush against her hair, smelled the soap and sweat of her. She put a hand to her ribs. It was so long since she'd been held and she could still feel Jean's fingers there.

Scrambling the wall, at last they were into the trees. It was cooler here, the light broken up, and far below there was the sound of water breaking over stone. They walked over a crumbled wash of dry leaves and a question rose in Lydia's mind.

'Why did you ask me today?' she said, but quietly, beneath her breath. Then she said it again, louder. 'Why did you ask me?'

This time Jean stopped and turned and, as she smiled, Lydia took a step towards her, put her hands on either side of Jean's head and kissed her.

20

Charlie held the frame in both hands. He felt its weight its honey gravity, while bees swerved around his head, lazy with the smoke.

'It's full,' he said.

'Shake it now,' Jean said. 'To get rid of the bees.'

Charlie shook the frame and the bees fell. He was glad of his bee suit and the gauntlets. With a long feather, Jean brushed the last of the bees free from the capped cells and Charlie lowered the frame into the empty super.

Steadily they cleared the supers from each of the hives, carrying them up to the shed, ready for the harvest. It was ten o'clock by the time they were done and the sun was already warm.

'Lemonade for you,' Jean said. 'I've got two patients to visit and then we'll be ready to uncap the cells.'

So Charlie sat at the kitchen table and drank his lemonade and watched Mrs Sandringham humming her tune, busy at the stove. He thought about Jean. She was as excited as he was today, but he wasn't sure that it was about the bees.

'Mrs Sandringham, why are you going to leave?' he said, addressing himself to another adult mystery. 'It's nice here. Dr Markham is a good doctor, and there's the bees.'

'Right now I'm cooking up a storm for your tea,' she said over her shoulder, 'in case you hadn't noticed.'

Charlie could hear her tone, but he carried on anyway.

'Dr Markham is sad about you leaving. I know, because she said so.'

'There's Mr and Mrs Marston and Emma and Meg all for tea. Come to try the new honey, like every year. Your mother too, so I gather, which is very nice, so I've a pile of work cut out.'

'She doesn't think anyone can replace you,' Charlie said. He paused, very puzzled by grown-ups. 'So why is she so happy now?'

Mrs Sandringham turned and studied Charlie's face.

'I'm going to live with my sister on her farm, help her out, with her husband died. As for the doctor, you keep your nose to yourself, young man.'

'But you'll be sad leaving, won't you? No more lemonade and cooking storms.' He dug a spoon into the table. 'I'm going to be sad.'

Mrs Sandringham shook her shoulders in a way that reminded Charlie of a dog beginning to shake off water.

'You just get on with what you're good at,' she said, 'and I'll get on with what I'm good at.'

'But Dr Markham –'

'No more about it now, thank you.'

Charlie knew how adults were sometimes, so Mrs Sandringham's brusque manner was no more than he expected and he didn't take it amiss. But she hadn't answered his question about the doctor, so he thought he would go down to the bees.

Jean watched Charlie from her bedroom window. He walked with such a boy's stride, swiping at the air with his gauntlets, kicking at a loose pebble. But the way he held himself and the turn of his head – he did those things just like his mother.

She had never been kissed like that before. They walked

into the woods and down to the stream. They found a flat rock with a strip of sunlight across it where they sat and ate sandwiches. Jean rolled her shirtsleeves up above her elbows and leaned back on her arms, lifted her face to the slant of sun. She shut her eyes.

I don't know where I am, she thought. I could be anywhere in the whole world.

Lydia had taken off her heavy shoes and socks and was dangling her feet in the stream.

'How strange they seem under the water,' she said.

Jean looked at Lydia's feet. They were two pale fish below the surface. She put her hand out and touched Lydia's hair, warm with the sun.

'You love this place, don't you?' Lydia said.

They barely spoke after that, and they didn't touch, but as they walked through the woods, up out of the valley and back to their starting point, the space between them was so charged that every move, every gesture Lydia made tugged at Jean.

Only once they were driving back and the town lay close below did a distance reassert itself and they spoke again, in oddly formal tones, about the weeks ahead. Jean was going to join Jim and Sarah at the seaside for a few days. Lydia would still be working all the hours she could. They spoke briefly of Charlie. Lydia didn't mention Robert and Jean didn't ask. Neither spoke of what had happened, or when they might see one another again.

Standing in her bedroom, pulling on old trousers and buttoning her shirt, Jean felt a surge of excitement. She loved this day; she loved the honey harvest, the process of it. After extracting, filtering and filtering again, she loved filling the jars with the pale, clear honey from her bees. From the weight of the frames she knew it was a good crop this year, and she'd already telephoned Sarah to have her bring more jam jars.

But she was kidding herself that the feeling in her belly was about the honey.

Jean hadn't spoken to Lydia since the walk. She could have taken her another book, or asked her for tea, and she hadn't. But Lydia's kiss had up-ended the world and Jean didn't know how to go on. Things were altered in a way she couldn't understand. Finally she had left it to Charlie: 'Your mother would be welcome to join us, if you think she might like to,' she'd told him, her voice steady and her heart beating a tattoo, and this morning he'd mentioned, like an afterthought, that she would come when her shift was ended.

Jean wondered whether Lydia was possessed by the same confusion. Waking up in the early morning, she imagined Lydia in her bed, maybe still asleep. Her head in profile on one pillow, hair caught across her cheek. On the other pillow a novel still open like a bird. Getting dressed, she'd see Lydia by the stream, pulling on her socks and boots, her shoulders curved down, fingers fiddling with laces.

Seated before Mrs Sandringham's cooked breakfast, she thought of Lydia snatching her own, chivvying Charlie, making sure he had his uniform straight, then pulling her bike round in the yard, leaning it into her hip to get the gate open, pedalling to the factory. And so it went on through her day. She conjured Lydia everywhere – her face, her neck, bent towards the stream, her shoulders, her breasts, her hands as she spoke, telling stories in the air, her laugh, her mouth – but she didn't know how to see her.

Uncapping was a messy business. Charlie had been told this a dozen times by Mrs Sandringham and he was taking his duties seriously. While Jean was seeing her patients, he had got things ready. The shed floor was covered with sheets of classified ads and minor news that lifted in the draught, and a bucket of water and one of Mrs Sandringham's clean rags stood by the worktop.

The bread knife, to be used for uncapping the cells, shone dully in the shed's half-light and a galvanized wash-tub was ready to take the cappings. Beside this stood the extractor.

'You any good at arm wrestling, Charlie?' Jean had asked him a few days ago, and they had sat at the garden table and tried their strength.

'You're strong for a lady,' he said, after Jean had pushed his arm down flush with the table. 'Stronger than my mum. But nowhere near as strong as my dad.'

Then Jean had showed him the extractor and explained how it worked. The frames of uncapped comb got spun inside the barrel so that the honey came spattering out against the sides and was then drawn off through the small tap at the base. It would be Charlie's job to turn the handle that made the barrel spin, but it was a tricky process. The handle needed turning gently at first and then faster. But turn it too slowly and the honey wouldn't come out. Turn it too fast, and the comb would break up. He would need to be strong and measured to do it well.

'That's why the arm wrestling,' Jean had said gravely. 'To be sure that you're strong enough for the job.'

A few bees, fellow travellers in the full frames, dunned on the shed window. Charlie had left an inch open at the top for them and soon enough they would find it and make their escape. Otherwise, the shed was quiet and still.

Jean was back from her calls; he had seen her return. He opened the extractor tap and imagined the honey running from it in a clear, slender stream. He imagined it running on and on, filling all the jars they had and then the bottles, and the bowls, and the cups and the pans, just the finest, slender thread that never stopped, like a wish in a fairy story his mother had told him as he dropped to sleep when he was smaller. Tilting the nearest frame towards him, he ran his finger down the wax cappings. A thimbleful of honey. That's how much each one held. That's how much a single bee could make in the whole of her lifetime, so Dr Markham said.

This would be something to tell Bobby about. This was better than the seaside.

Charlie rested the frame on the board and leaned it over the washtub. Beginning at the bottom, as Jean had done with hers, he began to saw at the wax cappings. The knife cut through them cleanly and the honey began to well up and drift down, heavy and slow. The top eighth of an inch, she had said, so he kept the bread knife as flat to the comb as he could. Honey dripped down from the frame, mixing in the washtub with the cappings. Anxious to finish quickly, Charlie started to saw faster, but Jean put a hand on his arm.

'Keep it steady. No rush.'

When he had taken the cappings off both sides of the frame, Jean slotted it into the extractor. Charlie turned the handle and the honey was tugged from the comb, spraying the sides in a viscous sheen.

The two of them worked slowly but steadily through the end of the morning, first uncapping, then extracting. They were happy at their task, absorbed, and when Mrs Sandringham knocked on the shed door and called them out for sandwiches, they emerged into the sunshine sticky and blinking, as if they had been away from the world a long while.

Harvesting the honey had quietened Jean's heart. But the day was half gone now and soon, very soon, Lydia would be here, seated at this table.

'The Marstons are coming this afternoon. Sometimes in the past Jim has helped me out with the harvest.'

'Does he like the bees?'

'No.' Jean grinned. 'Not really.'

'I've been good at helping you, haven't I?'

'You have.' Jean wondered how much she liked him because he reminded her of herself. This small determined boy who had become her friend. She looked down the garden, her mind's eye running on.

'Charlie, what would you like to do when you're older?'

She watched him study the table, pick at a flake of paint. His face was fierce when he looked up.

'Not what my father does,' he said.

'What does he do?'

'Works on the roads, keeping them good for vehicles. Different things, depending.'

'Why not?' Jean said.

'I'm going to be an insect man when I grow up.'

'An insect man?'

'I heard the word at school. We had it for a spelling test. When I told my mum the word, she smiled because she didn't think I knew what it meant.'

'And your father?'

'I'm not telling him. Besides which –' Charlie stopped.

'Do you want to be an entomologist?' Jean said. 'Was that the word?'

Charlie nodded. 'Our teacher tells us what they mean, the words, and it's what I want to do. Look at insects, how they live.'

'You'd be good at it, Charlie. You look at things very closely and you don't give up.'

For which she was glad. Because his passion gave the alibi for hers.

And Charlie gave Jean a smile that cut her straight to the quick – the way it took his eyes, the way it drew his lips – so she had to turn away and be busy with her sandwich again.

By the time the Marston family arrived, Jean and Charlie had finished extracting the honey. They had piled the supers ready for the bees to clean later and Charlie was down the garden, hunched by the pond. He was watching the water-boatmen skedaddle over the surface, each of their legs in a pool of its very own on the water, and every now and then putting his finger in to see them scarper. He didn't hear the girls until they were almost with him. He didn't have time to be ready.

They were dressed in pretty dresses; their socks were white and their sandals were white. They had pink knees and hair in ribbons.

'Jinjin said to us there was a boy down here,' the taller one said and she stood, arms folded, as if waiting for him to confirm himself.

When Charlie didn't reply, she went on.

'She said we were to come and say hello and play.'

'Hello,' Charlie said. He didn't want to share the garden with these girls; he didn't want to be polite.

'Why are you looking at the water?' said the smaller girl.

'Because there's things to look at,' he said.

'We've got a pond in our garden,' the taller one said.

'There's water-boatmen here, and frogs and dragonflies,' Charlie said, despite himself.

'We have fish. We don't like frogs,' said the smaller girl.

'I've been doing the honey harvest with Dr Markham,' Charlie said. 'All morning. I was in charge of the extractor.'

'Show me what you're looking at,' said the smaller girl.

She crouched down and Charlie pointed to the water-boatmen.

'Spiders,' she said.

'No,' he said. 'They're bugs. Not the same at all.'

'Are they clever then?' she said. 'Like Jinjin says the bees are?'

'They don't make honey or anything, and they live on their own. You watch long enough, you'll see one dive. It's how they get their food. Like tadpoles. Then they suck them empty.'

'You're called Charlie,' the smaller girl said, changing the subject. 'Jinjin told us. But you need to ask us our names.'

'Do I?' Charlie said.

'It's good manners,' she said, shuffling her knees closer to his.

'What's your name then?'

'Emma. My sister's called Meg.'

'Are you in special clothes, for doing the bees?' Meg said. She was standing a little way off now, not looking at the pond.

'No,' Charlie said. 'Ordinary ones. But I've got a bee suit and bee gloves. They're in Dr Markham's cloakroom.'

'Your sandals don't look very new,' Meg said. 'Emma gets my cast-offs, but we both get new sandals for the summer. Otherwise our feet might not grow well. We don't get cast-off sandals, or last year's.'

Charlie looked down at his last-year's sandals. They were a bit tight, but it was the end of summer now. He'd be needing new shoes for the winter, so these would have to do.

'What else can you see in the pond?' Emma said.

Charlie shrugged. 'Look for yourself. I'm going back to see about the honey,' he said, getting to his feet and brushing off his knees.

'Jinjin's talking to our parents. Our father is one of her oldest friends,' Meg said. 'Is she a friend of your parents?'

'My mother will be here soon,' Charlie said. 'She's invited for tea.'

'Isn't your father coming too?' Meg said.

Charlie strode away across the grass, his cheeks burning. But Emma caught him up and tugged at his shirt.

'Show me where you did all the honey-making. Please, will you?'

And by the time they had reached the honey shed, he striding and she walk-skip-walking to keep up, he had relented. He opened the shed door with all the ceremony needed for induction into a sacred rite and conducted her inside.

'He seems a nice boy,' Sarah said. 'Where did you come across him?'

'He came into the surgery a few months back. His mother was worried about him. I think he'd been in a fight.'

'And so he ends up helping you with the honey harvest?'

'He was fascinated by my honeycomb, Jim. The one you made for me. So I invited him to see the hives.'

Jean forced herself to concentrate. She was like a cat with a firecracker tied to its tail, turning at every sound, willing herself to stay seated, to drink tea, to talk with her friends.

But if Jim and Sarah noticed Jean's agitation, they said nothing.

'You must always speak quietly to them,' Charlie said. 'They don't like raised voices.'

Emma nodded and picked at a scab on her elbow.

'You can tell bees things. Did you know that?'

She nodded again. A daub of honey on the bench shone under the electric light. She touched a finger to it and licked.

Charlie put a hand on the ripening tank.

'One of the best yields ever,' he said. 'Dr Markham said so.'

Emma nodded solemnly. Charlie gave the ripening tank an authoritative tilt. He felt the slow shift of its cargo and set it back on the level. They looked down at the honey. Froth was forming on top.

'Why's it look like that?' Emma said, her voice deferential.

'It's all the secrets,' Charlie said. 'The bees hear them and hide them in the honey. Then we get the honey, and the secrets come to the surface and . . .' He made a gesture with one hand, closing it tight and then opening his fingers like a star. 'Whoosh – they disappear into the air.'

'Gosh,' Emma said, as if she'd only recently learned what you should say on this kind of occasion.

'It's called evaporation,' Charlie said, as if to clarify for the six-year-old girl.

'Shall we go out now?' she said. 'We could play at something. Do you like playing mothers and fathers?'

When Jean heard the doorbell ring, she put down her cup and sat very still in her chair. On one side of her, Charlie was telling Emma a story about a grass snake that lived in a sink. On her other, Jim was having everyone guess the number of honey jars they would have this year, and Sarah was telling Meg to eat up her crusts. Through the babble of voices Jean caught the sound of Mrs Sandringham's shoes on the hall tiles and the slam of the pantry door, caught in the through-draught as she let Lydia in.

Jean closed her eyes. What would Lydia be wearing? Jean had seen so many women undressed. Hundreds of women, their clothes slung over the screen, or folded neatly on the seat of the chair. She'd asked each of them to lie on the couch with a sheet to protect their modesty while she examined them, intimately, impersonally. If the day was chilly, she had the gas fire on, but still the room was never quite warm enough and she always apologized; she understood the instruments were cold, she knew they felt uncomfortable. She'd chatted to them, asked them questions about this and that, taken their mind off what her eyes and fingers were doing. Afterwards, once Jean had scrubbed her hands and the screen was folded to one side, once the patient was dressed again and seated in a chair, her handbag in her lap like a shield, then they could almost pretend it had all been an unpleasant dream, and the patient could look the doctor in the eye, shake her hand on leaving.

Jean had never stopped to think much about it till now. But now there was a woman she longed to touch, not examine, and a vision flashed through her mind of Lydia behind the screen and Jean with her, touching her, undressing her, feeling her hips, her belly, the curve of her breasts, her nipples. Jean dipped her head . . .

She gasped and gripped the table with both hands. She had never thought of a woman in this way.

'You all right?' Jim said, concern on his face.

She nodded, and put a hand to her side.

'Indigestion,' she said. 'Too much cake,' and Jim grinned, unconvinced, but polite at the tea table, and returned to his honey jar count.

Steady yourself, Jean told herself. She's just Charlie's mother, come to have tea, and she felt a rush of embarrassment at her thoughts.

When Lydia came out on to the terrace, smiling nervously, her step tentative, the rush of feeling was so strong that Jean didn't dare stand. But Charlie was on his feet and out of his seat in a single movement. He ran to Lydia, his face alight.

'Come and see the honey,' he said.

Jean watched mother and son; how he took her hand, how she smiled at him and looked him up and down. She watched their intimacy.

'In good time,' Lydia said, approaching the table, her eyes taking in Sarah and Jim, the two girls.

Jim got to his feet and pulled out a chair for her and Jean made the introductions in a voice that was steady enough.

The conversation started up again and Jean was relieved to see that Lydia was chatting quite easily with Sarah. She watched Lydia sip her tea, one hand resting on the back of Charlie's chair. Jean put a hand to her brow and shut her eyes. How could she be feeling like this? About someone she barely knew; someone from such a different walk of life; about a woman, for God's sake.

She looked beautiful, sitting halfway down the table, her hair lifted from her neck, her cheeks a little flushed. She was wearing the yellow dress Jean loved and a string of dark beads. How concentrated she seemed, as if everything else dropped away when she turned to look at someone. She was serious, listening to Sarah, and then Jean saw a smile cross her face, saw her lift her hand to her neck a moment, then drop it to her lap as though remembering where she was, at tea with strangers. The smile seemed to take Lydia by surprise, and Jean glimpsed what must be the first lines of her older self touching out from her eyes.

I know that about her, Jean thought. I know how she smiles, as if it were something precious to be stored.

She wished she had asked Lydia to tea on her own. She wished all the others were gone, that even Charlie was gone, and that the smile and the gesture were only for her.

'Jinjin?' From somewhere far away, Jean heard her name. 'Jinjin?' the voice said again.

She was staring at Lydia and Emma was saying her name. Now everyone was looking at her, and Lydia was looking at her, her expression telling Jean clear as day that their thoughts were in the same place. She pulled her glance away.

'What is it, poppet?' she said, stroking Emma's hair, breaking herself from her trance.

'Charlie told me about secrets in the honey,' Emma said,

'and how they come up to the surface and then go *whoosh*.'

Jean smiled.

'Will you show us?' she said to Charlie.

21

It was Friday, end of the week, and there were still two hours before the close of the factory day. All around Lydia, women worked doggedly, their thoughts on getting home, getting dinner. Lydia longed for a bath, and maybe a bit of a book. She wanted to see Charlie. She wanted to sleep. Next to her, Dot hummed something Lydia couldn't make out.

'You got any plans?' Lydia said, only half listening for the answer.

There was a pause and then Dot said, 'I'm not taking "no" any more.'

Lydia turned to look at her. She was binding wire around and around, the thinnest wire you could imagine, with a pair of tiny long-nose pliers.

'No to what?' Lydia said.

'And if you don't come, I'll wonder what on earth the point is, of being your friend any more.'

'Dot!' Now Lydia was listening properly. 'What are you talking about?'

'Fancy way of saying it, maybe. I could simply have said I've about had enough.'

Dot didn't look up from her task. You couldn't when you were doing that kind of work or you lost it and then the wire was wasted. If the supervisor was anywhere near, you'd have the cost of it docked from your wages.

Lydia waited and when Dot was finished, she asked again. 'What are you talking about?'

Dot stared at her. Her face was different to how Lydia had ever seen it before. No affection visible. No sympathy. Lydia's heart banged in her chest.

'Dot? What is it?' she said, her voice almost lost amid the hard, sharp business of factory noise.

Dot took a big breath, seemed to draw herself up, as if she had a whole speech prepared, and Lydia saw a flash of something softer cross her eyes and disappear before she spoke again.

'It's a speech, this,' Dot said. 'So bear with me.' She paused. 'All right. You won't help yourself,' she said at last, 'that's what it is, and I'm about done trying to do it for you. You won't look after yourself. Eat properly, sort out your rent, go out to the pictures, anything, and I've had enough. It's not only you you're doing it to, Lydia. Not only you you're hurting.'

'Charlie needs me –' Lydia began, but Dot broke across her.

'Yes, he does. He needs you to show him that you're worth treating well. So this is it. Come dancing tonight with the girls like you used to; show Charlie, show yourself. Or else maybe you should go and find yourself another best friend.'

'I'm going dancing,' Lydia told Charlie when she got home. He didn't say anything, but when she got upstairs, the factory day washed from her face and arms, she found her favourite dress, her high-heeled red shoes and her best lipstick laid out, and Charlie sitting on the bed, swinging his legs with pride. She smiled.

'You'll be all right,' Lydia said. 'Annie's going to look in.'

'Can I have fish and chips then?' he said, and Lydia laughed and clipped him a kiss on the top of his head.

Charlie stayed on the bed as she changed, playing with her beads, watching as she undressed to her slip, as she unclipped her stockings and found new ones. They'd always had this time. She liked to have him there, though there had been scant opportunity for it recently. But he was growing up. He looked at her differently and she could feel herself colour with the knowledge of his gaze.

She put the dress on – crossing it over her bosom, having Charlie tie it behind – then clipped up new stockings, fastened the ankle straps on her shoes and painted her lips.

'How do I look?' she said, picking up the hem, doing a half-twirl.

'So pretty,' he said, but there was something in his voice.

'But what?' Lydia said.

'But who sees you looking pretty now? Except me?'

So pretty. That was what Robert used to say. That's where Charlie had it from, though Robert hadn't said it to her for a very long time. She wondered when he'd stopped. She thought it must have been when he'd started saying it to some other woman.

The thought made her draw breath, the air punched from her. She'd known this in her body for a long time, but she hadn't allowed it to take hold in her mind. So pretty . . . What a smasher . . . Cute lady. He must have got that one from the Americans. He used to call her all those things in their first years, when Charlie was still a baby and they had been in love. It had been good then. Easy. She remembered how they had laughed about Pam. How he had warned her of his jealous sister and said he would protect her, and at first she hadn't believed him. She remembered how it had been, being a stranger to the town. But Pam hadn't mattered; the town hadn't mattered, because Robert came home to her. They had their baby boy, and their own pleasures. The sweet tea he brought to her in bed each morning; soaping his back when he came home filthy from the roads; Charlie's baby laugh as Robert tossed him in the air. The way Robert touched her neck, her arm, small touches when he passed by, reminders that she was his. Then at night they had each other in their bed bought new on HP, laughing at Pam asking them what did they want with such a big one. If Lydia had regrets then, they were no more than the unavoidable ones. That you chose one person, and so you couldn't choose another. Or so she'd thought.

She didn't know when all this was lost. But the start of it must have been when Robert touched another woman on the arm, smiled and said, 'So pretty.' She could imagine that now. Then there were the new words he spoke when he came home late, or was angry with her attention, or didn't want to touch her. She could see now how those moments were notched up, one by one, into something that couldn't be recovered.

'That baby gets all your love. Pam warned me, and she was right. You don't fit in; you don't understand. You don't want to. I should have married a local girl.'

But she didn't know how long it took for it all to be lost between them.

'So pretty,' Charlie said, and it was strange and sad to hear him use those words.

Lydia was still upstairs when Dot knocked on the door. When she stood at the top, all done out, Dot clapped her down and Charlie clapped too, his boyish face bright and smiling.

There was an edge to the air, the first cut of autumn. Lydia told Dot what Charlie had said.

'Too sharp by half, that boy of yours,' she said. 'Can't you just get dressed up for yourself, if you want to?'

'You know what he means,' Lydia said.

By the time they reached the Grafton, Lydia's reluctance

had gone. She was hungry to dance. She could feel it in her, the small ball of adrenalin in the pit of her stomach. She chafed with impatience as the others took time with make-up and drinks and finding a good spot to watch from.

'Haven't seen you out there for a good while,' Dot said. 'They won't know what's hit 'em.'

'Come on then,' said Lydia.

There was a big band playing, rows of trumpets and saxophones done up smart in bow-ties and red jackets, lifting the brass high and ducking it down. The dance floor was full, couples jiving, skirts swinging, no space to move into, no room to find your step.

The two friends made their way in. Lydia was nervous now, holding back a little.

'It's a long time since I last did this,' she said. 'I'd forgotten it was so busy.'

Dot took her hand.

'Come on,' she said, 'you've got this far.'

Then they were in the thick and Lydia's senses were full with the smell and the noise and the pulse of it. They began to find their feet, Lydia leading, Dot being the girl, and all at once Lydia was away, inside the music, dancing, flying. Her body was alive, the music ran through her, the rhythm beat in her blood and she had no thought of anything, of anyone. Just herself and the dance.

'Hit the spot,' Dot said, 'hasn't it?' Lydia grinned and put a hand on Dot's hip and spun her.

She'd forgotten how good she was. Better than good. When she was dancing, she could do anything. Change her heart, change her life.

'Excuse me, may I have the pleasure?'

The young man nodded to Dot as he took Lydia's hand, and with a quick wink to Lydia, Dot walked off to the side.

They began to dance, and Lydia couldn't see him. He was too close. All she could get was a sense of him. His cologne, his height, his dark hair. His feet were tight with hers, his body light and strong, as if they had danced together for years.

The man spoke softly. 'She didn't mind, your friend?' he said.

'Course not. She was longing to sit down for a bit.' Lydia smiled. 'Besides, it was an "Excuse Me".'

He was a real dancer. As good as the American from Minnesota all those years ago.

Too soon the dance was over and they stood side by side, a little out of breath.

'What's your name?' he said.

He told her he was visiting the town on a secondment, and she nodded, though she wasn't sure what that was. She told him she worked in the wireless factory. She didn't tell him she was older than he was. She didn't tell him she had a son, or a husband, though her wedding band was plain to see.

The band was finding its music for the next song and couples were drifting off and drifting on.

On the far side Lydia could see Dot. She caught her eye, and Dot lifted her glass with a smile and stayed where she was.

'Can I have the next?' the young man said, and when she nodded yes, he ran across the dance floor and called up to the bandleader. The bandleader turned to his musicians, the musicians shuffled their music again and the young man ran back.

'What did you ask him?' she said.

But he only said, 'The next dance is ours.'

As the band began to play 'Blue Danube', Lydia laughed.

'You want to lift me off my feet?' she said. 'They're playing it very fast.'

'I want the floor just for us.'

And the floor was theirs. They danced, their bodies as one, no space in between, as if there was nowhere else in the world they could be. When the music stopped he bowed to her, and she thought, I must not lose this.

The bandleader applauded them as they went to the bar, and Lydia caught his wink, though she knew it was meant for the young man.

'Can I get you a drink?' he said.

'A Singapore Sling, please,' she said, because she'd seen the name somewhere. In a thriller, or a film. She felt high, electric.

Her drink was red, in a long glass with a cherry on the edge and an orange umbrella.

She sipped. It was sweet and sharp and tasted of cherries, of course, and tinned pineapple.

'It's delicious,' she said.

'You're beautiful,' he said. 'And a fabulous dancer.'

'It's the first time for ages.'

'There's a first time for everything,' he said.

She drank her red drink.

'Come with me,' he said. 'Let's dance another dance and then go and have a drink somewhere else, somewhere quieter.'

'You know I'm married,' she said.

'It's only a drink.' His voice was gentle. 'Because we can't dance like that and then go our separate ways.'

So they danced again, a slow dance, and she lifted her hands up behind his neck and closed her eyes. She was back again in that quiet place with the noise of the water over stones, the broad, warm rock, and, for a moment, Jean's hand on her hair.

Beneath her fingers, Lydia felt the young man's smooth skin, the rise of his spine and then the sharp bristle where the barber had been. She thought of Jean that day, bent down to the stream, and saw again the small mole on the nape of her neck.

When the dance ended, Lydia smiled at the young man and thanked him. She was grateful for what he had let her feel, but she didn't want to touch him any more. He was careful here in the dance hall, but she knew how quickly that could change. She wanted to keep his tenderness, store it up. When he asked her again to go for a drink, she shook her head, thanked him for the evening, gathered up her coat and went home.

22

Sometimes in the night Charlie would wake suddenly and sit up. He'd wait in the dark a while, listening, and eventually he'd lie down again and drift off to sleep.

Charlie hadn't seen his father for weeks. He had a jar of honey labelled for him, and a list in his head of things to tell him. But his father never visited and Charlie began to wonder if he'd made a list of the wrong things, and he started a new list, of things he was sure his father would like. The new list wasn't all true. Charlie couldn't do ten press-ups and he hadn't been chosen for the football team. But he thought that if it brought his dad to the house, it wouldn't matter about the made-up bits and, anyway, he could always change the list at the last minute.

'It was nothing to do with you,' his mother told him. 'Nothing. He loves you, Charlie.'

But Charlie didn't believe her. That's why the list was so important. That's why he listened so hard in the night, because each time he was sure he'd hear his father's voice returned.

Charlie was at a loose end, the last days of summer. He tried going to the park, but there were no boys knotted round the memorial now and the pond was grey. The end of the fine weather had come on hard and fast, with rain, wind and closed-in skies. Charlie had huddled under the big beech tree and watched Dr Markham's garden give up its glory for the year. The first of the autumn leaves scattered the grass and the bare flowers ducked their heads in apology, their petals crushed and dull on the wet ground. The bees were as busy as the weather would allow, getting in supplies for the winter, but they had no time to do their dances now and if they could have spoken to him, Charlie was sure they would have told him to go home and make ready for the closing-in.

Charlie knew his mother was busy. He knew she was very worried, even though she didn't say. She was working long shifts at the factory. He often got the shopping for her and had the vegetables scraped before she got home. When she came in, she'd start cleaning, or mending things, and singing fierce tunes to herself. She'd been like this since the weather changed and he was glad she wasn't crying so much, but he wished she'd stop and play with him, or let him read to her.

He'd read Lydia's detective books to himself sometimes, picking one from the pile by her bed and opening it at random:

> *But there I was mistaken. My car slithered through the hedge like butter, and then gave a sickening plunge forward. I saw what was coming, leapt on the seat and would have jumped out. But a branch of hawthorn got me in the chest, lifted me up and held me, while a ton or two of expensive metal slipped below me, bucked and pitched, and then dropped with an almighty smash fifty feet to the bed of the stream.*

Charlie liked this kind of story, where cars tumbled down cliffs and heroes threw themselves clear; and he liked stories with gumshoe detectives slouching around the city with guns in their pockets, looking for hoods.

He'd try out bits of the slang, imagining himself as a hard-nosed detective. 'I gotta pack some real heat today if

I'm gonna catch those goons,' he'd murmur as he went downstairs for breakfast, patting his waistband as if to feel his gun. 'Kill the boiler, whacko,' he'd say, bringing Lydia's bike up hard to a standstill in the street.

The Sunday before school started, they went to the pictures and sat in the three-shilling seats with popcorn, and afterwards she cooked him his favourite, toad-in-the-hole. But when he talked about the film – how he wished his headmaster was like Alastair Sim and that Miss Gossage deserved a nice husband – she didn't seem to hear him and he had to say things twice, which wasn't the same. He didn't know if she was happy or sad, because she wasn't there.

Lying in bed, Charlie tried to work out how many bees it took to make one jar of honey.

'Half a teaspoon per bee,' Dr Markham had told him. She'd dropped a teaspoon into the honey jar and they'd looked at how little that was. More than a lifetime's work for less than a mouthful of honey. He imagined thousands on thousands of bees filling his bedroom, a swarm covering his lampshade, then the walls and the ceiling, moving and shifting, beating the air and filling his head with the drum of their buzzing.

Charlie hadn't seen Bobby since he went away to the seaside. But the day before they were back to school, Bobby knocked on the front door. He was carrying a stick of rock with the seaside written through and through.

'Brought it back for you,' he said. 'The water was icy, I'd have worn two pairs of swimmers if I could.'

Charlie grinned to see him.

'I can top you,' he said.

And he brought Bobby in and showed him the honey: six full, golden jars in a line on the table with brown paper labels.

'I wrote the labels for all the jars. But these ones are mine.'

Bobby leaned his elbows on the table and stared at them.

'Where'd you get it?' he said.

'Out of the hives.'

'You got it out of the beehives?'

Charlie nodded.

'One's got your name on it,' he said, picking out a jar.

'But didn't you get stung?' Bobby said, and Charlie nodded and held up seven fingers.

'Seven times!'

Bobby's wide eyes made Charlie feel proud and sure. 'I've got a bee suit and gauntlets,' he said, 'but you still get a few.'

23

Lydia walked fast through the night, and as she walked, she spoke to herself, hurriedly, below her breath.

'He's fine, he's sleeping. You know how deep he sleeps. Just don't think. You left the note in case he wakes. It's clear tonight, cool. It's autumn all right. Must put oil on my bike chain, Charlie will do it. Must mend the back gate. Maybe I can do that. But if he won't pay the rent, if he's going to get me out, if he's going to, but he wouldn't surely, not with Charlie, so mend the gate, Lydia . . .'

Talk, don't think. That's what she was doing. Because what she was doing was mad. Her body was doing it, not her mind. Her body that had woken her again tonight an hour, two hours after sleep at last; her body that had got up and pulled on some clothes, written a note for Charlie in case he woke, found her house keys and taken her to the front door and out into the quiet night. Just her body.

Lydia didn't like being alone on the streets at this time and she walked quickly, setting her shoes down sharp, clack-clack, like a warning, echoing up the sides of the empty streets and down again.

'Up to the corner and right; up to the corner, turn, cross the street, down to the pillar-box and there's the tree you like in spring but it smells of dog piss tonight, keep going to the bottom and then cross. Cross at the Belisha beacon, Charlie. No need to beware of motor cars tonight.'

Somebody cried out; a young woman, or an old man, she couldn't tell.

She walked down to the park and round the curve of its railings, touching a finger along the iron till it was grubby black, she could feel it, in the grubby dark.

Leaving the park, she was out of the streets and into the roads and the avenues. So wide at night, you could get lost crossing them, lose your bearings and forget who you were.

Lydia checked the road name by the light of the moon. Something flitted over the pavement, something else took flight. She crossed the road and walked more slowly. The house was there, in the space beyond her sight, just there.

The porch light was on. People needed to be able to see the doorbell when they came here in the night. People in an emergency. People who needed a doctor. She put out her finger, and then paused. What if Jean wasn't there? Had been called out? Lydia couldn't see the car. She pressed the bell.

The sound rang along her spine and out into the night, and afterwards the silence was even louder. Taking deep breaths to calm herself, she stood and waited.

A light went on upstairs, then in the hall and it shone through the stained glass so that Lydia stood in squares of drifted colour.

The door opened. Jean stood on the threshold, a dressing gown wrapped about her, her curly hair skewed with sleep.

'Lydia?'

'I had to come.'

'Are you . . . Is Charlie?'

'Can I come in?'

Standing in the hall, under the electric light's neutral glare, Lydia stared at the white-black-white-black floor. Jean's feet were bare and brown with white lines across them from where her sandals had been.

'Is everything all right?' Jean said.

'I couldn't sleep.'

Jean nodded.

'That's your doctor's nod,' Lydia said. 'But I'm not here because I'm ill.'

'You sound angry,' Jean said.

'I've barely seen you these last few weeks. I know why that is, but I went dancing two weeks ago, and I'm not sleeping and now I've come here.'

'Let's sit down,' Jean said, gesturing.

'I could easily find a nice man. Dot tells me so every time we go out. A nice man who'd be kind to me, and kind to Charlie.'

Jean put a hand through her hair and stepped back and leaned against the wall, her movements still freighted with sleep. She shut her eyes.

'I know you're tired,' Lydia said. 'I can go again.'

Jean kept her eyes closed.

'No, don't go,' she said.

'I've come without thinking,' Lydia said. 'I didn't want to think because I don't know how to. But here I am now and I still don't know what to think.'

'You're in my dreams,' Jean said.

Lydia felt her head spin and her heart race. 'I don't know what's happening,' she said.

She dug her nails into her palms until they stung and her sight cleared. Then she stepped forward, coming close enough to feel Jean's breath against her cheek. She smoothed away the curls of hair that lay like sleep across Jean's face and then softly, so softly that she shut her own eyes to feel it, ran a finger down the line of her cheek. She paused, waiting for Jean to shy away, or turn away. But Jean was absolutely still.

Lydia didn't know how long they stood like that in the

silence, in the dark hall, while she traced Jean's face with her fingers – around her jaw, her straight nose, feeling her smile, which came out of one side of her mouth when she was nervous. She ran a finger over her eyebrows feeling for, but not finding, the fine scar cut through above her left eye from a childhood fall. She touched her cheeks, the skin and the handsome cheekbones. This woman with her waiting face, her waiting body.

It seemed that she had waited all her life to be here. This time, when they kissed, there was nowhere else to go, no other place to be. Jean took her arms from the wall and closed them around Lydia, her fingers pressed into the small of her back and Lydia felt something she had never felt before, the curve of another woman's breasts against her body.

So close they were, so still, the force of Jean's heart beat in with her own. Gently, slowly, she kissed Jean's mouth again. She tasted Jean's lips with her tongue, their slight roughness giving way to something so smooth.

Lydia paused, suddenly unsure, and lowered her head away and down. What if Jean didn't want this? What if she didn't know how to say? But then Jean's fingers were on her face, touching, stroking, and under her chin, lifting her head, and Jean's mouth was on hers. They kissed again, thirsty, mouth on mouth, tongues exploring, hands restless with desire. Till Lydia couldn't bear it and she pulled away.

Around them, the house slept; the old pipes and the floorboards, the high, dusty ceilings over empty rooms. Lydia listened.

'Is it Charlie?' Jean said. 'Or is it what we've just done, kissing, do you think, that . . .'

Lydia shook her head and wiped her eyes.

'I never imagined,' Jean said. 'I've heard about such things but still I never let myself imagine.' She turned to

Lydia. 'You walked through the night and rang the door-bell and then . . .'

'I didn't know, don't know what I'm doing,' Lydia said. 'When I dance, it's you I dance with. I think about you all the time. I don't understand, but I'm so tired with keeping it in.'

'Is it about me, or Charlie? Or your husband?'

Lydia nodded. 'Everything. But please not now. I don't want to talk about it all now.'

'Why don't you sleep a little,' Jean said, 'and then I could drive you home?'

Lydia shut her eyes. 'No. I can't leave Charlie alone any longer.'

'Then I'll take you straight home. He won't even know you've been out.'

24

Lydia had never been so hungry before. She'd never felt this clamour, this need. In the weeks since that night-time walk, she made her way through her days with a constant nag in her side that pulled at her thoughts and marked out the time till she could next see Jean. She wanted this woman. She wanted to be naked before her, to feel Jean's hands on her skin, wanted Jean to kiss her; not only her mouth and her face and her neck, but further, and harder. Sitting on the assembly line, shopping, cooking, playing cards with Charlie or chivvying him, and most especially when she lay down to sleep, her longing bruised her eyes and flushed her skin.

'You're not listening, Mum,' she'd hear Charlie say, and she'd shake her head to clear it, blushing as though he could see what she'd been thinking, and she'd ask him to repeat himself. At work she felt as if an invisible wall separated her from the other women. She could see their lips moving, their hands gesturing, could see their heads go back as they let out a laugh, but they sounded as if they were in a different room from her.

When they met, Lydia and Jean talked with the same hunger that they kissed with, urgently, as if to make up for lost time. Each wanted to know what the other had experi-enced – what they felt, thought about, hated, desired.

'We had a stray cat for a while,' Lydia said. 'My mum

took to feeding her and she moved in. She slept on my bed. But my father didn't like it and she disappeared. He said she'd got run over, but I think he drowned her.'

'That's horrible.'

'That's how he is. Always puts things out of sight that he doesn't like. Kills them off, if he can. What about you?'

'We had cats and dogs, and I loved the dogs especially. Barney and Bruno. They went right through my childhood. Lived outside, used to get fed by the kitchen door. Every couple of weeks the cook would boil up a sheep's head, which stank the whole way down the back corridor.'

'Sheep's head. But just for the dogs, surely?'

Jean laughed. 'Yes, for the dogs. But we got fed in the kitchen as children, and if the cook had been boiling the head that day, the smell used to make me retch.'

'You didn't eat with your parents?'

'Not till I was about fifteen. I'd still much rather have stayed in the kitchen.'

'Is that why you eat in there now?' Lydia said.

'Perhaps,' Jean said. She ran her finger down Lydia's cheek. 'Come and eat there with me soon. I'll make you my one-pot wonder. I invented it when I was a medical student and hadn't money for much of anything. But it's delicious.'

Lydia nodded, listening out for any noises – Charlie was long tucked up, but they must be careful – and then she stroked Jean's hair.

'I will,' she said.

Sometimes their talk would take a different turn, and one or the other would speak of their fear. What if someone found out about them? What then?

'But we've only kissed each other,' Lydia said.

'When I was a medical student, I read books that said that what we've done is the sign of a condition, or an illness.'

'Something you catch?' Despite her dismay, Lydia laughed.

Jean nodded. 'Or something you're born with, like a club foot.'

Lydia drummed her fingers. 'But you don't think that, do you? Besides, I've been married ten years. I've got a son. I never dreamed I'd want to kiss any woman, not till I met you.'

'Inverts. That's what the books call us.'

'You were engaged once.'

'We often like cigars . . .'

'What?'

'. . . and the colour green.'

'I don't like cigarettes very much,' Lydia said.

'Maybe you're not one then,' Jean said. 'I don't like there being a word for what I feel. A medical word. It makes it sound unnatural and joyless, and it isn't like that. I don't know what I'm doing, I don't know what to do. Except that I want to do it with you.' She laughed. 'I would never have dreamed of kissing Jim the way I want to kiss you.'

'Did you go out with him then?'

'He wanted to marry me and I knew that I didn't want him to.'

'Jean, what would happen if someone found out about us? What would happen to you?'

Jean shut her eyes. 'I'd probably lose my job. People would go to other doctors. Nobody would ask me for supper. Except maybe Jim, because we're such old friends. I'd have to leave the town, I think.'

'If we were men, we could go to prison. Those men got convicted last year and whatever they did, it was inside their own homes,' Lydia said.

'I remember there were two women who graduated the year before me, and they were going to set up in general practice together. I'm sure they were . . . I heard them talking about it. But I didn't think anything of it.'

'Are they all right?'

Jean nodded. 'So far as I know.'

Lydia thought of Charlie, asleep upstairs. Then she pictured all the women at the works, imagined walking into the canteen.

'I wouldn't want people to think anything of us, either,' she said.

As she cycled to and from work, Lydia travelled in her mind. Her fears fell away, anything seemed possible, and she got lost in her thoughts. So she was still worlds away on the afternoon that Charlie came running out of the back door with a letter in his hand.

'I don't know where it's from,' he said eagerly, impatient for her to open it.

She stood her bike against the yard wall, lifted out her groceries and handbag, and smiled at her son.

'Let me get inside, Charlie, then I'll look at the letter.'

With Charlie at her elbow, Lydia examined the envelope. She couldn't decipher the postmark, except that it wasn't their town, and she didn't recognize the handwriting. Opening it, she took out the single sheet of Basildon Bond.

The letter was typewritten and short. It began with the heading: *Notice Seeking Possession*. Lydia's sight blurred. She put a hand on the chair back to steady herself. Then, lifting the letter out of Charlie's reach, she read quickly.

She'd known this would happen, though she'd put it out of her mind. But still the news came as a shock. Folding the letter, she sat down.

'Mum?' Charlie said. 'What's happened, Mum?'

'I need a few minutes on my own. Leave me be for a bit.'

Lydia closed her eyes. She crossed her arms, drew up her shoulders and tucked her hands into her armpits. Once, when she'd been very small, on a winter day, her uncle had carried her home from the fair inside his jacket, buttoned up so close that her hands were pressed into her sides. She remembered how it felt, to be held so firm she couldn't move.

Nauseous with panic, Lydia walked to Dot's. She kept Charlie close to her, calling him back to heel like a puppy, each time he strayed away. He didn't ask any more questions, but every few minutes he'd look up at her, and she'd glimpse his worried face. Every bone of her ached to keep him safe, and as they walked she struggled with unruly fears that taunted her and picked at her skin. Somewhere in her thoughts, Jean stood, smiling but uncomprehending. She couldn't know this kind of terror, coming from her order of life.

'Just looking at you I've got the kettle on,' Dot said when she opened the door. 'Get in here, girl.'

She patted the back of Charlie's head, and fished a couple of pennies out of her apron.

'Charlie, go on up and find Janie. These need spending. Don't disturb us till you're shouted for.'

In the kitchen, two more children were squabbling over a cat. Shushing them out and shutting the door, Dot sat Lydia down and put a finger to her lips. It was only when she had sipped from a cup of sweet, strong tea that Dot allowed her to speak.

'I know the answer to this,' said Dot, after Lydia had showed her the letter, 'but I've got to make sure so I'll ask anyway. Robert won't pay anything towards the rent. Is that right?'

Lydia nodded.

'There's nothing I can do to make him. I know you say

I can take him to court to make him pay up, but I don't think I could do it.'

'Bloody men. Think they've a God-given right to be better off than the women. Work, marriage, divorce, the lot. They do less, get paid more and act like they own the place. And we let them.'

'Dot,' Lydia said. 'Please.'

'Anyway, taking him to court would take an age and you've only got a month,' Dot said.

'If it came to it, Robert would leave town rather than pay me anything.'

'I'd say good riddance.' Dot gave a fierce poke at the contents of the pot on the stove. 'But it doesn't solve your problem. Got any savings? Anything on the divi?'

Lydia shook her head.

'You never mention your family. What about them?'

'My mother's dead. My father cut me off when Charlie was born. Said I'd married beneath me. Said it wasn't what he'd intended for me. I had an uncle who would have gone to the ends of the earth for me, but he died in the war.'

Dot sat down and took Lydia's hands in her own.

'Why didn't you say something before?'

'Wasn't going to change anything. I've been working all the hours I could.'

'But a problem shared . . . you know.'

'I had enough on my plate already. Didn't want to think about it. So I thought I'd just wait for the worst to happen and then decide what to do.'

They ate tea at Dot's and walked home in the last of the evening light. Buoyed up by her friend, Lydia played cards with Charlie and kissed him goodnight with a smile he didn't question.

Then she wrote a list:

1. *Father*
2. *Classifieds*
3. *To sell?*
4. *Take in ironing?*

Her father wouldn't have much he could spare her. Besides which, she didn't even know if he was alive. But she must write and tell him of his grandson – how his eyes were like his grandfather's and how he had his quick, strong fingers. She must write as though she believed he still loved her and she must ask him to help her. Though, unless he'd won the pools, his help wouldn't make the difference between staying and having to go.

Then on Thursday she would buy a paper and look in the Classifieds. Better to know the worst. Better to know where they might be living the month after next, though the thought of Charlie – her clear, bright boy – in some horrid, festering place made her face hot with anger.

Despair sat like a fiend at her shoulder, ready to lurch out if she should let go her concentration. The room grew cold as Lydia sat with the pencil in her fingers. Night climbed in through the uncurtained windows and a brisk autumn wind played its havoc down the chimney. She stared at the table and willed her mind to be still. She corralled crumbs into a heap with one finger, pressing it down to gather them up, then flicking them away. She did it again, watching them scatter and fleck.

'Remember what Dot said,' she murmured. 'Just think in little bits. Not all at once. Little bits.'

Somewhere in the room she could hear a song being sung and it was Robert's voice, keening and sweet: 'The trees they grow so high / And the leaves they do grow green . . .'

But he was somewhere else, singing to another woman. Too tired for rage, Lydia cried quietly.

She must have been sitting at the table for a good while when Jean knocked on the window. She got up cold and stiff.

'What's happened?' Jean said. 'I knocked on the door, but you didn't answer, and then I saw you, through the window. Lydia? What's happened?'

Lydia fetched a cloth from the kitchen and wiped the table clean. Robert's voice was gone from the room, but the song's soft melancholy was wrapped like a shawl about her shoulders.

She gestured to Jean to sit.

'I got a letter today. I'm going to be evicted,' she said in a voice that pleased her with its calmness. 'I can't earn enough to pay the rent, and now the landlord wants me out.'

There was silence for a minute. Jean sat down. She pressed her hands together and ran her fingers through her hair.

'When?' she said finally.

'I've got a month.'

Lydia watched. Jean looked bewildered, incredulous.

'Did you know it was coming?' she said.

Lydia shook her head.

'I've got behind on the rent since Robert left. He stopped paying into it months ago. But I didn't know I'd gone this far. I suppose I've been a bit distracted, what with one thing and another.'

She smiled, but Jean didn't seem to notice.

'Why didn't you mention it?' she said.

'Why would I? Anyway, I've been over it with Dot, and what I can do –'

Jean interrupted her, her expression hurt.

'You've been to see Dot already? Why didn't you come to me?'

Lydia shook her head. 'Get hold of yourself, Jean. It's not you being evicted, it's me. I'm the one that's had the terrible news, not you. You're being jealous, and it looks daft,' she said. 'I'm going to get a cardigan.'

When she came downstairs she could hear Jean in the kitchen, setting the kettle to boil. The blue flare of the gas threw a queasy light over the dark. Lydia watched Jean's tight, angry movements.

'Have you ever seen anyone evicted?' Lydia said.

Jean shook her head.

'Dot has. I have. I've seen a family put on to the street. Two bailiffs, red-faced, thick-necked men, carrying out the lot – beds, cot, chairs, clothes, pots, pans, the baby's doll. The children crying and the husband shouting first and then he's gone to the pub, and the woman standing in the middle, apron still tied round, baby on a hip, stunned. As if somebody's hit her with a sledgehammer. Then a policeman coming and telling them to move on, they're causing an obstruction.'

They stood silently in the kitchen's half dark, until at last Lydia spooned tea into the pot and lifted the roaring kettle.

'Do you see now why I might turn first to a friend who knew about that?'

'What did she suggest?' Jean said.

'But you do see, don't you?' Lydia said and Jean nodded. 'Then hold me now. I don't want anyone else to do that.'

And Jean held Lydia tightly to her, as if her arms could be proof against the bailiffs or the loss of love.

'I can hear this song,' Lydia said. 'So clearly I'd swear it was out in the room, not in my head. It's sung so beautifully, in Robert's voice, but it's like a taunt, because he used to sing it when we were first married. First married and still in love.'

She put a hand over her eyes.

'And now, somewhere else in the town, he'll be singing it to another woman, and all he's left me is the memory of it.'

When Jean left and the noise of her motor car had faded into the night, Lydia climbed the stairs, her body heavy with fatigue. For a minute she stood silent beside Charlie's bed, listening to the lift of his breath, before tucking his covers tighter against the night. Then she lay down and fell into an undreaming sleep.

25

Jean delivered Mrs Sandringham to her sister's small-holding, tucked up in the fertile flat fields to the south of the town. Mrs Sandringham sat in the back of the motor car like the queen, weeping and excited.

'But I know you, Dr Markham. You'll just eat baked potatoes, or you'll cook up that horrid pot of yours.'

'I'll be perfectly fine. Besides, baked potatoes and my horrid pots got me through medical school very nicely.'

'That's if you remember to eat at all. You'll waste away if you don't get more inside you.'

Watching Mrs Sandringham and her sister bustle about each other, making their first moves since childhood back into a shared household, Jean felt a surge of jealousy. She drank a last cup of strong tea, ate a slice of cake, and drove away with promises of visits.

As a child, Jean would set herself hard tasks. The first had been to run non-stop around the garden when she was nine, because her father said girls had less stamina than boys. It took several attempts. On the first she got as far as the bottom wall. On the second she reached the compost heap. On the third, she was all the way into the kitchen garden, rows of cabbages either side of her, when she thought that if she didn't stop, her heart would burst. But she kept on and then it was done, and she sat on a bench outside the kitchen door and grinned while her chest ached and her vision cleared again.

There had been a pile of other tasks after that, and though she told her father about only a few of them, they were all performed for him. Cataloguing butterflies, swimming to the far rock, eating quickly, jumping off high walls, knowing the direction of the wind: the list was long and diverse, the challenges ever greater. It culminated in Jean's determination to study medicine.

'I'm speaking for your father in this, too, and it's not what we want for you,' her mother had said.

'But it's what I want,' Jean said. 'What I've wanted for years.'

However, her mother had her speech to say and she would not be diverted.

'We've discussed it at some length' – Jean had heard the sound of their discussion the evening before; her mother's shrill, querulous voice, her father's voice careful, placating – 'and we're agreed that it is not an occupation suitable to your temperament, your turn of mind and so we will not support it financially. How will you find a good marriage if all your time is taken up with sickness and disease?'

'It's a profession, not an occupation,' Jean said. 'And why is it only you telling me this? Where's Father?'

'He's happy for me to talk to you, and I resent your tone. Your attitude just confirms that our decision is the right one.'

Jean's years of medical training made up the last and hardest of her tasks. She was not a natural scientist and her studies took much of her mental energy and kept her at her books for long hours into the night. Her parents' disapproval cast a shadow at the start and, though eventually, begrudgingly, they gave her a small allowance, she struggled through her student years. It was Jim, now a practising solicitor, and not her parents, who made sure she had enough to eat and coins for the gas. Often he would turn up unannounced and take her out to the Italian restaurant on the corner or arrive with a shopping bag full of canned food.

Driving home from Mrs Sandringham's new life, Jean felt that same fierce energy she had known in her growing-up. She felt it for the first time in nearly twenty years and so distinctive was it – like a mood that changed the very colour of the everyday world – that she stopped the car by a path into some woodland on a road she didn't know.

She got out and set off walking, then jogging, and then she was running, running hard in the wrong shoes over the gritty scumble of the path, to feel that old sense of exertion.

Jean dipped her finger into the glass and tasted the beer froth.

'The Red Horse has the best beer,' she said. 'And this is a new barrel. Am I right?'

'I wish you wouldn't do that,' Jim said.

'Am I right?'

'Yes,' he said, his voice sulky.

'Nobody can see us, tucked away in here.' She put her finger in again. 'You sound like my mother. Besides, I've always done it.'

'And I've always disliked it. Now for God's sake eat the crisps, so I can tell Sarah.' He pulled the packet open and sprinkled over the salt.

'I'm perfectly well,' Jean said.

'Perfectly well, but mysteriously unable to sleep and without appetite; both by your own admission. Losing weight hand over fist.'

Jean shifted on her seat and looked at the walls, but horse brasses and old prints of the town offered no diversion.

'Since Mrs Sandringham went,' she began, but Jim interrupted.

'Don't tell me. Since Mrs S went you've had an epidemic, countless sets of tonsils, a worrying bout of early-in-the-season bronchitis in the elderly population, a few industrial accidents and an uncommon number of births, all demanding your singular attention.'

'You sound angry,' Jean said, and Jim rolled his eyes. 'But why?'

'You've found a receptionist for the surgery – good. I'm sure she's doing a fine job with the filing, and ringing the bell nicely for the next patient. But she's not putting your dinner to keep warm, or making sure there's food in the house and neither are you. What have you done about finding a housekeeper?'

Jean shrugged, but said nothing.

'I don't know how to explain the state you're in, but we're worried. You're not eating properly; you're working too hard; probably listening to your jazz records till the small hours. You're burning the candle at both ends and in the middle.' Jim picked up his pint. 'I've said my piece, and now I need a drink.'

Jean glanced at her friend. He didn't know. He hadn't guessed. But she could only tell him the half of it.

'I've got some ideas,' she said. 'I'm just a bit short on time.'

Jim stared into his beer, then suddenly looked up and round at her.

'You haven't done something really daft?' he said. 'Been converted by one of those ghastly evangelical preachers, perhaps? Sneaked off to a tent when nobody was looking?'

Jean laughed. 'I couldn't bear the music.'

'Or discovered something else. I don't know – that the truth lies in the stars, so you're up all night with a telescope?'

'I will find a housekeeper,' Jean said firmly. She took out her cigarettes and offered them over. 'How are the girls?'

'They're fine. They'd be even finer if they got to see their favourite godmother occasionally. I can't believe you're out on call every night.'

'Please, Jim,' she said.

He got to his feet. 'I'm getting you pickled eggs now, and some of that fat pork.' From his tone she knew he was struggling to force a banter. 'Then I can add them to Sarah's list.'

Jean put the cigarette to her lips and breathed the smoke in deep. She felt her lungs fill, expand and then she breathed out slowly, letting the tension ride with the smoke into the tiny room.

As he left the snug, Jim turned.

'I know something's up,' he said, pointing his cigarette. 'I know you're not telling me. But as well as being desperately curious, I'm worried, because look how it's taking you.'

Jean went to the window. The wind was getting up and the Red Horse was rocking on its pole. She stood very still, looking out, sheltering the small flame in her mind. Jim was right; of course he was right, though she couldn't tell him why. But their conversation had given her an idea so obvious she couldn't believe she hadn't thought of it before and, standing there, she willed it to survive and grow stronger. Which it did and became the rising of a plan. So even as she waited for Jim with his eggs and fat pork, she began to chafe with impatience to be home.

It was newly dark and the air was fresh. It would rain soon. Jean opened the yard gate and let herself in. She looked across to the house. Charlie's light was off and Lydia stood at the kitchen window looking straight out at Jean's patch of darkness. Jean watched her, entranced. Then

Lydia moved away and the back door opened and she stood in the doorway, a dark shadow of a woman. Jean could make out a cup in her hands.

As Lydia sat down on the step, wrapping her cardigan round for warmth, it looked as if she might almost have been waiting for Jean.

Jean watched and her heart beat out the seconds like a percussive force. She was unavoidably, unaccountably in love with this woman who sat there on the cold stone, unknowing and unknown.

Stepping forward, past the bicycle and the dustbin, past the geraniums, their garish red veering into the drift of light from the open door, Jean called out softly, urgently.

'Lydia.'

She watched Lydia put down her cup and listen, shoulders wary, staring into the dark.

'Lydia,' Jean called again and unable to hold herself back any longer, so much energy awkward in that small space, she ran the last few steps, took her hands, tugged her to her feet and kissed her.

Lydia pulled away. 'The neighbours,' she said. 'Or if Charlie hears us.'

'I've had an idea,' Jean said, her words tumbling out.

'You smell of beer. You're not drunk, are you?'

'Listen. I've got to tell you.'

'It's late, Jean.'

'One minute, and then I'll go if you want. I can just slip away into the night.'

Lydia laughed. 'There's no need to be melodramatic. I can listen for your minute.'

She poured Jean a cup of coffee from the jug and they sat on the step, hip to hip, and Jean explained herself. The conversation in the pub with Jim; the swinging horse sign, the wind, which mattered for some reason.

'What do you think?' she said finally.

'Jean,' Lydia said slowly, 'you're a doctor, and I work in a factory.'

'It solves everything,' Jean said. 'Your crisis. My crisis. We can live under the same roof. Charlie would love it. The garden, the bees . . .'

'Wait a minute. Don't rush me.' She put her hands between her thighs and dropped her forehead to her lap.

'Lydia?' Jean touched her shoulder, the back of her head. 'You're cold. Let's go inside.'

'Let me think, please.'

Jean stood up and stepped away, her hands beating the dark in frustration. She went into the kitchen and put on the kettle. A picture of a man standing by a spaceship under a full moon was pinned to a cupboard door. Charlie had signed it with a tiny bee emblem under his name. Jean smiled, and touched it with her finger.

They drank the coffee in silence, hands nursing cups, and then Lydia beckoned Jean in.

'Let's talk now,' she said. She brought down blankets from upstairs, and they wrapped themselves up on the sofa.

'So what do you think of my idea?' Jean said.

'It's not as simple as you think,' Lydia said. 'For me to work for you.'

'Why not?'

'Jean, we come from different ends of the street.'

'What do you mean?'

'In fact, you don't even come from a street. You're from a house in the country that just has a name. A beautiful house with gardens all around and a gardener to keep it nice. You probably can't even see another building from the windows.'

Jean shrugged. 'But that was then. Growing up. I left it gladly. Now we're here, in your sitting room –'

'Front room.'

'It doesn't matter what you call it.'

Lydia looked round at Jean.

'But it does. It matters a lot. That's exactly what matters.' She shook her head, lips pursed with frustration. 'I don't want to be employed by you,' she said. 'My kind is always employed by your kind, but us, the two of us, we're not . . .'

Jean took her hand. 'But you'd be my companion, my friend, my –'

'You might know that, and I might. But it's not what everyone else would know. They'd see me doing your cooking and washing.'

'Sounds like your marriage,' Jean said. 'Only with friendship added in.'

'Don't,' Lydia said.

'It's a means to an end,' Jean said, rubbing her eyes, trying to see again what had seemed so clear, so simple, two hours ago. She stood up out of the blanket and put her hands against the mantelpiece, pushing, bracing against it, needing to feel something firm, unchanging.

'It's a way to be living under the same roof,' she said. 'It wouldn't be like that for ever. Just for now.'

'What about Robert? What about your friends? What about mine?'

'My friends like you already. Jim and Sarah.'

Lydia laughed a short laugh. 'But they don't know, do they? They don't know how you've kissed me. And when they do? Besides, they'll look at me differently when they know you're paying my wages.'

Jean turned back to face Lydia.

'Listen to me. Every week women come to me suffering from nervous exhaustion, or because they can't sleep, bags under their eyes, fatigued, worn out. Or it's their children, especially in the winter. Bronchial conditions, ear infections, weepy eyes. Upset stomachs, diarrhoea. Why? Because their mothers have to skimp on fresh food, so they're malnour-ished, more prone to infections. Some get pneumonia.'

'Stop it.' Lydia put her hands to her ears. 'You don't need to make a damn speech. You don't need to tell me all this.'

'I visit them in rooms where the paper is peeling with the damp and fungus is growing on the walls, on the ceiling even. Where the drains are blocked and the toilet doesn't flush and the water from the tap has a funny smell. As often as not the husband's nowhere in evidence; either gone altogether, or drinking the children's health away in the pub.'

'You're blackmailing me,' Lydia said, her voice furious.

'And I want to know why the Council hasn't condemned these buildings,' Jean said, 'or clapped the landlord in pri-son. I want to know how the husband can hold his head up and why he hasn't been shamed for his neglect. But the women, the mothers, the wives, sitting in my surgery with their handbag clutched to their lap, or laying their child out for me to examine on a bed I can smell the damp from – they think it's their fault.'

Jean stopped.

'So what do you think would be best for Charlie, Lydia?'

Lydia was silent, and after a minute Jean sat down be-side her.

'Lydia?' she said.

Lydia looked round at Jean, eyes blazing, mouth bitter.

'That's what I hate about your kind,' she said. 'Born with a silver spoon. Making out that I can't look after my son properly because I'm from the wrong class.'

'I don't think that,' Jean said.

Lydia shut her eyes.

'You haven't even got a child; you've got no idea what it's like.'

She didn't see Jean wince, didn't see the cut she made.

'I'm only saying what I see as a doctor,' Jean said. 'And what I see again and again is how hard things can be.'

Lydia made no reply.

'Please,' Jean said. 'Live with me.'

Still Lydia was silent, eyes shut, lips tight, but there were tears on her cheeks.

'Don't coddle me,' Lydia said at last, 'or blackmail me, or patronize me. Don't fool yourself that the best things are easy. More than anything else, for God's sake, don't try and fool me.'

They talked on until exhaustion took them, then slept, wrapped in blankets and one another's arms, till dawn.

26

Charlie raced all the way across the town, along the streets like his own, past the children like him and the grown-ups in their Sunday habits. The town looked like a Sunday and it smelled like Sunday, too, what with the factory chimney quiet, no smoke out of it, and every now and then the smell of dinner roasting. The day was bright and dry and Charlie went past children kicking leaves into clouds, and others coming from the park. Behind them, flicking the pages of a newspaper, or sucking on a pipe, would be a father. It looked to Charlie as if every boy in the town but him had a father behind him. As he ran he made a fierce face so no one would think he cared.

Annie was the nearest thing Charlie had to a sister and he'd missed her, these last two months. There were four precious jars of honey on his windowsill and one of them was for her. But they didn't go to lunch at Pam's on a Sunday any more, him and his mother; and Annie didn't come and visit them either. That was because of George. Leastways, that's why his mum said it was. So this Sunday he'd made a plan. He'd even written it on a piece of paper, very small, and rolled the paper up and pushed it under the skirting in his room where the wood was split.

He wanted to give Annie the pot of honey and tell her all about what he'd done for the honey harvest, but he wasn't going to cross the town with a jar in his hand, so it would have to wait a bit longer. Instead he slipped a photo in his pocket to show her. Dr Markham's friend had taken it on the harvest day: Charlie in his bee suit, standing beside a hive. Then he turned the knob on the front door all the way so it didn't make a sound closing, and set off.

Charlie ran as if his life depended on it, only stopping to get his breath back by the waste ground at the head of the street, and to pick up some pebbles. Three boys were standing under the trees along one side. They might have been the same three boys he'd seen all those months ago with the cat, the last time they went to Pam's, when his dad didn't stay for trifle. But if they were, then they looked younger than before, not frightening at all. They looked like boys with fathers who'd go home soon and eat their Sunday dinner.

Charlie was going to throw pebbles at Annie's window from the back yard. That was his plan. He'd throw the pebbles; Annie would look out to see what it was, see him and come down. Somehow she'd smuggle him into her room. He hadn't worked out that bit of the plan yet; he figured they'd have to play that bit by ear. That was something his dad always said.

Then once he was in Annie's bedroom, she'd bring him up a big plate with roast potatoes, meat, cabbage and gravy. He wanted to see Annie, but he was hungry, too. His mum was sick in bed since the day before. He'd felt her forehead today, but it was still too hot and she wouldn't be making any meal. Or if she did, it wouldn't be roast potatoes with thick gravy. So it was a good plan. He thought it was a good plan, though now he was here with the pebbles in his hand, there were butterflies in his stomach.

The alley smelled of old fish. Cats were digging at a pile of newspapers. Charlie walked down to Pam's back yard. He'd been reading one of his mum's thrillers today and now he had a slight swagger to him, his hands in his pockets. He was Johnnie Delaney checking out the territory in downtown Chicago. Casing the joint before putting the sting on a likely hoodlum. He thought his aunt Pam would make a good hoodlum. She could be scary enough.

Gingerly, Charlie lifted the gate latch. It wasn't locked. He wiped his brow clear of imaginary sweat and pushed. The gate opened noiselessly. So far so good. The yard was empty and there was nobody standing at the kitchen window. Ducking behind the coal shed, he rummaged in his pocket for a pebble, then stepped out, eyes raised to Annie's window. He could see her through the glass; her silhouette familiar, reassuring. Holding the pebble in his fingers, he got the window in his sights and drew back his arm to throw.

'I shouldn't do that, son.'

Charlie jumped and stared. His father stared back, eyebrows raised in a quizzical expression, ash dripping from the cigarette between his fingers. Up at her window, Annie looked down, her face pale, her mouth an 'O', her eyes unblinking.

'Dad!' The pebble still in his hand, he ran at his father, butting his head into Robert's stomach, wrapping his arms around his middle, breathing in the smell of him. For a moment, a whole moment, Charlie held him tight. Then Robert's hands were on his arms and Charlie could feel his fingers pulling him off, holding him away. He felt his old, cold dismay and wished he could be a different boy, so his father would hug him.

'This'll be a surprise to Pam,' Robert said, drawling slightly with the cigarette between his lips, keeping Charlie at arm's length, looking him up and down. 'Grown a bit since I last saw you, I swear you have. Don't know if there's enough in the oven for such a big extra mouth.'

He chuckled, and Charlie didn't speak. He looked at his father's face, searched it for something he couldn't have put a name to. He glanced up at the house. Annie was still at the window, and she was pointing down, mouthing something.

'Lost your tongue?' Robert said. 'Must have something to say, sneaking up like this.'

He let go of Charlie and took a long draw on his cigarette, tossed the stub in the corner, and tugged another from the packet in his breast pocket.

'Mum's sick,' Charlie said. 'It's why I've come here.'

'Sorry to hear it, Charlie,' Robert said, lighting up.

Charlie watched him and waited.

'What are you staring for?' Robert said, and Charlie shrugged and looked at the ground. 'Pam wasn't expecting you, but since you're here . . .' Robert didn't finish the sentence, just stood there, smoking.

Charlie looked across towards Annie again. 'Can I go in, Dad? Annie's in her room, I can see her in the window.'

Robert slouched back on his heels and shook his head.

'No you don't. Since you've turned up unannounced, may as well make the best of it. Tell you a bit sooner than I'd planned, that's all.'

Charlie's heart jumped. Perhaps his dad had changed his mind. Perhaps he was going to come back home.

'We made a den, Dad. We've got supplies in there, and a map. You couldn't see it was there from the path, not even from a foot away. Bobby's dad said . . .'

But Robert wasn't listening. He was turning away, walking back to the house. Charlie watched his father, uncertain, until Robert beckoned impatiently. Tugging the pebbles from his pocket, Charlie followed him and the pebbles dropped and bounced over the yard.

The kitchen was empty of people and humid with boiling vegetables, and Charlie could smell the meat from the oven. His stomach turned over with hunger and excitement. Robert walked straight through and into the next room, and Charlie followed. Pam was standing at the table close-shouldered with another woman Charlie didn't know, and they were speaking in low, women's voices as they laid the cutlery and the cruets.

Robert put a heavy hand on Charlie's shoulder. 'Look what the cat brought in,' he said.

The two women turned.

'Charlie!' Pam said, and he saw a blush rise fast on her face, which he didn't often see on an adult. 'What on earth are you doing here?'

'I said you might not have enough dinner for an uninvited guest,' Robert said.

'Specially not with his appetite,' Pam said, recovering herself. 'Doesn't know how to be grateful, your boy.' And the wash of resentment, which Charlie knew so well but never understood, crossed her face.

But it was the other lady that Charlie stared at. She didn't look much older than Annie and she had on shiny black shoes with heels and her hair all primped like a film star and he could smell her perfume from where he stood. But he was certain he'd seen her before, and she was looking back at him as if he ought to know her, smiling at him as if he ought to smile back.

Robert stepped forward and took the lady's hand, then lifted it at Charlie.

'Meet the future Mrs Weekes,' he said.

Charlie was confused. 'But that's my mum,' he said.

'No, Charlie. Mrs Weekes is my wife and Irene here is going to be Mrs Weekes soon as we can make it so and you can pay her some respect.'

Charlie shook his head slowly from side to side. He didn't understand, and then he did. He felt his limbs go rigid, and slowly he turned to face his father.

'She's not ever going to be Mrs Weekes. I hate her,' he said, and he turned for the door. But Robert got him by the scruff and lifted him from the floor, and he spoke in a voice clenched with rage.

'You turn back around and apologize, or I'm going to wallop you to the back end of tomorrow.'

Charlie shut his eyes. He felt his father's knuckles digging into his neck and his breath against his cheek.

'Open your bloody eyes,' Robert said. Then Charlie saw his father's face so close to him, it was all flesh and pocks and dark shadows.

'Apologize,' Robert said again, and Charlie could hear other voices, female voices, imploring, asking Robert to put him down, let him go.

'I'm waiting,' Robert said, and the room hushed around them.

'Charlie?' Annie's voice was quiet.

He squinted his eyes round to see her. She stood very still, and even as he was, Charlie could see how pale she was. Then she gave the slightest shake to her head and Charlie took as deep a breath as he could, smelling the cigarettes and perfume, but not his mother's, on his father's shirt and he dug an elbow hard into his father's side.

Robert dropped Charlie with a yelp of pain and before he could grab him again, Charlie was out, pushing past Annie to get to the front door. He yanked it open and was off running up the street. If Robert had chased him, he'd have caught him. But Robert contented himself with yelling from the doorway so once Charlie was a few streets away, he slowed down and walked. He was shaking and cold, but his hunger was lost for now beneath grief.

27

The room was at sea around her, the wallpaper billowing and the curtains vast breakers. Furniture mounted and toppled and the wind roared. Lydia's skin was scalded with cold and her eyes burned in her head. Let the storm out, someone, open the windows and let it go.

'Charlie!' She yelled his name, but the wind was so loud he'd never hear. 'Charlie!'

The moon was above her, round and pale, rising under the ceiling. The moon could swing the tide, quieten the storm. But it only lifted her head, 'Drink a little,' it said, and it wet her lips while the seas rose again, and again she was plunged under.

The room was silent when Lydia woke. Nothing stirred, nobody called or cried out. She lay still on the bed, listening to the sound of her breathing, staring up at the dark, exhausted, as if she had been running all day long, or carrying something heavy up a steep hill for ever. As her eyes grew accustomed, Lydia glanced around the room, turning her heavy head this way, and then that. Beyond the bedside table, someone sat on the chair, asleep maybe, they were so still. She stared, as if concentration would give her better sight. But the dark wouldn't yield, and eventually she fell into sleep again.

Light was drifting in around the curtains next time, and the figure in the chair was gone. She looked at her alarm clock. It was nearly half past eight and the house was quiet. She closed her eyes, and then opened them abruptly, panic beating in her chest. She had to get up; she had to get to work. She'd be late, locked out for the morning. What about Charlie? The teacher rapped them on the hand if they were late.

'Charlie!' she shouted, but her voice was thin and faint. It would never wake him. Ignoring the roll of the walls and her pounding heart, she pulled herself up to sitting and began to get out of bed. Placing her feet on the floor, she put a hand to the table to steady herself. It must have been the fever she'd had in the night, but she felt her head reel. She leaned forward and braced her legs to stand and the thought crossed her mind that it was strange to have to think about how to do this.

She fell hard, bruising her shoulder and catching her forehead on the wardrobe. Lying there with one ear to the ground, fatigue overcame her. She couldn't move, and so she let her worries go and watched them hover a foot above her body, like small bats. She'd have to ask Charlie because she didn't know if bats could hover, they seemed too twitchy for that.

She grew cold on the floor; dozed and then woke. Her worries had kept away, but now they seemed to be multiplying, growing. There was agitation in the air, wings beating. Robert was up there now, hovering too, with a faceless woman on his arm, it might be Pam, it might not be, and there was a building, drab and mean, with a grey front door and three small rooms that she knew were for her and Charlie. Above the building was her father, his mouth pinched and angry, mouthing silently at her.

'Stay up there,' she implored them, because the floor was hard and her body ached, though she didn't mind that if they would only leave her be.

Lydia didn't know how long she lay there with her ear

to the ground before she felt the front door open and close beneath her, jarring through the floorboards, and then footsteps on the stairs, firm but light-footed. Not Charlie's step, Lydia knew, and not Robert's. She should move, try to get up, but she seemed to have no power to do so. By reflex she put her free hand to her hair, which felt matted and stiff against her head, and then to her nightdress, rucked around her, tugging it weakly. The door opened and the footsteps stopped.

'I leave you alone for an hour and look what happens.' There were hands beneath her arms, helping her back into bed, firm fingers on her wrist, holding it.

'Jean,' she said. 'What are you . . .'

Jean didn't reply, but counted out Lydia's pulse below her breath, then put a hand to her brow.

'You're still running a marathon,' she said, 'and you're still too hot.'

Lydia's thoughts chased through her head.

'Charlie's late,' she said. 'His teacher hits them if they're late.'

'It's OK. He's there already.'

'I have to get to work.'

'I've sent in a doctor's note. You won't be going back for a while yet.'

Lydia shook her head impatiently. Jean didn't understand. She didn't have that kind of job. She didn't have a son to look after, or a husband who'd left.

'I have to go to work,' she began to say, but Jean interrupted.

'They don't want you there, not with what you've got.'

Lydia shut her eyes and tried to think.

'But I was fine, I remember I was fine. You were here that night, Friday. We slept.' She smiled at the memory. 'Then Saturday I went to work. I didn't feel too bright, but I've been working so much. Sunday, I was exhausted, and my throat was bad. Charlie brought me tea, but I couldn't drink it, and then he went.' She sat up suddenly. 'Where's Charlie? Where is he?'

'I told you, he's at school today.'

Lydia tried to remember. Her head burned and her thoughts danced at the edge of her mind like scraps of ash in the heat of a fire.

'He went out and when he came back, he was upset. I heard him. I heard him crying, Jean, and I tried to get up but the floor was moving away from the bed.'

'He's fine, Lydia. Dot gave him his tea one night, and his cousin Annie's been here a couple of times.'

'Why did he cry?'

'Charlie came to get me on Monday,' Jean said.

'But he doesn't cry.'

'He came to the surgery on Monday morning,' Jean said, 'and he was so pale, I thought something terrible had happened.'

'Annie was here? Why did Annie come here?'

'And he said you were ill, that you hadn't gone to work and that he couldn't understand what you were saying. So I knew you had a fever.'

'I'm glad Annie was here,' Lydia said. 'She's a lovely girl. Her and Charlie.' She smiled to herself.

'Lydia, listen to me. You're sick, and you're exhausted. Once the fever is down and you're through the worst, I'm taking you away for a few days. You and Charlie, both.'

Perhaps it was the illness, perhaps it was Jean's air of authority, perhaps it was the clean tide of her delirium, but over the next day, as the rage of fever fell and Lydia could see the bed and the curtains and the floor as just and only those things again, the landscape of her fears seemed changed. Nothing that was there before was gone, but things looked distinct now, clean, with their separate shadows, as if they'd been tumbled by the fever and washed up, each on their own pitch of beach. Lydia lay too, washed out, washed up, and when Charlie came in from school, he found her sitting up against her pillows, pale and returned.

'Come here, Charlie boy,' Lydia said, smiling, and she saw his face relax, and she wondered what he had seen.

He climbed on to the bed and sat with his legs swinging, his hands behind him, flat to the counterpane.

'You've been ill for ever,' he said.

'What have you been up to?' Lydia said, putting her hand against the small of his back.

He shrugged.

'Nothing much. Miss Phelps said why didn't I have my homework in.'

'Did you tell her?'

Charlie gave her the look he gave every time she did something that confirmed that she'd never been a boy and so didn't understand anything.

'Did you get a punishment?'

Again he didn't answer, but Lydia saw how he bunched his hand to a fist.

'Can I see?' she said.

He shook his head. 'Anyhow, Annie put some cream on for me days ago,' he said, the accusation clear.

'Good,' she said. She'd have a look at it later, once he was asleep.

But she wondered why Annie had come round. Jean had mentioned it too. She'd seen so little of her recently, what with everything. Hadn't stopped to think about her, and she wondered whether everything was all right with George, with Pam.

'Did Annie cook you tea?' she said.

'Sausages,' he said, 'and next night she made an omelette, which I ate.'

'Did you tell her?' Lydia said, and Charlie looked at her

in panic, and she didn't know what it could be that she'd said.

'Did you tell her you don't like omelettes?' she said gently, and he shook his head again as he slipped down from the bed.

'It's one of the things I like best now,' he said as he left the room. 'One of them.'

28

Dr Markham always did the things she said she would. She'd said she'd show Charlie her bees. She'd said she'd get him a bee suit. Charlie knew, when she promised to take them away in her motor car to the seaside once his mother was better, that she would do it. Charlie didn't really know why she had promised, but she had, and when he handed her letter to his teacher, he knew, even before she had opened it, that she would have to let him go.

So while everybody else was sitting behind their desks, two on two, dipping their pens in the blue ink and scratscratting over the long hours, Charlie had Dr Markham's promise in his eyes as they travelled right across the day to a beach full of sand and stones.

He fidgeted in his seat, stretching his legs, shifting his fingers under the seatbelt across his lap. He wasn't used to sitting in the front and now the novelty had worn off, he'd rather have been in the back, with all the seat to himself and the back of his mother's head securely in his view.

'Tell me again how long the beach is,' he said, looking over at Jean.

'As far as you can run, and then further, and then further still,' she said.

'And how much longer have we got in the car?'

He watched Jean slip a glance back to Lydia on the back seat. Dr Markham looked at his mother, and he looked at her. She wasn't like Dot, or any of his mother's friends. She looked at his mother in a different way. He was glad she minded about her, because his dad had stopped, but it was strange.

'Have you got a husband?' Charlie said, and he felt his stomach jolt, but he didn't know if it was the car, or if it was something inside him that swerved. He didn't know why he'd asked the question since he knew the answer.

He stared out of the side window, not looking, not thinking, eyes burning, ears hot with embarrassment. Hedges and gates and buildings, the black and white of cows, the black and white of empty trees, a man and a dog, a church, more hedges – things went past his eyes, and he couldn't hold on to anything. Dizzy-headed, he shut his eyes and pressed his forehead against the cold glass.

'If you keep your eyes skinned, you'll see a ruined windmill soon,' Jean said, as though he hadn't asked his last question. 'And a big tree right by it. It's half an hour more from there.'

Charlie turned and looked at his mother. Lydia lay across the back seat, covered with a blanket. She looked asleep. She looked very white, except for two points in her cheeks, as if she'd put her lipstick there by mistake. He turned back and stared out of the window again. He hated his dad. He'd kill his dad when he was older.

Lydia had slept for most of the journey, but Jean had told Charlie it was fine, it was what she needed to get well. Besides, he'd rather have anything than how she was before, shouting and not seeing him. Shouting about his dad, and the bits of songs she kept singing, then asleep so deep he couldn't wake her.

'Tell me again what you did when you were young,' he said, his head turned to the window again, searching for the windmill, so he didn't see Jean's smile. 'Tell me about camping out and running away.'

So Jean told him the stories she remembered, and about the time there was a storm and lightning and the vow she made not to go inside the house though she felt scared enough to die.

And after a few minutes they passed the tree and the ruined windmill, ivy climbing from its eyes.

'Half an hour,' Charlie said. 'Will we wake Mum up when we get there?'

'We will.'

They drove on into the flat, clear autumn sky and across the deep marshes where clouds of birds circled and rose and circled and fell and it smelled of earth and water. Charlie's chest was tight with excitement because Dr Markham had promised, if his mother allowed and if the weather held, he could sleep in the tent and make a fire to cook his tea on.

The flint-faced cottage was all on its own, a mile beyond a village, down a track with grass up the middle and sand at the edges. The dunes hid the cottage from the sea, but when they stopped the car and opened the doors, Charlie could smell the sea so strongly that it made his mouth water. He looked back at his mother, still sleeping, and over at Jean. She caught his glance and ever so slightly tilted her head.

'Go,' she mouthed, and he was out of the car and away, running at the sand, scrambling and falling, his feet sinking, his fingers scrabbling in the wiry grass, till he reached the top where the dunes sloped steep down to the beach, and there was the sea and the beach so long there was no end to it, just as Dr Markham had said. Charlie stood on the dune top with his arms spread wide and leaned into the wind. He filled his mouth with it and let it run tears from his eyes and whip his hair back on his skull. Then, taking off his shoes and socks and throwing them behind him, he stood tiptoed on the edge, and dropped, sinking into the fall of sand.

*

Leaning into the back of the car, Jean spoke softly. 'Lydia, we're here,' she said. She waited, and at last, as if these words had had to make a journey too, Lydia murmured and shifted under the blanket. Leaving Lydia to wake properly in her own time, Jean pushed the car door to and walked over to the cottage. She stood beneath the porch and put her hand up into the eaves for the key. Inside was the clean, musty smell she recognized, and she breathed it in as deep as her lungs would allow. There was a fire burning in the grate and fresh bedlinen stacked on the kitchen table. She grinned. Her telephone message had got through. There would be groceries in the pantry, and a new canister of gas, and plenty of dry wood.

Jean had been coming to the cottage since she was a young girl. It was the place she came home to in her dreams and, in bringing somebody else here for the first time, she felt a knot of anticipation. She put water on to boil and found the fresh tea among the groceries. Then she went to find Lydia.

Jean brought Lydia into the cottage and sat her on a kitchen chair, wrapped her round with a blanket and put a mug of tea between her hands. Lydia was pale and tired, but it wasn't illness that hung in her eyes now.

'Charlie's on the beach,' Jean said, before Lydia could ask. 'I couldn't see him for smoke. The minute we arrived.'

'Good,' Lydia said. 'He's been too much a man recently.' She stared into the tea. 'He was crying when I was sick, but I couldn't help him.'

'So he can be a boy here,' Jean said quickly. 'Nothing else for him to be.'

Lydia looked around the room, at the flagged floor and the cupboards with their red gingham curtains, at the walls three-foot deep and the oil lamps. 'It's nice. Old and snug,' she said.

'My mother always hated it. Being so far from other people, no electricity, the scruffiness, too much weather. It's exactly what I love. It's always been a place where I could go unwatched.'

Lydia nodded, but Jean could see her thoughts were somewhere else.

'It'll be good for Charlie,' Lydia said. 'But I'm better now. Only very tired.'

'And so?'

Lydia looked at the square of pale sky, all she could see through the small window formed to keep the weather out. 'We've been through this,' she said. 'I can't afford not to be back at work and I don't want your charity. There's nothing more to say.'

'Just for now, just for this time, put those worries away. For your sake, to get strong, because you're not well enough to work; and for Charlie's.'

'And for yours?'

Jean got up and started to unpack the groceries. Sausages, bread, bacon, butter, eggs.

'Yes, for mine too,' she said, angry with Lydia, angry with herself, and she busied herself noisily with the food.

When Charlie came in from the beach, it was as if he'd been coming here all his life, tugging the front door because it always stuck a bit in the sea air, catching a finger to the porch bell as he went past so that it sounded a soft, deep toll, just as Jean used to do as a child. Barefoot, his hair thick with sand, he came in with the sea and the wind still clinging and put his hands, cupped together, down on the table.

'Guess what,' he said, looking round at Lydia.

'You're full of sand,' she said, putting a hand to his hair. 'And where are your shoes and socks?' but her voice was pleased.

Charlie looked round at Lydia and uncupped his hands.

On his palm lay a large, shiny bean and a rectangular, brown sac from each corner of which a brittle tendril whisked into the air.

'Found them washed up,' he said, and he placed them carefully on the mantelpiece, between a lustre jug and an empty vase, as though he knew, Jean thought, that that was where she'd always placed her childhood finds. Then he hitched himself up on to the deep sill below the window as if that, too, were simply his place, leaned back against the wall, arms around his knees and looked back at Lydia.

'Can I sleep in the tent?'

Somehow Charlie's return dissolved the mood between the two women, as if their argument was done now. Jean scythed a square of grass in the orchard behind the house and together they helped Charlie put up the tent, and build a fire for his sausages.

'There's a bed made up too. In case of a hurricane or something,' Jean said, and she showed Charlie the little bedroom behind the kitchen.

'You know where your mum is sleeping?' she said and the boy nodded, impatient, hardly listening. Only when Lydia came to say goodnight did he clutch her arm hard, his face full of shadows in the torchlight.

Jean slept deeply that night and woke slowly into the day with a bridling of pleasure as she recalled where she was and who was sleeping in the room next door. Downstairs, there were small footprints on the kitchen flags and the bread looked as if a beast of some description had attacked it, but there was no other sign of Charlie. Jean made tea and poured two cups. She took one up to Lydia's room and knocked. No sound. Lifting the latch, she went in. Autumn sunlight blanched the room, but Lydia still slept. The doctor in Jean was at ease. Lydia's colour was normal, her fever was gone and with a few days' rest, her fatigue would lift. The patient was convalescing well; she wouldn't wake her, and she turned to go. But something else gave her pause, so that she looked again.

Lydia lay with one arm flung above her, her face turned to one side, though it wasn't her sleeping face that made Jean turn back. It was the sight of one breast, visible where the bedclothes had got flung off, visible beneath her night-dress, the nipple tight, which burned itself into Jean's mind. Suddenly all the force of her desire, put away this last week while Lydia was ill, came flooding through her so powerfully that it was as much as she could do to stand there in the middle of the room.

'Lydia,' she whispered. Every particle in her body longed to draw close, kneel down, touch, and perhaps she would have done just that, but there was Charlie's voice downstairs so she turned away again and shut the door on her desire.

The tide rose and fell across a perfect day. Charlie was as busy as a boy can be; raking for cockles, catching eels, hiding in the dunes till the sun fell below the sea. He made forays back to the cottage, always for a good reason – to fetch scissors, or string, or a towel. But each time he'd seek his mother out, make sure of her, before running off again.

For the two women, the day passed in a strange kind of calm. The air was charged with relief and anticipation, as if they were living in the calm before and beyond a storm. Lydia spent the day reading, moving with the sun around the cottage. The story was quiet and secluded and she was glad to keep to its path and away from her own. Charlie came to find her now and then and once she went with him, over the dunes and down to the endless beach. But the sea unnerved her, she didn't know why, so smooth and full, tipping over, breaking its bounds, and she soon returned to the stillness of the cottage.

It was only just dark when Jean saw Charlie into his tent. He climbed into the sleeping bag and laid back, his whole body stilled with exhaustion.

'Tomorrow,' he said. Jean paused to see what tomorrow held, but already he was halfway to dreaming and, raising her fingers to him in a kind of benediction, she closed the tent.

She walked up the sand hill to look at the sea, now just a darker space below the dark sky, stood there as she'd stood on so many other nights in so many other years, then turned and walked slowly back.

The lights were extinguished by the time she came inside, and in their place a dozen candles lit. Lydia sat on the sofa with her legs tucked up and a book spread open on her lap.

'Bet he was asleep fast,' Lydia said, her smile wavery in the flickering light.

'Before he was in his sleeping bag, almost.' Kneeling on the hearth, Jean spread her hands to the last of the fire. 'It's warm in here. Beautiful. I didn't know we had so many candles.'

'I'll have to tell him soon,' Lydia said. 'About the house. That Robert's left us.'

'He knows about Robert,' Jean said.

'Yes, but not from me. He needs to know from me.'

'Don't tell him while we're here. Let him have his holiday first.' She turned to Lydia. 'You need yours, too.'

Jean wanted to touch Lydia's face, to put her hands in her hair. She wanted to run her finger along her collarbone, unbutton her blouse and feel the swell of her breasts. She longed to take Lydia's hand and lead her up the narrow stairs, across the creaky boards, along past the cupboard she'd hidden in as a child, into her bedroom. But she knew that Lydia needed to lie Charlie down in her mind, settle him and say goodnight before she shut the door.

'Jean?' Lydia's voice broke across her thoughts. 'You're in a trance. Come here.'

As Jean kissed her, she knew that Lydia was here now, in this place, to be with her.

They kissed as if the universe began and ended there; as if nothing else existed but their two bodies, their two mouths, and the desire between them. Jean was breathless and there was an urgency in her she had never known before. She wanted to eat and drink this woman. Her body danced on a million points, and at the same time it felt so heavy, her desire lurching and churning like a broiling sea. She drew back from her own force, burying her head in Lydia's shoulder and clutching her hands to Lydia's sides. Breathing deeply, she tried to calm herself. She felt Lydia's fingers in her hair, stroking, soothing, and for a moment the earth was still.

'Touch me,' Lydia said, and she lifted Jean's hand to her breasts.

Jean undid the buttons on Lydia's cardigan, then her blouse. She'd never opened a blouse from the outside and it felt awkward, as if this were a different skill to learn. She fumbled a little, pressing at the buttons' pearly edges. Freeing the last of them, suddenly impatient, she pulled it open and off, tugging the arms away, in one movement. How often in her doctoring life had she stood before an undressed woman? But this was so different. This was for the very first time. Holding her breath, she ran her hands up Lydia's stomach, feeling the gentle swell of her woman's belly, her ribs, and then the soft give of her breasts. She traced the lines of Lydia's brassière, around from under her arms and over her shoulders.

Lydia was perfectly still, eyes closed. But as Jean's fingers travelled down towards her breasts again, she opened her eyes and watched.

Jean's heart thudded in her ears. Beneath the lace, she could feel Lydia's nipples sharpen and, unable to hold back any longer, she ran her tongue over.

'God,' Lydia said, her voice rough and dry.

Jean reached and unhooked the brassière, slipping it down, lifting it free. Pushing herself back and away, she stared at Lydia, bare-chested, her breasts heavy, nipples dark. She hadn't known how it might feel to bend towards a woman and find her rising, arching, for her. She'd never before felt this wish to enter and be entered; to be laid bare, exposed. She'd never felt such ferocity and such tenderness.

'You're beautiful,' she said. 'So beautiful.'

But Lydia was reaching around, gathering her clothes, getting to her feet.

'I can't,' she said. 'Not here.'

Jean looked at her bewildered and Lydia took her hand, pulled her up.

'Take me to your bed,' Lydia said.

'Is it Charlie?'

'I want to make love to you up there.'

They locked the door on Lydia's fear and thought up an excuse to give her boy, should he come searching for his mother that night, and slowly they made their way to one another, undoing and easing from their clothes, brushing and touching each other's skin, till they lay naked beneath the counterpane, looking up at the patterns on the ceiling that formed and unformed in the guttering candlelight.

Jean turned and cupped Lydia's breasts in her hands. It was miraculous to be here now. Even in these last weeks she'd never allowed herself to imagine this. Tenderly she kissed her. Then she took Lydia's nipple tight in her mouth and this time Lydia cried out in a voice so free, so wild, it sent a shock across Jean's scalp. Lydia's hand was on her wrist, pulling it down, across ribs and belly, past the points of Lydia's hips, till Jean felt the first turn of hair. Lydia reached high behind her, gripping the headboard, her breath coming harder, faster.

'Please,' she said, 'please God.'

Now Jean's fingers ran away with her, down through the coarse rise of hair, down and into the turns and soft equivocations of another woman's sex. Lydia's desire was slick as oil between her fingers and Jean dipped deep, circling and returning, her fingers wet, her movements steady, as Lydia rose and rose and then broke at last and cried out like a bird. Afterwards, soft and quiet, she curled herself inside Jean's arms.

'My body's singing,' Jean said. 'I never knew. Never knew it could . . .' But Lydia put a finger to Jean's lips. 'Sshh,' and then her mouth where her finger had been. Jean closed her eyes and found out what she had never known, that she could give herself up to someone else. When Lydia kissed between her legs, Jean looked at her there, at this woman making love to her, and laughed out loud in wonder.

They had two more days and two more nights before returning; the days they spent with Charlie and the nights they spent with each other. As Lydia's strength returned, she put her book aside and demanded that they go exploring, so they made an expedition to the eel smokery in a town by the sea and another to the church with the wooden angels. Charlie came to see the eels hanging from the roof, but he didn't want to visit the church. So Lydia and Jean went alone and looked up at the pairs of angels flying high from the beams.

'They're meant to be men in the Bible, but they look like pairs of girls to me,' Jean said.

And since the church was empty, they stole a kiss.

When they left the cottage, Lydia sat in the front of the

car and Charlie, in the back, looked out of the window and didn't ask how long till they were home. He'd cried a little, Jean knew. But, returning, he had his mother in view and, beside him on the seat, garnered from the endless beach, he had a box of treasure.

29

D ot stood stock-still. She shook her head.
   'I'm telling you, there must be a man. Look at you.'
Lydia smiled and shrugged, but her heart jumped.

'Maybe you don't know you've met him yet.'

They stood facing one another as people thronged past, faces grey-green under the strip-lighting. Irritated elbows caught at them, somebody muttered that it was a stupid place to stand and talk.

Lydia glanced high, beyond the sea of hurrying heads. Below the ceiling, thin strips of window draped in cobwebs gave out on to sky. In all her years here, she'd never noticed the windows before.

'There isn't a man. Really there isn't,' she said, and something in her soul sang as she said it.

This corridor smelled as it always did, of hot rubber and old sweat. All the years she'd worked in the factory she'd hated it, but now she was going, she almost liked it. She breathed deep. Only one day left, and then she'd hand back her pinafore and her tools, and cycle away for the last time.

'But being offered a nice place to live, and a new job. It is a bit of a turnaround,' she said.

That was a daft piece of understatement and Lydia felt herself blush, though under the nauseous shine of the factory lights she hoped it wasn't visible.

The bell rang and the two women turned as a reflex and merged into the flood, hurrying back to work.

'You've told them you're going?' Dot said.

Lydia nodded. 'Mr Evans did look a bit surprised, since I'm not still ill, or pregnant. Said they'd always found my work satisfactory and good luck in the future.'

'You lucky so-and-so. No more clocking on, no more going mad with boredom, no more canteen meals.'

'You'll have to keep me filled in on the gossip,' Lydia said.

'When are you out of the house?'

'I've started packing. We're moving over the weekend.'

'Does Robert know?'

Lydia felt her head spin and the blood rush from her face. She took hold of Dot's arm.

'Don't tell him anything. Please,' she said.

Dot looked at her strangely.

'Why would I tell him anything? I don't even like him.'

Lydia nodded, but Dot's voice was far away and Lydia's skin was clammy with fear.

'Let go of my arm,' Dot said. 'What's got into you?' She rubbed at her arm. 'I'll be out in bruises tomorrow. You won't be able to keep it a secret for long. He'll find out soon enough. A sister like Pam. You know that. Anyway, he might be pleased. What with him not giving you a penny. Takes the pressure off.'

'But he mustn't know,' Lydia said in a low voice.

'So did you ever hear from your dad?' Dot said, changing the subject.

Lydia shook herself like a dog coming in out of the rain, as if to clear Robert off. She nodded. 'He said I could come back and keep house for him if I wanted, but he wouldn't spare a penny for me otherwise.'

'Nice,' Dot said. 'Clear.'

Lydia went on, her voice artificial and breezy, as if she

was simply explaining what the weather was like outside.

'I'd gone to London when the war got going. The money was good in the munitions factory, but it wasn't what Dad had wanted. He already had a life lined up for me, right down to the pattern on my apron. A life and a husband. Pleasant enough fellow. He'd been Dad's apprentice. Would have taken over the business. I'd probably have married him if Robert hadn't sung so sweetly. If I hadn't fancied him so hard. If I hadn't got knocked up so fast. God knows, things might have been better with him.'

'Except you wouldn't have had Charlie,' Dot said.

Lydia nodded slowly. 'That's the clincher, isn't it?' she said. 'I wouldn't have had Charlie.'

Dot laughed. 'So you've got your father on one side not forgiving, Pam on the other and your sod of a husband in the middle. Nest of vipers.'

They sat down and got out their tools, ready to start the afternoon shift.

'What does Charlie think of it all, then? Going off to live in a posh house?' Dot said.

'He's happy. Near his beloved bees. With all that garden.'

The forewoman was making her way towards the switch, an eye to the clock, while the women waited. Dot fiddled with the handle on her screwdriver, looking up at Lydia, then down at her lap, then up again while they waited for the shift to start.

'I'm going to miss you, you daft thing. Lucky for you, with your doctor. I didn't know she was such a good friend,' Dot said, but the conveyor belt had started, its clatter rising, and the room was too noisy now for any reply to be heard.

Lydia brooded through the afternoon on what she should say, but by the time they knocked off, she still didn't know how to answer.

Thursday was Lydia's final day. After ten years' work,

the factory gave her the last day off, and a teapot in yellow and green.

That evening Dot called by to help her with the packing.

'Pam's been sniffing around,' she said. 'Wanting to know this, wanting to know that.'

'What did you tell her?'

'Not a blinding thing.' Dot opened one of the bags she'd brought and began to fill it with plates, wrapping them in newspaper, piece by piece.

'It's making her quite cross,' she said. 'Silly, because she'll find out pretty soon, but I think sod it, why should I tell her anything?'

'She doesn't have to see me any more,' Lydia said. 'Now Robert's left me, and I'm not working at the factory.'

'But it won't stop her wanting to know. Charlie's still her nephew.'

Lydia snorted. 'Not so as you'd notice. She's horrid to him.'

'Maybe that's because he's her nephew,' Dot said. 'Maybe he reminds her too much.'

Lydia looked round at Dot. 'What do you mean?'

'Well, he's the spit of Robert, isn't he?'

Lydia nodded. 'Sometimes it's strange, seeing the man who's left me in the face of my boy,' she said.

'Maybe that's what Pam feels too. She's always gone on about being like a mother to Robert, bringing him up single-handed and that. She thinks he's her boy. But he went and left her for you.'

Lydia paused in her packing. Dot's words made her shiver.

'She's his sister, not his girlfriend. And anyway, then she might be fond of Charlie, him looking so like his dad,' she said.

'But she isn't, is she,' Dot said flatly. 'Home truths, Lydia. She isn't ever going to forgive your Charlie for looking like her boy.'

'Quite the philosopher,' Lydia said abruptly, pulling open the cutlery drawer. She gathered up a rackety handful and dumped it into a box. The shot and clatter of metal felt good. She let the sound die and turned to her friend.

'Sorry, Dot. Not your fault.'

'Watch your back,' Dot said. 'She's got her knives out for you.'

'I hate her for taking it out on Charlie,' Lydia said. She gathered up another handful. 'In fact, I just hate her,' she said. 'First time I've admitted it. If it wasn't for Annie. Don't know how she got through so well, with a mother like that.'

'Doesn't look that well on it at the minute,' Dot said flatly. 'And I'm not sure her mother's even noticed.'

'Annie?' Lydia looked round. Something about Dot's tone tugged her out of her own rage. 'What's up with Annie?'

'At a guess, I'd say she was pregnant.'

Lydia bit her lip. 'And you think Pam hasn't noticed?'

'Odd, isn't it? A woman who can't leave anybody alone, least of all her own daughter. Maybe Pam doesn't want to notice. Maybe she hopes it'll go away.'

'You're sure?'

'Sure as you can be when you see a girl throwing up in the toilets and who won't meet your eye when you ask her, is she all right.'

'But not showing,' Lydia said.

'I'd say barely in there,' Dot said. 'She looked right as rain last week. But if I was Pam, I'd be setting up to collar that young George before he disappears in a puff of smoke.'

'Except she doesn't like young George. He's the last thing she wants for Annie.'

'Perhaps that's why Annie headed straight for him, then,' Dot said. 'It's what I'd have done with a mother like that.'

30

Outside a new dark was falling, a dark Charlie didn't know yet. He walked carefully, wheeling the bike. Like everything else here, the street lamps had bigger kingdoms and the pools of shadow between them fell wider and deeper than he was used to. He pushed the bicycle over the gravel and on to the pavement. It was quiet here. He could hear the sound of his own feet and the noise of the wind in the trees. On this road there were no clutches of gossiping women home from the factory, no children running between the houses, or playing out. There were no other boys with bicycles. He couldn't smell any other dinners cooking. He couldn't even smell his own, though he'd only just shut the door on it.

Straddling the bike, Charlie looked out on the road. His road. He'd walked along it dozens of times visiting Dr Markham, but it was different now, now that he lived here.

The bicycle was his. A gift. Leant up against the shed that afternoon, brand-new, with three gears, front and back lights and a label tied to the handlebars: 'Should help with the journey to school.' When he found his mother and asked her was it really for him, she caught him by the cheeks, which he didn't like her doing any more, and said it was, but it was Dr Markham he had to thank. Then she kissed him on the forehead and said his supper would be ready in an hour, so to be back by then.

It was freezing outside and Charlie wrapped his scarf tighter, rubbed at his fingers and pushed off. He'd ride the bike up and down a few times, get the hang of the gears, then maybe go to Bobby's house. He'd like to see Bobby's face. This was something of his that Bobby would really want.

The road stretched away for ever, with empty trees and deep grass verges, and big houses behind hedges. Charlie cycled harder, faster up the hill. Pushing the pedals, he looked into the dark and imagined that his dad was just ahead there, by that tree, in front of that house, or round the corner, leaning back, waiting to see him, to see his son Charlie. He sat straighter and set his jaw firmly in case, so his dad would see how strong he'd got, and how fast and able. He let himself imagine it for a time and then, because it was hurting, he stopped.

'Stupid,' he muttered, and then he tried other words.

'Damn and bloody fool. Bloody stupid.' But the words didn't work and he shook his head.

'I hate you,' he said. 'I hate you. I hate her. I hate her stupid face and her hair. I hate her stupid name. I hate her name and she won't ever be Mrs Weekes. Ever.'

He didn't want to go to Bobby's any more and he turned and let the bike freewheel down the road, murmuring under his breath, feeling how it got easier and easier.

'I hate you, I hate you, I hate you.'

He remembered the night that they'd come back from the sea. He'd been telling his mother a story, something funny, but she hadn't seemed to hear him.

'You know we've got to move?' she'd said when he stopped talking. 'That we can't stay here?'

They were eating fish and chips. Charlie was famished and happy. His box of treasure was at the foot of the stairs, waiting, not opened yet.

She spoke and he looked up at her, not understanding, and she picked a chip off the newspaper and started to study the crossword.

'But we live here,' Charlie said.

He watched his mother find a pencil in the drawer and write in an answer.

'It's because there's only the two of us here now,' she said.

'But I've always lived here. Since I was a baby.'

'I don't earn enough on my own to pay the rent,' she said.

She began to write in another answer, but she was holding the pencil very tight, he could see that, and maybe the fat from the chips had got into the paper because the pencil wouldn't make a mark.

'Why isn't my dad paying any?' he said.

She looked down at the pencil.

'I hate him,' Charlie said.

'Now, Charlie,' she said, but she was making shapes across the newspaper, digging into it, zigzag shapes, like lightning coming down.

Charlie wasn't hungry any more. He pushed his chips away.

'I can get some money then,' he said. 'I'll get a paper round, or run messages for the bookies on a Saturday. Mikey in my class does that.'

His mother shook her head.

'You're too young and, anyway, it wouldn't be enough, my love.'

'But you're working in the factory all the time,' Charlie said, 'except for being ill and after. You can't work any more.'

Then his mother had explained about Dr Markham's offer.

Charlie left the bicycle against the shed and went around

the side of the house through the side gate and into the garden. He went carefully in the dark, over the terrace, down on to the lawn, down beyond the beech hedge. Laying his hands on the rough, damp wood, he put his cheek to the hive.

'Remember me,' he said, and he made his voice smooth as smoke. 'Don't wake up, just listen out in your dreams, bees, and you'll hear.'

He cupped a hand around his mouth and spoke slow and low.

'My father is dead.'

He waited, and the bees still slept.

'I hate him. He's dead. Now you know.'

He had his own bedroom in Dr Markham's house, and his own name on the door, carved in metal like the doctor's name on her door. He had his own desk, and shelves on the wall that went up higher than he could reach. All the things he'd ever found could go there. For the best things, the smallest, most special ones, Dr Markham had given him a wooden box. It was a box that used to be hers, for her most special things. It had gold lines set into the wood and tiny drawers. There was a tiny shell still in the corner of one of the drawers. Dr Markham had told him it was for luck. It was pink, like his finger, and ridged like a washboard. He kept the box on the table by his bed, and some of the drawers he left empty for the future.

Charlie thought the shell had already brought him some luck. When he went to school in the morning, his mother stood on the doorstep and smiled and blew him a kiss that he pretended not to see. She didn't go to the factory and then come home in the dark so tired that he was frightened, when she fell asleep, that she wasn't going to wake up.

It was odd, how happy she was in Dr Markham's kitchen, in Dr Markham's house, but Charlie was glad of it.

Glad that she sang songs again; glad she didn't cry any more; glad she had her book propped open with a weight again. He didn't need to worry any more, when he wasn't there.

Sometimes in the evening, if it could be early enough, they all ate supper together and that made him happy too. His mother would tell stories about the factory to make them laugh, and Dr Markham would tell stories about doctoring so that his mother put her hands over her ears. But most often he ate his tea on his own; though his mother often sat with him, he felt sad.

'Are you happy, Charlie?' his mother would ask, and he always said yes, because he wanted to see that look on her face, made for him and no one else. But perhaps if it had been dark, then he'd just have shrugged.

Charlie's bedroom was next to the study, and then there was the bathroom. There were big tiles around the bath in blue and white and if Charlie pinched his eyes nearly shut, they looked like the sea. When you ran the water, it made the walls groan.

'Sounds like your grandfather,' his mother said, but he'd never met his grandfather, so he didn't know if that was true.

The bath was long, so long, he could lie with his head back and float and listen to his heartbeat till the water was tepid and his skin was white at the edges.

His mother's bedroom was across the landing, next to Dr Markham's. It was only a little room, with a bed like his, so that her counterpane had to be folded to fit. Dr Markham said it used to be a dressing room, where all the clothes were kept, and that's why it had such a big wardrobe, and two doors: one out on to the landing, and the other through to Dr Markham's bedroom. His mother put her chair against this door because there wasn't anywhere else to put it, and her clothes left half the wardrobe empty.

The first day they moved into Dr Markham's house, Lydia had told Charlie to come and find her if he needed to, night or day, it didn't matter. She'd gripped his shoulders so he'd know she meant it. Since they moved there, Charlie had woken in the night a few times. Twice he'd heard Dr Markham go out to a call, the motor car pulling away into silence, but the other times he couldn't have said what it was that woke him. Except that it wasn't nightmares and he wasn't upset, so he'd lain there with his eyes open, listening to the dark, till sleep had caught him up again.

But the night of the thunderstorm was different. Charlie was deep under when the first clap of thunder dug him from his dreams and flung sleep against the bedroom wall. It woke him so suddenly that for a minute he didn't know where he was, or whether he was sleeping or waking and he lay rigid against the sheets, eyes seeing nothing, hands over his ears, heart pounding, while the darkness echoed. Then the noise died away and there was silence. No rain, no wind, no nothing. Turning on to his side, he tucked his hands beneath his head, safe between the pillow and the cool sheet, and closed his eyes again.

Years ago, frightened by another storm, Charlie had scrambled down the stairs and found his parents on the sofa. Snuggled between them, head on his mother's lap, feet snug beneath his father's elbow, he'd fallen back to sleep, cradled in the sound of their conversation, cocooned against the storm.

And when the lightning broke now from the sky, cracking Charlie's eyelids open, filling the room with its blue dance, he was scared again, fear chasing up and down his body, and he longed to be there, tucked inside his parents' voices.

'Mum,' he cried out, but his voice was small inside the weather.

Heart racing, he got out of bed and opened his bedroom door. The storm had its eye on the house and the landing shook with thunder; the windows rattled with rain.

Charlie tugged open Lydia's door and made for the bed.

'Mum,' he said, his voice calmer now he was here, now he was close to her, and he reached down to the covers to put his hands on her shoulder, to shake her awake. But the bed was unslept in, the counterpane pulled tight over the pillows.

Charlie froze and for a second everything felt far away from him and he stood quite alone. Then he cried out again into the chilled, hard air for his mother.

Seconds later, Lydia was there with him, her arms around him, holding him tight to her. Charlie buried his head against her, dug his fists into her sides.

'I was scared,' he said, 'and then you weren't there.'

'But I am now. Sshh, sshh, it's all right,' she said, sitting down on the bed with him and rocking him in her arms. She smelled of sleep.

'Don't walk under pylons when there's lightning,' she murmured.

'Dad,' Charlie said sleepily. 'It's what Dad says.'

They stayed like that till he was drifting and then she picked him up to take him back to his bed. In this half-sleep, his eyes heavy, Charlie saw that the chair with his mother's clothes over was moved and the door to Dr Markham's room open.

'Is Dr Markham there?' he said, as Lydia tucked him into his bed and she stroked his hair and shushed him back to sleep.

31

The roads were empty and Jean drove fast to get home. Her mind ran with the wheels, steering tight to the straightest, fastest route. She was a woman in love. There was no point in taking the corners gently or pretending any different, not to herself at least.

The last visit on her list that day had taken Jean out beyond the edge of town, and she was tired now, her eyes weary. As she drove along the narrow lanes, the trees dipped in at her, their empty branches veering into the headlights, and she glimpsed strange creatures that slipped away beyond the spoons of light from the headlamps.

The visit hadn't been easy and, until recently, Jean would have played it over in her mind afterwards, working out what she could have done differently, defending herself from all her self-accusation. But tonight she left the patient where she was; and instead her thoughts travelled, light and slender, strong as a spider's thread, up over the roofs and gardens, over the factory and the park, across the pond with its first glint of ice, to home.

As she pulled into the garage, the headlamps lit up Charlie's bike leaned against the near wall, and the small trestle table covered with bits of rock and pebble, set up for his fossil hunt. A trowel and a sieve were lined up at one end together with a notebook and pencil. She picked up each thing, and then put each back in place. Charlie was careful in his arranging of things, and half of it was play and half of it was deadly serious. She knew because she recognized the same trait in herself.

So good, this was. This was what it was to be happy. Friday, home, tired, the lights on in the house and somebody else here. Rocks and oddments and Lydia's bucket of bulbs in a corner, ready for their winter soil, and a kiss to be snatched in the pantry and the promise of this woman's love.

Charlie nearly toppled Jean with his sense of importance as she came in, running up close before she'd had a chance to put down her bag.

'They're coming round now. I thought I could help with it, because she needs honeycomb for her homework, but you're back so that's better . . .'

He paused and took in Jean, still in her coat and scarf, still holding her black bag.

'If you didn't mind, I thought I could help her out,' he went on, more slowly.

Jean nodded. 'Good idea,' she said. 'Who's coming round now?'

'And Bobby's going to come over at the weekend,' he said, his thoughts in their own gauge. 'We're going to make things for the den.' He paused. 'Who?'

'Charlie, who's coming now?'

'Meg and Emma and Mrs Marston. Maybe Mr Marston later . . .' but he was already running on, away into the house, marshalling his equipment for the girls, ready to instruct them, to play.

Jean watched as he ran off and wondered what he understood. The night of the storm, Lydia had been terrified and so angry with herself.

'If he'd seen me in your bed. Imagine if he had.'

'He wouldn't have understood,' Jean said, but she knew he understood something already, despite their care and restraint.

Jean closed her eyes and listened to the noise. Voices, clutter, the flurry of more than one life in the house. The meal was impromptu, a casserole filled out with carrots, potatoes, swedes, to feed the extra mouths, apples stewed up with sugar and raisins to keep the little girls going a while longer.

Charlie had presented the jar of honeycomb, together with a detailed drawing of a portion of a hive.

'That's how I met Dr Markham,' he said. 'Because I'd hurt my ribs and there was the wooden honeycomb in her surgery.'

'But it wouldn't help your ribs, would it?' Emma said.

'No, silly. But he asked about it. Didn't he?' Meg said, turning to Jean.

'He did, and we discovered that some great minds have the same passions, and now look where we are,' Jean said, her swift glance catching Lydia's cheek, and Sarah's eye.

'So tell us, Charlie, how the bees make their comb,' Jim said, and as Charlie told, Jean looked at the faces around the table and basked.

The conversation turned and turned about. The children got down from the table, Charlie leading the way upstairs. The adults lit cigarettes. Jean brought out the whisky.

She described a house she'd been to for the first time, and how she'd walked through three rooms between newspapers piled almost to the ceiling to find her patient.

'Corridors made of newsprint and somewhere down them the voice of my patient, telling me to hurry up and to shut the door firmly. She can't have thrown away a newspaper for decades. Every now and then I'd get a headline in the eye – the top page of a dusty stack – and there were some that took me straight back to my childhood. The General Strike. My mother thought the leaders should be shot, usually over her breakfast coffee.'

She laughed. 'When I finally found the patient, we had quite a nice chat and then I examined her, wrote a prescription and left, thinking, well, it's not how I want to live, but I don't think she's mad.'

Then Sarah told a story about an old lady she'd visited as a child, carrying the basket of groceries for her mother, and Jim asked could he please have some of the stewed apple, now the children had finished with it.

Lydia fetched Jim a bowl for his fruit.

'So how are you finding it, working here?' Sarah said as Lydia passed her some apple. 'She's not playing her jazz records at all hours I hope?' Sarah said, and before Lydia could reply, Jim interrupted.

'Anyway, if she causes you any trouble, you'll have to give me a call. I'm her oldest friend, and that comes with certain privileges and responsibilities.'

'Jim,' Jean said, his words touching and exasperating her. But Jean knew that there was another, unspoken conversation going on here, a quizzing of this unusual friendship. She often forgot about their differences now; Lydia a factory worker and herself a doctor, middle class to the marrow. She forgot that in the normal scheme of lives, even their friendship was unusual. Housekeepers didn't sit down to supper with their employers. Not like this.

Lydia took a sip of her whisky and Jean watched her wince. It wasn't a taste she was used to and she put the glass down with a degree of certainty that suggested to Jean she might be a little drunk. Then she grinned, as if resolved upon something.

'She is a good employer,' Lydia said. She put a hand to her neck and turned to find Jean's eyes. 'Only,' she said, tapping a finger to the table, her expression serious, or was it mock-serious, 'only she does have this habit.'

Jean broke in, banging her glass on the table in melodramatic fashion.

'I need more whisky, if my housekeeper is going to give away my trade secrets,' she said, pushing the glass towards Jim. 'Come on then, what is it that I do?'

Lydia frowned slightly, as if running through a list of recollections. 'I'll mention the gravest,' she said, 'and leave the minor ones for another time.'

'Which is?' said Jim, grinning.

'You're enjoying this too much,' she said.

'Which is that she's very good with her patients. Diligent, attentive, thorough, never turns anyone away, even if she's about to shut up shop. But she will overfeed the fish. Every time she walks through the waiting room, she dips a finger in the fish food and sprinkles it over. I've seen it happen a dozen times. I swear, those fish swim to the top when they see her coming now.'

'That's outrageous,' Jean said, smiling. She loved this edge of humour that surfaced in Lydia nowadays.

Lydia raised her hands, palms upwards, affecting a disingenuous shrug. 'The fish will simply sink under their own weight soon,' she said.

'And that's simply not true, my love,' Jean said, laughing. 'It's an atrocious lie.'

Her words hung above the table, and the laugh guttered in Jean's throat. Blood rushed in her ears like white noise and she could feel the heat in her face rise. She stood up, more abruptly than she wanted to, and pushed her chair out from the table. She heard Jim's voice, and Lydia's replying.

'I'd better go and check outside,' she said. 'The dark, and Charlie doesn't always . . . things might be open, and if it rains.'

She didn't know how to excuse herself. The others were shifting, adjusting in their chairs. Before she dug any deeper, she left the room and headed for the welcome cool of the November night.

Out in the garden, Jean realized that she had given the bees no thought in the last few months, and there were things that needed doing in preparation for the spring. She'd decided to increase the number of hives, so there were new frames to make. She was going to do these tasks with Charlie, but tonight she needed the task for herself and, lighting a gas lamp to use in the shed, she set to with a vengeance. It was a relief to work with wood and wire, aligning side struts, working out the slender bee space. Slowly the noise in her ears quietened and the still air was soft like balm.

She'd been daft to think she could keep it wholly secret from them. But what was she going to say? What were they going to say? And she'd left Lydia in there, just marched out.

'Not true, my love,' she murmured. Did it sound so bad? Mightn't she say just that to Jim? Or to the children?

'It's not bad,' she said, bringing the hammer down. 'It's bloody marvellous. The most marvellous thing I could ever have imagined.'

And these words, this acknowledgement, spoken out, brought a rush to her heart, made her heavy with desire. Perhaps Sarah hadn't noticed the affection; perhaps Jim hadn't heard the endearment. Leaning the finished frame against the table, she rested with this thought till Sarah pushed open the shed door. With the plaid blanket from the sitting room round her shoulders, she looked like a refugee, someone rescued, someone you saw in newspaper monochrome.

Should be me wrapped in that, Jean thought, but she said nothing, only picked up two more lengths of wood. Sarah sat down on the end of the bench and pulled the rug tight.

'I've left the others talking shop,' she said.

Jean nodded and picked up a piece of sandpaper. The

wood didn't need sanding, but she needed to be doing something.

'At least, Jim is interrogating Lydia about the factory. She seems to know an awful lot about it.'

'She worked there for ten years, so she would do,' Jean said.

'Yes, but she talks in a way that . . . describes things in such a way –'

Jean interrupted her. 'Probably all her reading. She knows lots of long words,' she said, hearing her own sarcasm, her defensiveness.

Sarah picked up the chisel. She touched her finger to its sharp edge.

'She's making her way through my father's books now,' Jean said, conscious that she should make amends, but unsure what for. 'She's an unusual woman. If she'd had my schooling . . .'

For several minutes neither woman spoke and then they both began together.

'I'm sorry for . . .' Jean said.

'I didn't mean to sound . . .' Sarah said and they both laughed, relieved, at the collision.

'What are you going to do at Christmastime?' Sarah said. 'Does Charlie see his father?'

Jean shrugged. 'Not at the moment, I don't think so. I haven't got as far as Christmas. I'm glad he could help Meg out with her homework. He's a fine boy.'

'Jean,' Sarah said in a different tone, less open to diversion, 'I did hear you, in the kitchen. I'm not mistaken, am I?'

Jean was glad she was sitting down. Even so she could feel her legs weaken, as if someone had put an electric prod to her stomach.

There seemed little point in lying; now it had come to this. She shook her head.

'No,' she said.

Sarah nodded and took a deep breath, as if at least that was settled.

'Are you warm enough?' she said. It was true, now that Jean had stopped her furious activity and now the fact had been confirmed, the cold was creeping in through her clothes, pressing against her skin.

'It's a big blanket,' Sarah said, so Jean shuffled up and they sat together beneath it, watching their breath in the chilly light.

'It does explain a few things,' Sarah said at last. 'You've certainly had Jim puzzled.' She laughed. 'He thinks he has the last word on you, so it's really irritated him.'

'Well, now he knows,' Jean said flatly.

Sarah shook her head. 'I'm not sure he does. He was surprised you left the room so fast, but he didn't seem to know why. Men hear things very differently from women, Jean. Even Jim, who's better than most, and knows you as well as anyone. I don't think he heard you. At least, not as I did.'

'But you'll tell him,' Jean said. 'You'll have to.'

'Does anyone else know?'

'I don't think so.'

'God, Jean, you don't take the easy route, do you?'

'I didn't choose this bit,' Jean said. She drummed a finger on the wood. 'You know what they call people like me?'

'Couldn't you go to prison?'

'If I was a man,' Jean said. 'I've always felt sorry for those men when I've read about them in the newspaper. But now I am one, if you know what I mean.'

'She's from such a different background,' Sarah said in a solemn tone. 'Doesn't that make it even harder?'

'Not so as I've noticed,' Jean said, annoyed. Then she caught Sarah's expression and before she could squash it, a giggle rose in her throat and she heard Sarah snort, and both of them were helpless with laughter.

'We should go back in,' Jean said at last. 'Jim must be thinking something odd has happened by now. The children will turn into pumpkins soon.'

'But it has!' Sarah said. 'Something has happened.'

'Are you shocked?' Jean said.

Sarah looked at her steadily. 'Yes . . . I don't really understand. But I don't think your love is wrong, and I'll defend you against all comers.'

'Do you think I'll need knights in armour?' Jean said, amused.

'If this gets out, you'll need more than knights, Jean. If this gets out, have you thought what it'll do? To your professional standing? Your friendships? Have you thought what it'll do to that boy?'

Deep in their conversation, Lydia and Jim barely noticed the others' return. Jean caught phrases like 'repetitive frequency' and 'transmitting valves' and there was much nodding between the pair and an occasional 'mm' of acknowledgement. She filled the sink with hot suds and dirty dishes while Sarah rounded up sleepy children. Emma began to cry with exhaustion, which brought the conversation to a swift close.

'Take care, my friend,' Sarah said as she hugged Jean goodnight.

'We must speak again,' Jim said to Lydia. 'Delicious supper.'

Once Charlie was in bed and the house put to rights again, the two women sat, stunned, at the kitchen table.

'So is the cat out then?' Lydia said.

Jean hit her forehead with the heel of her hand and groaned.

'I'm sorry. It was so stupid,' she said. 'I suppose I was too relaxed.'

'It was the most exciting sentence I've ever heard,' Lydia

said. Reaching out, she stroked the back of Jean's hand. 'In front of your friends, to call me your love.'

'Sarah heard, and Jim didn't,' Jean said.

'What did she say?'

'She asked what if people find out.'

'Was she horrified? Or disgusted?'

'No. But taken aback. And she doesn't understand.'

'Nor do I,' said Lydia. 'But there it is. It's as real as the wood in this table.'

Jean gripped Lydia's hand, making a fist with it. 'What would we do? If people found out and . . .'

'Listen,' Lydia said, lifting their hands, banging them down, so that the warm band of her wedding ring jagged into Jean's knuckle.

'All your medical training means you go in and in to something and worry out the cause. Is it this? Is it that? Rule things out till you get to the centre of it. But maybe we need to do the opposite thing. Maybe we need to go and find the centre of it somewhere else. The centre for us, I mean.'

'You're sounding like one of your detectives,' Jean said, 'after he's hit the whisky.'

'I'm serious, Jean. Your father's got a shelf full of books about travelling, about people living their lives somewhere else. We can do that too. Go and live somewhere new.'

Jean saw how Lydia's chin was set strong and fierce.

'Make a virtue of necessity.' She squeezed Jean's hand. 'We could go anywhere, us and Charlie. People always need doctors. France, or Italy; America even. But listen,' she said, banging their hands on the table, 'the only person who knows so far is Sarah, and she's your friend, not your foe. Be calm.'

When Lydia came to her bed that night, Jean wrote out her love with a fingertip across her lover's shoulders, making the letters round and even.

'Don't use long words,' Lydia said, her voice gruff with tiredness. 'I won't understand them.'

And as Lydia curled away into her dreams, Jean slipped a hand between Lydia's legs, buried her face in her hair and smiled into the dark.

32

It rained for a solid week at the end of November, from the far hills where Jean and Lydia had walked, down to the town, and beyond, to the plain where Mrs Sandringham and her sister pulled potatoes from waterlogged fields. It was joyless rain from a blank sky. By the time it was done, it had forced the river far beyond its normal banks.

Charlie went with Bobby to the big bridge after school and they leaned over the parapet and stared at the angry mess of water rushing under the arches.

'You'd see a corpse if you looked for long enough,' Charlie said. 'It's a known fact.'

'There's just bits of wood and trees,' Bobby said. 'There aren't any bodies. How come there'd have to be a body?'

'Because,' said Charlie patiently, 'murderers often tip their victims into fast-flowing rivers and then the body gets bloated so it can only be recognized by its teeth, and anyway it's miles from where it started by the time someone sees it, so that helps the murderer get away.'

'But if nobody's been murdered, there won't be any bodies,' Bobby said.

'There will, because murderers like the rain. It brings them out, like rats.' Charlie tossed in a stick and the boys watched it get sucked below the surface in a second. 'The body might not surface for miles and miles. Like the stick, it gets dropped in and then disappears.'

The water roiled and churned and the boys leaned further. They saw a dead fish, flipped this way and that, silver belly nipping the light. Then they saw something and Charlie said it was a dog, and Bobby a sheep, but anyway it was enough with its matted pelt and limbs flung about.

'Let's go,' Bobby said.

'D'you want to try my bike?' Charlie said, because they both knew he'd won the argument and he could afford to be magnanimous.

So they left the angry water and got threepence of chips, and Bobby rode Charlie's bike up and down by the fountain in the park till he had to go home.

Charlie was about to go home too when he heard his name called.

'Charlie Weekes, look at you.'

Wheeling round, he saw Annie on the far side of the fountain, arm hooked in with another girl's. Cycling slowly towards them, he affected as much two-wheeled nonchalance as he could muster, sitting back in his saddle, one hand in his pocket, coming to a small skid-stop.

'That's quite a bike,' Annie said. 'I hope you came by it in a proper fashion.'

Charlie flushed and Annie's friend giggled.

'Got to go,' she said, and with a peck to Annie's cheek she strode off with that swinging girl's walk that somewhere in himself Charlie knew would be important to him one day.

'It was a present,' Charlie said defensively.

'You're such an only child,' Annie said. 'I was teasing.'

'Dr Markham gave it to me. For getting to school.'

'Lucky boy,' Annie said. 'Give us a croggie home then. I'm knackered.'

'But you're too big,' he said. 'Won't you be embarrassed?'

'I don't much care,' Annie said. 'I think it's you that's the embarrassed one.'

'What if Auntie Pam sees you?'

'She's got worse to see than that,' Annie said, but more to herself than to Charlie. 'Come on, I'll be careful of your precious bike. I haven't seen you in an age. I'll buy you a KitKat if you get me all the way home.'

It took all Charlie's strength and concentration to cycle Annie home, so it was only as they freewheeled down the alley that he remembered what had happened the last time he'd been to the house.

'Is Auntie Pam . . .' he began, because he wasn't coming in if she was there.

'She won't be home for another hour. She told me to get the dinner going. So I'll start on the food and you can sit and tell me how you're getting on.'

She opened the back door and let them in.

'My feet are sodden, so yours must be worse. Give me your shoes or Aunt Lydia will accuse me of causing your death when you get pneumonia.'

It was so easy, talking to Annie. He sat on the kitchen stool, his back against the wall, eating his KitKat while Annie made him tea and toast. While he told her all about everything, she scrubbed potatoes, fried onions and laid the table for tea, only interrupting with the occasional question.

Once the tea was on, Annie sat down opposite and started filing her nails.

'Do you all have tea together?' she said.

And Charlie explained how Dr Markham often had to eat late, and how she had to go out on call at night and had a bell rigged up in her bedroom so she could hear if anyone rang at the front door.

'It doesn't wake you up?' Annie said.

'No. Maybe it does my mum, but she's never said. Because her bedroom's right next door to Dr Markham's and there's a door connecting them from the olden days.'

'So they're good friends?' she said. 'Your mum and the doctor?'

He nodded.

'Because of Dr Markham we don't have to live in one of the houses that are all flooded out. We saw them today, me and Bobby. You could smell the water standing at the top of the street, and there were men wading through it carrying mattresses and cushions. Bobby said all the families have got to sleep in the church hall and when it goes down there'll be rats in their houses.'

'Nothing like that thunderstorm last month, though,' said Annie. 'That petrified me.'

'Me too. A bit,' Charlie said. 'A boy at school, his uncle was struck by lightning and his hair sizzled on the spot and never grew back.'

Annie laughed.

'That's a new excuse for baldness.'

'I thought my mum had been struck, when she wasn't in her bed, but then she came in, in her nightie, so it was all right.'

'Safe and sound,' Annie said, and Charlie looked up at her tone, because it was a bit sharp, as if he'd said something to annoy her.

'Does Aunt Lydia feel better now?' Annie said in a different voice.

Charlie nodded.

'She doesn't cry at all. She only sings while she's cooking. She says she's never had a best friend like Dr Markham before. She says she's the kind of friend you only make once in your life.'

'And do you like her, Charlie?'

'She gave me my bike, and she's nicer to my mum than my dad ever was.'

He stopped talking and scratched at a mark on the table. 'But you tell me some things now.'

Annie laughed and started to answer him, but then the kitchen door was pushed wide and Pam came in.

'What a nice surprise, Charlie. Nice to hear how your mother is getting on, these days.'

Annie was on her feet like a shot.

'Mum! You're back so early. Tea's all prepared. I bumped into Charlie and so he –'

'I can see, Annie, I have got eyes. You go bumping into things a bit often, I'd say. I can hear very well too.'

'Charlie was showing me his bike,' Annie said, and she was blushing, but Charlie didn't know why.

He didn't understand why Annie's voice was shaking. He didn't understand why she looked so frightened. He'd seen his aunt cruel and unkind a hundred times, but she was being quite nice today, he thought, for her.

Annie had come round the table and put her arm around Charlie's shoulders. She was pressing into his skin with her fingertips and pushing him towards the back door.

'He's got to go now, or he'll be late back. I'll see him off,' and she opened the back door and nearly pushed him down the step.

'Go on, Charlie,' she said. 'Go quickly before you're in trouble.'

Pressing a kiss to his head, she shut the back door and he heard the key turn in the lock.

He cycled fast through the dark streets, only stopping on the bridge to catch his breath.

Still the river rushed, crazy and bloated, and it sounded like something from a dream, something he might wake with the noise of and wonder what it was he was afraid of.

'Where have you been?' his mother said when he came in, and she brushed her hands off on her apron in such a way that he knew she was angry. 'It's pitch dark now, and I told you to be home half an hour ago.'

'I met Bobby on the big bridge. We watched the water

and we went to the park. Sorry, Mum.'

But he didn't tell her about the visit with Annie, and he didn't tell her about Pam.

33

The snow that fell in December was dry and hard, skittering on the road like oatmeal, and flurrying in the wind till the ground was white. The first morning, Charlie raced out to see, to stand inside it. He gathered up a fistful, cosseted it in his palms to make a snowball. But it wouldn't stick. So he scooped armfuls and flung them this way and that, whooping and crying out.

Lydia stood beneath the porch, watching. Charlie called to her. His voice was small, as if the thick air had taken all the substance from it and left only the bare cartilage of sound.

Charlie called to her, and she wished he had a brother or sister, because she didn't want to join him now. She didn't want to play. But there was no one else and so she went out and scooped and flung with him till the time was pressing for breakfast.

The weather had sent Jean out early on her visits, worried that the roads might be blocked soon. Because of it, Lydia made Charlie leave his bike in the garage and walk to school in his wellingtons, his shoes wrapped up and bulking out his satchel. She watched him stomp sulkily down the drive, casting a look towards the garage as he went, and she bit back a laugh. But as he walked out of the gate and out of her sight, she wanted to run after him and gather him into herself and hold him tight.

It had been more than a month now and what had felt almost like playing at first had settled down to being real. Charlie treated this house like his home, and Lydia was beginning to. She left her books in the kitchen and put out the few pieces of her mother's china in the sitting-room cabinet. Her shoes were stacked beside Jean's in the cloakroom and her shopping basket hung on the wall in the pantry. She worked out where the draughts came from and went to, which windows stuck and how if you put the wireless on in the kitchen at the same time as the kettle, then the lights wobbled in the sitting room. Each night she shared Jean's bed and though she now locked her door as a precaution against discovery, Charlie had slept soundly every night since the thunderstorm.

Lydia finished the washing-up and checked her list. There was plenty to be getting on with before the morning surgery, but something in her resisted. She put the kettle on, rinsed the breakfast tea-leaves with boiling water and poured herself a pale cup of tea. She plugged in the bar heater, took the library book from the dresser and sat down at the kitchen table. Taking a deep breath and holding it, she opened the book at the first page and began to read:

When questioned later, the only unusual thing the ticket inspector noticed was that the carriage blinds were kept drawn for the whole journey. But he had given it no more thought than to check in his ticket book for payment taken. After all, it could have been a couple freshly wed, for all he knew, or a wealthy man with much on his mind who wished for no interruption. Besides the inspector had more important things to think on.

But had his knocks for luncheon, then dinner, then breakfast been answered, had the door been opened a little and had he glimpsed in, past the man guarding it, then he might have noticed that a woman slept on one of the lower bunks; slept, that is, for the entire journey – and perhaps the woman would have been glad of his notice, had she not been drugged to oblivion.

Light-headed, Lydia breathed out into the quiet kitchen till her lungs were empty. She loved it when the story hadn't even begun and anything might happen. She loved it when you didn't know yet what was important. She wanted to hold on to it, keep the feeling.

With that uncanny talent for finding what they want, the cat turned up and curled into her lap. For half an hour she read and then she put the book back on the dresser shelf, turned off the bar heater and went about her tasks.

If it had been the factory, she'd have been at her place for an hour by now, hands moving quickly, precisely, again and again, eyes focused, only lifting every now and then to snatch a glance at the clock whose arms, she always swore, moved more slowly than time itself.

Lydia had no regrets, but it had taken her by surprise to find that she missed her old home. All her life she'd lived on a terraced street, thick with other people and she was lonely in this big house surrounded by trees and hedges that didn't think to speak. She wondered how Annie was – she missed the girl – and whether Dot was right. But she was sure she'd have heard, even up here, if she was.

She missed her old work. Not the labour of it, not the monotony or the condescension. But she missed Dot and the others, the bustle and chunter of the place, and she missed leaving it behind at the end of the day. Twice she'd been to visit Dot and they'd sat and gossiped, but there was something awkward in the air between them that they couldn't get around, and when Dot asked her to come out on Friday with the girls, Lydia made an excuse.

Last night, undressing for bed, Lydia had stood and looked at herself naked in the wardrobe mirror. The air was so cold in her little room, it almost hurt to stand like that, still and upright. She noticed the slope of her shoulders and the slight line of colour where summer just marked her arms. Her feet with their high arches still surprised her. They were like a dancer's feet, she thought, not hers. She smoothed her hands across her stomach, marking the lines made there by her pregnancy, and ran the flat of her hand over the dark triangle between her legs. At last she stared at her face, staring back uncertain, wondering, had she changed to have fallen in love with another woman? Had something in her body altered to make her a monstrous creature?

She laughed. It was silly to think so. But still it was what people said about people like her. About the men, anyway. You never read stories in the newspaper about women. It was silly because the truth of it was simple. She'd fallen in love with a man once, and she'd fallen out of love with him, and now she'd fallen in love with a woman.

The night before she'd had a dream that lingered in her mind after she woke like a trace of old perfume on a dress not worn for a while. She was standing somewhere sunny and warm and next to her was Robert with Charlie, just a little boy, perched on his shoulders. Charlie sat with his chin dipped into his father's hair, eyes dropping. Robert had his shirt open and she thought how handsome he looked.

Waking, Lydia turned to look at the alarm clock. Her hand brushed Jean's breast and, though her mind was elsewhere, she felt her body tighten with desire. But the dream had left such a taste of sadness in her mouth, such bewildering grief for a man she didn't believe she had loved for years, that she left Jean sleeping and got up and sat alone for a while before it was time to wake Charlie.

The surgery was quiet when Lydia arrived later that morning, just a couple of people waiting in the porch, blowing on their fingers and stamping their feet. She opened up quickly, drawing the curtains in the waiting room, lighting the gas fire, tidying the magazines.

She was glad not to recognize the faces waiting today. No one from the factory. There had been a few and everyone had been friendly enough, but Lydia felt uncomfortable with it. Jean wasn't back yet from her calls. The snow would probably have slowed her, just as it must have kept some would-be patients at home today. In the consulting room, Lydia touched the wooden honeycomb on the mantelpiece like a votive charm. Charlie's find, that first time. Something to keep them safe. She thought how different things would have been if he hadn't noticed it, if he hadn't been the boy he was. She would never have met Jean, or only on the far side of a doctor's desk; she wouldn't be here now. But still she couldn't shake her sense of sadness and she busied herself to push the feeling away.

'We'll never be able to hold hands,' Lydia said. It was lunchtime and they were eating soup. 'Not anywhere anybody might see us.' She cupped her hands around the bowl for warmth. 'Not even in front of Charlie.'

'No,' Jean said, and she began to eat, spooning the soup carefully, methodically into her mouth. She kept her eyes on her bowl.

'I loved holding hands, when I first knew Robert,' Lydia said. 'Claiming him. I didn't know it would feel so important.'

She looked out through the window, at the white beyond.

'I used to love it,' she said again.

'We can't, you're right.' Jean's voice cut in sharply. 'We can't hold hands because you're a woman and I'm a woman. So if holding hands is that important, go back to him, why don't you?'

Lydia looked at her. She'd never heard Jean speak like

this; never seen her angry like this. Her mouth was pinched, her hands were moving in angles, setting down the soup spoon with a sharp *clat* on the bowl, picking up her knife as if she wanted to write something in the air with it, then putting it down and resting her hands in two fists on the chequered oilcloth.

'But I don't want to,' Lydia said. 'Even if I could, I'd never go back to him. I was just thinking, just trying to understand something, something I've been feeling,' and she bit her lip to stop her tears.

They ate their soup in silence and afterwards Jean washed the dishes and Lydia put the kettle on for a cup of coffee. Jean's habit. Leaning her elbows on the counter, she stared at the wall as she waited for it to boil. She noticed the bobbles in the plaster, and a stray hair caught fast somehow on the wall, but drifting in the kettle steam. She paused for the water to fall off the boil, as Jean had told her, and poured it into the coffee jug. She didn't look at Jean. She didn't speak.

Then she felt Jean's hands on her shoulders, felt her kiss the back of her head.

'I didn't mean all that,' Jean said finally. 'I don't like it either, having to keep all this secret all the time.' And then, in a softer voice, 'I'm sorry.'

She pressed her finger lightly to the back of Lydia's neck and, soft as soft, ran her nail down over her skin. The touch was so gentle and so insistent, it drew Lydia's breath from her and she gave out an involuntary 'oh'.

'What's more,' Jean went on, 'if you ever tried to go back to him, I promise you, I'd physically manacle you to one of the beehives to stop you, or something else equally dramatic.'

Lydia snorted with laughter and turned round and they kissed, Jean lifting her hand to cup the back of Lydia's head and keep her close.

Only when they sat down to drink the coffee, nearly cool in the jug by now, did Jean tell Lydia what was on her mind.

'I'm worried. About where all my patients, all those ill people, are going,' Jean said.

'What ill people?'

'The ones who should be coming in to my surgery, or calling me for home visits.'

Lydia frowned, perplexed. 'But isn't it a good thing if not so many people are getting ill?'

Jean drank down her coffee and poured another cup. She banged it on the table, coffee gathering in a small pool.

'I shouldn't have time to do this,' she said. 'I should be too busy. I should be snatching lunch and longing for a cup of coffee. Like last winter, and the one before.'

'Maybe people just aren't as ill,' Lydia said again.

Jean shook her head. 'I bumped into Dr Glover. He told me he's run off his feet. He said he's got quite a few new patients and he doesn't know why.' She stood up. 'I'll give Jim a call. It's time we went to the pub.'

As the snow settled in over the week, and the town grew accustomed to it, so Lydia felt her sadness settle into something if not comfortable exactly, then at least known and contained. People moved solidly through the icy streets, eyes to the ground, taking care with their footing, and in the same way Lydia moved about with this grief. She kept it steady in her, didn't let it veer off and unbalance her, and she made her own ballast against it. She cooked up rich, dense stews to keep the weather at bay and made buns and cakes to welcome Charlie and Jean back in out of it, and her grief lodged like a pebble next to her joy.

On the Friday, Dot came to the house. It was eight o' clock and she was dressed up: high heels, fresh stockings, a new dress, Lydia was sure. It was bitter outside and Lydia ushered her in before they had even greeted one another.

'Nearly broke my neck,' Dot said. 'Wrong shoes for the job.'

She looked around her, then fished in her handbag and took out a compact.

'How do my lips look?'

'What are you doing, Dot?' Lydia said. 'It's perishing outside and you're dressed for a dance.'

'I am off dancing. After this.'

'After what?'

'Come with me.'

'I can't, Dot.'

'Anyway, you could say hello how are you, instead of the third degree.'

Lydia brought Dot into the sitting room. For a minute they sat silent. Dot put her hands out to the fire to warm them, slipped off her shoes and stretched out her stockinged feet.

'Charlie's upstairs,' Lydia said. 'I'll call him down, to say hello.'

'What about the doctor?'

'She's out on her calls still. The snow,' Lydia said.

'Got it snug here.' Dot inclined her head to take in the whole room, the whole house.

'I'll get us a cup of tea.' Lydia made to get up.

'No, it's all right. Don't call Charlie. I'm not staying long,' Dot said.

'But it's the first time you've come to see me. Through the snow, and on a Friday night,' Lydia said. 'Any news? I was thinking about Annie earlier. I miss her. Any news?'

Dot shrugged. 'Maybe I was wrong on that. She looks quite perky and nothing showing, so far as I can see.'

Lydia nodded, sad for a moment; she couldn't say how.

'How's Charlie getting on?' Dot said, something over-solicitous in her tone, Lydia thought. 'Janie says he comes to school on a bicycle now. She says the other boys are green with envy.'

'He's fine. He seems fine.'

'And you're living here now.'

'I've got my own room, and Charlie has his. Got all his bits and pieces out on the shelves.' Lydia gave a small laugh. She wasn't comfortable, and it was partly this house, being so big and so different. But partly she didn't know why. 'You know how he likes to collect things.'

She looked down the sitting room where old oil portraits faced one another sternly. 'My ancestors,' Jean had told her, laughing. 'Got them to thank for something.' Lydia looked, not seeing them, and turned back to Dot.

'It's not a social call, is it?' she said.

She watched Dot duck her head, not meet her eye. She watched her look down at her feet. She looked down too. Dot's toenails were painted fresh red. They twitched uneasily, giving the game away, Lydia thought, whatever Dot liked to say.

'It's not, is it,' she said again. Not a question.

Dot took a breath, gearing herself, Lydia could see.

'I don't mind what this is,' Dot said. She looked at Lydia, her eyes pleading, like a dog.

'What what is?'

'I'm glad you're out of trouble,' Dot said. 'I mean, since Robert. Somewhere to live for you both that's safe and comfortable. Those floods last month, those houses down there, they're already damp and filthy and now the river flooding. I'm glad you're both safe up here, and not ended up in one of those, and you with your job as well.'

She paused and Lydia waited. Dot was coming to it now.

'Something's going round at the factory,' she said finally. 'Pam, of course.'

Dot looked at her knees, at her shoes, her stockings,

brushed at something on her shins. Lydia waited on. Dot took a deep breath.

'She's saying that Charlie Weekes can't find his mother in her own bed in that doctor's house, and it's not all she's saying. I've waited a while to see if it'd fizzle out, but it hasn't.'

She spoke it in a rush and it seemed to take all the wind from her, as if she were smaller after, shrunken with her bitter news.

It was only the smallest pause after Dot had spoken, a second or two, and then Lydia widened her eyes and laughed.

'How stupid,' she said. 'How typical of her.'

'Yes,' Dot said uncertainly, but her features brightened with Lydia's laughter, and then she smiled and looked relieved. 'Yes,' she said again. 'And everybody knows what she is, of course they do. But you know how it is about smoke and fire. People always think . . .' and she tailed off.

Lydia's thoughts rushed and crashed. What did Pam know? How? What about Robert? What did it mean? Somehow she kept her voice calm.

'She's always been a jealous one. Thinks Robert's God's gift. She won't like it that I'm all right without him.'

'I never could stand her,' Dot said. 'Now you're not there any more, I've a mind to give the old cow what-for next time she opens her mouth.'

'Don't,' Lydia said. 'Leastways, not for me. Best just let it die down.'

Soon after the two women said their goodbyes, with promises and pledges for the future. But if Dot's heart was lighter as she tottered into the snowy night on her good-time heels, Lydia couldn't say the same for herself as she stood under the porch light and waved.

34

The sky was murderous, the day Robert came for Charlie. So black that the mothers at the school gates were pinching up their eyes to spot their own when the school doors opened, then ushering them home with protective shoulders. The snow was melting fast and odds on a white Christmas were lengthening. In the playground the snowmen were defeated, dropped to their knees, eyes and noses slipped, lives ebbing away beneath them. The youngest children, let out first, skittered over treacherous pools of grey slush to their mothers. Beyond the mothers, Robert leaned against the railings, sucking on a cigarette, eyes flicking between pavement and school.

It was the last week before the holidays and Charlie's class, like all the others, was busy in rehearsal for the Christmas performance. Charlie and Bobby were in charge of the sound effects – a bell, a horn, the shut of a door, some nonchalant whistling – and when the bell went for the end of the day, they stayed in the classroom some minutes longer to practise. By the time they had their coats gathered, the playground was nearly empty again, the mothers departed, the older children stomping towards home.

Charlie wasn't thinking of anything very much right then, and certainly not his father. He didn't notice the storm clouds directly, but it crossed his mind that it might rain and he frowned because his mum still wouldn't let him ride his bike to school and so he had a long walk home. Then he grinned, because Dr Markham had promised a big tree to decorate with proper candles and the tree was coming today.

'Race yer,' he said and he was off already. Bobby, shouting a protest, was running to catch up. They both knew Bobby was the faster runner, but Charlie still took it for a victory whenever and however he won.

Charlie went flat out across the playground, not minding the slush, laughing at his friend who kept on calling out from behind, went flat out to be first to the gate, till he was there and somebody was blocking his way, so he stopped and waited for the man to move, but he didn't and Charlie began to say 'Excuse me,' and then he looked up.

While Charlie ran head-down across the playground, Robert had walked slowly towards the gate. His assumed nonchalance was gone now, replaced by an almost feral poise, and he didn't take his eyes off Charlie. He'd been in doubt a moment before. Had he come to the wrong school? Or had Lydia and that woman moved him to a different one? The playground was nearly empty, hundreds of bloody children had come out, and not his. But just as he thought he would go, Charlie appeared, with that daft friend of his.

'So, Charlie,' Robert said.

Charlie looked up at his father's face, pale with cold, eyes glancing over Charlie's shoulder and back again. Charlie glanced back. Bobby had stopped a yard short of the gate. Bobby looked at him, a waiting look because this was Charlie's next move and he, Bobby, was sticking clear.

Charlie was out of breath. Exultation still beat hard in his chest.

'It's the Christmas show and we're doing all the sounds, me and Bobby. We were practising,' he said. Then: 'Why're you here, Dad?'

He felt guilty, he didn't know why, with his dad here,

and saying about the show sounded silly, babyish, soon as it was off his tongue.

'Because you're coming back with me today.' And Robert turned and began walking, crossing the road at a slant, not looking, not waiting, just walking.

The two boys stood by the railings and perhaps if the rain hadn't started up, then they'd have stood there for ever. But it was so heavy, so fast, that it struck them into action, shrugging their shoulders like they saw men do against the weather, pulling on their caps.

'Will yer?' Bobby said, and Charlie nodded, because how could he not.

He had to run to keep up and not once did his dad turn for him, slow his pace, or tip his head to say, 'Come along.' Robert walked without looking and he pulled Charlie behind him, like a man pulls a cur on a leash, paying him no heed and sure that he'll follow.

They walked for twenty minutes; Robert ahead, hands in pockets, collar up, hat pulled low against the rain, the boy behind. Charlie followed his father's back and he marked the streets as they went by.

'That's Foley Street and left at the end and on some for the chip shop. Now that's Church Street with no church, and along Monkton Street . . .' and so on.

He marked the streets and he didn't think. Only his body moved. There was nothing surprising about this to him, about his father at the gate or feeling he'd done something wrong, or following behind with his thoughts in his feet and his head empty. It was what he had expected, some-where in his stomach, in his gut.

One hand in his trouser pocket, he cupped himself for warmth. After they had walked for fifteen minutes, his father stopped before a house with a brown door, unlocked it and went in, Charlie behind him.

They stood in a small front room, awkward, nearly

touching, in the space between the table and the settee end, and for a minute Robert was at a loss. They were here, his goal accomplished, his plan done, and it had been easy. But he hadn't paid much thought to what came after. It hadn't occurred to him that he needed to. That there would be Charlie stood bang up to him, holding his satchel and looking at the wall as if he'd never seen this man who was his father before. He hadn't planned for this, and he should have, because the one reliable thing about this boy was that he'd never behaved like a boy ought, never behaved like Robert when he was a lad, and here they were again.

'Put down the bloody satchel,' Robert said. 'I took an hour unpaid to get you here. Stop staring at the wall.'

Charlie dropped the satchel and looked down at his shoes. He looked up at the settee and the table and he didn't know what to do; he'd never known what to do to stop his father's rage.

Taking Charlie by the shoulders, Robert looked hard at his son. Checking for signs, he told himself, but the boy didn't look much different. Skinnier maybe, but he was always short on flesh. The way Charlie stood there like that, it could have been his mother. She could make him angry just by standing. Provoke him by it. Robert shook his head and looked away. This wasn't how he'd imagined it.

'Come on, and I'll show you round.'

Following behind, Charlie looked at a kitchen and a scullery; he stood on the back step and stared out into the December dark. He climbed the stairs and looked at the bathroom and a small back bedroom.

'This is yours,' Robert said in the kind of rough voice Charlie knew for affection. 'The bricks are just for now, till I get something better done.'

Charlie looked and saw a bed and a chair, a small table and a cupboard. At the foot of the bed, two short planks made a pair of shelves, blocked up with bricks at either end. He went and stood at the window.

Opposite, there was a woman bent over a sink, only the top of her head visible, and looking back towards him from an upstairs room, an old man who seemed to be adjusting his braces. Charlie shut his eyes and when he opened them, the old man was gone and the woman replaced at the sink by a young girl, arms reaching towards the taps.

'Am I staying here then?' Charlie said, without turning.

He heard his father move his feet about and then the sound of him fishing out a cigarette, the rush of a match flare and the long breath out.

'We'll have some fun, Charlie. I've written to your mother. I've said to send your clothes and that.'

Things warred in Charlie. Rage, fear, bewilderment. He turned round. His father leaned in the doorway, easy with his cigarette.

'Why?' Charlie said.

Robert shrugged.

'Why not?'

'But she was doing my costume tonight,' Charlie said. 'I've got to be there.'

'Well you won't be.'

It didn't make sense to Charlie, his dad just wanting him now. He didn't understand.

'But you haven't got time to look after me,' he said, and this was heading into different territory, and he didn't want to, but he couldn't avoid it.

'Won't be just me,' Robert said, his tobacco ease shifting, darkening. 'Will it?'

Charlie was backed up against the bed, the metal frame pressing into the backs of his knees. He was light-headed and his legs felt wobbly. His mum always had something for him to eat when he got in, some bread and jam, or a bun sometimes. He sat down on the bed, the springs jinging beneath him.

'Could I have something to eat, please?' he said.

'Won't be only me, will it,' Robert said again. 'Remember? And she'll be a good thing for you after what's been . . .' He stopped. 'She'll be back soon,' he went on, 'and the sooner you get used to each other, the better.'

Charlie put his hands down on the bed, pressed his arms into his sides. Carefully he looked round to the doorway, to his father planted there. If he tried to run, he'd never get through. He pictured his mother standing in the middle of the kitchen floor, waiting. He saw himself come through the door, and her relief and then her crossness.

'She'll be worried by now,' he said.

Charlie sensed, rather than saw Robert move and when his father spoke next, standing hard up by the bed, his voice was clenched in the back of his throat and coming down on Charlie like splinters of sound that cut lines over Charlie's flinching skin.

'It's about time you got some proper bringing-up. If she's worried, that's her lookout. She should have thought about that before she went and took up with the doctor.'

'No!' Charlie shouted, because this was too sharp. 'Dr Markham is kind and my friend and she's given Mum a job, too. Because of her we didn't have to be flooded like the others.'

Charlie stopped. His father would hit him now; and worse, he'd shut the door and leave Charlie in this strange room that wasn't his. He waited, but Robert made no move, only said again: 'She'll be back soon.' He took hold of Charlie's arm and pulled him to standing. 'Wash your face. She won't want to see you crying.'

In the bathroom Charlie splashed water on his face. He stood on tiptoe and his face appeared, climbing up from the white tiles, red-eyed like the troll beneath the bridge. It was strange to see his father's shaving brush and the little mirror he liked to use in its stand, because although there was no shaving brush at Dr Markham's, Charlie hadn't really thought of his father doing his shaving somewhere else. Beside the brush were pots that Charlie recognized as women's pots, because his mother had one of them just the same. Charlie shivered; the pots, sitting there neatly, minding their own business, brought something home.

Walking slowly down the steep stairs, down to his father, hands shrugged deep into his pockets, Charlie began to hum. He didn't know the song, it was just one of the tunes Dr Markham liked to play on the gramophone and it would come drifting up to Charlie as he drifted into sleep. He didn't really even know that he was humming now. His eyes were planted on the centre of the stairs where an orange pattern curved and thrust all the way down. Charlie hadn't noticed it on his way up. It was horrid, something that would climb and strangle you when you weren't looking, when you were just walking down the stairs. So he hummed the tune like a magic weapon and stepped carefully down.

He found his father sat at the table, waiting, and on a plate some buttered toast and beside it a glass of milk.

'Growing, boy, you must be hungry,' Robert said, and Charlie sat and drank.

It was the first time Robert had ever fed his son. He'd never even bought Charlie an ice cream from the van. Feeding children was a woman's job. He watched the boy.

'Better for that?' he said and Charlie, eyes on his plate, nodded.

He was tense, course he was. They hadn't seen each other for a few months and you get out of the habit of it, of being a father, or a son. They hadn't seen each other except for that time at Pam's when he'd wanted Charlie to be polite and nice, like he could be if he chose, and pleased to meet Irene, pleased that his dad was making a proper home again. But Charlie was so damn rude, and he'd had a look on him that was so like one of Lydia's, it had made Robert furious. Still, perhaps the women were right, perhaps he had been a bit heavy-handed that day.

Robert put his hand flat on the table, fingers out, and slowly slid it towards Charlie's plate till his fingertips nearly touched the rim. This was an old game. Two pieces of toast were still stacked, and Charlie was eating a third. Smoothly, like a snake in a nest, Robert caught a piece beneath his fingers and dragged it away across the table towards him. This was Charlie's cue to yell out, to stop him if he could, and sometimes Charlie won and sometimes Robert would slip the food in his mouth at the last minute, laughing at Charlie's rage.

Today he didn't mind about eating it or not, he just wanted to remind the boy that here they were, father and son again. But Charlie didn't yell out or grab, he only watched, and his eyes dropped to his plate again. So Robert put the toast back, though the smell of the melted butter had his taste buds going, and he got up and went to the window. He was jittery. Could do with a cigarette.

Remember what she said, he told himself. The boy's done nothing wrong.

'We'll have fun,' he said again to Charlie.

He listened out. He'd hear her before he could see her, that clip-clip her heels made.

He lit up. He hadn't been able to sit still, ever since Pam had told him. He shook his head. You couldn't undo what was done, but if he'd known then. Christ, if he'd known then, he'd have taken a torch to that doctor. He looked back to the table. Charlie was still eating, on to the last piece. He was quite a good-looking lad, skinny but decent proportions. Could be strong when he was bigger. Not badly co-ordinated either. Handy with a ball if he'd put his mind to it. Robert was determined, now he had him here and away from his mother, that Charlie would put his mind to it and less of his fancy notions.

The silence in the room was beginning to beat in his ears. He stared through the window, willed her to be back soon.

'She'll get the dinner on when she's in,' he said aloud, to break the pressure, 'so that'll do yer till then.'

That day going to the doctor's, he hadn't wanted to take Charlie in the first place. The boy only had a few bruises. It was Lydia had badgered him into it, what with him off for the day he couldn't remember why.

Robert knew Charlie had been in a fight. You didn't get bruises like that by colliding with some slippery steps, or whatever nonsense it was the boy had said. He'd been pleased, though he hadn't said so to Lydia, because it meant the lad was showing some spirit at last. But she'd gone on at him till he'd given in, so he'd taken Charlie to the doctor's surgery and the doctor was that bloody woman.

He should have seen it. He should have spotted what was going on. All that stuff about bees. She knew what she was up to from the start. She was too bloody nice. Wouldn't get a man behaving like that. Gave him the creeps. He should have got up and gone that day, taken Charlie with him. He should have punched her in the face, woman and all.

Charlie had finished the toast and was watching his father, pale-faced and blinking.

'Well?' Robert said. 'Long time no see. Tell me what you've been up to. How's that pretty teacher been getting on, then?'

But he didn't hear the reply because he was thinking now. Once Irene was in and could watch the boy, he must be on with the next bit of the plan.

They'd talked it through, Pam and him, guessing at what Lydia would do, where she'd go when Charlie didn't come home, and what they needed to say to keep her off.

'Better if she hears it from me,' Pam said. 'I'll keep my cool, make sure she understands right.'

So he needed to be over to Pam's and tell her he'd done it. Because, whatever he'd said to Charlie, he hadn't written Lydia any kind of letter, and when she couldn't find the boy anywhere else, that was where she'd end up. Then she'd get it from Pam, good as if he'd told her, perverted bitch. If she was worried meantime, it was less than she deserved.

Charlie listened to his breath, the tiny whistle as he breathed in, felt the pull through his nose and down his throat. His hands were heavy on his lap, so heavy now that he couldn't imagine lifting them, and they were fused with his legs. He couldn't feel where his legs ended and his hands began, or the other way around. On the other side of the room, his father looked out of the window and smoked cigarettes and muttered. His father had asked him about a teacher, but he hadn't listened to the answer, so Charlie stopped speaking mid-sentence and since then he'd sat like this, perfectly still.

When the woman came in, Charlie watched his father kiss her full on the mouth and put his hand on her bottom. She had on high heels like his mother wore to go out on a Friday and a clingy dress that meant you could see the shape of her very well. Her bosom looked like two cones, but Charlie had it on authority from Bobby that that wasn't natural; it was the brassière that made them like that.

Charlie saw at once why his father put his hand on her bottom, what with the bosom and heels and the very red lipstick, and other things about her that Charlie recognized.

He didn't know how he recognized them, but he did. He felt them in his bones, though if anybody had asked him, he couldn't have described what they were. Charlie saw that she had more of these things he couldn't name than his mother did, and he hated his father for choosing her instead.

'Irene, listen,' he heard his father say, pulling her to the window. She turned and smiled towards Charlie at the same time as his father took her by the arm, and Charlie stared down again, at the plate with its crumbs. Their voices murmured for a minute or two, and then they stopped and the woman walked over to Charlie and kneeled by his chair.

'Pleased to meet you. My name's Irene.' She paused, but Charlie didn't say anything, and then she went on. 'Robert's got to go out for a bit, and I'm going to cook tea. Sausages. You'll like sausages, won't you?'

Charlie looked over at his father. He was putting on his coat, finding his hat, and as hard as Charlie looked at him, he couldn't get his father to look his way. Only at the last, before he went out, did Robert turn to his son.

'It's all for you, this,' he said. 'So you do as she says.'

'He'll be good as gold,' the woman said, and Charlie could tell that any minute now she'd pat him on the head. 'We'll have a nice time, getting to know each other.'

Then with a last scowl at his son, Robert was gone. Charlie sat on the chair and, quiet in his head, he hummed his tune again and tried not to wonder.

35

Neither of them spoke in the car. Jean drove slowly and hesitantly, not because the road was icy, though it was, or the car in some way failing. But because the future had become fearful and it was hard, driving into it. The streets were empty and glistened in the headlamps with a million pricks of ice where the day's melt had frozen again under the stars. Beside her, Lydia sat very still.

Jean stopped the car a street away, as they had decided, and with a last look to her, Lydia got out.

She walked the length of the street as though she had never walked it before, past the waste ground and past all the houses with their eyes curtained against the cold. For a minute she stood in front of Pam's door, then she lifted the knocker.

Pam didn't say a word. She only stood, arms folded over her flowered bosom, looking down on Lydia from her step above.

'I'm looking for Charlie,' Lydia said in a quiet voice.

'You would be.'

'When he wasn't home from school,' Lydia said. She waited. 'Bobby told me –' she said, but Pam interrupted.

'Bobby?' her voice sharp as acid.

Lydia went on. 'He said Robert had come to the school gates and taken Charlie with him?' her voice rising to an appeal, despite herself.

'Well, since you know it from Bobby, I don't see why you're here asking.' Pam turned away, back towards the inside. 'Excuse me, Lydia,' she said, spitting the name as if it tasted bitter. 'I've got better things to be doing than –'

'Where is he, Pam?' Lydia's voice wasn't loud, but it cut through the street air, and it made Pam glance back. 'Where is he?' Lydia said again, before Pam could shut the door on her. 'Where is he?' and her voice was getting louder now.

'Stop it!' Pam said. 'For God's sake. The whole street.' With another glance out, she gestured her in, pressing flat to the wall as Lydia passed, as if fearful of catching something.

Lydia stood at the end of the hall, neither staying nor leaving. Above her, the stairs rose. On her left, the door was open, but she didn't go in.

'He's not here,' Pam said.

The smell of dinner was thick and Lydia's gorge rose. She pictured what she'd left. They'd put the tree up in the living room and Sarah was there with the girls, making paper chains and cutting out stars. Leaving, she'd walked outside through square pools of light that fell from the windows. The house was like a beacon.

'Don't turn any of them off before we're back,' she'd said. 'I want it lit up like Blackpool pier.'

The two women faced each other off in the narrow hall.

'Where's Robert and where's my son?' Lydia said.

'He's holding on to Charlie now. I knew it years ago. You don't deserve to be a mother.'

The words cut a thin line through Lydia, a wound made but not yet properly felt.

'No.'

'Yes. His girlfriend, and she'll be his wife soon enough, she's getting him his tea tonight.'

Lydia shook her head. 'His supper's ready and he's been out long enough. I want him home now.'

'She's a nice girl,' Pam said, as though Lydia hadn't spoken. 'A secretary. I expect they're getting on like a house on fire.'

'His supper's ready at home,' Lydia said. 'I need to get him before it's spoilt.'

'Supper is it now?' Pam said. 'Too good for tea, are we? You always did have your airs.'

Turning her head away in frustration, Lydia looked down at the tiled floor, its simple geometry a moment's relief. She looked up at Pam.

'But Robert doesn't even like him,' she said. 'He left, he walked out. On Charlie, too.'

Pam leaned in at Lydia, her mouth distorted. 'Now we know why, don't we?' she said, her eyes chasing up and down.

'I don't know what you're talking about,' Lydia said. 'And I need Charlie back. I need him home.'

'It was him that told us. Him that let on what you get up to with that doctor. We should have guessed, her inviting you in to her home, giving you your cosy job.'

'Charlie?'

'It's disgusting.'

'What did he tell you?'

'So Robert's taken him now and don't you dare go near him.'

'Tell me where he lives. I need to know where Charlie is.'

'He'll get lawyers if you go near. Stand up in court for all the world to hear. Then you'll never clap eyes on Charlie again.'

Lydia didn't know what to do with her hands, so they held each other in front of her. Or her voice, so it stayed inside her mouth, a small sound coming out that didn't sound like her. Didn't know what to do with her eyes, which kept on looking at things. Through the doorway the table laid for two people, knives and forks and cups and saucers, Pam's work pinafore hanging on a chair. The basket with knitting, needles spiking up like a V for victory.

But the objects didn't make sense. She saw the clock on the mantelpiece and the mirror above, and in the mirror there was a face looking back, bleached under the yellowed light, a face that was staring at something she couldn't begin to fit in with tables and chairs and tea laid out.

'Pam, please,' Lydia said, but Pam set her lips hard and she pinched her eyes till they were pebbles in her face. Then something broke inside Lydia and such an ache rose in her chest, such a heat beneath her skin that she cried out in fury, in grief. She cried out of a pain that was new and raw, the edges still torn and ragged, and yet such a near familiar, as if it had been there all the time, just not felt till now.

'I need my son. Tell me where he is. I'm his mother.' And in the mirror she saw the bleached face crack.

Pam waited till Lydia turned to her. Then shook her head, slowly and carefully, and pointed back to the front door.

'Our tea's ready,' she said. 'Go back to your doctor. You're lucky it's not worse for you. But I shouldn't try anything. There's enough of us know about you now. We'd only have to call in the authorities and it would be horrid, that, for Charlie. Who knows what would happen to you.'

Lydia walked fast away from the house, everything in her held tight because she would not, must not cry. Not here, not in this street, not before other people's doors and windows. Jean was waiting for her a street away. She must get there, to the car. She was nearly to the top of the street when she heard the footsteps, running, coming nearer.

'Charlie!' She shouted his name as she turned, even as she heard, even as she knew already that it was not him.

But the figure that came to her and took her hand and held it was Annie, muffled up in a big coat and a scarf and a hat.

'I couldn't come downstairs,' she said. 'I couldn't see you there. But I heard. I heard what she said.'

'Do you know where he is?' Lydia said, but Annie shook her head.

'They don't trust me. They've told Irene – that's Robert's, you know – they've told her not to tell either.'

'She'll punish you, Annie. If she finds out you've come after me.'

'I don't care. There's more to worry about in the world than my mother.' Annie stepped back as if she'd said too much. 'I'll come and tell you, soon as I find anything out,' she said, and they stayed standing like that at the top of the street, till the sound of other voices coming towards them broke in.

'You'd better go back,' Lydia said, putting her hand on Annie's darkened cheek, and they held each other tight. Something broke through the thick of Lydia's mind and she remembered about Annie and what Dot had said. She wondered what Pam knew of her own daughter right now and would have asked her then, before grief pushed the thought away. But, as if guessing at it, Annie slipped from her arms and was gone into the night.

'Careful, love,' Lydia whispered after her, before turning back into her own, hard darkness.

36

The woman called Irene was still kneeling by Charlie's chair when his dad closed the door. After she got up, she had to brush off bits from the floor where they had stuck into her knees.

'Nice tune,' she said.

He didn't want to speak to her, so he went on humming, and she started cooking his tea in the kitchen.

His mum would be making his tea now. She would be asking him to do things, not letting him sit here and hum. He wondered if she was worried, or if she knew where he was. He wondered if she was missing him. He hummed harder.

'Charlie?' Irene said his name like a question. She was standing in the doorway, but he didn't turn his head, or stop humming. 'Do you like ketchup?'

Why did his dad have to go out? He'd come to get him at the school railings. He'd brought him here.

Irene gave him her handkerchief. She put it down on the table and she didn't ask him anything.

Charlie ate the sausages, the mashed potato and peas. Irene sat nearly opposite him and read a book. It was called *Appointment with Romance*.

She took his plate when he had finished and brought in a bowl of yellow jelly. Pineapple. It had a cherry on top and she made a noise as she put it down like *dah-dum*.

Then she went and lit the fire, kicked off her shoes and sat with her back against the settee. Charlie sat on at the table with the jelly before him and he hummed again in his head.

He liked jelly. He liked red best, but he liked yellow too. His mother had a mould like a rabbit and, when he was little, his dad would cut the nose off and laugh.

'You don't have to eat it,' Irene said. She was watching him.

'I only like it as a rabbit,' he said, which they both knew wasn't true.

She shrugged. 'Weren't any rabbits about this morning.'

He could see her out the corner of his eye. She sat doing nothing. She wasn't like his mother.

She'd left her book on the table. He looked at the picture on the cover. A woman with blond hair stood outside a big house. She had her hands behind her head. She looked a bit surprised. Behind her was a man in a dark suit with ripply hair. He was smoking a pipe and he didn't look surprised at all.

Charlie could smell the jelly. It smelled the same as the pineapple cubes from the sweet shop that left your tongue rough. He lifted the cherry off and ate it slowly. The sweetness made his mouth water. He didn't think about his mother, or the Christmas tree with its real candles. He didn't think at all.

'You must be getting freezing over there.' Her voice surprised him; he didn't know where he had been. 'You could come here, nearer the fire,' she said.

He sat at one corner of the settee. The fire had settled in and he wondered that she wasn't too hot. Her feet at least. She had her legs stretched out in front.

'When will my dad be back?'

'Look,' she said. 'Do you see these?'

He could see the coloured varnish on her stockinged toes.

'Wages of sin,' she said.

'My mum does that too. But only in the summer,' he said, like an accusation.

'No. These,' she said, pointing, and then he saw that she had lumps on each of her feet, like big knuckles grown on below her big toe. He looked at her face for an answer.

'It's the pointy toes,' she said. 'My shoes.'

'Does it hurt?'

She nodded.

'Why don't you wear different shoes?'

She shook her head.

'I wouldn't have the job without the shoes. You'll understand when you're older.'

But he understood already. The lumps on her feet and her pointy bosom. He bet his dad didn't mind about her feet.

When she got up, he eased down and sat as she had done, back against the settee, feet towards the fire. She came back with a bar of chocolate and a pack of cards.

'Don't tell your dad. We're going to eat the whole lot.'

Charlie knew what she was doing, and he ate the chocolate.

Irene could shuffle cards. Not like his mum or his dad did, but in a hard flick and then a long sweep.

'I'll teach you blackjack,' she said. 'It's a card game they play in the casinos.'

So she taught him and he counted numbers, filling his head till he had won a pile of matches. Then he lit them, end to end, nearly half a box, till the air was dense with phosphorous.

Charlie was asleep when the door handle turned, the flutter in his eyelids the only sign of his flailing dreams.

It was late. Robert stepped with the exaggerated steps of a drunken man.

'Bloody dark,' he muttered. 'Black bloody dark.'

Drawing close to the bed, he sank to his knees, patting the shadow of his son, murmuring densely.

Awake suddenly, Charlie lay still as stone in the vinegary dark. He felt hands on his hair, a heavy palm on his brow. He froze. Then he remembered where he was and he waited.

'Charlie,' Robert said. And again. 'Charlie. You listening?' His breath was rich with beer. Charlie moved his head. 'You listening?' Charlie waited.

'Good thing you're a boy. No trouble like the girls. Like Annie. Bloody trouble.'

Charlie felt his father's hand on his cheek, smelled it.

'You do as I say then.' Robert tapped a finger, bored it into the sleep-sodden boy. 'You do exactly as I say and we'll all be happy families.'

In the morning it was Irene's knock on the door that woke him. He dressed and went downstairs. Irene was in the kitchen.

'Where's my dad?' he said.

'Gone already. To work.'

'But he wasn't here last night either.'

'No, he wasn't, was he.' Her voice was snappy. 'Quick now, because I have to go to work soon.'

So he sat and ate his breakfast and thought how in an hour he would be at his desk. He wondered what his mother was thinking, and what to tell Bobby. He wondered why she hadn't come to find him, and if he could go back home today, because he didn't want to make his father angry, especially not with his mother.

Irene sat down at the table. He could smell her perfume. He looked at her. She was like the woman on the book, all the lines – her lips, her hair, her blouse – drawn just so.

'Your father left a message for you,' she said.

He waited. She looked at her nails, ran her fingertip round the curve of one. He felt his heart beat in his chest.

'He's got something to say to you, but he's left me to say it.'

She paused and looked back at him and he saw that she didn't want to.

'You have to go to work,' he said at last, and she nodded, as if there were an agreement then between them.

'He says that you'll live here now and that you're not to speak to your mother.'

He didn't understand. She was his mother. Why would he not speak to her, or be with her?

'Do you understand, Charlie?'

He couldn't answer.

'Charlie. Listen. You have to understand, or he'll call in the police and you'll go to court and a judge will stop you then. I know. He told me. If she comes to the school, you're not to speak to her. Or to the doctor.'

The words were like darkness. He didn't understand. They were too heavy. They hurt him. When he spoke, his voice sounded small and thin.

'Is he going to be at the school again?' he said. It wasn't the question he wanted to ask, but he couldn't ask that.

When he turned to look at Irene, she turned away from him and spoke to the wall.

'You're to come back here on your own today,' she said.

37

It was Saturday; it was four days. She stood, as if waiting for a third person to join them, or for something to happen; something to change what was. Then she sat, touching her fingers to her forehead, like a summons to herself.

'Each day I think it mustn't be true. All through the day I have that thought,' she said.

'Tell me,' Jim said. 'Did you see this coming? Any of it?'

Beyond their closed door, the little girls argued about something.

'Does it matter now?' Jean looked at the ceiling and the floor. 'Are you asking this as a friend or as a lawyer?'

Jim was still in his chair, waiting.

'No. I didn't,' Jean said finally.

Children's voices rose, pipsqueaky, imperative and then faded again.

'It's so quiet in the house. But differently. God knows, I was used to quiet. I lived alone for long enough. But Charlie.'

This last was nearly a cry. There was a weight in her throat. She got up again, walked to the window. The garden looked clean and empty. Ground, tree, hedge, sky. This early, the grass still shone like glass.

'I don't know what it's like to be a mother. But I am full of rage, Jim.'

'And Lydia?'

'It was the Christmas performance at his school yesterday.'

'She didn't go?'

'Imagine her seeing him there, no more than a few feet away. Imagine him seeing her. Then the leaving?'

Jim nodded. 'So she didn't go.'

'I had to stop her. She knew the truth of how it would be, but she couldn't stand it.'

'Literally? You physically stopped her?'

Jean looked again at the garden. The winter marked out the separateness of things. Knocked everything back into itself; told the tree to stand firm, drop its leaves and draw its sap in.

'You know Robert's sister, her sister-in-law, has been spreading gossip?'

'Sarah told me.'

'Lydia told me she dreamed she was at the school and everyone knew, mothers, teachers, children; everyone knew what Pam had said.'

'Do they?'

'Give me one of your cigarettes,' she said.

Jim opened the silver box on the table and she waited, sitting down in the chair at the window, lifting her head to watch. He had a ritual with this box, more elaborate than his functional flick and shake of a packet, and right now it calmed her.

'I can imagine you doing this in your office. Reassuring a client,' she said. She nodded to him to light it for her; he drew delicately and passed the cigarette over.

She should not have mentioned Lydia's dream. It had not been as she had told it. Lydia had woken shaking, her hands about her head, and when Jean held her, she had cried out in fear before her dreaming self retreated, and she'd opened her eyes.

'We were on the stage,' Lydia told her. 'We were performing and all the audience knew about us. We didn't know it at first and so we sang a song, I think. But they began to murmur, then shout.'

She'd broken into sobs and Jean was glad, because she didn't want to hear any more.

Jim drum-rolled his fingers on the coffee table. He lit a cigarette from the box for himself, but quickly, with no grace.

'You've spoken to your colleague,' Jean said. 'The divorce man.'

Jim drew on his cigarette again.

'And?' she said. 'Come on, Jim. If it had been good news, you'd have said already.'

His eyes dropped. He wouldn't hold her gaze. His voice was deeper than usual.

'You've said that Robert is living with his girlfriend, like a married couple?' he said.

'Yes.'

He looked up. 'In the same house?' She nodded quickly. 'Don't you think . . .' he said.

'Think what?'

'I'm sure she's being kind to Charlie,' he said.

'What are you telling me?' Jean's voice was calm, expectant.

'Well . . .' Jim was hesitant. 'There's already talk. You know, Lydia knows, how damaging that could be. You've said so yourself. She's having dreams about it. Perhaps it's not fair to drag him through it. It's not his fault. The way children are with each other. It could destroy his childhood.'

'Strong words. Drag. Fault. Destroy.'

He went on. 'Maybe it would be better for him to be in a home with a man and a woman.'

So he'd said it. She was relieved, in one way. Better to know what he thought.

'You haven't met Charlie's father,' she said, keeping her voice neutral.

'Better a father than no father.'

'And no mother?'

'Jean.'

She could hear his voice, appealing, appeasing. A dozen thoughts went through her mind. That she cared about Charlie. That his father didn't. That he'd only taken Charlie to get at Lydia. That her heart – hers, Jean's – was breaking. That if Jim saw Lydia now, he would think differently. But this last thought made her break her silence, because perhaps he would still think the same.

'Tell me what your colleague said.' And she turned away to end the other conversation.

Jim told her at last. That no judge would give Lydia custody of Charlie with such allegations made. That public feeling would be against her, or worse.

'Worse? What could be worse than a judge who knows nothing, who cares less, leaving a child with such a father?'

'I understand what you're saying, but you're too partisan, Jean. You've only got one side. Only got Lydia's account of things.'

'What did your colleague mean, worse?' she challenged him.

Jim was speaking to her now as if she were a child.

'People who don't know Lydia could make life very difficult for her. For you too. Ugly. Especially if they gang up. Crowds do things that people as individuals wouldn't.'

'All because I've given her room in my house to live? And Charlie?'

He shrugged. 'That's what you say. But Pam will say differently. So will Robert.'

Above them again they heard the noise of children, and a lower voice that was Sarah's.

'You're my oldest friend,' she said.

'My colleague gave me some advice on how she should conduct herself. I could have given it to you myself, but I think you might listen harder if it comes from another solicitor and not from me. Shall I tell you?'

'All right, and then let's leave this, please, because I can't . . . Let's make coffee and take the girls into the garden to run about as if nothing is wrong.'

'She should do all she can to hide any untoward affection . . .' Jim paused and she glanced round at him. He went on. 'That is what he said. Any untoward affection for you,' he went on in a tone that dared her to deny, or affirm, 'and, once the dust has settled, she should appeal to the father's kindness of heart.'

'His kindness of heart. Any more?'

'What?'

'Did he have any more advice for us?'

'For us?'

'Appeal to Robert's kindness. Maybe Lydia will try such a thing, but the man has no kindness of heart. We've done nothing wrong. Nothing I believe to be wrong. Meeting Lydia and Charlie. It is the best thing that has happened to me. Better even than not marrying you.'

Jim laughed at that, or at least he tried to, which was enough to let them leave the room for now.

38

There were times in the day when Lydia knew she was drowning. Some she could anticipate. First thing in the morning, or the time in the evening when she should be tucking him in. Others came upon her unexpectedly, catching at her heels, tugging the sand from under her feet. These times came like the seventh wave, which she could never see, even as Charlie counted it in for her on the beach those months back. But however the waters came, they swept over her, pressing the air from her lungs and filling her eyes with salt water till the world was a blur and each breath took her further under.

She started to wake in the night, sure she was hearing him, and just as she had done when he was tiny, she would be out of bed before her dream had even broken. Then, pulling her dressing gown around her shoulders, careful even in her half-sleep to come out of her door and not Jean's, she'd be halfway across the landing before she remembered.

He was not there, his sheets were smooth and tucked, his curtains open to the night.

It was only days. She could still count them on her two hands. A child learning to count could do the same. But she had never counted time so hard. She carried a photo with her in her apron pocket, or between the pages of a book she couldn't read. Jean had taken it not long ago. Charlie grinning, one tooth half-grown, his socks exasperatingly adrift, which made her hurt more than she could say.

Dot came again and they sat before the fire. Jean offered whisky. Behind them, the Christmas tree rose to the ceiling, painted angels with painted smiles, dull baubles turning slowly in the still air; on the floor the box of candles.

'The factory is full of talk,' Dot said. 'Rumours flying.'

'Is it about us?' Jean said.

'Some of it.' Dot looked at Jean, as if for confirmation of something, and Jean nodded slightly. 'Some of it is.'

'Tell us then,' Lydia said.

Dot hesitated.

'You came here because you had things you could tell us, Dot. Say them, or leave us be.'

'I'm your friend, Lydia. I came here because I'm your friend.'

'He has my child. That's all I care about.'

'Nothing can be worse than now, anyway,' Jean said.

Dot sipped the whisky, which she was not used to.

'Burning your throat?' Jean said.

But she saw courage flare in Dot's cheeks and then Dot spoke, steadily and evenly.

'It's being said that Robert knew there was something wrong. Before he ever met Irene.'

'Irene, is she,' Lydia said. 'Irene.'

'She's called Irene Meadows.'

'Irene,' Lydia said again. 'The name my boy, my son is saying. Now, while you talk here, Charlie is saying, "Irene".'

'What is she like?' Jean said.

'She's young. She works in an office.'

Lydia nodded, impatient. 'We know that. We know she is young. How would she not be young? But what is she like? With Charlie?'

'I've never met her,' Dot said. 'I don't know. But I've heard that she is kind.'

Lydia looked up to the ceiling to hold away the tears.

'Don't make her kind,' she said, her voice crying though her eyes were still dry. 'Don't make her kind.' She looked at Jean. 'Should she be kind?'

'It's better that she is. For Charlie. Until he returns.'

'I'd best go,' Dot said. 'I'll come another time. Tomorrow even. Or to the surgery –'

But Lydia pleaded. 'I'm sorry. Please don't go.' The tears she had kept at bay fell down her face.

'It's gossip, what I hear in the factory,' Dot said. 'You know that.'

'But it's all that anybody knows,' Jean said. 'So it might as well be true.'

'Please don't talk of Charlie any more,' Lydia said. 'Tell us what else is being said.'

But she could not sit and hear of the rumours that had spread like Chinese whispers around the cafeteria.

'I will go to bed,' she said. 'Tell it to Jean, so that we know.'

Lydia lay as still as a stone between the sheets so as not to feel too much. Her body had lost its way this last week, not knowing when it was hungry, or tired, or cold. She lay exhausted, bone-tired, but awake. This end of the night she could sleep, if she could only still her mind. So she did what she had learned to do when she was much younger and her head was buzzy, not with grief, like now, but with dancing and possibility.

She pictured an empty room, no colour on the walls, no window, nothing to look at except the small, plain table in its centre. On the table, a tin can, with no label. Once her mind had seen the can, she held it there. She would let her mind look nowhere else in this imagined room, would not let it leave.

Just beyond the table, just behind the dull walls and the

empty room, a terrible tide of feelings surged and sank, but she kept her eyes on the can; she would not look away. And at last, her thoughts beached, she slept.

It was still deep dark when she woke and her limbs felt drugged and heavy; her hair was across her face like weed. She had been dreaming. It was summer, not winter, and she was laughing with Charlie in their kitchen, which was bright with sunlight, and there were tiles on the floor and rough plaster on the wall, and outside, beyond, was the sea.

For a minute the dream was warm on her skin and then, just as certainly, it was ashes and she cried out. No words, only sound.

She cried out and Jean was there, but she had no answer for her pain. She could only hold her.

She held her, and it was seconds or minutes or hours that they lay like that. It was time out of mind. They lay so long, so still, that Lydia no longer knew where her body ended and Jean's began. Until at last she sought Jean out, hungry now, desperate for something, for another kind of falling, and Jean made love to her in that dark bed so that she cried out again, hard and loud, and covered Jean's wrist with her hand, holding her close inside, as if never to let her go.

'Did we do something very wrong?' Lydia whispered.

'No,' Jean said. 'Not wrong at all.' But when Lydia slept again, her body washed through with fatigue, Jean lay awake, wondering if indeed she had done something very wrong to this woman she so loved.

In the end, Jean went downstairs. It was late and it was cold. The kind of cold that has no time for pain. She sat before the last warmth of the fire. Christmas was in two days. She had discussed and organized with Sarah while they decorated the tree, and they would do what they could. But no one pretended that all this was bearable.

She had been down there for perhaps ten minutes when the bell rang fiercely. It surprised her. It had been a while since she had been called out in the night. She went to it quickly. Lydia was asleep upstairs, and the bell in the bedroom was disconnected, but Jean had watched her. Her sleep was fitful and would need little to undo it.

It was different when people called at night. They rang harder, as if the dark made things more imperative. Fears, needs, actions. If you didn't answer the door directly, they rang again, and then they knocked, banging their knuckles hard on the wood so that the hall echoed with their urgency.

Jean didn't recognize the woman standing in the porch.

'Dr Markham,' the woman said.

'Can I help you?'

The moon cut a thin curve in the sky and the night was very black. It must have been an awkward walk from wherever she had come. Though she wore a coat, she had no hat, no gloves, no scarf.

The woman seemed reluctant to speak.

'Do you want to come in? It's very cold,' Jean said.

The woman nodded slightly, so Jean shut the door behind them and they stood in the hall.

Still the woman hesitated, though Jean could see agitation in her movements, fear in her face. She saw her look around, more than a glance, as though searching for something.

'Is somebody ill?' Jean said, and as if called back to herself, the woman nodded.

'My daughter,' she said. 'She's very ill.'

'Who is her doctor?' Jean said. There was something familiar about this woman's face, but Jean knew she was not a patient of hers. 'It would be helpful –'

The woman cut her off. 'It must be you,' she said.

Jean leaned against the table. She was exhausted. She

didn't want to hear of anybody else's difficulties. She didn't want to see anybody else's difficulties.

'It must be me,' she repeated. She was too tired to help this woman over whatever trouble lay in the saying. So, not unkindly, she waited.

The woman looked down at the ground and then along the tiled floor till her gaze met Jean's shoes.

'My daughter is bleeding,' she said, lifting her head, looking Jean full in the face.

'Severely?'

The woman nodded.

'Then you should take her to the hospital at once,' Jean said. 'Phone for an ambulance. You can do so from here, if you want to.'

But the woman shook her head. 'I can't.'

'Why have you come to me? I don't know you,' Jean said.

The woman stumbled slightly and put out a hand. She was very pale.

'Sit down,' Jean said and, when the woman had sat down, 'Tell me your name.'

'Mrs Cranmer,' the woman said. 'Pam Cranmer.'

It was no more than a minute till she spoke again, but there was a girl bleeding the other side of the town and time had changed its texture. Into the silence, Jean said 'Annie,' and she saw Pam's nod. She knew immediately that whatever she did next, she would wish she had done differently.

'You know that I can't help you,' she said at last. She stayed standing. 'You must take her to the hospital.'

Pam stayed silent.

'When did it start? How soon after?' Jean said.

'About fifteen minutes after the woman had gone. I went to find her. But she wouldn't come back.'

Jean looked at her watch. 'It's eleven forty-five now. How long has she been bleeding for?'

'It's an hour.'

Pam sat on the chair with her hands on her lap. She sat straight and she breathed evenly; her colour returned a little. She answered the questions in a neutral, quiet voice. But she was brittle, as if she would just crack.

Jean looked at her, and then she thought of Lydia, sleeping above them. She thought of what this woman had done.

'What did the woman use?'

Pam's head jerked back, as though Jean had struck her. 'What?' she said.

Jean turned away, impatient. 'What did she use? Knitting needles?'

'I don't know,' Pam said.

Now rage broke in Jean, cuffing her hard, swinging blows to her abdomen and she turned to Pam, came close to her, so that she could smell the wool in her coat and the hairspray under the headscarf. She spoke in a voice not her own, intimate and brutal.

'You don't know? Where were you?'

'I didn't watch.'

'But you like sharp things. You like seeing what they do. You like poking things in and scraping them about and making people bleed.'

She remembered how Lydia had sat in the kitchen earlier that day, answering when she was spoken to, her fingers straying again and again to the photograph on the chair arm beside her, so that its corners were rubbed to grey paper now.

Pam's hands turned on her lap, squirming like blind things. Jean would pick her up and snap her.

'Maybe she used a crochet hook to try and get it all out. Always popular. Every home has one. Do you like that thought? Your daughter, your precious daughter and a crochet hook?'

Pam was turning her head to this side and that, her eyes closed, her breath coming in short gasps.

'Or maybe a pickle spoon. Then you don't have to get your fingers dirty on the jar.'

Picking up her doctor's bag, she dropped it at Pam's feet.

'You've taken everything you can away from us. Taken Lydia's son from her. Destroyed my practice. Now, now you want me to pick this bag up, put on my hat and coat, and come in the night to see your daughter. I would be struck off for this. I could go to prison.'

'Lydia loves her.'

Pam's voice was a blade in the air. It stopped Jean, held her on a point. She stepped away, back towards the wall. From somewhere Pam had gathered this voice, this sharp, thin force.

'She's always encouraged her. Annie wants to be a teacher. She won't be able to if –'

'But it's you that has stopped her. Lydia has told me. At every turn.'

'Lydia never understood. My parents died, I brought my brother up. My husband died, I brought up my children. I've worked in that factory all my life.'

'And Annie shouldn't want something else?' Jean shook her head. The conversation was mad. A girl was bleeding, maybe to death.

'I'm calling the ambulance,' she said.

'Please.' Pam was on her feet as she cried, reaching for Jean's sleeve. 'For my child,' she said.

'No!' Jean shouted and it echoed off the tiled floor and the cold walls. She listened, but there was no noise from above.

She left the hall and walked into the kitchen. Muted light streaked beyond her, washing the floor, casting her shadow out ahead. She burned with rage, her body coiled with it, her muscles were sprung tight. She turned in the empty room, and turned again, as though there were something to be found in there that would help her. But the room gave nothing away and, if only for the cool of it, she went to the sink and turned on the tap. The water fell over her hands, drawing her down, calming her. She stood, and something opened in her mind. An idea. Perhaps a choice.

The water ran over her knuckles, her fingers. She turned her hands over and it pooled in her palms, running down her arms, wetting her sleeves. She stood very still and waited, ordering down her rage, ordering down her battering self, to draw out this timid thought. On the draining board she saw cups and pans, objects from another time. An empty honey jar up-ended, the label just visible, the ink run on Charlie's careful hand. She picked up the jar, then set it down again.

'My price,' she said.

They found Annie on the kitchen floor, gathered in like an animal, knees drawn to her stomach, eyes dull. The sheets beneath her were soaked with blood. Blood slashed the floor.

Quickly Jean ordered Pam to ready the table again, to boil water, to find stronger light, and quickly she went to the girl, stroking her forehead, speaking low to her, and gently.

'Annie,' she said, 'I'm Dr Markham. Charlie's friend. I'm going to stop the pain and the bleeding. Squeeze my hand, so I know you can hear.'

They lifted the girl to the table. Jean looked at Pam.

'Don't forget,' she said, her glance steady. Then: 'Hold her. She needs you.' And she began.

39

Charlie went to the river with Bobby on Christmas Eve. It was the morning and he had all day. The sky was very blue and the shadow of the moon still hung in it.

Charlie said they should cross the blue bridge and go to the weir because there could be a body caught above. They clambered to it, slipping past the Danger sign and the red stick man tripping on his thin red line, and looked hard for bodies, or other things, above the sluice. They reached down to the water with their sticks, turning over the river's leavings like women at a jumble sale. The December sun shone on the back of their heads. The noise was glorious, crashing through Charlie's head. He couldn't hear himself think and he shouted back into it, loud as he could.

When they had had enough, they walked, swaggering a little, to the pipe factory and ate the chocolate sandwich biscuits Bobby had brought from the Christmas tin. He said when he was rich, he would have a speedboat and an aeroplane. Charlie said he would go to the Amazon, or maybe to Australia.

Their den was nothing now. A strip of corrugated iron, some rotten boards and a couple of rusty tins. The tarpaulin was gone, and the tin of sardines. Snakes were summer dreams too. So they found a different place and Charlie brought out the matches coaxed from Irene, newspaper and some strips of kindling and they lit a fire for winter.

'I've got to go by dinnertime,' Bobby said. 'My cousins'll be there. My mum said I'll be in trouble else.'

Charlie put his hands out to the fire.

'You at your dad's?' Bobby said.

'We could get some chips. Bring 'em back here,' Charlie said, as if Bobby hadn't spoken. 'Irene gave me a shilling.' He flipped it up for proof.

They'd built up the fire so that it flamed high. You couldn't see the flames in the sunlight; you could only see the air bend.

'They'll be gone in a couple of days,' Bobby said. 'My cousins. After Christmas.'

Charlie shrugged. 'Bye then,' he said.

He got some chips and went back to the weir, but bigger boys were there, and a dog with a studded collar. He didn't like the look of the dog. He walked back across the town, taking his time. The streets were busy. Women with full baskets, children running about, men drifting into pubs. At first Charlie kept himself busy by looking, but twice, and then a third time, he thought he saw his mother so he set his eyes to the pavement, only looking up to pick his way.

He didn't want to see her. He didn't want to think about her. His mind raged, and he banged his knuckles along the church railings so that they were black and sore. He hated his dad. But he didn't know what he felt about his mum except that if he saw her, he would hold on to her and the police would have to drag him away because he'd yell and kick and smash to stop it happening.

Slowly he walked back, taking the long way through the park. There was nobody else there. He kicked into dense piles of leaves, mulched down by winter. 'Take that. Take that!' till his shoes were glistening and picked all over with earth. He spoke under his lip like the detectives did in the thrillers.

'Gonna hunt that no-good deadbeat right outta town,' he muttered. 'Ain't that right, my friend?'

Charlie could smell the beer when he opened the front door, and he could hear the shouting. A man's voice – his father's – and a woman's. His mother's? He shoved down the narrow hall and turned the door handle, his heart thudding and his courage high. He would hit his father, he would strangle him, he would kick him between the legs. But as he pulled the door open, he heard not his mother, but his aunt. It was Pam, and she was shouting at his father. Charlie stopped, the door ajar. The argument went on. They hadn't seen him. He pulled it to again, stepped back and leaned against the wall.

His aunt adored his father. He'd never heard her like this before. She didn't like his mother, but she adored his father. Now they sounded very angry, and his father was drunk. Charlie knew about listening at doors. It wasn't safe, and so he started to climb the stairs.

But Pam's voice was so loud he'd have heard it in the attic, if they had one.

'You took him because you were angry. You don't even like him.'

'That's because of her.'

'No. You haven't liked him any better this week, and she's nowhere near.'

Charlie couldn't help hearing. He sat down on the stairs.

'Don't tell me how I feel,' his father said. 'You're always telling me how I feel.'

Chairs were being pushed and a bottle banged down hard, and then Pam's voice.

'My daughter damn near died last night.'

'Her fault. Should learn to keep her legs shut.'

There was no sound for a moment, and then Pam's voice again.

'What about you? You haven't had your fly done up these past five years. You can't blame Lydia for finding somewhere else to warm her hands. It's only because you like this girl when she's upright and making the tea as well as fucking her that you've come to this. What's more, I bet you like her better when she's not going soft over your little son.'

'You've changed your tune a bit. Since when did you care how Lydia felt? And anyway, so what?' His dad's voice, a bit shaky.

'So I bloody brought you up, and I've defended you against all comers all your bloody life, especially when they were telling the truth about you. You've never had a thought for anybody but yourself, and everybody knows it. Though it took your wife longer than most to find out. I can't help loving you, you're my own blood, but you're selfish to the bone. Now I'm asking you to do something for me.'

Then there were more noises and something from his dad like a curse, and Pam's voice again.

'I'm asking you to do something for my daughter. Give her a half-chance at respectability. You don't want your son here, except you're too bloody proud to admit it.'

Charlie put his arms around his knees and brought them up close. Pam went on like a road drill, and he wanted to put his hands over his ears, and he wanted to listen.

'There was a price, Robert. That doctor came to my house and I promised her. I had to promise her.'

'The price. My son for your daughter.' His father's voice was muted, as if maybe he had turned away.

'You don't want him here,' she said again. 'You want Irene to yourself.'

Charlie waited, and now Robert spoke as if he were picking up the words one by one and threading them on.

'He's not my son,' he said.

Charlie pulled at a scab on his elbow. Make it hurt, make it hurt was in his fingers.

'Not how my son should be,' Robert said.

Charlie dug his nail in and lifted the scab crust. Tears came to his eyes. Beyond him, the voices still spoke. Catching the scab between his fingertips, he tugged. Blood rose, a small dome of red.

A key was in the front door. Charlie should get up or he'd be seen there, listening.

'She's made sure of it,' he heard his father say.

The front door opened and Irene came in. Her eyes were bright with Christmas and she had her arms full.

'Charlie!' she said, a greeting.

He stood slowly, like an old man, but made no reply. The blood smudged his sleeve. As Irene pushed the front door closed, his father appeared.

Robert looked from Irene to Charlie and back again. Charlie could smell the alcohol now.

'You been listening,' he said, to Irene as much as his son.

'Listening to what?' she said.

'Pam's here. You better come in.'

And without another glance to Charlie, Robert went back inside and the door was closed.

Irene was crying when she came to his room. Crying and shaking her head. She held something out.

'Here,' she said, giving him the pack of cards. 'Nothing much else, is there?'

She picked up his satchel, gathered his few ends of clothing into it, and put it into Charlie's arms.

'Go down to your father,' she said.

Pam stood in the kitchen doorway and his father was slumped in the chair. Charlie waited. He watched the tinsel shift in the draught. It made a shivering, metallic sound.

'Go on,' Pam said to Robert softly, more like he was the boy here.

Robert beckoned to Charlie. He walked closer, to an arm's length. His father stared at him and he waited, light on the balls of his feet, for a swipe or a sharp word.

'Get him out then,' he said.

40

It was early in the afternoon and the light was sliding from a pale blue sky. This time of year, the dark came sharp as a flick-knife, quick between the ribs of the day. Lydia turned the pages of the book she still couldn't read. She felt leaden. She would be glad of the night.

She looked out of the window. Jean had been tired today, her mood strange and electric. Now she was in the garden, repairing some hive frames. Since breakfast she had been busy with tasks that didn't need to be done. Or at least not now. Not the day before Christmas.

Earlier Lydia had put a hand to her shoulder carefully, as if something about her would throw it off.

'Jean?' she said.

And when Jean turned to her, even as their eyes met, her glance had slipped off and gone elsewhere.

Lydia hadn't heard her go out in the night, but she had seen blood on her blouse in the morning. Though Lydia had asked her, Jean wouldn't say where she had been, or what had been wrong. Several times the telephone had rung and Jean had been quick to answer it, speaking in a low voice, turning away if Lydia was there. Once it had been Sarah and Jean had beckoned Lydia over to speak. But Lydia could hear the little girls in the background and it was unbearable, and so she had said she was sorry and put down the receiver.

Lydia tapped on the glass, and gestured with her fingers.

'Going for a walk,' she mouthed, and she took her coat from the hall and went out.

The road was always quiet. Few houses and, not so far beyond, fields.

Lydia strode, commanding her legs to walk fast, not caring that she stumbled in the coming dark, not caring to find a rhythm. She walked upwards into the night till she was out of breath, and finally she turned back, towards the litter of lights below. It was hard to keep her head up, too hard to look out, and Lydia kept her eyes on the road. She didn't see the figures till they were quite close.

She heard the woman's voice first, soft, enquiring. A question, Lydia could hear that. And she looked up to see two figures walking up the hill towards her, a young woman, and beside her, a small boy, head down, trailing something. For a split second she didn't recognize him. The boy paused to answer, lifted his head. Then her heart was in her throat and the blood roared loud in her ears. But she couldn't move, she couldn't breathe, she couldn't speak.

As if in slow motion, she saw him drop what he carried – a satchel, her mind told her somewhere, unimportantly – and then she saw him gather himself up and run.

Out of the shadows he ran towards her and she stood and waited. Behind him the young woman also stood and waited and another, unimportant thought crossed her mind, that she must be Robert's.

But now Charlie was in her arms and she didn't think any more.

41

The sky sat upon their shoulders, so low and so grey, and their movements in the cold day were thick and imprecise. The ground was soft with the rain, and earth soon clodded their boots. The hives were heavier than Jean remembered.

Slowly they lifted, slowly they manoeuvred. Every so often she would stop and look around her, as if storing up her fill of it against the future.

Charlie ran about, helping, and Lydia came out for a while, wrapped up in Jean's old coat.

There was everything left to do, and nothing at all. They had come to their decision in an instant three months ago but spoken of it to nobody, not even Charlie, till they knew they could go. Now they were leaving and, for the time being, they would take only what they needed.

Jim drove the car slowly across the silent Sunday town. Behind, in the trailer, the four hives and Charlie.

'You found someone quickly, for the hives,' Jim said.

'Yes.' Jean looked out at the town.

'You've gone already,' Jim said. 'Haven't you?'

'I didn't choose it.'

'You chose something. Are you taking the cat?'

'She'll like it. The heat. The insects.'

'And us?'

'You'll visit. For ages. We'll visit.'

They sat in the kitchen and drank coffee. Lydia sat with them. She wrote on a list, and crossed things off. Sometimes she smiled at what they said, but she didn't join the conversation. This was not her farewell.

Charlie was in and out, buzzing, excited. Often, Jean saw, he would brush by Lydia, or pause, and she would put a brief hand on his hair or drop a kiss to his shoulder. Jean saw that till he left the room, Lydia's eyes didn't leave him. She wouldn't let him go.

'You have money enough,' Jim said.

'I'll write before we're on the street,' Jean said.

'*Viale*, not street. Or *strada*.'

'What will you do?'

'I will not worry,' Jim said.

'We'll be careful. It'll be easier in a foreign country.'

'You're a doctor. Everybody sees you.'

Jean shook her head.

'Only if they need to. We'll be careful. We'll be strange already, for being English.'

'And I will not miss you in the Red Horse on Thursdays. I will find another oldest friend to put in your place.'

The doorbell rang and Lydia went to see.

'You know there was a whip-round at the factory,' Jean said. 'Like they do when a girl gets married.'

'That's a nice gesture,' Jim said.

'Pam organized it. She left the money in the porch with a note. Lydia didn't show it to me, but it made her cry a little.'

'Does she know what happened?'

'She knows that Annie lost her baby. Nothing else. She's been round with Annie every day almost. Made her promise that she'll visit us before the year is out.'

'Do you think she will?'

Jean shrugged. 'I don't know. But I don't think Lydia could bear to go without the promise.'

She got up and fetched the jug of coffee.

'Lydia's learning the language so quickly. More quickly than me,' she said. 'We have a book. But I've done my other homework. I've written some letters and made some telephone calls. I can practise over there and I've established that there are plenty of sick people. English-speaking sick people. So I'll get to work on them while I'm learning new words.'

'Then you are as set as you can be, though it might take some getting used to. A foreign country and foreign ways. What about here? Have you cured everybody here?'

'Everybody who will be cured.'

Sarah and the little girls came at lunchtime and Charlie showed the girls the four squares in the grass where the hives had been.

'They're like windows,' he said.

'What to?'

'It doesn't matter, so long as you can look through them.'

He chased them to the bottom of the garden, roaring like a lion; and a while later they went home.

They packed Charlie's shelves that evening, each thing wrapped in old news till the holdall was full. Though it was late now, he swore he would not sleep. Lydia turned off his light and went downstairs.

'Is he excited?' Jean said.

'He said it would be like a new world to look at. He said you had told him so.'

Jean kissed the woman she would leave her life for, run away for.

'He's right,' she said.

They stood an arm's length apart, Robert rocking slightly, Charlie standing stock-still. The street was quiet. There was that same pause now that they do in the films, and Charlie thought how strange it was that it could really happen like that.

'What do you want?' Robert said at last.

For a moment Charlie thought perhaps his father didn't know him. But something about the way Robert crossed his arms and waited answered that.

'I wanted to see you,' Charlie said.

Robert leaned his shoulder against the doorframe. His mouth was a piece of string and on his jutting chin was the forgotten haze of an old man's stubble. He put out his hands, like a performer when he's done a trick.

'So. Here I am,' he said. 'Not very hard to find, eh?'

'I heard about Pam,' Charlie said. 'Annie told me. I'm very sorry.'

Robert shrugged. 'Quick's best.'

Charlie nodded.

'She visits you over there, doesn't she?' Robert said.

Charlie nodded.

'Took your time, coming to pay your respects,' Robert said. 'Took your bloody time.'

Lives on his own, drinks on his own. That was what Annie had written, and Charlie could feel the drink in the air like a mood. There were stains on his father's trousers and his cardigan was grubby.

'Annie looks in, though,' Charlie said, surprised by pity. 'Calls in to see you. I know that.'

Robert shrugged. 'So why've you come back?'

Charlie told himself that he'd turned up here and his father had had no warning. That he was an ill man, and lonely. He told himself that he had gone away a child and come back a man.

'Like I said, I wanted to see you.'

'Nobody wears suits like that in this town. Get in before I die, is it?'

Charlie shook his head, because he didn't want it to go like this. Somewhere behind him he heard the sound of someone running, light, urgent footsteps. They were coming down the street.

'Let's go and have a beer. Or a coffee,' he said. 'Get off the doorstep, anyway.'

The afternoon sun trailed a dirty finger over the front window. Charlie felt cold. The sun had no heat here, no warmth.

Robert turned. 'I've got my tea on,' he said, and he walked back inside, stoop-shouldered.

His steps were awkward and slurred. There was nothing left of the swagger Charlie had tried to copy as a boy.

Charlie stood undecided. He put a hand to the bag on his shoulder, felt the jar of honey.

What are you going to do, Charlie? he said to himself.

Behind him the running steps drew closer and he turned. A boy ran down the centre of the empty street as if his life depended on it, legs flying, running like a demon, one arm like a piston, the other holding something, a box or a boat, tight to his side. He was close now, but he didn't see Charlie, a man in a suit on a doorstep. Didn't look, at any rate. His eyes were wide and his breath was quick, and he might be running to anywhere. He might be running from anything. He was just a boy going by, perhaps ten years old, in trainers and scruffy jeans.

Charlie turned back to follow his father.

'You bastard,' he said quietly.

The house was cold and unchanged, ornaments, curtains, tables and chairs. It smelled of old smoke and old food. In the kitchen Robert spread margarine on two slices of bread and poured orange soup into a bowl at the blue Formica table. He didn't look up. Charlie watched him sit down and dip his spoon, lift it to his mouth and suck. Watched him light a cigarette and lean it in the ashtray, waiting.

'Still eating your cockles?' Charlie said.

'You bring me some? In that pansy bag?'

Charlie took out the jar of honey and set it down beside the ashtray.

Robert picked up his cigarette, jabbed it in his mouth. He drew hard, pulling the glow towards him.

'I don't want to know about your fucking honey,' he said.

Charlie stood quite still. His legs were shaking and his mouth felt dry. It had come to it.

'No, you never wanted to know,' he said.

Anger shook his body, shook his voice. An old anger he knew too well, that had him whisper to the bees all those years ago.

'She took you away from me.' Robert's voice was plaintive, wheedling and he seemed to shrink into his chair. 'I had no choice,' he said, speaking each word slowly, separately.

'You always had a choice.' Charlie's voice was rough, peremptory. 'You could have written. Asked Annie. Done something.'

He walked over to the sink and looked out at the yard. The back gate was half off its hinges. He willed his father to speak. To say that he'd tried. This was the hope that had brought Charlie so far, and he held his breath in the dingy kitchen.

Come on, he thought. Please.

But when he turned back, his father only sat on, slumped, his cigarette burning up towards his fingers.

The boy in Charlie pleaded to go. But he was an adult now, a man taller than his father, and he had come a long way to ask this question.

'The day you sent me back,' he said. 'Why did you do it?'

Robert flicked the cigarette stump towards the ashtray and looked his son in the eye.

'You left, your mother left. Pam, Irene. Everybody's bloody left me.'

Pushing his chair back, he crossed his arms as if he'd made his speech now and that was the end of it.

'You're talking bollocks. Annie's still here, though God knows why. And Pam didn't leave you. She brought you up. Thought the bloody sun shone from you,' Charlie said.

'When the children get born, then the women leave you,' Robert said. 'Every time.'

Charlie shook his head impatiently. 'You came and got me, you told me we'd have fun and then you sent me back again.'

Robert took another cigarette from his packet. 'You come back to tell me you didn't have fun?'

He was watching Charlie like a boxer in the ring when he gets his man down.

Rage struck Charlie like an electric bolt. He stepped forward and lifted his fist to punch his father. Hard in the face. Half a step, that was all he took, and he saw Robert's fear.

'That's what I came back for,' Charlie said.

He flicked his fingers open, grazing the air an inch from Robert's face and he saw his father flinch.

'You're scared of me,' Charlie said in wonder, and he

leaned back against the sink and laughed, a hard, electric laugh.

'But it's more civilized to talk than fight,' he said. 'You haven't asked about my mother.'

Charlie pictured Lydia with her coffee and her book, waiting for him in the Café Nazionale. He hadn't told her about the trip, and he'd meet her there in two days' time and tell her nothing. Jean had made him promise not to.

'It was our choice to leave, not yours,' Jean said. 'But this life has been too hard-won. Leave her with her peace.'

'I don't want to upset her,' Charlie said. 'But I want to see my father for myself. As an adult.'

'I know you need to. But it will change things. Wait a while before you speak to her, till your feelings have settled a little,' so he had he agreed that he would say nothing for now.

Robert didn't speak, only watched him with wary eyes.

'You haven't asked, so I'll tell you about her,' Charlie said, because now he understood Jean's fear and he wanted to hurt this man.

What he said to Robert then was true, but it wasn't the only truth; things had been hard at the start for Lydia and Jean and they'd struggled. People aren't nicer somewhere else. He had felt this as a boy, though not much was said; but he knew it as a young man because they had spoken to him about what it had been like.

'She's happy and they're still together. They're still sleeping in the same bed.'

Robert put the cigarette to his lips and rummaged in his pocket for matches.

Charlie watched the suck of his cheeks and the pull of the flame and pity washed through him. He wondered what the hell he was doing here, a thousand miles from home, stuck in this hopeless conversation with this old man who didn't want to be his father.

His throat ached and his eyes throbbed, as though he'd

been crying for hours. He felt like someone who has sleep-walked their way into somewhere and then woken up.

'I thought it would be different,' he said to his father.

In the late afternoon sun a boy in trainers and scruffy jeans bent to the pond's edge. He pressed his finger to the black box beside him, its antenna waving slightly at his touch, then stretched out his arms like a small god. Lifting his boat out, he turned and stood proud. Above, on the hill, Charlie stood watching.

Placing the boat and its black box on the grass, the boy wiped his hands on his T-shirt and was off, shouting to a friend, running to the far side.

The town was still full of boys, Charlie thought, though he was twenty years away. His memory reached across, like the boy's dancing shadow in the water, etiolated, awkward.

He stood perfectly still, unseen, barely there.

The minutes passed and the wind arrived to whip the surface of the water. The boy returned for his boat and Charlie looked at his watch. It was time to go.

Acknowledgements

I would like to thank the Royal Literary Fund for their financial assistance during the writing of this novel. Ledig House in New York State offered me a sanctuary within which to finish the novel: I am grateful to D.W. Gibson and the wonderful staff there, and to my fellow writers, with whom it was a pleasure and an inspiration to spend those weeks.

My thanks to Elizabeth and John Horder and Peter and Sue Tomson for their reflections on what it was like to be a GP in the 1950s; and to Danielle Walker Palmour for giving me a taste of beekeeping.

Thank you to Karen Charlesworth, Jean Downey, Anna Maria Friman, Sandy Goldbeck-Wood, Liz Grierson, Susan Orr, Adam Phillips, Martin Riley and Dave Tomson for all their backing in so many ways.

Thanks also to the following for their kind permission to reprint short extracts from other works: A.P. Watt for John Buchan's *The Thirty-Nine Steps;* and Pan Macmillan for Eric Ambler's *The Mask of Dimitrios.*

'Roses of Picardy', words by Frederick E. Weatherly, music by Haydn Wood © Chappell Music Ltd (PRS). All rights administered by Warner Chappell Music Australia Pty Ltd. Reproduced by permission.

Many thanks to Alan Mahar and Emma Hargrave at Tindal Street.

Above all, my thanks to Clare Alexander for her unstinting support.

Fiona Shaw lives and works in York. She is the
author of several books, including *Out Of Me*,
The Sweetest Thing and *The Picture She Took*.